LESPADA

A MEDIEVAL ROMANCE

BY KATHRYN LE VEQUE

Printed by Dragonblade Publishing in the United States of America

Text copyright 2010, 2014 by Kathryn Le Veque
Cover copyright 2010, 2014 by Kathryn Le Veque

Library of Congress Control Number 2014-007
ISBN 978-1479178902

Kathryn Le Veque Novels

Time Travel Romance: (Saxon Lords of Hage)
The Crusader
Kingdom Come

Contemporary Romance:

Kathlyn Trent/Marcus Burton Series:
Valley of the Shadow
The Eden Factor
Canyon of the Sphinx

The American Heroes Series:
Resurrection
Fires of Autumn

Evenshade
Sea of Dreams
Purgatory

Other Contemporary Romance:
Lady of Heaven
Darkling, I Listen

Multi-author Collections/Anthologies:
With Dreams Only of You (USA Today bestseller)
Sirens of the Northern Seas (Viking romance)
Ever My Love (sequel to With Dreams Only Of You) July 2016

Note: All Kathryn's novels are designed to be read as stand-alones, although many have cross-over characters or cross-over family groups. Novels that are grouped together have related characters or family groups.

Series are clearly marked. All series contain the same characters or family groups except the American Heroes Series, which is an anthology with unrelated characters.

There is NO particular chronological order for any of the novels because they can all be read as stand-alones, even the series.

For more information, find it in **A Reader's Guide to the Medieval World of Le Veque.**

TABLE OF CONTENTS

"And what is better than wisdom? Woman.
And what is better than a good woman? Nothing."
Geoffrey Chaucer c.1343 – 1400

CHAPTER ONE

London, England
The Ides of March, 1264 A.D.

THE EVENING WAS still and hushed, the hour late. The sounds of the gentle waters of the Thames drifted over the moonlit houses, roofs, and avenues like the caressing soothe of a lullaby. Hardly a soul stirred on the dirty, dangerous streets. Even the Tower of London was bathed in nocturnal peace, a bastion normally wrought with violence and tension. But the tranquility belied the chaotic heart beating within the fortress, with friction pulsing through halls like the veins of a living body.

It was a foregone conclusion that a variety of factions resided within the old stone walls of the Tower, and these days were particularly strained. There were those allied with the king, and there were those against. The ancient fortress had seen its share of political strife and the future could only threaten more of the same. Though the evening was peaceful and the mood still, there was an underlying element of pandemonium that threatened to explode. Each man and woman at the Tower lived moment by moment in anticipation of this. It was an exhausting existence.

But not all allowed themselves to be sucked into the tension that surrounded them. In the tower wing on the eastern wall, two brothers shared a fire and a carafe of blood-red wine from Sicily. These men were key components to the political strife enveloping the Tower, and one man in particular. He was the one with the heavy yellowed vellum in hand, his jaw ticking with disbelief as his eyes perused the writing.

"I do not believe it," he growled.

"Believe what?" asked the other.

1

The man continued to stare at the missive until finally settling it in his lap. There was a long sigh.

"Mother."

"What has she done now?"

Davyss de Winter handed his brother the message. Hugh took the vellum, reading the contents hesitantly as if fearful of what it might say. When he came to the end, he closed his eyes in acquiescence. The vellum collapsed in his lap.

"God give us strength," he muttered. The deep brown eyes opened to look back at his brother. "She has been threatening you with this for months. I did not believe her to be serious."

Davyss gazed steadily at his younger brother, a knowing smile playing on his smooth lips. "You should know her better than that, little brother. The Lady Katharine Isabella Rowyna de Warenne de Winter never threatens. Her oath is more trustworthy than that of any knight I know." He took back the vellum, eyeing it with something of regret. "I just thought it would be later rather than sooner."

"What are you going to do?"

Davyss glanced at the missive one last time before setting it aside. It had been a harried day and this had been the first chance he'd had to sit in one place and unwind. Yet in his position, relaxation could be deadly. He didn't think he'd truly relaxed in fifteen years.

"I am not entirely sure that I have a choice in the matter. Should I refuse, she will deny me my inheritance. She has told me thus."

"So you will do it?"

Davyss fell silent. His thoughts revolved around his overbearing mother, ill with age and bitter with life, and the inheritance that was his due. Nearly everything the de Winter family had come from his mother's side, including the castle in which she currently resided. As the only sister of the Earl of Surrey, she had been granted Breckland Castle in Norfolk by her brother. It was a glorious stronghold, well-regarded and well-fortified near the dense Thetford Forest.

The de Warenne fortune came with it from his mother's sire. Davyss had worked too hard in the course of his thirty-four years to watch it all slip away to Hugh because he was too stubborn to do as his mother bade. It wasn't often that she dictated to him, but when she did, she meant it. He understood her want for her heir to marry and bear offspring to carry on the name. It wasn't unreasonable. He just wished he had some say in the matter.

He heard his brother snort. He glanced at him. "What is it?"

Hugh's handsome face was contorted in a smirk. "I suppose I find all of this ironic."

"How?"

Hugh snorted again, just for effect, and rose from his over-stuffed leather chair. He moved to the hearth and tossed another hunk of peat onto the blaze. Sparks flew up into the dim room.

"Because you are Henry's champion, for Christ's sake," he poked at the smoking fire. "The king of the mightiest country on earth turns to you for protection. Men are humbled at your feet and your reputation is second to none. A weak man did not achieve this. You have the will of the nation to command by sheer strength alone, yet your mother issues forth orders and suddenly, the champion is subdued like a submissive child."

The irony wasn't lost on Davyss. Hugh wasn't attempting to be condescending but that was the message.

"I cannot be selfish in this matter," he said simply. "I have the de Winter lineage to think of. I do indeed want sons to carry on my name"

"So you let dear Mummy arrange a marriage?"

Hugh was becoming taunting now. A long look from the quick-tempered Davyss quickly curbed any thoughts of furthering the torment. Under no circumstances would Hugh tangle with his older, and by far larger, brother.

"According to Mother, she is a woman of good bloodlines. Her father is Lord Mayor of Thetford and Sheriff of the Shire." He sounded suspiciously as if he was attempting to talk himself into the agreeable arrangement. "So I will marry her, she will bear my sons, I will stay in

London and still collect my inheritance, and everyone will be happy. I see no issue with this."

Hugh didn't believe him, but he did not let on. When pushed to the breaking point, Davyss' temper was unpredictable and, at times, deadly. He had no desire to be cuffed. He sat back in his chair.

"So what is my new sister's name?"

Davyss stared into the fire, digging deep into his memory. His mother had told him, once, during the few discussions they had exchanged on the subject.

"The Lady Devereux Allington."

"Family?"

"Saxon lords. A grand sire, several generations over, was king of the ancient Kingdom of Dremrud. She comes with some wealth."

"What does she look like?"

Davyss lifted a dark eyebrow. "You can tell me that upon your return."

"Return from what?"

"My wedding."

CHAPTER TWO

Thetford, Norfolk

THE ONLY MAN not in attendance at the wedding was the groom. Unwilling to leave London with the current political situation between Henry and the volatile Simon de Montfort, he remained at his post. Moreover, his absence was a statement to his mother that he could not be so easily pushed about. So he sent his knights, all five of them, to attend the marriage for him. Most importantly, he had sent his sword with Hugh. The lady would marry the weapon, by proxy, and become Lady de Winter. Davyss would therefore have a wife he'd never even met, a very neat arrangement for someone who did not wish to be married at all.

If the groom was reluctant, the bride was positively adverse. Hugh had been the first man to lay eyes on her, a petite woman with the body of a ripe goddess and luscious blonde hair that fell in a thick sheet to her buttocks. He had been momentarily dumbfounded by the glory of her face, so lovely that he was sure the angels were jealous. She had enormous gray eyes that were brilliant and bottomless, and a rosebud mouth that was sweet and delectable. But his glimpse of unearthly beauty had been fleeting as she slammed the door in his face. That action set the tone. The de Winter knights had, therefore, broken down the door and set chase to the fighting, scratching animal otherwise known as the Lady Devereux D'arcy Allington.

Hugh led the group with enthusiasm. One of the shortest knights, he was built like a bull. His dark hair, dark eyes and square jaw gave him a youthfully beautiful appearance and he was no stranger to women's attention. Usually, he could soothe any manner of female fits. Much to his chagrin, however, his brother's betrothed had not fallen under his spell. As she fought him like a banshee, his enthusiasm waned and he backed off to let the rest of the group have a go at her. He was embarrassed she had not swooned at his feet but would not admit to it, not even to himself.

Sir Nikolas de Nogaret was the next in line to deal with the hysterical lady. A tall man with blue eyes and wide shoulders, he ended up with a black eye when the lady swung a broken chair leg at him. Sir Philip de Rou took over when Nik acquired the hit to his face; a slender, blonde man with a decidedly suave manner, Philip was as over-confident in his persuasive abilities as Hugh had been. The lady opened a door into his nose when he had chased her into a wardrobe and, in that gesture, damaged his fragile ego as well as his face.

With two knights down, the final pair took over. Sir Andrew Catesby and his younger brother, Sir Edmund Catesby, were ten years apart in age. Andrew and Davyss had fostered together and were the closest of friends.

Cool, calm, and exceedingly collected, Andrew stepped over Philip's prostrate form on his way to corral the lady and was met by a flying taper. Her aim had been true and almost put his eye out. Edmund, young and newly knighted, tucked in behind his older brother and used him as a shield. When the brothers finally cornered her in her father's chamber, it had been Edmund who had taken the glory of finally subduing her.

Victory was attained for the moment but there was more bedlam to come. Carting her, bound and gagged, to Breckland Priory had been no easy feat. Though small, she was oddly strong. The men didn't want to injure her but the woman struggled like a wildcat. They were frankly astonished at the resistance they met and tried not to look like vicious brutes as they carried her through the town. She screamed and fought as if they were taking her to be hanged. The entire berg turned out to watch and their procession transformed into a bizarre parade, with knights on foot carrying a reluctant captive.

Fortunately, they made it to the priory without anyone losing fingers. The lady's father, a short man with silver hair and gray eyes, followed them from the cottage and lingered near the door of the chapel as they lugged his daughter inside. He had readily agreed to the union between his only child and Davyss de Winter due to the prestigious connections with the House of de Winter, but now he wasn't so sure his decision had been a wise one. The knights were enormous men, built and bred for battle, and his stubborn daughter was caught in the middle of the storm. She was, in fact, the tempest. He said a prayer for her health as she was half-dragged, half-carried, to the altar.

The interior of the old priory was spartanly furnished and dimly lit, with long thin tapers trailing ribbons of smoke into the musty air. Massive columns supported the ceiling, flanking the central area for the congregation. A few priests lingered in the shadows, hiding behind the supporting pillars and watching the drama unfold. But their fears were for naught, for not one of them would be forced to execute the wedding Mass. Davyss' personal priest, a man named Lollardly, stood waiting to perform the ceremony.

Lollardly had seen battles, and participated in them, for nearly twenty years and had earned a reputation for himself as a fighting friar. But the brawl happening before him was something not even he had ever witnessed and he was, truthfully, astonished.

"Here, here, do not injure the lady," he commanded the knights. "Untie her, you animals. Have you no respect?"

Andrew and Edmund had Devereux between them. Ever the gentleman, and with a healthy respect for the clergy, Andrew gently righted her on her feet. Once balanced, she tried to run. Andrew grabbed her before she could get away and wrapped his big arms around her torso, holding her fast.

Devereux cursed him through the gag. Lollardly lifted a disapproving eyebrow, took a step forward, and pulled the sodden wad from her mouth.

"My lady," he said sternly. "I would suggest you calm yourself and fulfill your duty. Your behavior is harming none but yourself and you are creating an embarrassing spectacle."

Devereux licked her chapped lips, a gesture not missed by Hugh and Philip in particular. They were rather intrigued by the pink rosebud mouth, especially when it wasn't gnashing at them.

"You should be protecting *me*," she hissed at the friar. "How dare you ally yourself with these devils."

"Devils or no, they represent your husband and you will obey."

"He is not my husband *yet*."

Lollardly had little patience for the inane. Beautiful or no, the lady was ridiculous as far as he was concerned and he would waste no more time. He glanced at Andrew behind her.

"Let us kneel."

The knights dropped to a knee and Hugh produced the blade of his forefathers; *Lespada,* the sword of high warriors. It was a magnificent weapon that had seen many generations of de Winter men, now carried by Davyss. Andrew tried to force Devereux down but she stiffened like a board. Not wanting to create more of a scene, and slightly perturbed that he was not in complete control, Andrew tried a few methods to force her to kneel. The last resort was to throw his knee into the back of her right knee. The joint buckled enough to allow him to shove her down to the cold stone floor. He knew she must have cut her skin with the force of her fall but she did not utter a word of pain.

"Curse you," she hissed. "Curse all of you. I hope you burn in hell for this. I hope you rot. I hope you…!"

Andrew slapped a hand over her mouth, smiling thinly at the friar. "Proceed."

Lollardly lifted an eyebrow and began the liturgy. It really was a pity, he thought. Lady Devereux was a stunning example of the glory of womanhood. She also had the manners of a wild boar. Davyss would not be pleased.

The friar droned on in Latin. The lady's bright gray eyes blazed with fury, Andrew's hand still over her mouth. Somewhere in her glare,

Lollardly could see the tears of fright, of sadness. Strangely, he saw no outright defiance, only self-protection. At least, he hoped that was what he saw. Given the opportunity, they could ease her fears to soothe her manner. But they could not curb blatant insubordination.

"*Quod Jesus refero said unto lemma, liberi illae universitas matrimonium, quod es donatus in matrimonium,*" Lollardly intoned the liturgy, reading from the dog-eared mass book he had copied himself many years ago. Gently closing the book, he formed the sign of the cross over the lady's head.

"*Bona exsisto vobis.*"

It was the union blessing. Devereux understood Latin and her loudly-thumping heart beat faster still. Andrew removed his big hand and Hugh placed the hilt of the sword in front of her lips.

"I will not kiss it," she said through clenched teeth.

Hugh tried to put the metal against her mouth in an effort to force her, but she would have no part in it. She bit her lips and lowered her head. Andrew, though it was not a gentlemanly gesture, grabbed the back of her blonde head and pulled her skull back. With a violent twist, she threw them both off balance and they tumbled to the ground.

"No!" she screeched.

The lady ended up on her back, with Hugh on top of her. The sword was in his hand. His weight, coupled with Andrew against her legs, rendered her immobile and Hugh found himself gazing into bright gray eyes.

The lady knew she was cornered. The knights had her and there was nothing more she could do, nowhere for her to go. She could feel herself breaking down, the fight in her veins leaving her. Still, she could not let go so easily.

"Please," she whispered in a strained tone. "Please do not force me to do this."

They were the first civilized words she had spoken. Her voice was like liquid sugar, soft and sweet and low. She was such a lovely creature that Hugh found himself listening to her. But he chased away his misgivings before they could control him.

"This is not my doing, my lady," he said neutrally. "Kiss the sword and we shall be done with it. Then I am to take you to London to meet your husband."

The lady shook her head. "But… but you do not understand. I will not. I cannot."

"Why?"

She wouldn't answer him and he was suddenly seized with anger. The fingers of his left hand bit into her upper arm. "Are you compromised?"

She gasped in shock at the suggestion. "No, my lord, I swear it," she insisted. "But… I will not marry de Winter."

Hugh gazed at her, baffled by her words, thinking it was surely another ploy. She was trying all avenues to resist this marriage. Before he could reply, however, a voice filled the stale air of the priory.

"Hugh!"

Lady Katharine de Winter strolled into the hall, leaning heavily on her cane. Behind her came a procession of properly submissive ladies-in-waiting with their severe wimples and pale faces.

"Get off of that woman, you beast," she told her son. "What are you doing to her?"

Hugh pushed himself off of Devereux, making sure that Andrew had a grip on her. His dark brown eyes warmed to his mother as he approached her.

"Darling," he kissed her on both cheeks. "How good to see you. You are as lovely as ever."

She let her youngest flatter her. "I can see that you waited for me." She cast a long glance in the direction of the lady, picking herself off the floor with Andrew's assistance. "What is she doing on the ground?"

Hugh took his mother's elbow and they began to walk towards the altar. "Nothing to worry over, Mother."

"Hmmm," Lady Katharine carefully inspected the disheveled woman from a short distance. "That is not what I think. I think someone has worked this young woman over." She paused before the knights, her sharp brown eyes scrutinizing every one of them. "Can anyone tell me what has truly happened here?"

Andrew had known Lady Katharine since childhood. His soft blue eyes twinkled at her. "The lady is reluctant to marry, my lady," he said. "We are simply helping her fulfill the pledge."

A withered eyebrow lifted. "Abusing the lady is *not* the same as helping her," she said flatly. Her wizened brown eyes peered more closely at the girl. "Lady Devereux, I have seen you since you were a child. I know your father. I have always known that you would be a match for one of my sons, although I sorely doubt the youngest is worthy of you and the oldest lacks the time and effort for the undertaking. Would you kindly explain why these men tell me you are reluctant to marry?"

Devereux faced the elderly woman with as much dignity as she could muster. From the instant she had been informed of her betrothal to Davyss de Winter until this very moment, the entire event had been a nightmare. Now, in front of these strangers, she must explain herself. She had no choice.

"I do not want to marry your son, my lady," she said quietly.

"Why not? And speak up, girl. My ears are not as they used to be."

Devereux started to reply, more loudly, but she glanced at the men surrounding her and the words died in her throat. She took a deep breath as she gazed into ancient, wise eyes.

"May I speak with you privately, my lady?" she asked.

Katharine cocked what was left of her eyebrow. "You will speak here. There is nothing you can tell me that these men cannot hear."

Something in the woman's attitude fired a spark in Devereux; there was no kindness, no compassion. Just like the men surrounding her. The realization fed her resistance and her attempt to be moderately tactful disappeared.

"Because your son supports a tyrant of a king," she said through clenched teeth. "I will not marry one so entrenched in oppression and politics."

The knights stirred in outrage but none spoke; they would leave that to Lady de Winter, whose tongue could cut more deeply than the sharpest knife. The old woman's eyes glittered with unspoken intensity as she sized up the blonde woman a few feet away; there was calculation to the gaze as she dissected the statement for both content and intent. She made her move accordingly.

"Your statement could be considered treacherous but I will give you the benefit of the doubt," Lady Katharine replied after a moment. "Since I believe that every woman should be given the right to speak her mind, I will give you that same courtesy. Tell me, then, Lady Devereux, why you would make this slanderous and uneducated statement about my son?"

It was a direct slap but Devereux would not back down. She was not weak by nature and would not let this bird-like woman, no matter how powerful, push her around. Lady Katharine had already done quite enough of that when she forced Devereux's father into a marriage contract. It had been a shock to Devereux those months ago when her father had informed her of the agreement. It made no sense, in any arena.

"It is not uneducated, my lady, I assure you," she said as evenly as she could manage. "There is not a man, woman or child in this country who does not know the name Davyss de Winter. Everyone knows that he is the king's champion and that men fear his power and wrath." She took a step towards the frail old woman, her bright gray eyes glimmering with more curiosity than defiance. "I am the daughter of a minor noble. I have no great rank or power, nor do I come with a dowry of a thousand fighting men. I am not a particularly suitable match for your son and I would ask why you seem so determined for me to be his wife."

Lady de Winter met Devereux's gaze with equal force. "For precisely the reasons you have indicated," she said quietly. "You are not politically connected. You cannot betray my son to an enemy who has coerced you or your father into submission. You do not come to this marriage with a secret agenda for power or money. You only bring yourself."

"That makes little sense to a politically connected family such as the de Winters."

Lady Katharine lifted a sparse brow. "It makes perfect sense. My son does not need a woman attempting to bend him to her will for her, or her family's, political gain," she paused a moment, studying Lady Devereux's exquisite face. The woman was genuinely beautiful in spite of the fact that she had been roughed over. "He needs someone strong and unconnected and true. He needs someone to keep his attention and show him that the true meaning of manhood comes from dedication to one woman, not the plaything of many. You are this person."

For the first time since being cornered in her father's home, Devereux felt her defiant stance waver. As Lady Katharine explained things, it made perfect sense. But it did not erase facts.

"How would you know that I am true?" she was genuinely curious.

The old expression was confident. "Because I have watched you grow up and, as I have said, I know your father. I have known your family for quite some time. You are aware of this, lady."

Devereux nodded faintly. "I know that you rule this shire. Your family has for generations. Everyone knows of the de Winter might."

"Then you are aware that I speak with some knowledge when I say that I know of you and of your character. You are the mistress of The House of Hope, a poorhouse that provides to the needy of the shire. You are held in high regard for your generosity and charity."

Devereux was growing increasingly perplexed. "Generosity and kindness do not necessarily seal a suitable match," she replied with less boldness and more awe. "The de Winter family came to these shores with William the Bastard. My family is Saxon, a conquered people. My mother died a few years ago and it has only been my father and I since that time. I tend the poorhouse and help my father manage the small village of people that depend upon us for their lives. A marriage into the House of de Winter is beyond my comprehension. I do not want to be involved in a family that so allies itself with the king."

"Why not?"

Her tone turned cold. "Because I do not believe in his absolute rule. I believe the country should be governed by the people as a whole, not by a monarchy that cares little for its subjects."

Lady Katharine almost looked amused. "Are you so sure of all things?"

Devereux was not so arrogant that she presumed to know everything. But she was resolute in her opinion.

"I am not, Lady de Winter," she said with some hesitation. "'Tis simply that I believe the Earl of Leicester is a man of the people, a man who understands how a country should be governed. It is his ideals that I support, not a king whose sense of entitlement is only exceeded by his arrogance."

One could have heard a pin drop in that cold, unfeeling chapel, surrounded by stone and effigies of barons long dead. Devereux was feeling increasingly uncomfortable as Lady Katharine simply stared at her. Then, something odd happened; the harsh glare faded from the old woman's eyes and she reached out, patting Devereux on her tender cheek.

"I like this one," she said to the men surrounding them. "Tell Davyss that I will expect him to treat her well. She will bear sons of character and strength." She refocused on Devereux, the twinkle in her eye once again hardening in a frightening manner. "You will now kiss the sword. Let us be done with this."

Devereux very nearly refused again; defiance shot up her spine and she could feel herself stiffen with the force of rebellion. But more than the threat from the knights and the physical battle that had consumed the majority of their acquaintance, the look in Lady de Winter's eyes suggested that she would not tolerate any further disobedience. Devereux didn't know why she suddenly felt herself submitting. The power in the old lady's eyes was unwavering and unkind. Devereux knew when she was beaten.

Lady de Winter did not wait for any words of agreement or refusal; she crooked a gnarled finger at Hugh, who brought about *Lespada* and held it to Devereux's lips. With her bright gray eyes still focused on the old woman she instinctively respected and naturally feared, she brushed the cold steel with her soft pink lips. Without any further struggle or fanfare, it was finally done.

And with that, Lady Katharine de Winter turned around and headed for the door of the priory. Hugh followed his mother to the entry, speaking softly with her and helping her through the portal as her ladies congregated around her. Then he turned around, his dark gaze suddenly focusing on something just over Devereux's right shoulder.

There was a figure in the shadows, something he'd not noticed until his mother just mentioned it. He instantly recognized the shape, and was silenced from speaking when a massive hand lifted to quiet him. It did not take Hugh long to deduce that his mother's arrival must have been a diversion so they would not have seen Davyss enter the priory; they had all been focused on the snarling bride and Lady de Winter, so much so that they would not have given thought to a vaporous figure in the darkness. And it was from that darkness that Davyss had witnessed the entire ceremony.

So his brother had decided to come after all. Hugh wisely assumed that the man would want time alone with his new bride, if for no other reason than to set her straight on the course their marriage would take after her natty little display of manners. Snapping his fingers at the knights, he jabbed a thumb at the door.

"Gather your mounts and secure transportation for the lady," he commanded. "I will join you in a moment."

Devereux was still standing near the altar with Lollardly; she was frankly a bit dumbfounded from her conversation with Lady de Winter. She was still trying to reconcile the event in her own mind. But the old priest eyed her critically as he moved past her and Devereux gazed back as if daring the man to speak harshly to her. She was still upset with him for going along with this travesty of a marriage ceremony.

Surprisingly, she did not try to run when the knights moved out. She stood where they had left her, watching her father bolt from the chapel and thinking the man to be a horrible coward. She knew he had only married her to de Winter to be part and parcel to the de Winter fortune. He was greedy that way. Feeling the least bit abandoned and, not surprisingly, exhausted in the light of her embattled wedding ceremony, she watched with some trepidation as the knights and the priest filed from the hall.

All except for Hugh; he marched upon her with an expression of hostility. Since all he had known from her since the moment of their association was violence, she hardly blamed him.

"You will wait here until we can bring about suitable transportation for the trip to Castle Acre Castle," he eyed her. "If you give me your word that you will not try to escape, I will not bind you."

She gave him a look that suggested she was bored with his statement. "If I wanted to flee, your bindings could not hold me," she fired back. "Go get your horses. I am not going anywhere."

"Do I have your word, lady?"

"I said it, did I not?"

"That is not an answer."

"It is enough of an answer for you. Do you doubt me?"

Hugh almost entered into an argument with her that would undoubtedly end in some manner of fist in his eye. But he caught himself in time, begging off for the sheer reason that Davyss was only a few feet away; he knew his brother would handle this banshee of a woman and they would all be the better for it. Still insulted with the fact that his charming and debonair self had not melted her with a first glance, he cast her a withering glare and quit the chapel.

When it was finally cold and empty, Devereux emitted a pent up sigh. Like a bubble of tension bursting, she suddenly felt deflated. She realized that tears were close to the surface but angrily chased them away, feeling despondent and disoriented.

She would wait for the knights to return to take her to her prison of Castle Acre Castle. It wasn't far from her berg, the great castle with the massive ramparts. Lady Katharine de Winter lived there at times; when she was not in residence, there were always groups of soldiers in and out of the place. Sometimes they would come into town and wreak havoc in the taverns. Devereux had spent her life knowing when to stay indoors and locked away when the soldiers were about. She had spent her life staying clear of the knights and other warriors who would, at times, pass through her town. She had never even seen her husband although she knew he had spent time at Castle Acre Castle periodically. She had often heard rumor to that effect. Now she was a part of that world she had attempted to stay clear of. She tried not to hate her father for it.

From the corner of her eye, she caught sight of the altar. It was beautifully carved and had the rarity of a cushion before it on which to kneel. Devereux found herself wondering where the priests were that usually inhabited this priory. She wondered if de Winter's knights had chased them off. With another heavy sigh, she made her way to the altar, gazing up at the gold-encrusted cross and wondering how drastically her life was going to change from this point.

Soft boot falls suddenly distracted her and she turned to see an unfamiliar knight entering the sanctuary. He was a colossal man, dressed from head to toe in armor and mail and weaponry. He was without his helm and as he emerged into the weak light, Devereux could see his very handsome features; his dark hair was in need of a cut, a bit shaggy and curly, and a dark beard embraced his granite jaw.

The longer she stared at him the more she realized that he was, in fact, extraordinarily handsome. It was something of a shock. Devereux continued to watch with a mixture of apprehension and fascination as the knight drew closer, his hazel eyes fixed on her flushed and weary face. It was a piercing gaze that sucked her in, holding her fast until she could hardly breathe.

"I apologize for disturbing you, my lady," he said. "Were you praying?"

His voice was deep and silky, like sweet wine. Devereux felt an odd flush of heat at the sound of his delicious tone, momentarily speechless as he gazed upon her. She managed to shake her head, however, and the knight came to stand several feet away. Even when he gazed toward the altar and crossed himself reverently, she couldn't take her eyes from him.

Davyss felt her stare, turning to look at her again. Christ, if she wasn't the most beautiful woman he had ever seen; even more beautiful at close range. She had long, straight blonde hair that was thick and silky, and eyes of the most amazing color. They were a shade of blue that was so pale that they were silver. Big and bottomless, he could see the fringe of soft lashes brush against her brow bone every time she blinked. And her face was sweet and round. He had witnessed the wedding ceremony from the shadows, stifling the roar of laughter as Hugh and Andrew had wrestled with her in an attempt to force her to kiss his sword.

But the more he watched, the more curious and strangely mesmerized he became with this woman who was now his wife. She was a hellion, a misfit, and he should have been disgusted with her behavior. But her spirit impressed him strangely, a woman who was not afraid to speak her mind or resist men twice her petite size. And when he witnessed the confrontation between her and his mother, calculated though it had been for his benefit, it had oddly cemented the deal. For some reason, he was no longer reluctant. But she clearly still was.

When the lady had finally kissed the sword to seal the marriage, Davyss realized he could no longer stay away. In spite of his own reluctance, he realized he had to discover her for himself.

"My lady is... weary," he cocked an eyebrow at her slovenly state. "May I assist?"

Devereux's bright gray eyes regarded him. "Nay, my lord," she turned away, her cheeks flushing and her confusion growing.

He continued to gaze at her, the marvelous blonde hair that cascaded from her head to her thighs. "Then why do you stand here if you are not praying?" he asked.

She shrugged weakly, refusing to look at him. "I was left here."

"By whom?"

She didn't reply. Davyss' eyes roved her body with interest, noting that she was deliciously curvaceous. She was petite in height, clad in some sort of rough garment, a leather girdle binding her small waist and emphasizing her full breasts. She looked like an angel but dressed like a peasant. He found himself shaking his head with awe, hardly believing this woman was his wife. She was a most startling paradox.

"You did not answer me," he said after a moment. "Who was foolish enough to leave you here alone?"

She sighed heavily. "Terrible men. Horrible men."

He raised an eyebrow. "Is that so? Why are they so terrible, other than the fact that they left you here alone?"

She turned to look at him, feeling that same odd heat she had experienced the very first time their eyes met. Even so, she found she could not tell him the whole situation. It was too embarrassing.

"They will return for me, I am sure," she said, avoiding his question. "They have probably gone to fetch my husband."

"And who is your husband?"

She made a face and Davyss had to conceal a smile. She looked like a child forced to swallow foul-tasting medicine. "Sir Davyss de Winter."

"Ah, yes," he nodded in acknowledgement. "De Winter."

Her expression darkened. "Then you know him?"

"A fair man."

"A fiend!"

"Is that so?" he realized he was very close to breaking a smile. "Why would you say that? I hear he is a wise and powerful man. Handsome, too."

Her eyes flashed. "This I would not know, my lord, for he does not even have the courage to face me."

"What do you mean?"

"I was only just married to him. But instead of showing me the respect of coming himself, do you know that he sent his sword in his place?"

It was at that moment that Davyss began to see that perhaps sending *Lespada* in his place had not been a wise decision. Whatever animosity the lady was feeling had been exacerbated by it. He began to regret his decision although, at the time, it had been the correct choice. Still, he could see she was very offended by it. For whatever reason, he felt the need to soothe her ruffled feathers.

"Would you sit, my lady?" he indicated one of two benches in the place. "I find I am exceedingly weary from my ride and wish to continue this conversation seated."

She lifted an eyebrow. "You look strong enough."

He fought off a grin and went to take the bench himself, thinking that she would follow him. He was wrong in that she did not and he almost laughed; clearly, nothing about Lady Devereux was predictable.

"You must understand that to marry to your husband's sword is a distinct honor," he said quietly. "The sword of a knight defines who he is as both man and warrior. It is as much a part of him as his heart or his head. When you are presented with the sword, he is offering you his very soul. When he presented you with his sword in his stead, he was asking you to become part of his life and his being."

Devereux's unhappy expression eased somewhat. It was apparent that she was thinking heavily on his words. After several moments, she simply shook her head.

"But I don't want to be part of the kind of life he leads," she said, all of the defiance out of her voice.

"Why not?"

She just looked at him. "You will forgive me, my lord, but that is truly none of your affair. I should not have said as much as I have only...."

"Only what?"

She shook her head again and turned away from him, moving away so she would not have to speak with him any longer. He watched her glorious hair, so beautiful and lush, the way it fell down her graceful back. After a moment, he stood up and wandered, slowly, in her general direction.

"I am sure had your husband known the offense you took at him not attending your wedding ceremony personally, he would have made the effort to come," he said in a low voice. "You must not judge the man too harshly. The sword is quite an honor."

She turned to look at him. "You will not come any closer, my lord."

He stopped. "Why not?"

"Because my husband's knights are near and should they see you in conversation with me, they might do you great harm."

He smiled faintly. "So you are concerned for me? You do not even know who I am."

Devereux looked him up and down, from the top of his dark head to the bottom of his enormous feet. He was tall and although she'd seen taller men in her life, the sheer width of the man's shoulders was astonishing. And his hands were positively enormous. He was an extraordinarily big man.

"You are a seasoned warrior," she said after a moment. "I can smell death on you. That is all I need to know."

His smile faded. "Your arrogance is astounding."

Her back stiffened with outrage. "Arrogance? You overstep yourself, sir."

He lifted an eyebrow. "That is because I have spent a mere two minutes speaking with you, enough to know that you are judgmental, closed-minded and arrogant. Do you believe you are so perfect, lady? Do you believe that you walk this earth with perfect thoughts and perfect deeds? Do you understand that it is men like de Winter who have fought and died a thousand times over so you may live in your nice manor home and lead a pleasant life in your pleasant little world? How dare you judge men for their determination that England should know a better future."

By the time he was finished, the gray eyes were wide with astonishment. "It is not arrogance I present but distaste for death and destruction," she explained earnestly. "Those men you speak of have killed innocents along with their enemies. They care not who they kill so long as they are victorious."

"And you believe de Winter to be this sort of man?"

"He is the king's champion. He did not achieve this position through grace and gentleness. What other sort could he possibly be?"

"If you have not met him yet, you might want to set your prejudice aside and come to know him before you pass judgment."

She opened her mouth to argue with him but thought better of it. She began to look at him strangely, as if paying closer attention to this knight who not only seemed to be exceedingly wise but also who seemed to know de Winter very well. A little too well, in fact; he seemed to be very defensive of the man. Furthermore, there was no earthly reason why he should be standing here, alone, speaking with her. Where were all of de Winter's knights while this was going on? Devereux was many things but she was not foolish; she began to suspect who the knight before her really was.

With that knowledge, she seemed to calm. An odd twinkle came to her eye. "Very well," she said. "Since you seem to know de Winter so well, then perhaps you will tell me what you know of him."

Davyss crossed his muscular arms and lifted an eyebrow thoughtfully. "Well," he said slowly. "As I said, he is a wise and powerful man. And very handsome."

"You said that."

"It's true."

"I am sure he is humble, also."

"Indeed."

"And chivalrous."

"Of course."

She shook her head sadly. "Then he will not want me," she turned away, a very calculated move. If the man was going to play games with her, then she was going to play to win. "I have none of those qualities. For certain, it is the entire reason behind my reluctance to marry him."

Davyss watched her luscious backside. "Is that so? Do tell and perhaps I can advise you."

She feigned distress, casting him a very sad glance over her shoulder. "I drink to excess. And I have been known to steal."

Davyss bit his lip; he almost burst out laughing. "Truly? A pity."

She was adding drama to her act now. "I have never been punished for my crimes because my father is Sheriff of the Shire and clearly, no one will accuse his only child of misdeeds. I have also been known to go on rampages and burn and pillage. That has to do with the excessive drinking, I think, but my father tried to have the priest purge me of these urges. He says the devil is in me. But… but the worst part is the children."

"What children?"

"*My* children," she wandered to the narrow window, gazing out into the greenery beyond. "I have six of them. All from different fathers." She suddenly whirled around and faced him. "Do you think he will still want me for his wife now?"

Davyss was very close to collapsing with laughter. It was difficult for him to speak and not sound like he was straining for every word. "Where are these children?"

She turned away with exaggerated distress. "All gone," she sighed. "I sold three into slavery, one to a passing nobleman, and two ran away. I think wild animals ate them."

Davyss had to turn away lest she see him grin. "I am sure it will matter not," he finally said. "At least he will know that you can bear him many strong sons."

Devereux whirled in his direction, her mouth opened in outrage. "What kind of man would want such a lowly woman?"

Davyss turned to look at her, rubbing his chin so she would not see the hint of a smile. "Me," he replied frankly. "I am Davyss de Winter and I am quite pleased with my acquisition."

Devereux didn't act overly surprised by the revelation. She leaned back against the wall, a soft breeze from the lancet window lifting her golden hair gently.

"I do not believe you," she said flatly.

He walked towards her, lifting his eyebrows. "'Tis true."

She shook her head. "Davyss de Winter is nine feet tall and breathes fire, so I have been told. You do not fit that description."

He grinned; he couldn't help it. "I assure you that I am he."

Devereux felt an odd flutter in her chest when he smiled; his teeth were big, straight and white and she could see, even with his beard, that he had big dimples in each cheek. If she thought the man to be handsome before, she could clearly see that her observations were correct; he was astonishingly so. The idea brought a strange quiver to her body. She folded her arms, protectively, across her chest as he drew close. Something inherent told her to protect herself from him.

"I was right," she said quietly, eyeing him as he came to a stop fairly close to her. "You are a seasoned warrior. I can smell death on you."

His smile faded. "Perhaps," he said. "It is regretful that you do not see marriage to me as an honor. Most women would, you know."

"Most women are given to silly romantic whims and dreams of god-like knights as their husbands," she said. "I, in fact, am not."

His smile was gone completely as his gaze moved over her, the lovely shape of her face and the delicate drape of her hair. "A pity you have such distain for those who are sworn to serve and protect you."

She shook her head. "You are not sworn to serve and protect me," she contradicted, a hint of irony in her tone. "You are sworn to serve and protect the king, sworn to carry out his commands right or wrong. Knighthood has the power to unite a country yet you do nothing more than squabble between yourselves and perpetuate war. It is those motives that I distain."

He was simply watching her now, analyzing her words, attempting to figure out what was at the heart of this woman that made her so bitter. There was something more than idealism there although he couldn't put his finger on it. He moved forward and grasped her gently by the elbow, encouraging her to come with him. Reluctantly, Devereux followed.

"Have you had much exposure to the knighthood, then?" he asked quietly as they moved through the empty church.

She faltered slightly. "My father has two knights who have served him for years as Lord Mayor and Sheriff of the Shire."

"Who are these men?"

"Older men who served King Henry. One of them used to serve Eleanor of Aquitaine."

"Are those the only knights you have ever known?"

She looked at him with those bright eyes. "Aye."

"Then your opinion of the knighthood is based solely upon these two men."

She paused, gazing up into his handsome face. "I am an active member of the community and take my duties as the daughter of the Sheriff of the Shire very seriously. I hear much and I see much. Do not think I live an isolated life, my lord. My opinion is based upon tales and information that has come to me over the years."

He looked down at her; she was such an exquisite creature but, truth be told, he was coming to feel some disappointment. She was not honored by the marriage, that much was clear; she also had a very bad opinion of his profession and, consequently, him. If he were to admit it to himself, it was somewhat of a blow to his self-esteem. He'd never met a woman who hadn't been overjoyed at a mere word from the mighty and powerful Davyss de Winter. Now he had married one who didn't care in the least. He tugged gently on her elbow to get her moving again.

"I would like to give you a bit of advice, my lady," he said as the door to the church loomed before them; he could see his men waiting outside. "I do not presume to discount your opinions because they are your own. They are not truth as I know it. But if I were you, I would think twice before insulting men who have spent their lives fighting and killing for their cause. The men that serve me are battle-born, hard to the core, and have demonstrated that fierceness in battle time and time again. The stories I could tell you about them would give you nightmares for the rest of your life. You have expressed your reservations to me so let that be the end of it. From this moment on, you are the wife of Sir Davyss de Winter, Champion to our illustrious King Henry and an honored knight of the realm. Whatever you think of me personally, I should like you to at least show some respect for that position. It is an important one. Is that clear?"

She paused just as they reached the door, the sunlight glistening off her miraculous hair as she turned to look at him. "Our parents made this arrangement, my lord, and for that fact alone, I will respect my father's wishes. My acceptance of this marriage has nothing to do with you or your standing. I do it because my father wishes it."

"And I do this because my mother wishes it."

"Then we are clear."

Davyss took her outside to his waiting men, who couldn't help but notice she was far calmer with him than she had been with them. They assumed Davyss had worked his usual magic and convinced the lady to be calm and compliant. He was particularly good at convincing women of his wishes.

The lady was mounted on Davyss' charger and he mounted behind her. With a piercing whistle from Davyss, the group thundered off in the direction of Castle Acre Castle.

CHAPTER THREE

"SHE DOES NOT want anything to do with me. Do you now see how miserable you have made us both?"

Lady Katharine sat patiently as her eldest son ranted. In the lavish solar of Breckland Castle with its massive walls and elaborate gardens, Davyss had been pacing around for over an hour. His source of agitation was his new bride, now locked in a chamber in the powerful keep of Castle Acre Castle. Davyss was afraid what would happen if he didn't lock her in, so he had bolted the door and headed for his mother's castle to let her know what, exactly, he thought of her little matchmaking scheme.

"It matters not how either of you feel," Katharine replied steadily, carefully stitching the *petit poi* in her hands. It was a colorful collection of birds. "You are married and that is the end of it."

Davyss' jaw ticked faintly. "It is *not* the end of it. She hates all I stand for, Mother. She will not be an agreeable or compliant wife in the least."

Katharine continued to stitch. "Is that what you were expecting?" she didn't look up from her hands. "Mere agreement and compliance?"

"What else is there?"

Katharine lifted her thin eyebrows. "There is much more, my son. Perhaps that is why I arranged this marriage so you would understand that there is more to life than kings and compliant women."

He faced her, a scowl on his face and his hands on his slender hips. "What are you talking about?"

Katharine glanced up at him, a hint of a smile on her old lips. "You have seen thirty years and four, Davyss. What have you learned in that time? That the more men you kill and the more power you wield, the more women will fall at your feet unconditionally? Have you ever had a conversation with a woman that was not foolish courtly flirting? Have you ever known a woman to show strength of character or courage in the face of adversity? Or do you simply view them as sheep as you select your *dame du jour* from the flock?"

His scowl was gone by now. After a moment, he sighed heavily. "I am sure you are driving at a point but I cannot see what it is."

"Aye, you can," Katharine set her needlepoint down. "I am trying to tell you that there is more to life than fighting, dying and cheap women, Davyss. You are a wise, intelligent man and God has given you excellent character and judgment. You are at an age where you need to understand that family is as important as those things you have fought all your life to achieve; a good wife, intelligent and strong without political aspirations, and sons to carry on your name. And, if you are lucky, you and your wife will be fond of each other like your father and I were. It makes life worth living to rise every morning to the face of someone you are very fond of. It means more than all the money and power in the world."

He lifted a dark eyebrow at her. "If you wanted me to experience a fond wife, then you have most definitely cursed me. She shall never be fond of me."

"She will make a man out of you."

Both eyebrows lifted in outrage. "Is that what you think? That I am not a man yet?"

Katharine's smile broke through. "You still have a great deal to learn. Telling a woman how powerful and handsome you are is not the mark of a true man."

He snorted and turned away. "I doubt there is anything my new wife could teach me."

The old woman's smile faded. "Allow me to tell you something about your new wife, Davyss, and perhaps you will understand what type of woman it is that you have married," she set the needlepoint on the table and leaned back in her chair. "From a young age, Lady

Devereux has known the true meaning of service and charity. Her mother started the poorhouse on the northern edge of Thetford several years ago and your wife helped her mother feed and shelter the needy. I have heard tale that she has gone without so that others less prosperous could have just a little. I began hearing rumors of this years ago so I started giving money to the poorhouse to continue the charity work that Devereux and her mother started. All the while, I kept my eye on this girl. I knew she had depth of character and morals that most women could only hope to bear. And I knew, someday, that I would marry one of my sons to her."

By this time, Davyss' belligerent expression was gone. "I know that place you speak of."

"Of course you do. You pass by it every time you come from London to visit me."

"They call it *La Maison d'Espoir*, I believe."

"Aye, they do. The House of Hope."

He actually looked surprised. "She is a part of that place?"

Katharine nodded, eyeing her son and realizing the information was having its desired effect. If nothing else, she knew her son well; he was hot-tempered and conceited, but he was not afraid to admit when he was wrong. It was a good trait.

"Not only is she a part of that place, but she has seen to its operation since her mother passed away," Katharine said. "Do you remember that epidemic that swept through the town about five years ago?"

He nodded. "I was in London at the time. I remember you told me of it."

His mother dark eyes were piercing. "Do you know that she nursed a great many people during that time?" When he shook his head rather weakly, she continued. "While others fled the area, including her father, your wife and her mother stayed to nurse the sick. Eventually Devereux and her mother were taken ill with the same affliction; the mother died but Devereux was spared."

Davyss stood there, staring at his mother as he processed what she had told him. Eventually he found a chair and sat, struggling to come to grips with the situation.

"Then I am sure she is selfless and true," he replied. "But she holds no respect for me at all."

"What do you think of her?"

"Are you seriously asking me that question after all I have told you?"

"I am asking what you think when you look at her. Is she beautiful?"

He thought on the silken blonde hair and gray eyes. "Aye," he admitted. "She is damn beautiful, in fact. I have never seen such beauty."

"And if you had seen her in London, would you have pursued her based upon her beauty alone?"

"Absolutely. She is a fine prize for any man. I will be the talk of court when people see the beauty of the woman I have married."

Katharine cast her son a rather disapproving look. "Based upon her appearance alone she is worthy to be seen on your arm, eh? Was there nothing else you found attractive about her?"

He pursed his lips irritably, thinking on their brief encounter. "She... well, she was rather humorous."

"Humorous?"

"She made me laugh."

"I see," Katharine looked down at her sewing so he would not see the smile on her lips; he sounded utterly distressed that the woman had the power to make him laugh. "So she is beautiful and humorous. And this distresses you because she does not view you in the same light?"

He could hear a mocking note in his mother's tone and he refused to look at her. "She despises me. She said as much."

Katharine shrugged. "Perhaps she will overcome that with time," she said softly. "Give her a reason to respect you, Davyss. Sometimes esteem is more than simply handling a sword better than most or bearing the honor of the king. It comes from the heart, not the hand."

He looked at her. "She is not perfect, either. She is proud and arrogant."

Katharine picked up her needlepoint and resumed. "Perhaps," she said faintly as she began to sew. "If I were you, I would try to get to know her before making such judgments."

He lifted an eyebrow, hearing his own words in them. Rising from the chair, he exhaled sharply and puffed out his cheeks. He wasn't sure what to think anymore.

"What would you suggest I do, then?" he ventured. "You started this. What brilliant stars of wisdom do you have for me in dealing with my new wife?"

Katharine scrutinized her son; he favored her with his dark hair and hazel eyes, something that his father had lamented. Grayson Davyss de Winter had been a handsome man, no doubt, but his son's handsome appearance had eclipsed him. Davyss was a spectacular example of the male species and he was well aware of the fact which was why, his mother suspected, he was so baffled at Lady Devereux's reaction to him. The possibility that the woman would not swoon at his feet had never occurred to him.

"Shave off that forest on your face and cut your hair," she told him. "You are not usually so shaggy in appearance"

"I have been traveling for weeks."

"That is no excuse for your lack of attention to your appearance," she sniffed. "You may want to bathe as well. I can smell you from here."

Davyss gave her a look that suggested he thought her to be ridiculous. "I apologize that I am so offensive."

His mother fought off a grin. "And bring her a gift," she said. "Go into my chamber upstairs and collect what you will for her."

"Like what?"

"Jewels. Clothing, if you think it will fit her. You just married the woman; ply her with gifts."

He puckered his lips wryly. "Anything else?"

Katharine shook her head and returned her attention to the needle in her hand. "You will have to figure it out for yourself."

He pursed his lips irritably, his gaze moving to the window that overlooked the bailey below. Business went on as usual below, in sharp contradiction to the unexpected turn his life just took.

"I do not need this additional burden," he muttered. "I have more pressing problems in London at the moment. I do not need the addition of a cantankerous new wife."

Katharine stopped sewing, casting him a sharp glance. "That is *exactly* what you need."

⚃

THE ROOM WASN'T particularly large or well appointed. In fact, it was rather sparse with its single unused bed and old table. Having only heard of Castle Acre Castle, Devereux had been told it was a mysterious place, full of military implications, and now she found herself in the heart of it. It only heightened her sense of misery.

It was an enormous compound with massive ramparts built up around an enormous bailey to the south and a motte to the north. She'd never seen anything so large.

The group had entered the castle on the southwest side of town through a massive stone gatehouse, entering the complex that was vast and fortified. Several hundred soldiers were in residence at this time because of de Winter's presence and they were camped out in the enormous bailey, creating a quagmire of mud, chaos, men and animals. A vast great hall sat in the middle of the bailey along with several outbuildings. The whole area smelled like a swamp.

Built within a circle of ramparts to the north was a powerfully con-structed keep, although the keep had been partially demolished by Henry II because it had been an unlicensed fortification eighty years prior. Lady Katharine's ancestor, William de Warenne, had built it during the conflicts between Empress Matilda and King Stephan, giving rise to a very fortified and illegal bastion. Henry, when he assumed the throne, went through the countryside destroying all of these unlicensed castles in the hopes they would never be used for an uprising ever again.

But somehow, he failed to demolish all of Castle Acre Castle's massive keep. Two stories of it still remained.

Davyss had brought her to the second floor of the crumbling keep and left her in one of the two chambers, bolting the door from the outside. He'd barely said a word and she, exhausted from her day of struggle and upset, hadn't shown any resistance. From the lancet windows to the north and west, she could see the small town beyond. It was a quiet place, certainly not as large as the berg she came from. Thetford was much bigger. As the day waned, her sense of homesickness and despair grew.

He left her with no food, no drink. Devereux spent a good deal of time and energy attempting to figure out how she could climb out of the windows and not kill herself, but the room was so barren that there was nothing she could make a ladder or a rope with. She could have jumped, of course, but it was several feet to the ground and she didn't want to break something. So she gave up on the idea of escaping and sat down in the chilly room, waiting for the moment when de Winter would decide to let her out again. She was thirsty and growing hungry. As the wait became excessive, so did her animosity.

It was late afternoon by the time she heard the door rattle. Startled from hours of silence and inaction, she instinctively leapt to her feet as the door opened. The first face she saw was that of the de Winter priest. She took a closer look at him, noting he had wild gray hair, wild gray eyes, and huge scarred hands. He didn't look like any priest she had ever seen. She couldn't help but notice he stood somewhat behind the door, as if using the panel as a shield against her.

"My lady," he greeted, eyeing her warily. "I came to see if you required anything to make your stay more comfortable."

She lifted a well-shaped eyebrow at him. "Can you seriously ask me that question as you look at this desolate room?" she wanted to know. "I have been locked in here for hours with no food, nothing to drink, and no comforts whatsoever. And you think to *now* come and ask me that question?"

He looked around the room, sighing faintly. Then he took a step inside and stopped using the door as a shield.

"Perhaps we started out on the wrong note," he said with some regret. "My name is Lollardly. We were not formally introduced earlier, but I am Sir Davyss' personal priest."

Devereux eyed him. "Is this how the de Winters normally treat women? Locking them in cold rooms with nothing of comfort?"

He grunted softly and scratched his head. "My lady, this was not my doing. It would be exceedingly more pleasant for us both if you would stop being so confrontational. I realize this day has been something of a shock for you but surely you know this was not my doing. I was following orders. If you choose to hate me because of my sense of duty, then so be it. But you should also realize that our association will be as pleasant, or as adversarial, as you make it. The choice is yours."

Devereux simply stared at him. Without a response, Lollardly saw no need to stay and he began to close the door quietly. Just before he closed it completely, Devereux spoke.

"Lollardly?" she said.

He stopped. "My lady?"

She took a step towards him, her expression a mixture of loathing and resignation. She finally settled for complete resignation.

"If it is not too much trouble, I should like something to eat," she said quietly. "I have not eaten all day. And perhaps a fire would be nice; it is cold in here."

Lollardly nodded firmly, as if she had just given him an intense command. "It shall be done, Lady de Winter," he said. "Anything else?"

She felt as if she had been struck by an unseen hand at the formal mention of her new title. It took her a moment to recover her shock and distaste.

"My things," she said. "Everything was left behind at my father's house. I will need my things."

Lollardly nodded. "A few of Davyss' knights rode for your father's home a few hours ago. They should be returning shortly."

She frowned at the thought of warriors handling her clothing and personal items. She hoped her father had sense enough to have his servants pack her trunks before the knights got their blood-stained hands on everything.

"Will there be anything else, my lady?" the priest interrupted her thoughts.

She eyed him, shaking her head after a moment. "Nay," she replied softly. "Except… well, if this is to be my bed, there is no mattress on it. I will need one."

"We are already seeing to that, my lady."

There was nothing more to say and he shut the door softly. She didn't hear the bolt slip through the bracket but she couldn't be sure that there wasn't a knight out there, just waiting for her to open it. If it was a test, she would pass it. Quite frankly, there was no use escaping and returning to her father. He would only turn her back over to her husband.

So she sat on the floor against the wall opposite the hearth and waited. Except for an occasional bird flying past the windows, her environment was largely silent. Her thoughts had settled somewhat from the turbulent day although her distain at what had happened was still a powerful thing. She mostly blamed her father but knew, deep down, that the man had only been doing what he thought best for his daughter. An advantageous marriage that had been proposed to him by Lady Katharine de Winter had been both a surprise and a blessing. Only a fool would have refused. If she was honest with herself, she understood why he did it.

Time was shiftless and shapeless up in her prison. She truly had no idea how much of it had elapsed when she heard the door latch give and the panel push open. An enormous man entered the chamber clad in a tunic, breeches and massive leather boots. Seated against the wall, Devereux watched with trepidation and curiosity as the man entered with a tray in his hand.

He was clean-shaven with cropped dark hair. Devereux truly had no idea who the man was until he looked at her. Sultry hazel eyes and a face that surely Adonis was jealous of gazed steadily at her. He smiled faintly.

"My lady," he said in a soft, deep voice. "I have brought you something to eat."

She had to look again; realizing it was Davyss, she rose stiffly from the floor, inspecting him as if she was just seeing him for the first time. He was completely without armor, his face as smooth as a baby's bottom and his dark hair clean and cut. The rough linen tunic fit his powerful chest and enormous arms like the skin of a grape and she could see the muscles flexing as he moved. He had a tight waist, tight buttocks, and massively muscled thighs. And those hands... she imagined that his fist would be almost as large as her head. *My God*, she thought to herself. He was the most handsome creature she'd ever seen. But handsome or no, it did nothing to ease her animosity towards him.

"So you have come to feed your caged animal?" she moved towards him, slowly. "How chivalrous."

His smile faded. "I apologize for locking you in," he said. "You must understand that this is a military encampment. I have hundreds of men on the grounds that would not think twice before molesting a woman. What I did, I did for your safety."

She reached him and the food. "If that is true, then you should have had me bolt the door from the inside so no one could get in. As it was, you put the bolt on the wrong side of the door. Anyone could have unlocked it."

He shook his head. "The door was guarded on the landing. Moreover, had I told you the threat when I first brought you here, in your current hysterical state, I doubt you would have believed me. You would have disregarded my warning and tried to flee into an encampment of five hundred men who would have gladly taken you to sport."

She eyed him, attempting to determine if he was telling the truth. Unable to reach a conclusion, she reached out for a piece of hard, cold bread. She was starving and took a large bite.

"You could have at least left me with food and water," she scolded.

"This keep has been unused for years. I had to send my men to collect even basic necessities." He watched her stuff her mouth with the bread, feeling rather caddish about locking her up without any comforts. He moved swiftly for the door. "I have something for you. I shall return."

He slammed the door, leaving her rather startled at his swift disappearance. But her puzzlement at his departure did not outweigh her appetite and she returned to the food he had brought, set upon the old table. There was the bread plus a hunk of tart white cheese, two small apples and a handful of walnuts. There was also a cup of something, although she wasn't quite sure what it was. It smelled rank but she drank it anyway, thirsty, and realized it was old ale. She made a face of disgust.

She sat on the bed frame and finished off the bread, half the cheese and one of the little apples. By the time Davyss came back, she was in the process of trying to crack the walnuts by stepping on them. He saw what she was doing, picked the walnut off the floor, and cracked it with his bare hand. When he handed her the meat of the nut, Devereux tried not to look too astonished at brute strength.

"My thanks," she said, eyeing his massive hands and wondering what else he could crack with them.

He silently acknowledged her and proceeded to set a big satchel on the table next to the food tray. It was a leather bag with intricate embroidery on it and leather handles. He opened it up and proceeded to pull out the contents.

"Here," he handed her a great bundle of material. "This is for you."

Puzzled, Devereux unrolled the fabric and realized it was a surcoat. The material was fantastic; some kind of silk, it was dyed a brilliant blue yet when the light hit it, there were high-lights of black and iridescent green. Before she could thank him, he was piling more garments on her arms. Carefully, she began to lay everything out on the bed frame and realized, when he was finished, that she had four new surcoats, three delicate shifts, one heavy lamb's wool shift with gloriously belled sleeves and gold tassels, at least four scarves, two gold belts and several smaller pieces of jewelry. Astonished, she looked up at him.

"I… I am not quite sure what to say," she said. "I have never seen anything so glorious."

For the first time since they had met, Davyss felt like he had the upper hand. She was humbled, speechless, and he felt in control. He was also quite pleased by the awestruck expression on her face. He felt as if he had done something right.

"I hope they are to your liking," he said. "They are gifts on the event of our marriage."

Her expression went from awestruck to somewhat concerned. She actually looked worried.

"They are beautiful, of course," she said, daring to look up at him. "But I do not have any such gifts for you. I am not sure that it is fair for you to give me such riches and not expect something in return."

He smiled that brilliant, toothy smile and Devereux's heart began to race. The man was excruciatingly handsome and even she wasn't immune to it.

"Your beauty is gift enough, my lady," he said gallantly. "How fortunate for me to have married the most beautiful woman in England."

She didn't look particularly comfortable with that declaration. Seeing that his words did not have the desired effect, Davyss reached into the bottom of the satchel and pulled forth a small silk purse to retrieve another weapon in his flattery arsenal. He pulled forth a gold band with a massive yellow diamond in the center. It was a spectacular ring that glittered madly, even in the dim light. He held it out to her.

"This is the ring my father gave to my mother on their wedding day," he said. "My mother wanted you to have it. Would you honor me by wearing it?"

For the second time in as many minutes, Devereux was speechless. The ring was magnificent, larger and richer than anything she had ever seen. She knew the de Winters were wealthy but the concept truly had no meaning until this moment. For lack of a better response, she held out her hand to take it. But Davyss took her hand, flipped it over, and slipped the ring on the third finger of her left hand. It was a little snug, but the fit was secure. Devereux pulled her hand back to examine the beautiful piece.

"Again, I have nothing so magnificent for you," she said, with obvious humility. "I am not sure I can accept such extravagant gifts."

"Of course you can," he assured her. "I am your husband. It is appropriate that you should have these. A de Winter must be richly and lavishly dressed."

She looked at him. "Why is that?"

He snorted. "Because we are one of the most powerful families in England," he said as if she was in need of an education. "We must always be aware of that station and display it accordingly. Moreover, you have married the king's champion. You, my lady, must be the most beautiful and well-dressed woman in London. You must honor me in that regard."

She stared at him, beginning to see the egocentric man behind the handsome face. The man was full of himself; she'd seen a hint of it earlier in the chapel and she saw even more of it now. Her animosity and distaste for the union, so recently eased, suddenly returned with a vengeance.

"I see," she said. "So I must parade around like a peacock so that all men will look to you and envy your good fortune."

His brow furrowed slightly. "You have married well, my lady. Do you not understand that?"

She lifted an eyebrow. "And do you understand that I do not care?" she fired back. She grabbed one of the surcoats and shook it at him. "You ply me with gifts because you want me to be the best dressed, most beautiful woman in England, not because you are joyful at our marriage. All you have shown me so far is that you are only concerned with yourself and how I will make you the envy of all men. You have helped me to understand that my opinion of the knighthood was not wrong; those who participate in it are vain and self-centered. You only care for your own glory."

She tossed the garment down and turned away from him, wandering towards the lancet window where the sun was now beginning to set. Streams of pink and gold filtered in through the opening and cast beams of light on the floor.

Davyss stared at her, the gentle curve of her backside and that glorious hair that he felt the urge to run his hands through. He was struggling to see her point of view but found, at the moment, that he could not. He did not understand her resistance to that which he considered important and felt his irritation rise.

"I am sorry you do not appreciate the important station you have been given in life," he rumbled. "I was hoping you would at least understand what is expected of you."

She shook her head, unsure how to reply. The truth was that she was feeling hollow and hurt. They could not have been further apart in ideals if they had tried and the realization that she was married to such a man sank her spirits tremendously. She was going to be miserable the rest of her life and she knew it.

"You do not know me, my lord," she said quietly. "You do not understand what is important to me and I am sure you do not care. Give me time to adjust to your expectations because, I am sure, you will not adjust to mine. I do not expect it. If you want a wife in name only, then you must give me time to provide it."

He almost walked out of the room. He just didn't see any point in speaking further on the subject. But something made him stay; he wasn't sure what it was, but something deep inside told him not to leave her. Perhaps it was his mother's advice that did not allow him to move. Whether or not she was in the room, Lady Katharine was telling him to stay. *Get to know her before you pass judgment.* Crossing his enormous arms, he leaned against the wall thoughtfully.

"My mother told me get to know you," he said softly. "She told me that I must earn your respect. But I am not sure that is possible."

Devereux turned to him. "Why would you say that?"

He lifted his massive shoulders. "Because you have already formed your opinion of what kind of man I am. You did the moment you married me. I am not sure I can change that."

"You have given me little else to go on, my lord. The words out of your mouth are extremely pompous and your actions thus far have been self-serving."

He looked at her pointedly. "I have worked hard to achieve my station and reputation. I am not ashamed."

She gazed steadily at him, a faint sigh escaping her lips. "You do not have to be," she said. "But there is something called humility that is the most attractive quality anyone can possess. Do good deeds, earn your reputation, but be humble and gracious and endearing. Those qualities are more valuable than the greatest status on earth or the biggest chest of gold. It is those qualities that will cause people to bow at your feet and a wife to respect you. Does that make any sense?"

He could see she wasn't being condescending or confrontational. In fact, she spoke the words in a very gentle yet sincere manner. At that moment, he began to see something beyond the beauty. He saw something tender and benevolent. He wasn't used to those qualities in a lovely woman; he didn't think he'd ever seen it before. It made him uncomfortable, perhaps feeling exposed, but it also brought about greater interest. He wanted to see more.

"It does," he said after a moment. "But I am who I am, lady. I do not expect to change."

"I did not say change. Yet there is always opportunity to grow."

He grunted and averted his gaze as he kicked distractedly at the floor. He looked very much like he was fidgeting. "You sound like my mother. Did she tell you to say all of this?"

When he looked back up, she was smiling. Davyss had to catch his breath; he'd never seen her smile. Never in his life had he seen anything so lovely. She was an exquisite creature in any circumstance, but when she smiled, her entire face turned as radiant as the sun. It was breathtaking.

"Nay," she said with a chuckle. "I have only briefly spoken to your mother and it was not under the most pleasant of circumstances."

He pursed his lips wryly; then, he nodded and pushed himself up off the wall. "You sound just like her."

"Then she is a wise woman."

Davyss looked at her as if to retort but ended up chuckling. He made his way over to her. "Aye, she is, but do not attempt to outsmart her," he stopped a foot or so away. "She will beat you every time."

"I would never attempt to outsmart her."

"Good. And do not attempt to outsmart me, either, because that is not such a difficult task and if I lose I shall become very angry."

She fought off a grin. "Is that so?" she appeared to take his suggestion seriously. "What are the consequences, if I may ask?"

He frowned and shook his head, although there was clearly humor to it. "You would not like it."

"May I at least have a hint?"

"Are you sure you want one?"

Her grin broke through. "Is it so terrible?"

"I am not sure."

"Try."

He didn't know why he did what he did in that moment, only that it seemed like the most reasonable thing to do. Reaching out, he grabbed her by the arms and pulled her against him, planting his smooth lips firmly atop hers. When he felt her stiffen with resistance, he put his arms around her and held her fast. His embrace was warm, his hands caressing.

Devereux struggled to pull away from him, to turn her head, but every time she moved he seemed to be there, in all directions. His kiss went from firm and cold to gentle and warm. After several long seconds of defiance and struggle, she began to give in to the inevitable chemistry. The warmth, the magnetism, was irresistible and she naturally succumbed.

Davyss meant to dominate her and he had. She was small against his size and no match for his strength physically. But an odd thing happened; a gesture of dominance quickly turned into to something curious and warm. She was delicious and soft, and he took great delight in tenderly suckling her lips. When he felt her curious response, he licked her lips sensuously and gently plunged his tongue into her mouth. He could hear soft protests in her throat and she briefly struggled against him again, but just as quickly, she relaxed again. He held her closer.

He'd never known anything so sweet and pure. Because she had collapsed against him completely, his hands began to stroke her body, moving up her back and to her glorious hair. He entwined his fingers in it, feeling the silk against his flesh, and what had started out as an act of control was quickly becoming one of desire. Soon, the tables were turning and he was the one surrendering. He was losing his mind.

He lifted her up so that she was braced against him and he pushed her back against the wall. Trapped against the wall with his enormous body, Devereux had nowhere to go. His hands were everywhere and as caught up as she was in the firestorm of passion they were experiencing, she began to feel some fear when his hands moved, however tenderly, over her breasts. When she tried to protest, he merely covered her lips with his own. When she tried to physically remove his hands, he grabbed both her wrists and pinned her arms above her head.

Fear began to pound in her chest at the helpless position he had put her in. His mouth was on her neck, her face, and although there was large degree of excitement to it, she was still a maiden and everything he was doing to her was new. This wasn't anything she had ever experienced before. When he suddenly grabbed the top of her surcoat and ripped it wide-open, she shrieked. But he quickly covered her mouth with his, his tongue engaging in intimate delights, as her breasts sprang free and his hand began to grope her.

The fear bloomed and her struggles increased but he effectively had her trapped. There was nowhere for her to go. Davyss was out of control, his hand moving over her breasts and teasing her nipples into hard little pellets. When he lowered his head and capture a nipple between his lips, suckling firmly, Devereux felt excitement and desire such as she had never known shoot through her body. Bolts of lightning raced through her limbs and, for a moment, she stopped fighting him. He was warm, overwhelmingly manly, and passionate. As his mouth moved from one breast to the other, she gasped with pleasure. Whatever the man was doing to her was overpowering her senses and she began to surrender.

But that was until his roving hand ripped away the last of her surcoat and shift, leaving her entire body wide-open for his attention. The hand that was so powerfully yet tenderly caressing her breasts moved to the fluff of curls between her legs and stroked her intimately.

The fear was back in force with Devereux; she bucked with shock and he took it as desire. He wedged himself in between her knees and pried her legs open. His mouth was on hers again and she couldn't say a word; he heard the gasps and thought they were cries of passion when they were really cries of fright. He should have known the difference but he did not; when he finally inserted a finger into her warm, wet passage, Devereux screamed but he stifled her cries with his heated mouth. He stroked in and out of her, feeling her tight body, and it drove him mad like no other. He'd never been so aroused in his entire life.

With his free hand, he lowered his breeches, exposing his stiff and enormous erection. Quick as a flash, he let go of her wrists and grabbed her behind both knees, pulling her legs around his hips. Using his body, he kept her pressed firmly against the wall as hands held her pelvis against him, his arousal pushing insistently into her virginal passage.

Devereux was pounding on his enormous shoulder, terrified and aroused at the same time, as he thrust forward and almost seated himself completely on the first try. She cried out and he put his hand in her mouth to stifle her noise, his lips suckling her nipples as he firmly, carefully, withdrew himself and thrust into her again. She sobbed again and bit his hand, drawing blood, but he didn't feel it; he was only aware of his throbbing member enveloped by her tight, wet body.

And then he began to move. Slowly and carefully at first, withdrawing almost completely before pushing into her again. She was incredibly slick and his pace began to increase. His hands moved to her buttocks as he held her tight against him, his mouth on her neck and shoulders as she sobbed and weakly struggled. The more he moved within her, however, the more she seemed to surrender. With his hands on her buttocks, his mouth claimed her own and she showed the last shreds of her resistance. Soon, the hands bashing his shoulders stopped hitting him and fell still. His kisses eased into a tender and delicious assault and her hands, once still, began to caress his wide shoulders. She was starting to feel the power, too.

He stroked in and out of her, holding her beautiful body tightly against him as he moved. His mouth was everywhere; her lips, cheeks, neck, breasts. There wasn't any part of her upper body that had escaped his tender assault. As he suckled her nipples, he could feel her body drawing at him and he thrust hard, grinding his pelvis against hers and feeling her first release around his swollen member. As Devereux cried out softly, this time for an entirely different reason, Davyss thrust into her a few more times before finding his own blinding release. He spilled himself deep.

The room was full of the sounds of panting and sobs. Davyss' body was still pressing Devereux against the cold wall, his hands on her buttocks and his face buried in her neck. He originally thought her sobs were those of passion but it took him a moment to realize she was weeping deeply. It was not the sounds of joy. His head came up and he stared at her. An enormous hand flicked away a tear and she jerked her head away from him sharply.

"Stop," she wept. "Please… just stop."

He was genuinely concerned. "Why do you weep? Did I hurt you?"

She sobbed louder, putting a hand over her face so he could not see her confusion and fear. Davyss was truly at a loss; he squeezed her buttocks again, thrusting what was left of his arousal into her and gently kissing her neck. She gasped at the movement.

"Was that not to your liking, Lady de Winter?" he kissed her neck again. "We must consummate the marriage. Did you not enjoy it?"

She was weeping so hard that she couldn't speak. Davyss watched her face, thoroughly puzzled, before his gaze trailed down her slender white torso, inspecting his bride at close range. She had an incredibly beautiful body and already he could feel himself growing hard again. His hungry gaze moved to the junction where they were joined, the curls between her legs that were now mingled with his.

Her slender white legs, parted to receive him, drew his lust and he ran his hands down her thighs, feeling her stiffen to his touch. Caressing her buttocks again, he withdrew himself slightly with the intent of making love to her again but caught sight of a slight amount of blood on them both.

The sight was like throwing cold water on him. It took him a moment to realize that he had just consummated the marriage with his virgin wife and hadn't been entirely considerate about it. He'd treated her just as he treated any other woman he bedded. He should have been more thoughtful and compassionate, but the truth was that he'd been so overwhelmed with lust for the woman that he hadn't thought about anything other than quenching his own desire.

He hadn't thought of her feelings in the least; why should he? He was the great and powerful Davyss de Winter. He always took what he wanted and he had wanted her. But this was different; this wasn't some courtier or lady to be used and cast aside without thought. This was his wife, a good woman he'd been told, and he had just seriously abused that relationship. He'd thought only of himself. Pangs of remorse began to claw at him.

Carefully, he withdrew completely and set her on her feet. Sobbing, Devereux pulled the tattered ends of her surcoat tightly around her and stumbled away from him, pressing herself into the wall as close as she could get. The entire time Davyss reclaimed his tunic and secured his breeches, his gaze never left her. There was something in his expression, something unreadable and confused, that reflected the mood of the room. There was devastation here. He could feel it.

He left without another word.

CHAPTER FOUR

L ADY KATHARINE WAS greeted by Hugh at the great gatehouse of Castle Acre Castle. She'd traveled with fifty men-at-arms the nine miles from Breckland Castle to Castle Acre Castle to spend the evening with her eldest son and new wife. Given her conversation earlier in the day with Davyss, she thought it might be a wise thing to do. She'd sent word ahead of her arrival and was met at the bailey gate by Hugh, Nikolas and Philip.

The sun had set and a line of torches lit the road from the bailey gate into the heart of the compound. The glow they gave off into the velvet night was eerie, the only light amidst a vast sea of darkness. Hugh greeted his mother with a kiss to each cheek while Nikolas and Philip each showed how gracefully they could salute her. Lady Katharine eyed Nikolas in particular.

"Nik," she said. "Come closer."

Nikolas stepped forward, gazing full-faced at Lady Katharine. She reached out a bird-like hand and grasped his chin, turning his face slightly. She was looking at something in particular.

"Where did you get that black eye?" she asked.

Nikolas didn't falter although Philip, next to him, fought off a smirk. "In the struggle with Lady de Winter earlier today, my lady," he replied steadily.

"Did she strike you?"

"Not with her fists, my lady," he replied. "She hit me with the leg of a chair."

Lady Katharine's eyes narrowed at the injury and she unfortunately caught a glimpse of Philip; his nose was swollen and purple. She jabbed a gnarled finger at him.

"And what happened to you?" she demanded.

Philip's smirk was gone and he cleared his throat softly. "A door to the nose, my lady."

"Lady Devereux?"

"Aye, my lady."

Lady Katharine shook her head. "God's Blood," she breathed. "I have never heard of such nonsense."

Hugh stood next to his mother, still feeling the sting of embarrassment and inadequacy from earlier in the day when they had all failed to charm, or subdue, Lady Devereux. Davyss' collection of knights were some of the most powerful warriors in the court of King Henry the Third but they had failed to effectively restrain one very small lady. It was a shameful display that they hoped would never become public knowledge.

The carriage carrying Lady Katharine moved from the gatehouse towards the massive lower bailey beyond. At sunset, the smells of cooking fires and roasting meat were heavy in the air. Hugh rode beside the carriage astride his big bay charger.

"All that is in the past, Mother," he assured her. "She surely understands her place now."

Lady Katharine cast him a long look. "What makes you say this?"

"Because she has been confined to her chamber since arriving here earlier today," he replied. "Davyss spent a good deal of time with her earlier. I am sure he explained things to her."

"Where is your brother now?"

"In the hall."

"And how is your brother's mood since his undoubtedly productive discussion with Lady Devereux this afternoon?"

Hugh looked at her; he resembled his mother a good deal with his dark eyes and angular face. "Why do you ask?"

"I am curious. Answer me."

Hugh shrugged as they passed into the vast bailey with its collection of cooking fires and scent of men and animals. "He seems well enough."

Lady Katharine didn't say any more as the carriage neared the great all, a massive thing planted in the middle of the lower bailey. Its stone walls soared skyward and the roof was sharply angled, covered with a matting of pitch and sod. The enormously long lancet windows cast bright streams of light into the darkened bailey, the result of a massive fire in a hearth that could have easily fit ten men inside it. Hugh helped his mother disembark and escorted her into the hall. Her severely wimpled ladies, three of them, followed close behind.

There was one very big table near the hearth, large enough for fifty men. Servants moved around the room, lighting tapers and bringing food to the table. The hall itself was spartanly furnished with a cluttered dirt floor and dogs huddled in the corners. It smelled almost as bad as the bailey outside. Davyss was sitting facing the door when his mother and brother entered. He watched his mother come near, his expression unreadable, and took a long drink of his wine.

Lady Katharine reached the table and was helped to sit by Hugh and Nikolas. The bench was dusty, with bits of old food on it, and they brushed it off for her. Nikolas took her cane and leaned it against the hearth as Lady Katharine's women took position behind her; never would they dare sit in her presence.

Katharine watched her eldest closely; there was something about his expression that had her curious as well as concerned. The man seemed to have difficulty holding her gaze which was unlike him. Davyss was, if nothing else, fearless and confident. He always looked people in the eye because he believed you could tell a good deal about what they were thinking simply by the countenance of their eyes. Were she to use her son's logic, his thoughts were not good.

"Davyss," she accepted a cup of wine from one of her women. "You did not greet me at the gate."

Davyss eyed his mother. "My apologies."

He didn't sound as if he meant it but she let it go. "Where is your wife?" his mother asked. "I have traveled a great distance to spend time with her."

Something in Davyss' eyes darkened; Lady Katharine saw it. After a moment of holding her gaze, he averted his eyes and took another swallow of wine.

"In her chamber, I would presume."

"You do not know?"

He looked at his mother then. "I left her there some time ago. She was there when I left."

Lady Katharine was growing edgy at her son's evasive manner. She smacked the table and demanded her cane, which was brought to her by one of her cowering women. Cane in hand, she rose stiffly.

"Davyss," she said firmly. "You will attend me."

Davyss knew better than to argue, although he was fairly drunk and in no mood for his mother's imperious manner. He knew what was coming. Still, he did as he was told; slamming his cup to the table, he went to his mother and gently took her elbow. He led her from the hall, out into the starlit night beyond.

The bailey was muddy with excrement, a stark contrast to the crisp and pure sky above. Lady Katharine was unsteady on her feet and the uneven walking surface nearly toppled her, so Davyss swung his mother into his powerful arms and carried her across the muck.

"Where did you wish to go?" he asked.

"Take me to your wife."

Somewhere low in his throat, he growled. Lady Katharine's eyes narrowed at her boy.

"What has happened, Davyss?" she asked, although there was no true force behind it. "Why is she not down in the hall?"

Davyss was not in a chatting mood and he didn't feel like answering foolish questions. He would not look his mother in the eye as he headed for the distant, lonely keep.

"I do not know what you mean," he rumbled.

She smacked him on the shoulder. "You know very well what I mean. Where is your wife and what has happened since you and I spoke at Breckland? Did you not speak to the woman and try to reconcile your rough beginning?"

He didn't answer until they reached a portion of the bailey that was hard-packed earth. Gently, he set his mother to her feet. Before them loomed the motte and keep, stretching long and dark against the starry sky. Instead of escorting her forward, he simply stood there. Lady Katharine sensed great turmoil but waited patiently for him to speak. She was, in truth, surprised to see him so agitated, an unusual condition for the usually-cool man.

"If you must know, I fear that I have irrevocably damaged whatever chance Lady Devereux and I had of having an agreeable marriage," he finally said.

"What did you do?"

Davyss looked at his mother, realizing that he was embarrassed to tell her. But he knew he could not avoid it. He averted his gaze, taking a deep breath as he tried to delicately phrase the situation.

"I consummated the marriage," he told her. "It was not... pleasant."

Lady Katharine lifted an eyebrow. "What do you mean?"

He grunted, scratching his neck in a nervous gesture. "I took her by force."

Lady Katharine's dark eyes cooled dramatically. "You raped her."

He shook his head. "Nay, not in the true sense," he said. "I thought... I thought we were of one mind at the time. I thought she was agreeable but I realized that... I did not even realize she was resisting me until after it was over. It never occurred to me that...."

He was having difficulty spitting it out and Lady Katharine's attitude grew colder.

"It never occurred to you that she could resist your charm and your wit because no woman ever has," she moved closer to him, her dark eyes blazing. "Davyss, you are the greatest knight in the realm. Do not believe for one minute that I do not hear of your every triumph and every exploit. I know of your fearlessness, your strength and your bravery. I also know that you have every woman at court mad for you. God knows how many bastards you have about; it makes me ill simply to think on it. But for all of your strength and skill and dashing good looks, you are a fool when it comes to women. Do you hear me? I have raised in idiot!"

He took her scolding; nothing she said was untrue. He hung his head, unable to look her in the eye. Furious, she grabbed him by the chin and forced him to face her.

"Did you hurt her?" she demanded.

"Other than the obvious, I do not believe so."

"Where is she?"

"I left her in the chamber on the second floor."

"And you have not talked to her since? Not even to see if she is well?"

He tried to shake his head. "Nay," he replied. "But I did send Lollardly to her with food and her trunks. He saw to her needs."

Lady Katharine's features tightened and she dropped her hand. "You sent that lecherous drunk to see to your wife?"

"I did."

"Did he speak to her?"

"He brought her food and drink. Beyond that, I have not spoken with him further about her."

Lady Katharine's dark eyes glittered; there was great displeasure in the dark and stormy depths, unusual for the woman who was much like her son in that she did not readily show emotion. Then she smacked him on his taut buttocks with her cane.

"Get up there," she growled. "Go to your wife and beg for her forgiveness. Make every effort to make amends because if you do not, so help me, you will not like my reaction. Is that clear?"

He sighed heavily. "I doubt she wishes to see me. 'Twould be better if you went. Perhaps she would not be so hostile."

Lady Katharine's eyebrows flew up. "If I...?" she sputtered. But, after a moment's thought, she cooled. Perhaps he was right; perhaps she should be the ambassador for peace and beg forgiveness for her inept son. "Very well," she agreed after a moment's deliberation. "I shall see if

I can make a masterpiece out of the mess you have created."

"I would be grateful."

"Would you really? I wonder."

He was properly, and genuinely, contrite. "I fear that I need your help, Mother."

"You have not needed my help since you were four years old."

"I need it now."

Lady Katharine shook her head and turned towards the towering keep. She could see a soft light at the top. "I would have done better to marry her to Hugh," she growled. "What on earth was I thinking when I pledged this woman to you?"

Davyss truly didn't have an answer. For the first time in his life, he was doubting himself. His confidence had taken a tremendous hit since the moment he first laid eyes on the Lady Devereux Allington. On the battlefield, he was invincible, but where women were concerned, he apparently still had a good deal to learn. Everything was cloudy to that regard but he knew one thing; he deeply regretted what he had done. He'd spent the rest of the afternoon brooding on it and coming to the conclusion that he had more than likely ruined any chance of an amicable marriage. And he was deeply upset by it.

He found himself reverting back to the original plan; he would leave his wife in Norfolk and return to London. She would bear his children and he would carry on his life at court as if they had never married. But even as he convinced himself of the proper course of action, the one thing he hadn't gambled on was the fact that his new wife was extraordinarily lovely and intelligent. There was something very different about her and he wasn't at all sure he wanted to be parted from her. As he watched his mother make her way into the keep, he found himself hoping she could right his wrong.

CB

A SOFT KNOCK on the door roused Devereux from her dozing state. Seated in a crude wooden chair before the peat fire that Andrew had started for her, she was exhausted both physically and mentally. But at least the room was warm now and a mattress had been produced for the bed. Stuffed with fresh straw, it was covered with the linens that had been brought from her father's house. They were linens that she and her mother had sewed together when she had been young. Her trunks were lined up neatly against the wall and Andrew had even had fresh rushes brought to the chamber. The room was far cozier than it had been hours earlier.

The knock rapped a second time and Devereux rose, both anxious and defensive. The past several hours had done nothing to ease her devastation at what had happened with Davyss. If anything, her sense of desolation had deepened, ingraining itself into her heart. She wasn't sure she could ever look at the man again and not think of what had happened. The worst part was, if she would admit it to herself, was the fact that for the most part, she had enjoyed it. Davyss had awakened a part of her she never knew to exist. She was deeply ashamed.

"Who is it?" she asked as she drew near the door.

"Lady Katharine," came a voice from the other side. "May I enter?"

Devereux well remembered her last conversation with the woman but there was no way she could avoid her. She bade her enter.

"Aye," she replied.

The door opened and the frail old woman stepped through. On the landing outside, Devereux could see at least two soldiers guarding the door. They shut the panel as the old woman moved into the room. Devereux stood several feet away, gazing steadily at her, waiting for the lashing that was undoubtedly to come.

But a lashing was not immediately forthcoming. Lady Katharine faced her new daughter, inspecting the woman in the firelight; she was clad in the heavy white woolen shift with the belled sleeves and gold tassels hanging from the cuffs. The shift was more of a heavy surcoat than an actual shift, with a stiff collar around the neck and a plunging neckline with gold embroidery around it. It was, in truth, an exquisite garment, made more exquisite by Devereux's beauty. Lady Katharine sighed with satisfaction.

"My husband brought me that coat all the way from Rome," she indicated the off-white garment. "It never looked so good on me."

Off-guard with the compliment, Devereux looked down at herself as if confused by the woman's observations. After Davyss had left and she had pulled herself together, she had dressed in the warm garment simply because the room was cold. She had then pulled her silky hair into a single thick braid, tied at the end with a golden scarf. She had no idea how angelic and radiant she looked.

"This belongs to you?" she smoothed her hands over the feather-soft wool. "Your son gave it to me as a gift. I was unaware that it was yours."

The old woman waved her hand. "I told him to give to it to you. It was made for you."

Devereux didn't know what to say. She wasn't feeling particularly amiable towards any member of the de Winter family at the moment but she would not forget her manners. She indicated the chair to Lady Katharine.

"Would you sit, my lady?" she said.

Lady Katharine made her way to the chair and sat heavily. Her gaze moved over the room, the fire, the over-stuffed mattress before finally coming to rest on Devereux again. Her dark eyes were piercing as she appraised her and it was a struggle for Devereux not to back away. She met the woman's gaze steadily.

"How may I be of service, my lady?" Devereux asked.

Lady Katharine's attention remained steady. "I understand you and my son experienced some conflict this afternoon. I am here to see if I can assist."

Devereux's brow furrowed slightly. "Did he send you?"

The old woman shifted slightly. "He did."

Devereux's silver eyes regarded the woman a moment. She was careful in her reply. "Lady Katharine, surely you realize that this marriage is not palatable for your son or for me," she said. "Why, exactly, did he send you?"

"To see if I could ease your anger towards him."

Devereux pondered that a moment; so he feared that she was angry with him? Odd, he didn't seem the type. He seemed more like the kind who didn't care what anyone thought. Still, she was deeply confused and deeply hurt by the events of the afternoon. She turned away from the woman and moved towards the hearth, feeling the soft heat on her skin.

"What I feel is not anger, my lady," she said. "He is my husband. He had every right to take what belonged to him. For this, I cannot fault him."

"But you are upset."

She suddenly looked at the woman, sharply. "I want to go home," she hissed. "I was abducted from my home by four monstrous knights, married to a sword and forced into submission by my husband in a brutal act of consummation. Today I have endured more than any woman can be expected to reasonably endure. As I told you earlier today, I do not want to marry your son but it is done. Now I am his wife whether or not I want to be. He has consummated the marriage and we have done our duty. Now allow me to go home in peace while my husband returns to London and the intrigue that infects it. I want no part of it. I simply want to go home."

Her last words were spoken on the verge of tears and Lady Katharine watched her turn away. The old woman had to admit that the lady had had a rough day. She did indeed feel pity for her.

"I am sorry that you have had such a difficult time," she replied evenly. "But you were not innocent in all of this. You fought like a banshee which is why the knights were forced to take steps to restrain you. I have seen Sir Nikolas' black eye and Sir Philip's bruised nose. I did not imagine those injuries, perpetrated by you."

"I was defending myself."

"Against what?"

"Against men determined to abduct me."

"They were not determined to abduct you. They had come to take you to your husband and you started the battle. The abduction was a direct result of your violent behavior."

She looked at Lady Katharine angrily. "Do you condone their behavior, then?"

"I certainly do not condone yours. Think carefully before you accuse others of misdeeds, lady. You started it."

Devereux could see that she wasn't gaining much sympathy. Infuriated and hurt, she refused to look at Lady Katharine.

"I want to go home," she whispered again. "I do not want to be a part of this life. I do not want to be a part of the de Winter war machine."

Lady Katharine leaned on her cane. "But you are now chatelaine of Castle Acre Castle. This is a prestigious post. Does this not bring you joy?"

Devereux shook her head. "It does not," she said honestly. "Do you not understand? I have never wanted anything like this. I must return to my charity work; it is something I have devoted my life to. I would feel useless and silly being chatelaine of a great castle. There is no joy in it for me. My joy comes from helping those in need. It is that life I would return to."

Lady Katharine drew in a long, thoughtful breath. "Your charity work is well known, Lady Devereux. That is one of the things that impressed me so much about you."

"Then let me return to it," Devereux suddenly turned to her imploringly. "I am not needed here. Please, Lady Katharine; let me go home."

"You *are* home."

Devereux shook her head. "This is not my home. This is a prison."

The old woman gazed steadily at her. "And you do not believe you can be happy here?"

Devereux's expression washed with sorrow. "Nay," she whispered. "This place bears only misery for me."

"Is there nothing my son can say to you to change your mind?"

Devereux moved away from her, back towards the fire again. "He has taken what is his right," she said softly. "I will bear his children and carry his name. But in return, I want to go home. I want to continue what is important to me. I do not want to be a part of Davyss de Winter's world nor part of the rule he supports because it is the king's tyranny that creates a good deal of the misery I see."

Lady Katharine suddenly felt very weary. She was starting to think that perhaps this idea of hers had not been wise. Perhaps this woman could not benefit her son as she had hoped. But the marriage was consummated, making it impossible for an annulment. They would have to make the best of it until the emotions of the situation had settled. Perhaps there would be a chance at a later time for the two of them to come to some sort of amicable existence. After a moment, Lady Katharine rose from the chair and leaned heavily on her cane.

"Very well," she said quietly. "If that is your wish, I will not deny you. You may leave with me when I return for Breckland. I will return you home."

Devereux nodded, silent and brooding. With a lingering glance at the lowered blonde head, Lady Katharine made her way from the chamber and down the narrow stairs of the keep. Out in the moonlit night with a hundred torches lighting the lower bailey against the dark sky, she found her son just where she had left him.

Davyss saw his mother coming and went to meet her. She hadn't been with his wife very long, something that both concerned and encouraged him. He met his mother just as she was descending the steps from the keep. He took her arm to steady her down the big stone stairs.

"Well?" he asked. "What did she say?"

Lady Katharine sighed heavily. She was feeling her age tonight. "She does not want to remain at Castle Acre Castle and she does not want to remain with you," she said pointedly. "Whatever has happened between the two of you, it is clear that tonight will not see it mended."

Davyss felt his disappointment. "Did she tell you that she did not wish to remain?"

Lady Katharine nodded. "On all accounts. I am therefore taking her with me when I return to Breckland. I am taking her back to her father, Davyss. Leave her be for a while. Let us see if time cannot mend this episode."

Davyss' gaze moved to the two story keep. He could see a weak light in the window of the second floor chamber. "Let me go and speak with her," he said with a mixture of resignation and determination. "Perhaps I can make amends."

Lady Katharine grabbed him before he could move. "Nay," she said firmly. "Leave her alone. I fear you will only make things worse if you try."

"But…"

"Nay, Davyss," she said, more firmly. "The woman needs time to heal. Let her reconcile this marriage in her own mind. Give her time before you approach her again."

Davyss didn't want to listen to her; that much was clear. But he acquiesced with great reluctance, escorting his mother back to the great hall even though his mind was on his new wife in the bower high above the bailey.

Devereux left before sunrise.

CHAPTER FIVE

Six weeks later

T HE STRUCTURE THAT was *La Maison d'Espoir* had originally been a barn thirty years ago, put together with strips of wood, thatch and an oddly well-made frame. But it was eventually abandoned and subsequently confiscated by the Lady DeHaven Devereux-Allington. The lady wife of the Lord Mayor of Thetford, Lady DeHaven took her duties as the mayor's wife seriously and as the king's wars with his barons intensified, she sought to help the increasing number of people who were left homeless and injured as a result. Much of Devereux's opinions on kings and warfare had come from her peace-loving mother. Commandeering the abandoned barn on the north edge of the city had been a starting point to helping those that war and famine touched.

Lady DeHaven and her young daughter, Devereux, had cleaned up the place as much as they could in order to shelter some of the homeless and ill. Soon, more people joined them in their quest to aid the less fortunate and more and more poor, sick and homeless came to The House of Hope as the years passed. Word of the benevolent Allingtons had spread. Eventually, the structure housed hundreds and Lady DeHaven and her daughter cooked for and tended to the needy. The House of Hope was legendary throughout the area for its compassionate and necessary work.

When Lady DeHaven died, the legacy was left to her daughter. It was the place that Devereux called home even more than the fortified manor she shared with her father. She had been back from Castle Acre Castle for a little over a month and had settled back into her routine, following the schedule she and her mother had set all those years ago. It gave her peace and comfort to be back in familiar surroundings, but more than that, she was back with those people with whom she shared the same ideals. She had a good deal of help with townsfolk who pitched in to help her; at any given time there were upwards of fifty people helping her feed and tend the sick and poor. More than her father, certainly more than her husband, these people were her family. She had struggled for a month to put memories of Davyss de Winter out of her mind. It was still a struggle.

As the sun rose on this clear and cool day, Devereux had been up before sunrise, as was usual. A farmer she did business with had delivered a wagon full of oats that she and several other helpers had taken from the wagon to the kitchens where three cooks were preparing great iron vats of cooked oats with vast quantities of dried cherries thrown in. There had been a bumper crop of cherries last fall and they had been lucky enough to receive the overflow from a farmer north of Ipswich. They had barrels of millet that had been ground into flour and mixed with a lesser quantity of buckwheat to make bread, the smell of which was wafting heavily in the air from the large earthen ovens built to the west of the building.

There were also huge amounts of walnuts and hazelnuts in the kitchen area as well as bushels of small, sour crab apples. With monetary donations that Devereux had received from Lady Katharine de Winter no less, she had worked a deal with a local dairy farmer for wheels of soft, tart white cheese. All of these things, plus the cooked oats, would provide food for the nearly two hundred people staying under the roof of The House of Hope.

Dressed in a heavy surcoat of dark blue wool, Devereux was wrapped tight against the cold morning as she directed the workers. Her luscious hair was pulled away from her face with a kerchief, revealing her lovely and cold-pinched face. Seeing that her helpers had transferred most of the oats into the kitchen, she moved into the main structure of the house itself to make sure that everyone began their orderly mobilization towards the feeding area. It was moderately warm inside, smelling of bodies, as people began to rise for the day. A little lad, no more than two, suddenly crashed into her in his eagerness to get his food and she laughed softly as she righted the child.

"Lady Devereux?"

Someone was addressing her from behind and she turned around to see a young man she'd known all her life. Stephan Longham was a man of lesser birth, a year older than her, but strong and handsome. His father was the smithy in town and his mother a midwife. He had three younger brothers who all helped at The House of Hope. Devereux had always greatly depended on the Longham boys as laborers, cooks, surgeons and friends.

Stephan smiled as the little boy who had just crashed into Devereux almost smacked into him as well in his haste to get away. Together, they watched the child dash off.

"What can I do for you, Stephan?" Devereux asked.

Stephan returned his attention to her. "Sedgebow is outside. He has a wagon full of salted pork and said that he was told to bring it to you."

Her brow furrowed slightly as she began to move back towards the kitchens. Stephan followed.

"The pig farmer from Westley?" she clarified, puzzled. "I have not spoken with the man in months, not since the last time he tried to bargain with us for his salt pork. 'Tis always far too expensive."

Stephan followed her into the steamy kitchens. "I told him to go away but he would not leave without speaking with you first."

Devereux braced herself for the confrontation. "The man is a thief and a liar," she growled. "I will not purchase his salt pork no matter how much he is willing to bargain."

Stephan didn't reply; he had been serving Lady Devereux at The House of Hope for almost ten years. He knew how she did business and he knew what was expected of him should Sedgebow not leave if the lady asked him to. Stephan knew Lady Devereux very well and had loved her nearly as long as he'd known her; although beneath her station, it did not ease what he felt for her. Her marriage to Davyss de

Winter had devastated him.

Lady Devereux wouldn't speak of her marriage to de Winter or why she had returned to Thetford and no one would dare ask. They had all either seen or heard of the spectacle of the marriage a month past, how Lady Devereux had attempted to fight off de Winter and his men. It had been a frightening and curious thing. So Stephan had stuck to her closely since her return as both friend and assistant; she was back and he didn't care why. It was the closest he could get to her without overstepping both his boundaries and social station.

Devereux burst into the dusty, cluttered delivery area just outside the kitchen yards with full force, preparing to argue with the wily pig farmer. Stephan was right behind her; somewhere in their march they had picked up his youngest brother, Cullen, who was absolutely enormous. A big, bald young man, he was mostly fat but strong as an ox. He and Stephan made for an intimidating pair as Devereux faced off against the pig farmer from Westley.

"Sedgebow," she began with annoyance in her tone. "I told you the last time we had dealings that I would no longer be purchasing any of your salt pork. I thought you understood me clearly."

The fat, toothless farmer lifted a lazy eyebrow. "You did not purchase this, m'lady," he said. "I was directed to bring it to you."

Confusion outweighed her annoyance. "Who directed you?"

Before the farmer could answer, the sounds of thunder could be heard in the distance. Startled, Devereux instinctively stepped back as a herd of chargers entered the area, kicking up great clods of earth with their sharp hooves. The sounds of snorting filled the air and the glint of mail and armor flashed in the dawn's early light. After her initial start, Devereux realized she was looking at Davyss and his men.

The power of the de Winter war machine was unmistakable. The men bore tunics of black and gray with the red de Winter dragon stitched on the front. Devereux was suspicious and resistant to their appearance, apprehensive of Davyss. They had parted on an unpleasant note and she feared that the song between them was still unpleasant.

Truth be told, she wasn't sure what to think. For a man she had sworn to loathe the day she had left Castle Acre Castle, at the moment, she didn't loathe him as she hoped she could. Some odd sensation in her chest told her that she was glad to see him. Her heart thumped and twisted oddly and her gaze remained fixed on him, as if she could look at nothing else, as his massive charcoal steed with its glinting plate armor pushed its way forward.

Davyss flipped up his visor, his gaze falling on his wife. He was not disappointed; she was more beautiful than he remembered. He'd spent forty-two days attempting to convince himself that she was of no consequence to him; it was a marriage of convenience and he would treat it as such. But even as he attempted to resume his normal routine, he found one portion of that routine that he could not resume. He did not take a woman to his bed during those forty-two days; not one.

He had his share of admirers and regular playmates, but he found that he could not bed them. Something deep inside him prevented it, although he knew not what. The last woman he had intimately touched had been Devereux. Like it or not, she had marked him. He couldn't get her out of his mind.

More than that, his mother, oddly, had not tried to speak to him of his marriage at all. Lady Katharine had remained unusually quiet on the subject, which only caused Davyss to think more strongly about it. As the days passed and the duties of the king's champion consumed him, he found his thoughts lingering on the woman he had married. He reached a point where he could think of nothing else. He needed to discover why.

"Lady de Winter," he greeted, bracing an enormous fist against a thigh as he gazed down at her unearthly beauty. "I hope you can put this pork to use."

Her eyebrows lifted. "*You* purchased the pork?"

He nodded, tearing his gaze away to look over the enormous, patch-worn barn that was The House of Hope. He gestured at the structure. "I thought you could use it."

Devereux was twice stunned; not only by his appearance but by his donation. It was overwhelmingly generous. Rather speechless, she separated herself from Stephan and made her way hesitantly towards her husband.

"Of course we can use it," she stopped a few feet from the charger, her lovely face upturned to him, knowing she should at least thank the man. "Your... your donation is exceedingly generous, my lord. Thank you."

He flashed a smile at her, a brilliant gesture that had sent many a maiden's heart fluttering. But for Devereux, the gesture was genuine. He wasn't trying to gain favor or make a woman swoon. He was genuinely glad to see her. He dismounted his charger.

"I would see this place that you have made famous," he winked at her. "Would you show it to me?"

She blinked; he seemed almost jovial. It was not the sort of reaction she was expecting from him considering the animosity between them when they last parted. But here he was, standing before her as if nothing had happened and actually appearing happy. She began to suspect that the salt pork was more an offering of peace than anything else and something in her softened, if only slightly. She dipped her head graciously to his request.

"If that is your wish, my lord," she replied.

"It is. And it is also my wish to have you call me Davyss, please. It seems terribly formal to address your husband as 'my lord'."

Stunned, she blinked at him. "V-very well, my... I mean, Davyss."

He smiled at her. "That was not too hard, was it?"

A bit overwhelmed by the entire situation, she simply shook her head. Davyss took her elbow chivalrously and began to lead her towards the structure. He couldn't help notice that she was having difficulty looking him in the eye but he wasn't surprised; they had parted with indifference and hostility. He was, frankly, surprised she hadn't ordered him away when he had appeared with the pig like some sort of offering to an angry god. Pleased that his gift of pork had produced the desired effect, he was determined to continue the momentum. Perhaps if he could bombard her with his overwhelming and suave personality, she would forget her anger. But deep down, he knew she wasn't that shallow, yet it was the best plan he had at the moment.

"I hope you have been well since we last spoke," he said pleasantly.

Devereux nodded. "I have," she replied. "And… you?"

There was some hesitation to that question, as if she had been forced to ask it out of courtesy, and he fought off a smile. "Well enough," he said, eyeing her lowered head. "You are more beautiful than I had remembered."

It sounded like a contrived compliment that was uttered far too smoothly. Devereux sensed he was attempting to soften her somehow with sweet words and irritation began to bloom, with perhaps some disgust mixed in. They entered the structure at that moment and she extended her arm, indicating the warm, musty and crowded great room beyond.

"This is our main hall," she told him, sounding rather clipped. "We can house up to three hundred people in here but today, we only have around two hundred. But that will change."

Davyss noted the tone and was puzzled; what he had done already to provoke her irritation? For lack of a better response, he simply observed the dim hall with the straw floor and rough-hewn benches. There was no comfort to it whatsoever but in spite of that, the place was warm and smelled of hay and porridge. The combination was oddly soothing.

"Why will it change?" he asked curiously.

She looked at him. "Because the winter and spring were very difficult and cold. Most peasants in the area have run through their food stores."

Lollardly, having followed Davyss into the building along with the rest of the knights, entered the conversation.

"Your charity work is well known, my lady," he said with approval. "God will reward you well for your work."

Devereux turned to the scruffy, smelly priest. "I would rather that God reward these people. They need it much more than I do."

Lollardly gazed steadily at her, still seeing the defiance but now seeing something more. There was something wise and settled about the woman. He had known of Devereux Allington's charity from the onset, but seeing it the flesh was a sight to behold. He wondered if it was having any impact on Davyss, the man who usually thought only of himself. Lollardly could see for himself how completely different Davyss and Devereux's worlds were. No wonder she had fought this marriage like a banshee.

"God rewards the meek, my lady," he replied, a bit more subdued. "Have no doubt he shall take care of these people."

Devereux wasn't sure what more to say so she said nothing. Davyss, however, continued to look around the room, littered with the old as well as the very young. He'd never seen a place like this, a place for charity where even the smallest bit of food was a matter between life and death. His version of life and death involved sword and battle, not food and shelter. But this was humanity as he was unused to seeing. It was simple, desolate and powerful. Without realizing it, he began to walk through the masses.

He passed by families with young children huddled around bowls of steaming porridge. They had the look of hungry animals. He passed by old couples who were sharing food between them. He watched as an old man fed an old woman who couldn't seem to muster the strength to do it herself. The old man was very sweet with the woman, petting her cheek as if to remind her to swallow. As he watched the pair, Devereux sat on the bench next to the woman and reached out to take the porridge from the old man.

"Thelred, I shall feed her," she told him gently. "You have not yet eaten. Go and get your meal and I shall take care of your wife."

He shook his head. "Thank ye, m'lady, but I will tend the wife me-self. We've spent a lot o'years together. She needs me."

Devereux smiled faintly at the joy the old man exhibited; he seemed very happy in his life, something she admired a great deal. The man had absolutely nothing but as long as he had a roof over his head and food for his wife, he was content.

"Are you sure?" she pressed gently.

The old man nodded firmly. "We'll be just fine, thanks to ye."

Devereux patted his leathered hand. "As you say," she said softly. "I respect your devotion, Thelred. Your wife is a very fortunate woman."

The old woman suddenly vomited, spilling out porridge all over herself, her husband and some on Devereux. Devereux did nothing more than show concern to the woman; she called quickly for rags and between her and the old man, managed to clean the old woman up adequately. Devereux even helped Thelred direct the old woman to a pallet where they carefully laid her down to rest. The entire time, other than wipe her hands clean, Devereux never once lamented the fact that she had vomit on her clothes. She was simply concerned with the health and welfare of the old woman.

Davyss watched the entire event. In that moment, that space of time, he sprouted a healthy respect for his wife. He'd never seen anyone so selfless or kind and his initial treatment of her began to gnaw at him like nothing he had ever experienced. He had indeed been cruel and callous to this glorious creature, someone so gentle that she treated the poor as if they were God's greatest creatures.

Given his background and noble status, he should have found her behavior repulsive but he did not; there was something holy and compassionate about it. As Devereux returned to him, only now beginning to clean the vomit off her sleeve, he watched her through new eyes.

"Is there something more I can do?" he asked, nodding his head in the direction of the old couple. "That woman is ill."

Devereux glanced at the pair as the old man began stroking his wife's hair. "She is old and sick," she said softly. "I am afraid there is nothing anyone can do, although I thank you for your offer."

Davyss wasn't sure what more to say; he suddenly felt uncomfortable, as if he didn't belong at this place. He only brought death and destruction. This place brought hope. He gazed down at his wife, so lovely he could hardly believe it. But she had something more than beauty, something his mother had seen. He was beginning to see it, too. He took a moment to summon his courage and swallow his considerable pride.

"I must be honest with you, my lady," he finally said. "I am not entirely sure why I came here today, only that in the month we have been apart, I have thought of little else but you. Our marriage got off to a very bad start and for that, I am sorry. I will accept the blame but in that blame, I find that I must also accept responsibility for rectifying the situation. I am hoping you will allow me."

She looked up at him, her suspicions on his appearance confirmed; the pig had indeed been a peace offering. She was oddly touched by the gesture and by the fact the man wanted to make amends for his boorish behavior. In fact, she could hardly believe he had voiced an apology. If he had put aside his conceit to show her some honesty, then perhaps she should as well. She reasoned that she at least owed him that chance if he was willing to try. She realized, as she gazed into his handsome face, that she was willing to try as well.

"Our rough beginning was not entirely your fault," she admitted, although it was difficult. "I did not make it easy."

He smiled, a genuine gesture. "I am not quite sure how else you were expected to react when four enormous knights broke in to your home and abducted you."

She heard her words echoed in his statement and it brought a grin. Somewhat sheepishly, she averted her gaze. "They did not exactly break in," she informed him. "They did, in fact, knock."

He laughed softly. "Ah, then I am glad they at least showed some manners," he said, sobering as he watched her lovely features. There was something more he wanted to ask but was fearful of her reaction; even so, he continued. "I was hoping you would sup with me tonight so that we may discuss the situation further."

She nodded after a slight hesitation. "I would be agreeable."

"Good." Relieved, his eyes twinkled as he continued to watch her, every move she made. "When shall I return for you?"

"Return?" she cocked her head. "Are you leaving, then?"

He shook his head. "Not really; we are moving on to Castle Acre Castle for a while. I will return at sundown if that is acceptable."

"It is."

"Will you see me out?"

She nodded and he thought he saw a blush. Enchanted and thrilled, he took her hand and tucked it into the crook of his elbow. The entourage that had followed them into the hall now fell in behind them as they retreated, suspicious glances and expressions passing between the Longham brothers and Davyss' knights.

Hugh was especially suspicious, casting threatening expressions at Stephan, who simply gazed back without response. Lollardly actually had to put himself between Hugh and Stephan for fear that something would erupt. Devereux and Davyss, oblivious to the posturing going on behind them, didn't say a word to each other as they returned to the brightening morning outside.

Davyss motioned to his men to mount their horses before turning to Devereux, still clutching his elbow. Their eyes met and they gazed at each other for several moments, silently, each re-evaluating the other. This visit had been something of a new introduction for them both. Davyss could only pray the meal that evening was equally successful.

He smiled faintly. "I shall see you this evening, then."

She nodded. "I will be here."

His smile broadened and he took the hand on his elbow, bringing it to his lips for a gentle kiss. Devereux tried not to react, but it was difficult; in that kiss, she remembered his scorching touch as he had consummated their marriage, making her feel and behave in ways she never knew possible. It was enough to flush her cheeks.

Devereux watched as he mounted his horse and winked at her before donning his helm. The destriers were kicking up loads of earth as they began to tear off down the road and she stood back, watching Davyss balance atop his dancing animal as he finished securing his helm. Once the fasten was closed, he lowered his visor, raised a hand to her, and then spurred his charger after his knights. Dust swirled and dogs barked as the thunder of hooves faded into the distance.

Devereux wasn't sure how long she stood there, her thoughts lingering on Davyss. It took her some time to realize that Stephan was standing next to her.

"He is a big brute," Stephan muttered. "Thank God he has gone."

Devereux glanced at the young man beside her. She wasn't sure how to respond so it was best she say nothing. Turning back to the hall, she made her way inside with Stephan on her heels.

During the day that followed, she made her way back to her father's home to change out of the vomit-stained dress. Although she did not understand why, she took her time dressing. Something in the way that Davyss had looked at her made her want to appear presentable and elegant. Odd thoughts, but the more she thought on Davyss, the more consumed with him she became.

When Davyss returned to The House of Hope promptly at sunset, she was waiting.

CHAPTER SIX

PROMPTLY AT SUNDOWN, Davyss appeared.

The man, Lollardly, Hugh, several knights and several men-at-arms appeared at The House of Hope like a great thundering herd. Devereux, standing just inside the door that led to the yard outside, heard them coming.

As the evening meal was in full swing around her, she had been playing with a little girl who had a horrible cleft palate but who was joyful and sweet. The little girl was a particular favorite of Devereux's. When the chargers filled the muddy yard, the little girl grew fearful so Devereux gave her back her little poppet, which was nothing more than a doll made out of straw, and the child ran off. Eyeing the noisy group outside with both irritation and anticipation, Devereux proceeded out into the yard.

She stood just outside the door, watching the chargers circle. The great beasts snapped and snorted, sending anyone within proximity running. Davyss finally pulled his charger forward of the pack, his helmed head focused on Devereux. She was wearing one of the surcoats he had given her, the brilliant blue with the exotic highlights of black and iridescent green. Her lovely blonde hair was pulled away from her face, revealing the sweet shape of her jaw and emphasizing her enormous gray eyes. She stood by the door, gazing up at him very calmly and expectantly, and he felt his heart leap. She was an exquisite creature, and a smile of appreciation creased his lips before he ever lifted his visor.

"Greetings this evening, Lady de Winter," he used her title with pleasure. "You look beautiful."

She faltered in her confident stance, gazing down at the garments she wore. "This is one of your gifts," she said as if he did not remember. "I am glad that you approve."

He nodded, his eyes riveted to her. "Approve indeed," he murmured. "Are you ready to depart for supper?"

"I am."

Davyss nodded to Hugh, who dismounted his steed and made his way towards her. Devereux well remembered the last time they came within close contact of each other and she instinctively flinched when he held his hand out to her. She eyed the hand and eventually put her hand in his palm. Hugh, ever the lady's man like his brother, smiled brilliantly at her and led her quite genteelly toward Davyss' steed.

"I hope you are hungry, my lady," he said pleasantly. "My brother and I have secured a meal at the best inn in town."

She looked up at him; Hugh had very dark eyes and hair, and an extremely square jaw that gave him an almost stubborn appearance. He was handsome but nothing like the rugged male beauty of his older brother. Still, she could see that he fancied himself the object of every young maiden's heart. And from the way he was looking at her, she suspected he would be disappointed if he wasn't the object of her heart as well, married or no. She resisted the urge to frown at him.

"Aye, I am hungry," she replied evenly. "Which inn are you referring to?"

"The Fist and Tankard, of course," Hugh replied as if she was in need of an education. "It is the finest in town."

Devereux lifted an eyebrow; she had heard of the place, all right, but it wasn't because of its fine food. It was because it had the largest selection of whores in town.

"If you like trollops and dirty women, then I supposed it is," she replied. "But if you want good food, the Swan is the place to go."

By this time, they had reached Davyss. Hugh was looking between his brother and his brother's wife with some anxiety. It was obvious that Devereux had shot an arrow into his bubble of happiness and he had no idea how to deal with it.

"Then you… you prefer the Swan?" he asked, loud enough for Davyss to hear him.

Devereux hesitated a brief moment, thinking on her answer; Davyss had come to make amends and she did not want to start the evening off being demanding and rude. She could see that Hugh looked very concerned by her comment and she shook her head at him.

"Not at all," she replied pleasantly. "I was simply pointing out my own experience. Perhaps the next time you visit, you will allow me to introduce you to the Swan."

The sun shone again and Hugh grinned. "It would be a pleasure, Lady de Winter."

She forced herself to smile in return; Hugh's polished performance when dealing with a woman was almost as accomplished as his brother's. Both of them were quite talented when it came to the most flattering words and the right time to flash that brilliant de Winter smile. She found the charade they put on disgusting and struggled not to roll her eyes at him.

Davyss, meanwhile, was impatiently holding his hands down to his brother. Devereux caught sight of them, the biggest hands she had ever seen. Hugh took the hint.

"Up you go, my lady," Hugh lifted her up to his brother.

Davyss settled her in front of him on the saddle, adjusting her skirts so they flowed like a banner. Devereux shifted a couple of times to get comfortable, glancing around at the men in armor that surrounded them; they were all the men that had come to take her to her wedding, men who forced her to marry a sword rather than a man. She met Sir Nikolas' steady blue-eyed gaze, remembering how she had clobbered him with a chair leg. Next to him was Sir Philip, the handsome blonde who had tried to talk her into surrendering peacefully. She had opened a door into his nose. Next to Sir Philip were Andrew and Edmund, brothers that faintly resembled each other. Andrew nodded his greeting while his younger brother Edmund simply gazed at her with some trepidation even though he had been the one to subdue her after everyone else had failed. Perhaps he thought they were in for another row. Rounding out the group was Lollardly, who appeared as if he might have actually washed his face for the event. His dark eyes glittered with some friendliness when their gazes met.

Devereux didn't have a chance to speak to any of them before Davyss spurred his charger forward. The beast had an excited gait and she held on tightly as the group roared into the main street of the town.

Thetford was a larger settlement with approximately three thousand people at any given time. In that respect, it was enormous and more than likely the largest town in Norfolk on average. There was a large main street that cut a path through the town with a variety of smaller roads that sprung off from the main avenue like branches from a tree trunk. The closer to the main road, the more businesses and merchants there were. Further off the main road were residential areas and inns.

The Fist and Tankard was one such inn off the main street, off to the northeast and in an area peppered with run-down brothels. It was little more than a brothel itself. The sun had just dipped below the horizon when Davyss and his men arrived at the inn with ten men-at-arms, swarming the entire front of the building with soldiers and weapons. The night air was cool, smelling of smoke and animals. Davyss pushed his way forward and dismounted, carefully and politely helping his wife down from the horse. A soldier took the charger's reins as Davyss escorted his wife inside the two-level establishment.

It was crowded inside, full of bodies and smoke. Tendrils of gray spiraled up from a hearth with the defective chimney, causing a steady haze to settle across the room. Most of the tables were full with men sharing an evening meal, talking and drinking loudly. The innkeeper caught sight of Davyss and his men and waved them over to a large alcove where he had a table waiting for them. The table was nothing more than a few planks thrown over some empty ale barrels, and Davyss took the stool at the head of the table and indicated for Devereux to sit. He sat next to her and the knights settled in around them, bellowing for ale and food. Lollardly sat on her other side.

They were swarmed by the innkeeper and several wenches bearing trenchers and wooden trays of steaming food; brown bread, butter and a berry compote were put all over the table along with boiled turnips with dill, carrots with honey, and half a pig that had been roasted over an open pit. The pork was cooked so that it was falling off the bone and Davyss went to work making sure Devereux received the best meat and the first helping of everything. He yelled at poor Edmund when the young knight made it to the bread before he did. Lollardly even slapped the young man in the head to punctuate the error.

The entire time, Davyss hadn't said a word to her. The men around them were chatting, laughing uproariously at jokes Devereux did not understand, but Davyss remained largely focused on his wife. He even served her himself. All the while, Devereux kept her head down, focusing on her food and her husband's polite attempts to help her.

"So, my lady," Hugh began, well into his tankard of ale. "I would assume this is better fair than The House of Hope is having tonight?"

Devereux fixed on him with her big gray eyes. "Any food at The House of Hope is welcomed and appreciated," she replied. "It is not an inn or a fine palace. We eat what God provides and do so happily."

Hugh's smile faded somewhat, glancing at his brother. "I did not mean to offend," he said, hoping she wouldn't fly into a rage. "I was simply… I suppose I was simply asking if the food was to your liking."

Devereux struggled not to react to his arrogant stance. The man really had no idea what it meant to be hungry and homeless; he was a typical young knight with an over-inflated sense of entitlement.

"The food is very good," she replied, trying to keep the distain from her voice. "Thank you for asking."

Hugh looked relieved and turned back to his meal but Lollardly growled at him.

"Foolish whelp," he rumbled. "The lady does not want to hear your ridiculous wit."

Hugh glared at the hairy priest, a man who had known him since birth. "I was making conversation, old man."

"You were making an ass of yourself."

The knights snorted at Hugh's expense, which only seemed to inflame him. But the laughter faded into awkward silence and Devereux returned her focus to her meal.

"Did the old woman recover?" Davyss' voice beside her was low and sultry. When Devereux turned to him, puzzled, he clarified. "The old woman who became ill when I was there. Did she recover?"

Devereux nodded in realization and swallowed the carrots in her mouth. "Ah," she wiped her mouth with the back of her hand. "She did not recover as far as I know."

Davyss nodded, watching her mouth as she spoke; she had the most beautiful mouth, one he remembered as being particular delicious. "I would imagine The House of Hope does not exist simply to provide food to those who need it. I imagine tending the ill is just as important."

She could see he was genuinely trying to carry on a conversation and her heart softened towards him, just a little. "We have more ill than we can handle," she replied honestly. "A surgeon from town comes to help a few days a week, but much more is needed. We have an entire section of the building that is dedicated to the ill. In fact, we seem to have become the place of choice for the destitute to give birth to their children."

Davyss' eyebrows lifted. "How many children are born there on a daily basis?"

"'Tis hard to say; but we have at least five or six born every week."

"Then you are an expert midwife."

She looked at him before answering, knowing that midwifery was considered an inappropriate skill for noble women. It was unseemly and lowly. She couldn't tell if there was disgust in his voice or not.

"The surgeon usually delivers the baby if a midwife is unavailable," she replied evenly. "But if no one is available, then I am not ashamed to admit I have delivered my share of children."

His hazel eyes twinkled. "I would not expect that you would be."

"What?"

"Ashamed."

She wasn't sure how to reply but his gaze was warm upon her. Uncertainly, she lowered her gaze and resumed her meal. As she ate, she was unaware that Davyss was making eye contact with every man at the table, silently ordering them to find their meal and evening's entertainment elsewhere. Hugh was the last to go, ignoring his brother's request until Davyss kicked him in the shin under the table. Hugh grunted with pain, causing Devereux to look up from her food and peer strangely at him. He smiled wanly and excused himself, his gaze shooting daggers at his brother as he quit the table. At that point, Devereux realized that she and Davyss were alone and her eyebrows lifted at the sudden silence.

"Was it something I said?" she quipped. "We appear to have been abandoned."

Davyss grinned. "Well and good. I find that I do not wish to share you with anyone tonight."

She looked at him; her spoon was halfway to her mouth but she lowered it without taking a bite. Her gaze upon him was intense.

"My lord," she said quietly. "May I speak freely?"

Davyss collected his cup, leaning back in his seat as if getting comfortable for what was sure to come.

"I wish you would."

She nodded. "Very well," she thought carefully on her words. "This is the first time that you and I have seen each other since our wedding. Our parting at that time was not the most pleasant."

His smile faded somewhat. "It was not," he took a deep breath, blew out his cheeks and sat forward. He stared at the cup in his hand a moment before continuing. "My lady, you and I have distinctly different philosophies on life. I do not suppose we could be much different if we tried."

She grinned wryly. "Nay, I do not suppose we could."

His smile returned. "I suppose what I am attempting to say is that I have done a good deal of thinking in the time we have been apart," he said quietly. "Perhaps I needed to reconcile this marriage in my own mind. You see, I never wanted a wife. I did not want to marry you but my mother threatened to disinherit me if I did not, so I was forced. As much as you were pushed into the marriage, so was I. That is why I sent *Lespada*, the sword of my ancestors, to the marriage ceremony instead of appearing myself. It was my personal rebellion against my mother and I suppose in doing that, from the beginning, I earned your anger. It was a very bad way to start off the marriage and for that, I apologize profusely. I should not have done that."

Devereux was listening to him intently, surprised at his admission. His honesty touched her and it caused her guard to go down somewhat. "It was not your fault entirely," she relented. "As I said earlier today, I did not make it easy for your men. Your mother was right; my behavior dictated theirs. They responded because I was breaking noses and giving knights black eyes. Sending your sword to our wedding ceremony was not the true problem; the entire situation was."

He nodded with regret. "I realize that," he said. "I suppose we both could have done things differently."

"I would agree with that."

He grinned at her, taking a swallow of ale and savoring it as he thought on the next part of the conversation. His expression sobered.

"I must apologize for something else," he said softly.

"What is that?"

"For being beastly and inconsiderate when I consummated our marriage," for the first time, he looked uncomfortable. "It simply never occurred to me... my lady, I swear to you that I am not a brutal man by nature when it comes to women. But I do take what I want and, God help me, I wanted you nearly the first moment I saw you. You are by far the most beautiful woman I have ever seen and I suppose my lust got the better of me. I am deeply sorry for my actions and I hope you will someday forgive me for being so callous."

Devereux stared at him, struggling not to be embarrassed by the thought of that brutal and exciting night. But it was a difficult struggle and she lowered her gaze.

"You had every right to consummate the marriage," she whispered. "You need not apologize for assuming your right."

"I realize that I had every right," he said, almost irritably, but quickly cooled. He lifted his enormous shoulders helplessly. "I suppose I... well, I suppose I should have taken your feelings into consideration at the time. It simply did not occur to me."

Devereux looked at him, her gaze guarded. She watched him as he fidgeted with his ale cup, seemingly awkward with the subject at hand.

"Forgive me if I am on a path of insult and injury, but it seems to me that you are unaccustomed to having your wishes denied," she ventured.

He lifted an eyebrow, almost regretfully. "One does not refuse Davyss de Winter and live to tell the tale."

He said it lightly and she took it lightly. "I would imagine that holds true with women as well," she pushed further.

He looked at her, then. "I would say that is a fair statement."

"Then it probably would not have mattered if I had refused you or not. You would have taken what you saw as your due."

He was beginning to feel like a cad. "Probably."

She smiled faintly at the fact that the man was exhibiting less than confident behavior. He looked like a child who was about to be scolded but, strangely, she couldn't summon the energy. The man had apologized for their rough beginning; she wasn't the type to beat him over the head with it.

"Well," she folded her hands on her lap and fully faced him. "How would you recommend we rectify the situation and salvage this marriage?"

He stopped fidgeting with the cup and puffed out his cheeks again. "I am not entirely sure," he admitted. "But I will tell you this; I have thought on nothing but you since the day I left. You have occupied both my waking and sleeping hours. I always thought my marriage, to anyone, would have been one in name only. It was my original plan to leave you here to your life while I continued with mine in London but I find that I do not want that any longer. By hook, crook or black magic, you have somehow bewitched me, Lady de Winter, and I find that I want you by my side. I want to get to know you in the hopes that...."

He suddenly trailed off, leaving Devereux on the edge of her seat. "Hopes that what?" she invited him to continue.

He looked sheepish. "I will only tell you if you promise not to laugh."

She lifted an eyebrow, slowly. "One does not laugh at Davyss de Winter and live to tell the tale."

He chuckled, letting go of the cup and reaching out to take her hand. The palm was slightly calloused but the back of her hand was like velvet. Learning a little of her character as he had, he wasn't put off by the calluses at all; in fact, he kissed them sweetly before fixing her in the eye.

"My mother and father were quite fond of each other," he said in a low voice. "It never occurred to me that I actually admired that union until I found myself with a wife. What a glorious thing it must be to be married to someone you are fond of."

His touch had her electrified, so much so that she could hardly think. But she focused on his words, laboring for a reply. "I... I suppose we must get to know one another better before we can make that judgment," she stammered.

"True," he said, stroking the back of her hand. "I suppose we are both going to have to make adjustments."

She nodded; his touch was causing her breathing to become labored and heavy. "Per... perhaps we should make a list."

He looked thoughtful. "Very well," his brow furrowed as he pondered what that list might entail. "I suppose my list would start with the request that where I go, you go. I would have you with me always."

She looked rather distressed but didn't argue. "That is more than likely fair," she replied, thinking of The House of Hope and all of those who depended on her. She didn't want to leave it. "We cannot get to know each other if I am here and you are in London."

"True."

"I have something for the list."

"What?"

"That you cease your empty flattery."

He looked shocked. "Empty flattery?"

"Aye," she nodded quickly to explain herself. "Your flattery is far too practiced to be sincere. I would wager to say that you use it quite often."

He was about to argue with her but couldn't. "From this moment forward, I will not use it on anyone but you."

"I do not want to hear a word of it unless you mean it."

"God's Blood, woman, I mean every word when I speak of you. Are you serious?"

"Of course I am," she insisted. "I never say anything I do not mean."

Still holding her hand, he scratched his chin with his other hand, eyeing her. "I want to add something more to the list."

"Very well. What is it?"

"That we do not discuss or debate our political views for the next thirty days. Let us get to know one another before we allow that undoubtedly contentious intrusion."

Her light mood was fading, growing deep. "I was wondering when the subject was going to rear its ugly head."

He grunted. "I am afraid we cannot ignore it. But I would ask that we not discuss it until we come to know one another better. I fear any discussion of politics by either of us will kill whatever chance we may have of an amicable union."

She took a deep breath, thought on his words, and nodded shortly. "Very well," she agreed. "No discussion of kings, wars or politics. But how are we going to manage that feat given that you are the king's champion?

"I can keep quiet on the subject if you can."

"I will do my very best."

His smile was returning as was the warmth in his eyes. "Good," he was back to caressing her hand. "Do you have anything else to add to the list?"

She thought a moment, watching his fingers as they stroked her skin. She cocked her head slightly, suddenly looking mildly uncomfortable. He saw her expression.

"What is it?" he asked gently.

She grunted reluctantly. "I… well, I am not…."

"I have something more to add to the list."

She looked surprised. "What?"

"Complete honesty and truth, always. When I ask a question, I would like the courtesy of an honest answer."

She gazed steadily into his hazel eyes. "As would I."

"I swear it upon my oath."

That seemed to embolden her. "Very well," she pursed her lips as the correct words came to her. "Will you swear something else to me?"

"Is this another item for the list?"

"Aye."

"Then proceed."

She looked at him, dead on, and he was swallowed by the intensity of her gray eyes. "I want you to swear that you will be faithful to me," she whispered. "I realize that it may be a foolish request, but it is not foolish to me. I would never dream of shaming or betraying you, no matter what our differences are. I would like the same respect from you for the sheer fact that I am your wife, whether or not you wanted me."

His hazel eyes glittered in the dim light as he gazed back at her. "What would prompt you to make such a request?"

She did not back down. "Your mother told me that you needed someone to show you that the true meaning of manhood comes from dedication to one woman, not the plaything of many. Did I misunderstand her?"

He watched her sweet face, the strength behind those amazing gray eyes, and felt himself relent. He could not lie to her. "Nay," he said after a moment, suddenly having difficulty looking her in the eye. "You did not."

"Do you wish to elaborate on what she has told me so I am neither surprised nor offended by gossip or truths I might hear?"

He sighed heavily, looking particularly miserable. He felt as if he was about to confess his most grievous sins and not at all happy about it. "I thought perhaps we could come to know each other better before we delved into that particular subject."

"Why?"

He shrugged. "Because I am trying to establish something pleasant between us. Speaking on that particular subject might cause you to change your mind about me."

"Does this concern you so?"

"Of course it does."

She gazed steadily at him. He was still toying with her fingers and she suddenly squeezed his hand, forcing him to look at her. "If you wish to establish an honest and truthful marriage, then you must be honest and truthful with me. Tell me why your mother would say such a thing."

He puckered his lips, appearing both regretful and frustrated. Given their rough beginning and that fact that she virtually knew nothing about the man, Devereux was afraid that she might have overstepped her bounds. Men kept and took mistresses all of the time and it was not unusual. But she felt strongly that there needed to be honesty between them; it would be his choice to honor her request or not, which would largely determine the character of the man she had married. It would most certainly determine the wall of self-protection she would keep up around her when dealing with him and she held her breath as he regarded her.

Davyss suddenly pulled on her arm, strongly enough that it lifted her out of her seat. Reaching out, he wrapped his enormous arms around her torso and pulled her down onto his lap. Startled, Devereux was nonetheless a willing participant and she remembered well the feel of the man's arms around her; he was big and powerful and manly, and the combination was enough to cause her head to swim. She'd never been held by a man until the event of Davyss de Winter. Everything about his embrace was enough to cause her to forget any resentment, bitterness or disgust she had ever felt for him.

Davyss held her tightly on his lap, his great head against her left shoulder. His eye level was at her collarbone and his gaze rested pensively on the rise of her breasts.

"It is true that I have not led a pious life," he said softly. "I have experienced my share of women. But the day I married you is the day all of that ended. I have not as much as thought of another woman since that day."

"How many women?" she asked, hoping the tremble of excitement at his touch wasn't evident in her voice.

He shook his head. "It does not matter."

"More than I can count on both hands?"

"Aye."

He didn't sound prideful about it at all; he was, in fact, rather subdued. Devereux watched the top of his lowered head as it rested against her shoulder. "Anyone special I should be aware of?"

"Nay."

"Bastards?"

He grunted with hesitation. "Two that I am aware of. Twin girls."

"How do you know they are yours?"

"Because they look just like me."

She didn't say anything for a moment and when the silence became excessive, he dared to look up at her. He was surprised to see a faint smile on her face, the gray eyes glittering. When their eyes met, her smile broadened.

"I imagine it was very difficult to tell me this," she said softly.

He lifted a big shoulder. "You asked for truth. I gave it to you."

"I appreciate your candor."

His gaze was somewhat guarded as he continued to watch her. "Maybe so, but does it change your mind about me?"

She shook her head. "Nothing has changed."

His smile returned, this time one of relief. "You are most kind and understanding, my lady," he said graciously, then froze. He looked stricken. "Do you consider those words to be empty flattery?"

She broke into soft laughter. "Nay," she sobered. "They were genuine."

He laughed with her, pulling her closer in the process. She was warm and soft and absolutely delicious. His relief, his joy in the conversation, was so great that in little time he was slanting his lips over hers, very gently. He couldn't help himself. Much to his surprise, she didn't pull away, so his kiss grew more insistent and one of his great hands found its way into her hair.

The intensity of the kiss did not increase; it stayed heated and curious, his fingers drifting over her face, acquainting himself with the texture of her skin and the shape of her jaw. The same hand moved to her neck, gently caressing, as his lips began to move across her cheek and jawline. He heard her sigh faintly and her body began to quiver, like the swift flutter of butterfly wings. It only served to excite him more.

Davyss took his time as he sampled his wife. He had never in his life known anything so soft and pure. Other than holding her in his arms, his hands never moved below her collarbone; they remained in her hair, on her face, against her neck. He'd handled her so caddishly the first time they had met and he didn't want to repeat that mistake. He wanted her to become comfortable with his touch and hopefully learn to crave it. He already craved her almost beyond his ability to control.

Back in the smelly and smoky great room, the front door suddenly slammed back on its hinges and several knights spilled into the room, hollering for food and ale. It was enough of a commotion that Davyss tore himself away from Devereux long enough to realize that knights bearing the yellow and green colors of the Earl of Gloucester, ally of Simon de Montfort, had entered the tavern. He immediately set Devereux on her feet.

"Stay here," he growled, his eyes tracking the movements in the room like a predator. "Do not stray from this spot for any reason."

Devereux, her head still swimming from his delicious kisses, simply nodded her head for lack of a better response. She watched as Davyss entered the great room with his proud, stalking gait, making his way towards the men who had just entered. Hugh and Nik saw Davyss first, crowding in behind him as Lollardly, Philip, Andrew and Edmund shortly followed. The six most powerful knights in the arsenal of Henry III and one fighting priest faced off against the new visitors.

There were eight knights in total facing Davyss and his men. The knight in front was an older man with curly dark hair flecked with gray. He had a dark beard and a weathered face, but his eyes were as sharp as a hawk's. His lips curled in a smile as he beheld the mighty and powerful Davyss de Winter.

"De Winter," he said with satisfaction. "I should have expected to see you here."

Davyss was as cold as ice. "You are in the heart of my holdings, de Reyne," he said. "You must have a death wish coming here."

De Reyne lifted his shoulders casually. "There is no law that says I cannot travel where I wish," he replied. "We are simply passing through."

"Passing through to where? You serve Gloucester and you are far from his territory."

"That is none of your business, I fear."

"I made it my business when you came onto my lands."

De Reyne's smile grew. "You needn't worry," he put up his hands in acquiescence. "We are heading north to Peterborough. We shall eat and be gone before you know it."

Davyss eyed him; not wanting to create a brawl, which would undoubtedly happen if these men were denied a meal, he simply backed off. His gaze never left de Reyne as the man, sensing that de Winter was unwilling to instigate a battle, motioned to his men to find a table. Davyss watched them make their way into the heart of the great room before turning to his men.

"Do not let them out of your sight," he rumbled. "Once they are finished eating, they are to be evacuated from this inn. Is that clear?"

Hugh and the others nodded. "Why did you let them stay?" Hugh wanted to know. "They will only cause trouble."

Davyss scratched his head, wondering if he let them stay because his wife was watching. She had accused him of being a war machine and perhaps he was taking the opportunity to prove that he wasn't some blood thirsty fiend who thrived on the thrill of the kill. Under normal circumstances, he would have thrown the lot of them out and have taken great pride in it. At the moment, he couldn't really answer his brother's question and that frustrated him.

"Never mind," he flicked an irritable hand at his knights. "Spread out in the room and watch them. When they are finished eating, I want them gone."

The knights acknowledged the command but it was Andrew who suddenly caught sight of what he knew would be the trigger to a very big battle. He grabbed Davyss by the shoulder and turned him in the direction of the alcove.

"You will want them gone now," he pointed.

De Reyne and two of his men were speaking with Devereux while the rest of Gloucester's men commandeered Davyss' former table. Davyss didn't even blink; before he realized it, *Lespada* was unsheathed and he was charging towards his wife. It was like a tide of death and men as it all rushed into the small, cluttered alcove.

Devereux never saw it coming.

CHAPTER SEVEN

T HERE WAS A single lit taper in The House of Hope this eve. It rested on a crude table next to the bed of a dying old woman. All was quiet and still as Devereux sat next to the woman, applying cool cloths to her head to bring her some comfort while the old woman's husband sat on the other side of the pallet, seated on the floor as he prayed endlessly. The night had been a vigil for the elderly woman who had vomited earlier that day. Death was closing in.

And that was where Davyss found his wife, crouched next to a dying peasant and trying to give the old woman some comfort in her last hours. Clad in battle armor with blood on his hands, he had marched into The House of Hope with fire and terror on his mind that was immediately doused at the sight of Devereux, healthy and whole. In fact, he had been weak with relief. He stood there and watched her for several long moments, composing himself, before approaching.

"Lady de Winter," his voice was quiet, rumbling, as he addressed her.

Devereux didn't acknowledge him. She continued gazing at the dying old woman's face. But gradually, she turned to see his boots standing a few feet away, her gaze trailing upward on his bloody armor until their eyes met. The impact was physical. Davyss gazed steadily at her before lowering himself into a crouch. His eyes were imploring.

"Are you all right?" he whispered.

She nodded and looked back to the old woman. "How did you get back here?" he pressed gently.

She wouldn't look at him. "I walked."

He sighed. "That was not safe."

Her head snapped to him, the gray eyes blazing. "It was safer than the inn. I would have been killed had I stayed there for the mighty battle going on around me."

He knew she was upset and he knew very well why. He remembered seeing de Reyne speaking with her and little else after that but a blinding battle that ended up with two of Gloucester's knights being killed and Nik being slightly wounded. At the end of the brawl when he had looked for Devereux, no one could locate her. Terrified she had been abducted or worse, he and his knights had torn apart the inn and several other establishments in the near area. Still unable to locate her, they had taken to the streets calling her name. It was Lollardly who finally suspected where she might have gone and Davyss rode hard for The House of Hope.

The old priest had been right. Davyss found her tending a dying woman and his relief had been so great that it had nearly brought tears to his eyes. But on the heels of that relief was the knowledge that he was going to have to do a great deal of damage control to repair their fragile relationship. He'd damaged it yet again.

She had turned back to the old woman as he continued to watch her from his position a few feet away. He could see that she was having a great deal of trouble looking at him.

"Devereux," his voice was so low that it sounded like a purr. "I must explain what happened back at the inn."

She shook her head, so hard that tendrils of blonde hair escaped their pin. "Nay," she said firmly. "There is no need"

"Aye, there is. Will you please allow me that courtesy?"

She was about to refuse again; he could see it. She was angry, confused and frightened. Everything she hated about knights had been demonstrated right before her eyes as Davyss and his men had clashed violently. But she suddenly stopped what she was doing and sighed heavily, closing her eyes as she did so. When she turned to him, she spoke with more sadness than anger.

"What is there to explain?" she asked. "You did as your instincts bade. I understand that."

He shook his head. "Nay, you do not," he replied softly. "The men speaking to you were knights of Gloucester, allies of Simon de Montfort. Other than de Reyne, they are not particularly honorable men. They would have gladly taken you to sport, or worse; if they had discovered you were my wife, then you might have known torture and fear such as you have never dreamed. What I did, I did to save your life."

She gazed steadily at him. "They were not harming me in the least and their words were not unkind."

"I know. But please trust me when I tell you this; the situation would have changed very shortly. You are a blindingly beautiful woman and that fact did not escape them. The small talk they offered was only the calm before the storm, believe me. I have known these men many years and know what they are capable of."

Her gaze remained steady and he found himself sucked into the brilliant gray eyes. But just when she opened her mouth to speak, her eyes filled with tears and she turned back to the old woman. Even as she picked up the cold compress and wrung it out, she began to sob. Davyss watched her, his heart just about breaking.

"I am sorry, Devereux," he murmured. "I know you hate violence and I know you believe me to embody the stench of death, but please believe me when I tell you that I did what I did for a very good reason. I did it to protect you."

She sobbed harder and covered her face with the hand that held the cold compress. On the opposite side of the old woman, Thelred the husband removed the compress from Devereux's hand and gently grasped her fingers.

"Up with ye, m'lady," his old arms tried to pull her to her feet. "Go with yer husband now. I can tend me wife."

Devereux only wept harder as the old man tried to help her. Davyss stood up and gently took her from the old man, nodding his thanks to the tired old face. He pulled her away from the elderly pair and put his enormous arm around her shoulders, gently walking her from the building. In his arms, Devereux wept like a child.

The night outside was cold and damp. It was also exceedingly late. Davyss took her to his horse, mounted her, and then took the saddle behind her. She didn't resist. The charger took off at a gentle trot into the dark, silent edge of town.

Devereux cried until they reached their destination. By then, she was exhausted and had little concern for where he had taken her. Davyss dismounted his steed and pulled her off, carrying her into the dark and silent building and up a flight of stairs. He took her into a room and closed the door, throwing the bolt softly behind them. A warm fire burned low in the hearth of the little room and Davyss set her down gently on the small bed.

Devereux didn't particularly care where they were; she was weary and spent. Wiping her eyes, she accepted a piece of cloth that Davyss handed her and blew her nose daintily. Davyss, meanwhile, began removing his armor in pieces and propping the plate pieces up against the wall. He pulled off his mail coat, followed by his hauberk, and laid them out carefully near the door so any moisture on them would dry out. All the while, his gaze lingered on his wife as she sat on the bed and sniffled.

He wasn't quite sure what to say to say to her. He removed his linen vest, followed by the heavy tunic, and laid them near the hearth to dry. The boots quickly followed. Clad in only his breeches, he made his way over to the little bed.

"Are you hungry?" he asked quietly.

She shook her head. "Are you thirsty, then? Would you like some wine?" he pressed.

She sighed heavily and shook her head again. The crackling hearth filled the silent air between them. Lacking any further response, Davyss sat down on the bed, wrapped his arms around her, and pulled her down with him. She stiffened, but only for a moment. Snuggled up against his warm and powerful body, Devereux could feel some of her fear and confusion flee as the flesh of his body created a heated envelope around her. It was a new sensation, one of extreme warmth and security. She'd never known such comfort existed.

Davyss shifted so that she was clutched up against his chest, his arms tightly around her and his big hands on her back. He caressed her shoulders, her hair, acquainting himself with the feel of her in his arms. They had never lain together, at least not in the still of the night with nothing to distract or trouble them. In fact, Davyss had never lain in bed with a woman that he wasn't having sex with. Leisure snuggling was unheard of. This was an entirely new experience for the both of them, the significance of which was not lost. For Devereux, it was like being in another world.

For his part, Davyss had never felt so complete or content; it was difficult to describe for a man who had known more than a few women in his lifetime. But they had all been fleeting interests; no one that had truly marked his heart. Not even the baron's daughter who had borne him twin daughters. The more time he spent with this woman he had married, the more she touched him on levels he had never known to exist.

His mouth was near her head and kissed her hair a few times, stroking her back with gentle caresses. He felt sorry for her, this woman who hated violence and found herself in the middle of a vicious sword fight. He knew she was shaken. He was shaken, too.

"I would like to say one thing before this night is through and we put all of this behind us," he murmured. "In spite of the view you have of the knighthood, I hope you understand that I do not go around looking for fights. Every time I raise my sword, I am risking death and I certainly do not want to die. I am also risking the deaths of my men and I have no desire to see any of my men wounded or killed. What I did tonight, I did with the sole motivation of protecting you. Those men would not have thought twice before taking advantage of you and it is my job, as your husband, to protect you from that. Do you understand?"

She sighed faintly, calming, and he felt her nod her head, just once.

"Aye," she responded. "I understand what you are saying but I tell you again that they made no such move against me."

"Would you rather I had waited until one of them grabbed you in places only meant for your husband?"

She pulled back, gazing up at him with a lifted eyebrow. "Nay," she replied. "But they had done nothing when you came charging in with your sword lifted. And that man who ran at you... you cut off his...."

She couldn't continue but did not have to; he knew what she was about to say. He had cut off the man's head with the mighty *Lespada*. He pinched her chin gently between his thumb and forefinger, forcing her to look at him.

"Would you rather it had been my head that got cut off?" he asked.

She tried to shake her head but had difficulty moving it because he held her chin. "Nay," she said, more softly.

"Had I not killed him first, he most certainly would have tried to kill me."

"I would not wish that at all."

He smiled faintly, holding her chin still as he kissed her cheek. "I am glad to hear that," he replied, sobering. "I am, however, sorry if we frightened you. It is an unfortunate byproduct of battle."

She gazed up at him, this man she had married yet who was a virtual stranger. His appearance that morning had brought what seemed like a man very willing to try to make amends. He understood her fears and her point of view; he'd tried very hard to. Yet she'd made little concession to him from the very beginning. Her guard had been up since the moment his knights came to claim her for their wedding. It simply wasn't fair that he was making all of the effort and she was making virtually none. Her guard began to dissolve.

"You do not need to apologize," she said quietly. "You acted on instinct and I cannot fault you. If anyone should apologize, it should be me. You have been trying very hard since this morning to make amends and I fear I have not made it easy for you."

He smile broadened. "Nonsense," he said. "You have been agreeable and charming."

She gave him a look suggesting he was lying simply to be kind. "I have not, but it is sweet of you to say so. And I am sorry that I ran from the inn; I will admit that I was very frightened and I simply wanted to get away. I do not know what I was thinking, really; all I could think of was getting away from the battle. I am unused to such things."

"That is understandable," he said. "But I will admit something also; I was terrified for you when we discovered you were missing. I had no idea what had happened to you."

She gave him a wry smile. "Again, my apologies," she said. "Perhaps... perhaps tomorrow will bring a better day for us both."

He nodded, gazing into her spectacular gray eyes. "I must leave for London on the morrow," he said, watching her expression change. "And I should like for you to come with me."

She nodded in resignation. "I know," she said. "And it 'tis not as if I do not wish to go. 'Tis simply that I worry for The House of Hope."

"It seems as if you have many who help you."

"Help me, yes. But I ultimately make the decisions and oversee everything."

"What of your father?"

She shook her head. "He is too wrapped up in his duties as Mayor and Sheriff of the Shire. He always thought The House of Hope was foolish, anyway. He used to scold my mother on it constantly as a waste of effort and money."

"I see." He could see the thought of leaving her charity truly distressed her. "Is there no one else to run the place in your stead?"

She nodded. "Aye," she said honestly. "Stephan Longham and his brothers are capable."

"Who is Stephan?"

"You saw him this morning," she replied. "He is the young man with the long blonde hair. We have known each other since we were children."

Davyss thought back to the morning when they had toured the

place; he remembered the blonde man, alright. He remembered that he was young and strong and handsome. A bit of jealousy flared in his chest, a surprising reaction.

"Then perhaps Stephan will tend it while you are in London with your husband." He didn't know why he made a point of reminding her that he was her husband, but some odd possessiveness prompted him to. "I will leave him with plenty of coin so he will be able to procure food and whatever else he may need."

She looked at him, curious. "Coin?" she repeated. "But… why would you do this?"

He looked at her as if she was mad, although it was gently done. "You are my wife," he said as if she needed reminding, again. "The House of Hope is your charity and it is my duty to support it and you. Do you disagree?"

She was astonished; the thought had never occurred to her. "Nay, Davyss, I do not," she peered at him. "Are you sure you want to?"

It was the first time she had used his Christian name; he liked the way it rolled off her tongue, spoken in her soft and sultry voice. "Do not be ridiculous," he chided softly. "The place does look rather run down. I noticed that the roof was much worn."

"Aye, very."

"Then I shall leave enough money to have it thatched while we are in London. In fact, I shall leave enough money to have the entire structure reinforced. Would this please you?"

She gazed up at him with her bottomless gray eyes, shocked beyond the ability to express it. "You would do this?"

He smiled warmly into her lovely face. "I would do it for you."

Devereux had never had someone speak so sweetly to her. The first sweet words out of the man's mouth had been contrived and practiced; that was what she expected from him. But this day seemed to have erased all of that from her mind because the words coming forth now were sincere and kind. She could only pray he really meant them; as much as she wanted to believe him, there was still a small part of her that was suspicious. She simply couldn't help it.

"Thank you," she said sincerely. "You are extremely generous."

His smile faded as his eyes took on a hungry glow. Devereux watched as he dipped his head low, closing her eyes as his warm lips captured hers. As she remembered from the afternoon, he was musky and gentle and titillating. She had enjoyed it quite a bit. She was enjoying it more now.

Davyss' hands were caressing her, giant appendages that were gentle and warm as they touched her. Devereux remembered his touch from their wedding day, hands that had caused her to momentarily forget all of the hatred and frustration she was feeling. His musky scent overwhelmed her nostrils, his heated palms overwhelming her nubile body. But this time, his kisses were far more gentle and passionate as opposed to lustful and powerful. She responded to his touch, timidly at first, but with increasing ardor. As much as he was tasting her, she was learning to taste him as well. The path of discovery had begun.

The first thing Devereux realized about Davyss was that he had a distinct scent and taste; both were very musky and very manly, something like leather and pine and earth. And his skin had a distinct texture as well; it was warm and smooth. His mouth moved to her jaw and neck, allowing her a moment to breathe. It was more like a ragged gasp. Her hands were on his enormous shoulders, feeling his warm skin beneath her palms. Soon her fingers were in his hair, acquainting herself with the thick inky strands. They smelled like leather.

Davyss' hand moved to her breast and Devereux started; he froze, lifting his head from where he was feasting against her collarbone. His hazel eyes were hazy with lust and concern.

"Did I hurt you?" he whispered.

She shook her head. "Nay,"

She was fearful to tell him what she was really thinking but he could read it in her expression. Cupping her cheek with one big hand, he kissed the side of her face.

"I did not mean to frighten you," he murmured. "If you do not wish for me to continue, I will not. I do not want you to be uncomfortable."

It was a far cry from the man who had so willingly taken his right on the eve of the marriage. She gazed intently at him.

"You are my husband," she said. "It 'tis your right to… to touch me."

He lifted a dark, well-shaped eyebrow. "I am well aware of my rights, madam," he said. "I was trying to be considerate of your feelings."

She looked into his eyes, trying to determine if he was simply humoring her or if he really meant it. But her gaze ended up moving from his eyes to his handsome face, to his thick neck and broad shoulders. His naked chest was her next destination, smooth tanned skin with a soft matting of dark hair. He had an exceedingly muscular chest and her female instincts, as naïve as they were, began to swamp her. It made her feel hot just to look at him. He was a glorious example of a man and naïve or not, frightened or not, she was not hard pressed to admit that she found him extraordinarily attractive. Embarrassed at the new feelings consuming her, she averted her eyes.

"I… I am not uncomfortable," she muttered. "I will not protest if you wish to continue."

Davyss fought off a smile; he couldn't help but notice she wouldn't look at him. He would have thought her disgusted with what was happening had he not seen the faint mottle to her cheeks. He dipped his head, trying to look her in the eye.

"Am I to understand that this is pleasurable for you, my lady?" he teased her gently.

She lowered her head further and he laughed softly. "So you will not admit it, you little fox?" he pushed.

She covered her face with her hands, but not before he saw a grin spread across her lips. Laughing softly, he wrapped his big arms around her and growled like a bear, nibbling at her neck enough to make her squeal. He continued to nibble and she giggled uncontrollably, finally begging for him to stop. He wouldn't stop until he extracted a kiss from her, which she did hesitantly; she wasn't used to love play. But he thought her innocence to be very charming and was pleased that she was at least willing to play along. The woman had been on her guard for most of the day, with good reason, and he was thrilled that she was starting to warm to him. With a tender smile, his lips claimed hers more powerfully than before. He wanted her more than he had ever wanted a woman in his life.

He laid Devereux back on the bed, shifting his weight off of her as his fingers went to work removing her from her shift. Devereux was focused on his gentle kisses, his tongue seeking intimate places inside her mouth, and unaware that he was intent on removing her from her clothes.

He was so careful with her that she didn't realize when he had unfastened the surcoat; she was only aware of it when he lifted her swiftly to pull it off. He kept her propped up as he pulled the shift over her head, leaving her nude but for the hose on her legs. He purposely left them on, deeply aroused by the delicate hose held in place by blue ribbons. Her legs were slender and shapely and he paused a moment to admire her form, running his hand gently down her torso, to her hip and down her thigh.

Devereux shuddered as his fingers danced along her skin. His kisses resumed, more gently, and Devereux's head was swimming with the sensations he was creating within her. Gone were any reservations she might have felt, the bitter memory of their first coupling. It was as if an entirely new man was holding her in his arms, someone kind and gentle and inordinately considerate. His mouth was heated, his kisses firm yet gentle as he moved from her lips to her breasts. She was ready for him.

Davyss suckled her nipples, feeling her twitch beneath him. He held her tighter, feasting on her delicious breasts and savoring every movement, every soft gasp she was emitting. His groin was painfully engorged and he lowered his breeches, wedging himself in between her legs. She twitched again, this time with some trepidation, as his fingers gently stroked the thick lips that covered her woman's center. He stroked her for a few moments, acquainting her with his touch, before carefully entering her with his enormous manhood.

Beneath him, Devereux groaned softly as he thrust gently into her. Her legs came up and he held her behind the knees, lifting her legs as he thrust again and again, sliding his full hard length into her. Seated to the hilt, he began slow and even thrusts, feeling her tense body relax with each successful push. Soon she was completely relaxed and he held her lovely legs high while his lips reclaimed her mouth once more. There was nothing more erotic than kissing her deeply as he thrust into her, feeling his new wife's body responding to him. Never in his life had he experienced such excitement. He wanted more.

His hands left her legs and moved to her hips holding them firmly as he continued to thrust. Devereux wrapped her legs around his, instinctively, as if to hold him deep inside of her. Her hips began to move with his, awkwardly at first but with increasing rhythm. It was an innate pulse, a primal mating movement that consumed her as she wrapped her body around her husband and gave herself over to him completely.

As Davyss' powerful body moved within her, Devereux imagined that this was what their first coupling should have been like; passion, tenderness, heat and power. She never knew such things existed. When the heat in her loins suddenly exploded in a shower of sparks that coursed like rivers throughout her body, she was vaguely aware of Davyss shuddering against her. Even when the sparks faded and the tremors died, he continued to move within her, stroking her, feeling every last ounce of pleasure that he could. The experience went on well into the night.

They fell asleep in each other's arms, Davyss's member still embedded in her body. He awoke before dawn and made love to her twice more before the sun rose.

It was if that horrible experience forty-two days earlier had never happened at all.

CHAPTER EIGHT

I T WAS BEFORE sunrise, the time right before dawn when the world was still and magical. The town of Thetford was quiet for the most part; the only movements on the streets or in homes were the merchants preparing for the day or the farmers getting ready to head to the fields. But in the barn behind the inn known as the Swan, there was a faint light glimmering in one of the stalls.

Several enormous chargers were tethered within the building, their bright black eyes blinking at the activity now filtering into the barn. Men the horses recognized were congregating and the beasts snorted as familiar scents filled their velvety nostrils. They knew that their day was about to begin and they began to grow excited.

It was relatively quiet as the de Winter knights began to prepare for the day. They milled about, grooming the chargers, unwilling to let local grooms tend their expensive and vicious war beasts. Edmund was sitting on the ground next to his black and white steed, yawning as he cleaned out the animal's hooves. The charger nibbled at his dark hair and he irritably swatted at it.

Andrew was in the stall next to his brother, snorting at the young knight as he wrestled with a charger that was more like a pet. Andrew was busy currying his own hairy horse that still hadn't lost his winter coat. Philip and Nik were across the aisle, in various stages of charger preparation while Hugh grumbled and complained at the end of the building with an animal that kept banging on him with his massive head. The preparations early this morning were in anticipation of leaving for London. They were all anxious to return to the living, breathing heart of England, each for his own different reason.

Davyss entered the barn, checking to make sure all of his men were up and moving. He had just left Devereux sleeping in a warm bed, his mind still on his bride even though his attention was on his men. Something had happened to him yesterday although he wasn't sure what it was; all he knew was that his new wife had gone from a pressing thought to an overwhelming need. He couldn't seem to think of anything else but her, even in this dawn of a new day. But this particular day was important and he struggled to focus.

Lollardly entered the barn right behind him. The old priest with the hairy eyebrows watched Davyss as the man inspected his knights. Davyss was meticulous in his command, always making sure his men were properly attired, alert and ready at a moment's notice. When Davyss was satisfied with his inspection, Lollardly caught his attention and motioned to him. Davyss followed the priest out into the growing dawn and they paused somewhere in the middle of the quiet, dirty yard.

Lollardly spoke. "I have just come from the abbey," he murmured quickly. "The Brother had a message for you."

Davyss suddenly looked displeased and taut. He gazed steadily at Lollardly for a moment before responding. "What is the message?"

"Simon requests you meet him when you arrive in London," Lollardly's voice was a whisper. "He must speak with you."

Davyss' eyebrows rose. "Simon is in London?" he repeated, incredulous. "God's Blood, the man takes risks. What in the hell is de Montfort doing there?"

Lollardly shook his head. "I would not know," he muttered. "But he is apparently desperate to see you."

"Henry is in London."

"I know. Will you meet Simon, then?"

Davyss scratched his head, pondering the deeper implications of such a meeting. He'd been pondering the deeper meaning of these clandestine meetings ever since he'd been knighted. After a moment, he emitted a heavy sigh. "I do not know if I can."

Lollardly nodded his head. "Aye, you can," he grumbled. "Davyss, you and Simon have known each other too long for you to avoid him now. Perhaps he needs something. Perhaps he wants to...."

Davyss held up a sharp hand. "Cease your prattle," he growled. "You do not have to tell me of Simon de Montfort, for I have known him since the day I was born. He and my father were the best of friends. Our families were close; we lived together and fought together until...."

Lollardly smiled faintly, clapping Davyss on a massive shoulder as the man trailed off. He knew how Davyss felt about his father's oldest, and dearest, friend. It was a dark secret he carried; the champion of the king and the leader of the baron's rebellion were still life-long and deep friends. Henry knew of the de Winter relationship to de Montfort, of course, but he assumed like everyone else that the link died when Grayson de Winter had. But the link remained. It was a secret that, if discovered, could mean Davyss' death.

"You do not need to tell me of your relationship to Simon," the old priest protested. "Lest you forget, your father, Simon and I fostered together. I watched Grayson and Simon grow into strong men and with strong ideals. I was there the day you were born and Simon was there to bless you. It was a difficult day when Grayson and Simon split; Grayson with dreams of serving the king and Simon with dreams of a different England. But that bond that Simon shares with you, as his best friend's son, has never been severed."

Davyss watched Lollardly through guarded eyes. "He risks my life every time he contacts me."

"And you risk his."

Davyss sighed sharply and crossed his enormous arms. "So what do you want me to do? Talk to him?"

"He will meet you at the Temple Church in Blackfriars," Lollardly told him. "I will tell my brother to get word to Simon that you will meet him at sundown upon the morrow."

Davyss was staring at his feet. It was a long and pensive pause. But eventually he nodded, barely, and Lollardly took it as a sign. The old priest disappeared, heading back towards the abbey that had given the town its name as Davyss continued to stand there and wonder what tomorrow's meeting would bring. He hadn't seen Simon in some time and no matter what their politics, he missed his father's friend. He wished again, as he had wished daily for many years, that things were different; that Simon wasn't a rebel and he wasn't the king's champion.

He wished they were on the same side.

⚃

DEVEREUX HAD BEEN to London, once, with her father when he had traveled there on business. She had been eleven years old at the time and nine years later, it was bigger than she had remembered. As Davyss' group entered the outskirts of London from the northwest, a massive settlement emerged with the blue ribbon of the River Thames running through it.

The de Winter war machine had brought six knights, including Davyss, one priest, three hundred men-at-arms and five wagons. It was a large group that traveled through the outskirts of London and people turned out to watch. Little boys stood by the side of the road, thrilled to see the knights, while women tried to garner the favor of the men who passed by. In a covered wagon with a fully armed escort, Devereux watched the little boys and loose women, waving at the children when they waved at her first.

One little girl with a few wilted flowers in her hand ran out in the road. She was holding the flowers aloft as she headed towards the carriage but almost got run over by Sir Philip's charger. The child stumbled, fell to the road, and began wailing. Devereux leapt off the wagon before anyone could stop her and rushed to the child's side.

The wilted flowers were scattered all over the dirt as Devereux knelt beside the little girl. She picked the child up from the road.

"There, there, sweetheart," she crooned. "You are all right. Every-thing is all right."

The child sobbed and held up her scraped elbow. Devereux smiled gently and pretended to take a good look.

"'Tis not too bad," she assured the little girl. Then she began looking around for someone to help her. Her gaze fell on Philip, now off his charger and standing next to her. "I need some wine or ale and a strip of cloth; any cloth will do. Can you please bring me these things?"

Philip was in motion, snapping orders to a few men around them. The entire column had come to a halt and Davyss was making his way back from the head of the group, bellowing his frustration that they had stopped as he went. But Devereux was only focused on the child at the moment, not three hundred men who had come to a dead stop because of her.

Lollardly arrived at the scene before Davyss, watching the situation with curious eyes. Lady de Winter was so unlike any woman he had ever known that he paused just to watch her tend the child, her gentle manner and her sweet words.

The more time he spent watching her, the more he was coming to like her. His first impression of her as a rebellious wench had not been her true nature; it had been the fear that had caused her to act like an animal. What he was seeing before him and what he had seen the day before, he suspected, was this woman's true character. She was special.

When Davyss arrived and bailed from his charger, Lollardly put his hands on the man's chest to stop his advance.

"What goes on?" Davyss demanded, flipping up his visor. "Why have we stopped?"

Lollardly pointed to Devereux, several feet away, cleaning the scrape of a peasant child. "Your wife is helping this child."

By this time, Hugh had come upon them, watching the scene with impatience. "It is simply a peasant," he grumbled. "She should not be wasting her time or ours."

Lollardly shushed him. "Jesus tended lepers," he reminded him. "Do you not see the noble self-sacrifice of Lady de Winter?"

Hugh fixed him with an intolerant look. "She is wiping away dirt from layers of dirt on a dirty child. There is nothing Christ-like about that."

The big priest thumped Hugh on the neck, the only weak part in the armor the man was wearing. As Hugh yelped and rubbed the spot, Lollardly glared at him.

"You would do well to pay attention to your new sister, Hugh de Winter," he hissed. "She is on the path to heaven. You could live for one hundred years and never know the same Godliness, you pathetic sinner."

Hugh frowned and continued to rub his neck. "It is one peasant child in a sea of thousands," he snarled as he turned away. "'Tis a waste of time and effort. The child will die before she sees her next birthday, anyway. Lady de Winter is not helping the child to live longer by wiping off a smidge of blood."

As Hugh stomped off, Lollardly shook his head. "Your brother is unsalvageable, Davyss," he lifted an eyebrow as he looked at the older brother. "But what of you? Is your new wife starting to make a mark upon your spirit yet?"

Davyss was watching Devereux as she finished tying the bandage in a puffy bow. The little girl seemed very pleased by it. He continued to watch her smiling face as she watched the child skip away, his heart softening for reasons he could not understand. He didn't respond to the priest's question as he made his way to his wife.

"Is everything all right, my lady?" he asked her pleasantly.

Devereux turned to him, a smile on her lovely face. She was particularly rosy cheeked this day, her humor far better than he had ever seen it. Since that morning when they had departed for London, she had been kind and sweet, and he was growing more and more enchanted.

"Everything is fine," she told him. "That little girl was trying to give me flowers and tripped. I fixed her scrape."

He smiled at her. "So I saw," he said. "May we continue?"

She nodded. "Of course," she started rushing back to the carriage. "I am sorry to have delayed you."

He took her by the elbow and slowed her pace. "No trouble," he said. "We should be at our destination within the hour."

They reached the covered wagon and Devereux shielded her eyes against the sunlight as she gazed towards the south. "Where will we be staying?"

Davyss put his hands around her slender waist and lifted her up into the wagon. Then he wiped at the sweat on his brow, gesturing off in the direction of the city.

"At Wintercroft," he replied. "It is my family's townhome. I think you shall like it; there is an expansive garden and a large pond. It is also where Nik and Philip's wives reside, so you will have ladies in residence to serve you."

She looked down at him. "They are married?"

"Aye."

"And the women stay in London while the men are about with you?"

He nodded. "We do not travel with women."

"And you would have me stay in London while you are traveling, also?"

He could see where this was leading and he grunted, scratching his forehead. This was not one of those "safe" conversations between them.

"I think it is a little premature to discuss that at the moment," he moved away from the wagon so she couldn't press him further. "Hold fast, my lady. We will be home soon."

Devereux watched him mount his charger and plow his way to the head of the column. Her thoughts lingered on the wives that were sequestered while their husbands were out running about. Davyss didn't give her an answer which made her suspect that he expected her to remain sequestered, too.

Truth was, she wasn't sure how she was feeling after yesterday. Everything she had initially thought about Davyss de Winter had been dissolved for the most part and she was becoming acquainted with a man who was kind, compassionate, gentle and wildly handsome. He had a quick wit and was humorous, something she found very appealing. But she still wasn't sure how she felt about being married to the de Winter war machine. Not that she had any choice; she was married, like it or not. She would simply have to deal with it.

The road widened and sturdier buildings began to come into view. They were larger estate homes and she watched with interest as they passed one after another. The homes were well spaced, perhaps a half mile or more in between them, and the area was fairly heavily forested as they began to near the moist air of the river. The land was very green and small ponds littered the area.

They traveled a little further when they came upon a road that branched off to the right from the main road. The column began to turn down this road, moving like an army of ants as they tramped down the moist dirt. Devereux strained to see what was at the end of the road and gradually, the heavily foliaged trees parted and she could see a gray stoned wall come into view. The wall was inordinately high and she could see a massive wood and iron gate cut into the middle of it. The gate was cranking open, allowing the army to enter.

Wintercroft loomed before her; although it was a fortified manor, it looked more like a small castle. It was pale-stoned, bulky and gloomy. The yard was littered with small outbuildings and a fairly large stable block. The house itself was odd; there was a heavy iron door on the first floor but no windows anywhere on the floor. All of the windows were on the second floor but there was also a strange addition that projected off the north side of the house, creating a third and fourth floor. It was like an enormous tower had been added to half of the house.

As the wagon pulled into the yard and drew close to the house, Devereux noticed two women standing by the front door. As she watched, the front portion of the column began to disband and two knights dismounted their steeds and approached the women. Philip pulled off his helm, his fair blonde hair glistening in the weak sunlight as he smiled broadly at his wife and took her in his arms. Nik, nursing a damaged arm from the skirmish in the inn, was less enthusiastic about greeting his wife. He simply kissed her on the cheek and they stood and talked like two acquaintances.

By this time, the wagon had pulled up to the front door and Davyss was suddenly standing next to the wheel. Devereux hadn't even seen him approach; she had been watching Philip and Nikolas with their wives. He smiled at Devereux and reached up to gently help her from the seat. Once her feet were on the ground, he claimed her hand and tucked it into the crook of his elbow.

"Welcome to Wintercroft," his hazel eyes moved over the structure affectionately. "My grandfather built this as a present to my grandmother. My father was born here."

Devereux inspected the odd building. "Is it a castle?"

Davyss shrugged. "Somewhere between a castle and a manor," he replied. "I think my grandfather wanted a stately manor but ended up adding fortifications for protection. You will find the interior of the keep to be a cross between the two; comfort and functionality. My mother hates the place."

She looked at him. "Why?"

He gazed down at her, smiling faintly. "She thinks it is ugly."

Devereux suppressed a grin as her gaze returned to the peculiar structure. "It is... interesting, to be sure. Where does she stay when she comes to London, then?"

"She has her own home in the city called Hollyhock."

Devereux lifted an eyebrow. "So she leaves the ugly house to her sons?"

"Exactly; what do we care what it looks like?"

Devereux wasn't sure what more to say, giggling when Davyss lifted his eyebrows at her as if he knew what she was thinking. It really was an ugly place. He patted her hand and fondled her fingers affectionately as they moved to where Philip, Nikolas and their wives were standing. As Davyss approached, the couples broke from their conversation to face de Winter and his new wife.

Davyss was focused on the women. "Lady Lucy de Rou and Lady Frances de Nogaret," he indicated Devereux. "This is Lady Devereux Allington de Winter; my wife."

Lucy de Rou was a delicate little blonde with big brown eyes and a big smile. She dipped in a curtsy for Devereux, followed quickly by Lady Frances. Frances was pretty and dark-eyed. Both women were prim, proper and pleasant.

"'Tis an honor to meet you, Lady de Winter," Lucy said in a sweet, baby-like voice. "We were told you would be coming and have prepared the master's chamber. I hope it is to your liking."

Devereux smiled. "I am sure it is fine," she said. "Thank you for your kindness, my lady."

Lucy just grinned, smiling up at Philip as if to seek his approval. He smiled sweetly at her. Frances, however, seemed a bit more reserved. In fact, Devereux got the distinct impression that the woman was sizing her up.

"We have prepared a bath for you, my lady," Frances said. "We thought you would want to refresh yourself after your journey."

"Again, you are thoughtful and kind," Devereux nodded. "I am most appreciative."

"Will you come with us, my lady?" Lucy indicated the open door, glancing at Davyss. "With your permission, my lord?"

Davyss waved a hand at them. "By all means."

Devereux looked at Davyss even as Lucy took her by the arm. There was something hesitant in her expression and Davyss smiled reassuringly. She smiled weakly in return, perhaps with resignation, and allowed the women to take her into the manor. Davyss' gaze lingered on the doorway even after she was gone, his mind fixated on the vision in blonde.

Hugh stood next to him, watching his brother as he stared at an empty doorway. "Davyss?" he nudged him. Receiving no response, he nudged him again. "Davyss?"

Davyss seemed to snap out of his trance, almost embarrassed, and began snapping orders. "Get the army quartered and secure the gate," he barked. "I want my knights in the hall in an hour."

Hugh began echoing his brother's orders, repeating them to all who might not have heard rather than actually doing anything. He was an excellent fighter but he was under the impression that menial tasks were beneath him so he tended to give orders rather than take them. But that was normal and Davyss simply ignored his brother's bossy manner; his own manner was rushed and brusque. He wanted to be done with the chores so he could return to the lovely young woman who had so recently been ushered into the keep.

He almost couldn't think of anything else.

ᙅᙐ

INSIDE THE BULKY keep of Wintercroft, Devereux was receiving the whirlwind tour. Lucy and Frances had whisked her into the very small foyer and up the massive stone stairs that were immediately to the right. They went up to the second floor and into a series of rooms that were linked; there were no hallways. One room opened up into another and into another, like a line of rooms. They were massive and fairly well appointed.

They passed through two enormous rooms and into a third, which was larger than the rest. There was an enormous bed in it, two massive wardrobes and a scattering of tables, chairs and other possessions. A colossal tapestry hung on the wall near two windows, partially rolled up; Devereux could see that when the tapestry was unrolled, it covered both windows.

The women paused when they reached the room. Devereux stood in the center of it, slightly awed by her surroundings, as Lucy and Frances bustled about with a couple of old servants. Devereux didn't even know what they were doing; she was paying more attention to the room around her. The rooms on the second floor were surprisingly light and airy with scrubbed, wide-planked wooden floors and great stone walls. There were great pieces of furniture in the rooms, from giant wardrobes to luxurious and expensive tables, candlesticks, sideboards and chairs. The wealth of the de Winters was fully evident and on display in this place, as it was meant to be.

Devereux gradually became aware that the ladies were attempting to direct her into a small door in the corner of the room. She obediently followed and ended up in a small chamber that had an enormous copper tub in it. Someone had lined it with linen and clear, clean water steamed into the air.

Off to her right, there was a smaller wardrobe, a vanity, and tucked into the corner was a stone seat built into the wall with a hole in it. There was a wood and fabric screen around it, partially blocking her view, and it took her a moment to realize it was a privy. Devereux was shocked; a privy in the *house*?

The ladies were attempting to help her remove her clothing. Devereux snapped out of her awestruck observations and allowed them to untie the surcoat she wore, one of the new ones that Davyss had given her. It was a yellow linen garment with lovely long sleeves and a matching shift underneath. The women stripped her to the shift and suddenly, Devereux was very self-conscious. She always bathed and dressed in private, so this was something of a new and uncomfortable experience. True, there were servants at her father's house who did the cooking and cleaning and that sort of thing, but she'd never had a handmaiden. She had always fended for herself. When pretty young Lucy tried to help her from the shift, she balked.

"Ladies," Devereux clutched the shift around her neck as if to hold it tight so they could not lift it over her head. "If you do not mind, I would like to bathe in private."

Lucy looked confused, looking to Frances, who simply shrugged her shoulders. Lucy returned her puzzled gaze to Devereux. "But... my lady, we are here to assist you. We wish to help you bathe. Do you not need help?"

She asked it with such bafflement that Devereux almost smiled. "My lady, I mean no offense, truly," she said carefully; she did not want to get off to a bad start with these women. "'Tis simply that... well, it is my preference. I believe bathing is a private activity."

Lucy blinked, still puzzled, but nodded unsteadily. This time, it was Frances who spoke.

"It is because you do not know us, Lady de Winter," she said confidently. "I understand. But please believe me when I say that we only wish to assist you."

Devereux turned to the handsome brunette; there was still something odd about the woman, an appraising look to the eye. It put Devereux on her guard.

"That is not necessary, Lady de Nogaret," she informed her. "If you and Lady Lucy will leave me now, I will bathe in private. Please see that my baggage is brought up."

"But…," Lucy protested weakly.

"That will be all, Lady Lucy. Thank you very much for your consideration."

Lucy nodded, looking somewhat like a kicked dog, and began to leave the room. Realizing that Frances wasn't moving, she took the woman by the arm and practically yanked her from the room. Devereux stood there, waiting until she was sure they had gone, before moving to the wood and fabric screen that partially covered the privy and moving it to the open chamber door. Even if anyone entered the enormous chamber beyond, the screen provided some privacy.

With a heavy sigh, she looked around the small chamber as if gathering her thoughts. She noticed that the ladies had set out a sponge, a bar of white soap, a glass phial with some kind of oil in it, and a scraper. They all sat upon a small table next to the tub. There was also a robe of some fashion, white and fine, strewn across a chair by the vanity. Throwing off her shoes, she pulled off her hose, pantalets and shift before plunging into the tub.

It was clean, hot and glorious. Devereux sighed with contentment as she went to work with the white bar of soap that smelled strongly of hyacinth. She washed her hair with it, twice, before moving to soap up her body. The tub was so big that she could move easily in it, submerging her head as she scrubbed every inch of flesh. Soon, the chamber was filled with the scent of flowers and it was into this lovely sanctuary that Davyss entered.

He had brought up her trunks, depositing them against the wall in the master's chamber. Lady Lucy had told him, somewhat sadly, that his wife had not required any help with her bath, so he had come up personally to see if she was in any manner of distress. She seemed to be such a sensitive woman that he found that he worried for her moods and mental state constantly during this time of change. He didn't want to see her upset, not even for a minute.

After setting the trunks down, Davyss removed his gloves, his plate armor, his hauberk and mail coat, and laid them carefully on the frame in the corner so any moisture would dry out. His squire would collect them later to clean them. In his breeches, sweaty tunic and massive knee-high boots, he went to the screen blocking the door and knocked on it.

"Lady de Winter?" he called softly. "May I enter?"

He could hear splashing before she answered. "Of course, my lord," she replied, sounding rather breathless. "Please come in."

He slid around the screen without moving it, his hazel eyes riveted to the figure in the enormous tub. As he approached, he could see that she was covering her chest with a piece of linen she had yanked off the side of the tub. He suppressed the urge to laugh at her but he couldn't keep the grin from his face. He stood over the tub with his fists on his hips as if inspecting the entire activity.

"Well?" he said with mock sternness. "I hear you wish to bathe alone. Does that mean I cannot participate, either?"

She gazed up at him with the linen pulled up around her neck, unsure how to answer. "I ... well, I suppose so. You are my husband, after all."

He lifted an eyebrow. "I know who I am," he removed his fists from his hips and crouched next to the bath. "But you chased off Lucy and Frances. They are most distressed. They think you do not like them."

She looked genuinely concerned. "I did not mean to distress them," she struggled for the correct words. "I am simply unused to bathing with help, much less with the help of women I do not even know. I am more comfortable alone, 'tis all. Please tell them not to be distressed. It was not my intention to upset them."

He smiled faintly. "I am sure they know that but I will remind them," his smile faded as his gaze trailed to the linen covering her chest, the soapy water. "I told you that they would be your ladies-in-waiting. You will have to get to know them sooner or later."

"I will. But right now, I would simply like to bathe without the assistance of strangers."

His eyes lingered on the peaked nipples showing through the linen. "May I help you bathe? You know me, after all."

The sheer tone in his voice made her blush to the roots of her hair; she may have been fairly naïve but she had heard that tone before, before he made love to her. "I am finished bathing, my lord," she said, avoiding his eyes.

He leaned forward and took her in his arms, pulling her wet body up against his damp and dirty tunic. She shrieked.

"You are sweaty and filthy," she pushed against him. "Now I will have to bathe again."

He laughed softly, released her, and yanked off his tunic. The gleam in his eye was strong. "Exactly."

The tub was big enough for two; before Devereux could protest, Davyss pulled off his boots and breeches and plopped his enormous bulk into the tub. Water sloshed all over the floor and Devereux yelped as a tidal wave engulfed her. As she wiped the water from her eyes, there was a white bar of soap thrust in her face.

"Here," Davyss said. "You may wash me so I am not so offensive."

She blinked the water from her eyes and hesitantly accepted the soap. "But it smells of flowers," she cocked an eyebrow at him. "You are going to smell like a woman."

"Would you rather me smell of horses?"

"Nay."

"Then wash me."

After a few moments of reluctance, she did as he asked. Davyss closed his eyes as she crept forward in the tub, planted herself between his massive legs, and began to soap him. She started with his dark hair, rubbing soap into it and creating white froth with her fingers as she worked it in. As Davyss sat there, still as stone, he could tell she was very hesitant. Her fingers were unsure, as she had never done this sort of thing before, and he could tell she was somewhat embarrassed and uncertain. But at least she was willing to try. He felt a good deal of confidence in that, confident that their new beginning was working. After the bumps of the past day, he sincerely hoped so.

He lifted his head, eyes still closed, as she soaped his face and neck. The more she worked, the more sure her fingers became. By the time she reached his hairy chest, she was soaping him quite vigorously. He grunted when she came to his belly, twitching, and she abruptly stopped and looked at him.

"What is wrong?" she asked, concerned. "Did I hurt you?"

He grunted again and shook his head, his eyes still closed. "Nay."

She eyed him as she went back to work, watching him twitch again as she soaped his ribs. She paused, he stopped twitching. Then she started again, stronger than before, and watched him shudder uncomfortably. It took her a moment to realize that he was very ticklish. She stared at him, the mere notion that the most powerful knight in the realm was ticklish overwhelmed her thoughts. She fought off a grin, then laughter, as realization dawned. Suddenly, she dug both hands into his ribs and tickled mercilessly. Davyss groaned and grabbed her by both wrists in his iron grip.

"You evil little wench," he growled. "You will not exploit that, not ever again. Do you understand?"

He opened his eyes and looked at her, seeing that her face was red and she was struggling to hold back the laughter. When their eyes met, she erupted into great peals and yanked her wrists free, digging her fingers into his ribs again. Davyss responded by throwing her in a big bear hug, holding her tightly enough that she couldn't move. She laughed uproariously as he held her tight, cradled against his mighty chest, his face mere inches from her own.

"Do that again and you shall pay the price," he growled, although a grin played on his lips. "Well? Swear you will never do it again or you shall feel my wrath."

Her laughter faded as she gazed up at him. "It is my secret, my lord," she said as if she held a great weapon against him. "I promise I will only use the knowledge in times of great need."

His eyebrows lifted as his loins grew heated; she was warm and soft and slippery against him and his lust bloomed full force.

"Times of great need?" he repeated, having a difficult time focusing on something other than her sweet body. "What on earth could that be?"

"I am not sure yet."

"I see," he lifted an eyebrow, pretending to be properly worried when all he really wanted to do was kiss her. "So you intend to abuse your power, do you?"

Her smile bloomed. "Not at all. But it is a good thing to know, don't you think?"

He just shook his head, completely charmed by her playful manner. "You are a horrible woman."

She laughed softly. "You knew that when you married me."

He nodded his head as if in complete agreement. "I know," he murmured. "How utterly fortunate I am."

His lips slanted hungrily over hers before she could reply. This time, she didn't stiffen in his arms. She remained cooperative and pliable, and Davyss could feel passion exploding within him such as he had never known. His mouth quickly left her lips, moving over her neck and shoulders as he captured a full breast in his grip. Soon his lips were on her nipples and he could hear Devereux gasping with awakening desire. He had her out of the tub and onto the floor before she could draw another breath.

He moved her to a cow hide rug that lay on the floor near a softly glowing bronze vizier. His massive body covered her, his mouth on her breasts and torso, suckling her delightfully damp skin that smelled strongly of flowers. Beneath him, Devereux continued to gasp and pant. He suckled her lower belly, her right thigh, before grabbing hold of her hips and flipping her onto her stomach.

His massive hands massaged her shoulders, her back, and finally her smooth buttocks. He gently pulled her legs apart, wedging himself in between her knees. Devereux lay there, acutely aware of every sensation, aware of his hands on her buttocks, her thighs, before he gently grasped her by the pelvis. He lowered his enormous body down atop her and carefully entered her from behind.

It was a completely different sensation from anything she had experienced with him thus far. Devereux groaned as he thrust into her, her slick body drawing him deep. He thrust again and again, covering her with his massive body as he supported his weight on one elbow. His free hand roamed her body, his lips on her head, her neck and shoulders. Then the hand moved to her pelvis again and he pulled her slightly onto her left side as his hand snaked underneath and began to play with the fluff of dark curls between her legs.

Davyss knew how to make a woman scream; that much had been clear from the beginning. Within seconds of the thrill of his expert fingers, Devereux buried her face in the cow hide rug and cried out as he manipulated her into a powerful climax. When her convulsions died down, Davyss flipped her onto her back and drove into her again, kissing her deeply as he thrust into her. After a few more thrusts, he spilled himself deep into her body but continued moving, not wanting the moment to end. Every time he took the woman, it was better than the time before. There was such power and desire between them that he could hardly comprehend it.

They lay on the cow hide rug for some time, feeling the warmth from the vizier and each other's bodies. Davyss shifted so his weight wasn't crushing her but he refused to let her go. Holding her sweetly and tightly was the best possible thing he could imagine, creating this warm little haven of flesh and beating hearts. But there was something more than just physical contact; there was something odd stirring in his chest that he didn't yet understand yet. All he knew was that it grew stronger by the moment.

"I am afraid I disrupted your bath," he murmured, kissing the side of her head. "My apologies."

She gazed up at him with her bottomless gray eyes, studying the lines of his handsome face. Moment by moment, day by day, the man was growing on her and she wasn't sure how she felt about that still. But it was becoming increasingly difficult to have any resistance at all to him. She was becoming swept up in whatever was developing between them, something she'd never even known to exist. It was magical.

"No need," she said softly. "You are my husband. You may do with me as you wish."

The warm expression faded from his face and he abruptly pushed himself up. His hazel eyes were glimmering with confusion, perhaps disappointment, as he stared at her.

"Will you stop saying that?" he demanded, though it was without force. "I know I am your husband. I am well aware of what my rights are. I do not need you to remind me every time we have any manner of physical contact."

Devereux sat up, watching his frustrated face. She began to feel some confusion as well. "But it is true. I… I am not sure why you are…."

He waved a big hand at her and stood up. "I know it is true," he almost snapped. "But you say it so coldly, as if … oh, hell, I do not know… as if you are removed from the situation. Is that what you truly wish? That you remain removed from this marriage in every way?"

She eyed him with some shock, digesting his words. Silently, she rose from the cow hide rug and collected the white robe that had been laid out for her. Wrapping it around her body, she seemed lost in thought as she turned to Davyss. He was still standing naked in the middle of the room, looking for an answer. She was struggling to supply one.

"I am not sure what you mean," she said honestly.

"Do you not *feel* anything?"

She seemed shocked by the question but just as quickly, he could see that she indeed knew what he was asking. She took a deep breath and squared her shoulders.

"Davyss," her sweet voice was low, firm. "You and I were married a little over a month ago and to say that we had a rough beginning is an understatement. You have acknowledged this. Until two days ago, I had resigned myself to the fact that I had married a man in name only. But then this man reappeared and seemed to be nothing like the one I remember from my wedding day. He was kind, considerate, generous and attentive. He was completely different from the Davyss de Winter I married on that turbulent day. Do I feel anything? Of course I do. Am I terrified? Absolutely. I am terrified that I am going to wake up and this all will have been a dream. I do not want to become attached to a dream."

He looked as if he was pained somehow by her answer. His hazel eyes flickered and he hung his head for a moment. Then he made his way over to her, putting his massive hands on her upper arms in a labored, if not thoughtful, gesture. His fingers caressed her as he thought on his reply.

"I will confess something," he whispered. "It was never, under any circumstances, my intention to become attached to anyone, least of all you. I do not know what it is about you that draws me to you, but something does. Whether it is what my mother said to me on our wedding day, or simply what I feel, I am not sure. All I know is that I feel something for you, something that terrifies and puzzles me. But it is the most wonderful feeling I have ever had."

By this time, he was looking at her. Devereux met his gaze; she could feel something from him, something warm and fearful. She understood the feeling well. After a moment, her expression softened.

"I understand completely," she smiled faintly. "I am experiencing it myself. But you scare me."

"I know. You scare me, too."

She sighed thoughtfully. "We simply cannot go through this marriage afraid of each other."

"What do we do?"

She cocked her head. "We should add something more to our list."

The corner of his mouth twitched. "Ah, yes, the list. I'd almost forgotten. What should we add?"

She sighed again, thinking. "We should add that we promise to never intentionally hurt one another. Maybe that would help."

His smile broke through. "It might," he agreed. "I swear upon my oath that I will never intentionally hurt you."

"So do I."

He laughed softly. "You swear on your oath?"

She grinned as he chuckled. "And why not? My oath was my marriage vow."

His laughter faded as he looked her in the eye. There was something deadly serious in his expression. "So is mine."

She continued smiling and he kissed her on the cheek, then on the lips. He put a big hand on her head, stroking her hair as he gazed into her lovely gray eyes.

"You are such a beautiful woman," he murmured. "I cannot believe that I am so fortunate."

"Nor I."

"You have me afraid to utter sweet words, you know. I am afraid you will think them insincere."

"I am coming to know the difference."

"Good."

He kissed her again and with a final stroke of the hair, went to the screen that blocked the door and moved it aside. He strolled into the master chamber beyond, stark naked.

Devereux followed, torn between embarrassment and pleasure at the sight of his bare buttocks. She wasn't used to men parading around nude and struggled not to stare as he went to one of the enormous wardrobes and threw open the doors. He began pulling garments out, throwing them around the floor and tossing a few up onto the bed until he came across what he was looking for. As Devereux watched, he pulled on a pair of leather breeches and a pale linen tunic with short sleeves.

"Sweetling," he turned to her as he fussed with the neck of the tunic. "My boots are in the dressing room. Can you get them for me?"

Devereux nodded and returned to the room with the big tub in the center of it. His boots were scattered on the floor and she picked them up. They were massive, heavy and dirty, and she struggled not to get dirt on herself as she carried them back to him. She handed him one and he took it with a grateful smile. He took the second one with a kiss.

"Now," he faced her, fully dressed, with his hands on his hips. "Do you wish to see the rest of the manor?"

She shook her head. "I cannot. My hair is wet and I must dry it first."

He nodded shortly. "Do you require help?"

Again, she shook her head. "I can do it myself."

"Will you be ready for the evening meal?"

"I will."

"Very well." He pulled her into his arms and kissed her sweetly, his lips lingering on her cheeks before pulling away completely. "I will return in a while."

Cheeks flushed with the power of his kisses, Devereux could only nod. He winked at her as he left the chamber. She stood there long after he was gone, going over their conversation, the encounter in general. Thoughts of the man made her feel giddy and warm, growing worse by the moment. And something additionally odd was occurring; thoughts of him seemed to suck every other idea out of her head. She found that didn't want to think of anything other than him.

But she forced herself to move, to focus on something other than his beautiful hazel eyes or amazing physique. She retreated back into the privy chamber where the tub still sat, the water now cool, and the cowhide that had cushioned their lovemaking lay. She stared at the hide a moment, a chill running through her as she thought of his hands on her body. It was still somewhat embarrassing to have such sexual thoughts, being a lady who had led a relatively sheltered life, but they were not unpleasant thoughts. She knew she could come to like them.

Pulling up a small stool, she sat next to the vizier and flipped her head over, running her fingers through her hair in front of the heat. As she did, her mind began to wander again to the massive knight who was her husband. She couldn't seem to get him off of her mind.

She didn't try.

CHAPTER NINE

T HE EVENING MEAL was the first introduction into what kind of man Davyss de Winter was, at least prior to his marriage and pledges of faithfulness. It was during this meal that Devereux began to see what Lady Katharine had meant about the numerous women in her son's life. It started with the serving wenches.

Seated next to her husband in the center of a very large table in Wintercroft's enormous great hall on the first, windowless floor of the structure, Devereux was dressed in a beautiful yellow surcoat with gold embellishment. Her hair was braided over one shoulder and she looked positively angelic; Davyss' reaction when he had first seen her and his constant attentiveness told her that he appreciated the effort she put forth in dressing. She was truly enjoying his company when the parade of serving wenches started.

She didn't notice it at first; she simply thought the servants were bringing the meal. Every time Davyss would take just a few sips of wine, a woman would immediately fill his glass. She noticed one of them at one point as she bent over her husband's left hand with a pitcher. All she could see were white breasts, spilling out over the top of a leather girdle. The woman brushed them against Davyss' arm as she poured his wine. Shocked, Devereux looked at her husband's face; he was focused on his meal.

Although they were surrounded with his knights and their wives, Davyss seemed to have eyes only for Devereux. He made sure her cup was always full by the same wenches who were so intent to seduce him and he also made sure she had the first serving of everything. He was attentive and sweet in spite of the parade of whores who were vying for his attention.

Lady Frances was sitting on Devereux's right hand. The woman hadn't said a word all evening, instead, sitting silently with her meal and responding to her husband on occasion. But Frances noticed the steady flow of serving wenches challenging Devereux for her husband's attention; that was a normal occurrence at Wintercroft. She was frankly curious how Lady de Winter was going to handle the situation and unsure how to feel about it. At some point, she caught Devereux's eye when a particularly busty wench brushed against Davyss. Devereux smiled weakly.

"The meal is lovely," she said. "Who is responsible?"

Frances was pleasant. "Lucy and I share the duties, Lady de Winter. However, now that you have arrived, you are in charge. We shall defer everything to you."

Devereux nodded faintly, studying the attractive woman; Nik, seated next to his wife, seemed more interested in the men around them. Frances sat quietly while her husband carried on a lively conversation with others. When Davyss turned to Hugh, seated on his left, Devereux took the opportunity to speak further with Frances. She felt sorry for the woman.

"How long have you and Sir Nikolas been married, my lady?" she asked politely.

Frances swallowed the bite in her mouth. "Three years, my lady," she replied. "We were married in London but I have lived at Wintercroft since."

Devereux's brow furrowed slightly. "He does not provide you with your own home?"

Frances looked both surprised and distressed by the question. "He serves Davyss de Winter, my lady," she said quietly. "I live where he lives, and right now, he lives with Sir Davyss."

Devereux was afraid she had upset the woman. "I did not mean to offend you," she said quickly. "I simply meant…to ask if you have a home of your own to attend to. I should not like to keep you from your home or family."

Frances shook her head. "My home is here. I hope this does not disturb you, Lady de Winter."

"Of course not," Devereux replied, thinking it would be wise to change the subject. "I want to thank you again for preparing a bath for me today. It was most thoughtful of you."

"It was our pleasure, my lady."

The conversation died a bit but Devereux tried to keep it going. "What do you do for entertainment?" she asked as she pulled apart a soft white piece of bread. "Do you draw?"

"I do."

"I am sure you are very good at it."

Frances smiled weakly, the first such gesture from the woman. She seemed rather quiet and sad. "I try, but I believe I am better at sewing."

"Truly?" Devereux pretended to be very interested. "Perhaps you will show me some of your work."

Frances seemed pleased by the request and nodded graciously. Lucy, far down the table on the other side of her husband, seemed upset that she was not included in the conversation that was clearly going on between Lady de Winter and Frances. When Devereux caught a glimpse of her sad young face, she caught the woman's attention and motioned her over. Lucy leapt up and raced to the women, even when Philip demanded to know why she was leaving him. He was more interested in his ale and manly conversation, anyway, which Lucy promptly reminded him. The men around Philip snorted.

As Lucy drew near, she tripped over a hovering serving wench in her haste. The woman was intending on pouring more wine into Davyss' cup but ended up spilling it on Frances' surcoat instead, prompting Devereux to shoot to her feet in outrage. She jabbed a finger at the wench, at her end of patience with all of these loose women hanging about and creating a nuisance.

"You," she snapped. "Get out. I do not want to see your face again."

The woman looked shocked, then angry, but quickly she did as she was told. Seeing the wench vacate gave Devereux the excuse she had been looking for; to get rid of the half-dozen women who were circling their section of the table like vultures. All of them were trying their hardest to gain Davyss' attention. Another woman bearing empty cups came near and she snapped at that woman also.

"And you," she growled. "Get out of my sight. Take the other whores with you. If I see another wench within the walls of this hall, you will not like my reaction. Consider yourself warned."

By this time, Davyss was watching his wife with interest. He saw the return of the woman he had met on their wedding day, full of strength and fury and indignation. She was truly a force to be reckoned with when roused. This time, however, it did not distress him. He found it comical and he was oddly proud. The wenches that crawled the hall of Wintercroft promptly vanished as word of an angry Lady de Winter spread. Across the table, Lollardly was watching the scene also with growing amusement.

"Here, here, Lady de Winter," the priest banged his dented pewter cup against the table. "You have done what could not be done. You emptied the hall of the rubbish that plagues it."

Devereux turned to the priest; he was drunk but not out of his senses. Davyss answered the old man before his wife could.

"Untrue," he reminded him. "My mother has done the same thing, although with less authority than Lady de Winter shows. Mother simply trips them with her cane or smacks them on the behind until they steer clear of her."

Devereux looked down at him. "She does?" she struggled not to smile. "Apparently the wenches need to be whacked with the cane, not tripped by it."

Davyss smiled up at her, tugging gently on her arm until she sat. "Reclaim your seat and have no worries," he put an arm around her shoulders and pressed his face into the side of her blonde head. "I know what is occurring. But rest assured that I have eyes only for you."

Devereux felt shivers run up her spine at his hot breath. "Is this a normal happening?" she asked frankly.

He paused as he kissed her head. She heard him sigh faintly. "Aye," he whispered.

"Am I to assume you took advantage of this?"

He didn't reply. He continued to hold her, his big arm around her shoulders, his face in her hair. She finally turned to look at him; due to his proximity, their faces were very close. Hazel eyes met with brilliant gray.

"What would you have me say?" he murmured. "I have already admitted my shortcomings."

She digested his statement carefully. "Then it would be fair to say that you have bedded every woman at Wintercroft?"

"Not every woman."

"I meant every young female servant."

He lowered his gaze. "It is possible."

Devereux fell silent and Davyss dared to look at her. She was staring off into space as if lost in thought. He began to feel an odd sense of desperation, fearful for the first time in his life that his rutting behavior may have cost him dearly. Up until now, he'd never cared. He had taken what he believed his right. Now he was coming to wish that perhaps he had shown more self-control. It had never occurred to him that someone else might be offended by his behavior. Someone he was very much coming to care about.

"What would you have me do?" he whispered, almost pleadingly. "Tell me what you want me to do and I shall do it."

She looked at him. "Do? Do what?"

He shook his head, growing frustrated. "I do not know," his brow furrowed as he grasped for words. "Repent, beg forgiveness, and seek atonement. This is not the first time you will be reminded of my past behavior and I do not want it to constantly break apart what I am trying to build up."

She lifted an eyebrow, curious. "What are you trying to build up?"

He lifted his enormous shoulders weakly. "Us."

She could see how frustrated he was, perhaps embarrassed. But he could not undo the past. She also sensed his sincerity and it softened any annoyance or shame she was feeling.

"Very well," she responded quietly. "You may do something for me."

"Anything."

"Dismiss every female servant at Wintercroft. I want every one of these women gone, women who sampled my husband before I have. I will be greatly shamed if they stay as constant reminders."

He nodded without hesitation. "It shall be done."

"Before sunrise."

"Immediately."

He kissed her cheek and rose, snapping orders to Andrew, who was seated on the other side of Hugh. Hugh, halfway through his second helping of meat, heard the command and his dark eyes widened. He bolted to his feet even as Andrew moved to do Davyss' bidding.

"What are you doing?" he grabbed Davyss by the arm.

Davyss gazed into his brother's eyes, knowing he was going to have trouble with Hugh. Hugh was a great connoisseur of women, perhaps even more than Davyss, and would undoubtedly bed at least three women before the morrow. In fact, Davyss and Hugh used to be very much alike in that respect. They used to have contests about it. Until now.

"My wife wants the serving wenches gone," he told him steadily. "So they are leaving."

Hugh's eyes widened. "Why?"

"Because she is uncomfortable having women that I have bedded living in the same house and hold with her. I wish to make her happy so I am removing them."

Hugh's jaw flexed. "*What?*" he hissed, dropping his hand from his brother's arm. "Why would you do such a thing?"

"I told you; to make her happy."

Hugh couldn't believe what he was hearing; he'd not talked to his brother in depth since they had arrived at Thetford to retrieve Lady de

Winter, so he was well out of the loop of what his brother was feeling and thinking about the woman. For all Hugh knew, the marriage was still only an unpleasant situation that Davyss must grow accustomed to. He hadn't even paid any attention when Davyss kissed and behaved attentively towards his wife. He hadn't cared in the least. If he thought about it, he hadn't really talked to his brother in a couple of days. Therefore, the latest news was a blow.

"You cannot make her happy," Hugh seethed. "We all know that she is a spoiled, arrogant bitch that will never…."

Hugh didn't see Davyss' fist coming until it was too late. Massive knuckles made contact with Hugh's jaw and the younger brother sailed over the table, right into Lollardly's lap. The priest, caught off guard by the flying knight, spilled food and wine everywhere. Devereux and the other women shrieked as Davyss vaulted over the table and went after his brother with a vengeance.

It was a nasty brawl from the start. Hugh had no idea why he was defending himself from his furious brother and, after several hard punches, began to fight back. Andrew put himself between Lady Devereux and the fight, not knowing the reason behind the brothers' battle but wanting to make sure Davyss' wife was protected. Philip grasped his wife and Frances and whisked them from the hall while Nik stayed behind to observe the situation. Young Edmund came to stand beside his brother, his eyes wide at the battle going on.

"What do we do?" he hissed at his brother. "Why are they fighting?"

Andrew shook his head, his soft brown eyes tracking the combat. "I have no idea."

"Should we stop them?" Edmund pressed, distressed.

Andrew shook his head as Lollardly, still wiping wine off his neck and arms, barked an answer.

"Stay out of it, young Catesby," he, too, was watching the rather brutal bout. "Whatever is troubling them, they must settle it."

Devereux was watching in horror. It was clear from the beginning that Davyss was much stronger than his brother and he was delivering

Hugh a righteous pounding. At one point, he hit Hugh in the face and blood spurted everywhere. Devereux was aghast; she suddenly leapt onto the table and screamed as loud as she could.

"Stop it!" she cried. "Stop it this moment! You are going to kill each other!"

Andrew went to grab her but she scooted out of his arm's length, leaping off the other side of the table and running in the direction of the battle.

"Davyss, stop!" she hollered. "Stop this instant!"

Through his haze of fury, Davyss heard her terrified voice and paused. But his brief moment of cessation gave Hugh an opportunity to clobber him in the jaw. As Davyss spun away, he clipped his brother on the back of the head with an enormous fist. Hugh went down as Davyss fell to his knees.

Devereux rushed to her husband, her hands on his shoulders. "My God," she breathed, looking at the blood on his face. "Are you all right?"

He nodded unsteadily, rising slowly on shaking legs. "I am fine," he grunted.

Devereux gazed up at him, gravely concerned. "Are you sure?"

"Aye."

"Why did you hit your brother?"

Davyss eyed Hugh, wallowing on the ground in semi-consciousness. "It does not matter," he grumbled. "Come along; let us retire."

Nik and Edmund had rushed to Hugh by this time, helping the man to his feet. Andrew stood with Lollardly as Davyss and Devereux walked slowly towards them; Davyss had his arm around his wife as if she could support his weight, wiping the blood from his nose.

"Are you sure you are all right, Davyss?" Andrew asked quietly. "Should I send the surgeon to your room?"

Davyss shook his head, almost knocking himself off balance. "Nay," he muttered. "My wife will tend me."

Devereux watched his face as he spoke; there was sadness and frustration and confusion in his manner. She could not fathom why; the entire event had been lightning-fast and frightening. In a new hall, in a new marriage, she was understandably distressed.

"Davyss, will you not speak with Hugh before we retire?" she asked softly. "Do not walk away from your brother angry. Speak rationally of your quarrel and settle it."

Davyss wouldn't even respond; he was emotionally as well as physically exhausted. But he did pause a moment, looking to Devereux before looking to his brother. Hugh was on his feet, barely, and glaring balefully at his brother through one good eye. The other was already swelling shut.

"You are mad," Hugh hissed at him. "Mad and bewitched."

Davyss twitched in his brother's direction but this time, both Andrew and Devereux held him fast. Lollardly put himself in the precarious position between the two brothers, holding up his hands as if to push them away from each other.

"Hugh, you will curb your tongue," he demanded of the younger man, then looked to Davyss. "Get out of here and let your brother cool down."

Davyss' jaw ticked as he glared at Hugh, ignoring the priest completely. "Do you understand why I punished you?"

Hugh gave him an expression that suggested he thought his brother was insane. "Nay," he insisted strongly. "The only explanation is that you are mad."

When Davyss spoke, it was through clenched teeth. "If you ever question my wishes again, I will deal you worse than what you received," he lowered his voice to a growl. "I am the head of this family and this is my keep. You will not question my wishes, ever. And if you ever speak of my wife that way again, I will kill you."

Hugh just stared at him. "Is that what this is about?" he looked truly stunned. "Because I called your wife a bitch?"

Davyss lurched again at his brother but Andrew threw himself in front of his liege, holding him fast with all his might. Edmund jumped in, inadvertently shoving Devereux out of the way as he moved to aid his brother. Devereux managed to scamper back to her husband, wedging herself between Andrew and Edmund, her small hands against Davyss' chest. The brilliant gray eyes blazed up at him.

"Nay, Davyss," she whispered firmly, an inkling of what was happening between the brothers sparking in her mind. "You will not hurt him. Let us retire for the evening."

Davyss was staring at Hugh, an odd flicker to his eye. Nik and Edmund pulled Hugh from the hall, away from his volatile brother. Davyss just stood there, long after his brother was removed, before eventually sitting heavily on the cluttered table. Devereux whispered something to the priest, who disappeared for a few moments, soon returning with a bowl of steaming water and a rag. Devereux thanked the man.

She returned her attention to her husband; he was bleeding from his mouth and had a small cut above his eye that was streaming blood. She dipped the rag in the water and wiped carefully at his mouth, then his eye. Davyss watched her silently, the hazel eyes riveted to her face as she worked. Devereux did not look at him as she surveyed the damage.

"Well," she sighed, fussing with the cut above his eye. "I do not believe I need to stitch this. It will heal well enough."

Davyss didn't respond; he was still looking at her. When the silence became excessive, she finally met his eye. He smiled weakly.

"Thank you, my lady," he said softly. "Shall we finally retire? It has been a full day."

He moved to get off the table but she grasped him, firmly but gently. "Davyss," she whispered. "Whatever has occurred between you and your brother, it is none of my affair. But I will say this; no one person or one thing should come between you and your brother. He is your blood. Everything else is secondary."

Davyss' gentle expression faded. He could see that she wasn't trying to pry or tell him how he should handle the situation; she was simply offering her opinion. He patted the hand resting on his arm.

"Although I appreciate your advice, you will understand when I say that I alone must make that determination," he replied quietly. "For now, I am exhausted and wish to sleep."

"Will you not speak with your brother first?"

"Nay."

"But why?"

"That is between me and Hugh."

He was firm and she did not argue further. But she knew, from words and actions that somehow she was at the root of the problem. Perhaps if she was the cause, then it was her duty to fix it. She felt oddly responsible. Just because Davyss would not speak with his brother did not mean that she couldn't.

CB

WAITING FOR DAVYSS to fall into a deep, snore-inducing sleep had been the hard part. He slept as a knight sleeps, very lightly, so even when he fell asleep, he wasn't quite as unconscious as she had hoped. In truth, sleeping in the same bed as the man was an odd sensation; she'd slept alone her entire life. Now the bed was full of an enormous man who fidgeted constantly. But he eventually stilled, and when she stirred from the bed, he instantly awoke but she assured him that she was simply seeking the privy. He accepted her explanation and she waited until he fell back asleep before slipping from the dark chamber.

Since three massive chambers were linked in a row, she emerged from their chamber into the next one where Philip and Lucy slept. They were awake, however, quietly making love in their large bed in the far corner. Embarrassed at her intrusion, Devereux scooted into the next connecting room where Nik and Frances slept. They were both sound asleep on their respective sides of the bed.

Devereux hadn't yet been shown around the complex so she truly had no idea where she was going to find Hugh. Descending the spiral staircase into the windowless bottom floor, it was very nearly pitch black but for a few lit sconces in the direction that led to the hall. She crept along the wall, finally emerging into the great hall that was lightless but for the chimney opening and a softly flickering fire. Several servants were sleeping near the fire and she tentatively approached one, nudging the man in the foot. On the fourth nudge, he awoke, saw who it was, and bolted to his feet.

She had the man take her to Hugh. She would have never found him otherwise. He was up in the odd-shaped tower, in a smaller chamber on the third floor. He wasn't asleep, however; he answered the chamber door irritably, his eyes narrowing when he saw Devereux. As the servant scampered away, Hugh faced off against his brother's wife, standing in the doorway as she stood on the landing.

He wasn't pleased to see her; that was obvious. "What do you want?" he growled.

Devereux didn't know Hugh at all; he'd made a point of staying away from her since their rough introduction and she didn't blame him. She was suddenly uncertain as to why she had come at all, trying to apologize to this hostile stranger for something she didn't fully understand. But she squared her shoulders and summoned her courage.

"I… I came to apologize," she said softly. "Sir Hugh, I know we had a turbulent beginning and I suppose I am to blame. But your brother and I are married, like it or not, and we are coming to terms with it. In fact, we realize that this may be an amicable union. I am sorry if that offends or upsets you, but I am here tonight because you and Davyss and I will be family for the rest of our lives and I do not want bad blood between us. I would like to make amends."

He just looked at her. "There are no amends to make," he replied. "You and my brother may be married, but you and I are not. We have no relationship whatsoever. You are simply my brother's wife."

She was somewhat discouraged by his attitude but did not let it deter her. "You are correct," she shrugged. "I do not know what I expected in coming here, but I simply wanted to speak with you to let you know that I am sorry for our rough beginning and I do not wish for our association to be hostile."

Hugh's gaze moved from her head to her toes and back again, in a manner that suggested he was bordering on disgust. "I have nothing to say to you," he wiped at his nose. "Whatever you have done to my brother to convince him that you are worthy of being his wife is his business, but you'll not use your same witchcraft on me. I have no regard for you."

His words inflamed her and she fought to keep down her ready-temper; could the man truly be so cold? "As I have no regard for you," she lowered her voice, the friendliness out of it. "I simply do not want you and your brother fighting because of me."

"Why in the hell do you care?'

She lifted a well-shaped brow. "About you, I do not. But I do care for my husband because he is, in fact, my husband. I do not know how your relationship was before he married me, but I suspect you two did not fight as you did down in the hall tonight. I am simply attempting to apologize if I inadvertently caused that. If I did not, then I will apologize for disturbing you."

Hugh's handsome face was impassive as he watched her turn to walk way. But he couldn't resist jabbing at her, so righteously confused and so righteously envious at the same time. When she wasn't fighting tooth and nail, she was well spoken and lovely. Very lovely. Perhaps he could see what Davyss saw in her but he would not admit it. He couldn't seem to think straight.

"You may think you have Davyss' attention at the moment," he said. "But trust me; he will lose interest in you quickly enough. He will no longer be pliable to your will and the wenches you sent away tonight will return in droves and there will be nothing you can do about it."

She paused, eyeing the man and realizing he was attempting to get a rise out of her. She wondered if she should respond at all but, like Hugh, she couldn't resist the confrontation. The man was arrogant and hurtful, and she would hurt him back.

"Are you so certain?"

He was smiling now, although it was not a smile of humor or warmth. "I know my brother well."

"Do not be disappointed if you are wrong."

His smile faded somewhat. "I will not be wrong."

She cocked an eyebrow. "It is quite possible your brother is discovering that devotion to one woman is better than pursuing many," she used Lady Katharine's words, inspecting Hugh from head to toe, as he had inspected her just moments before. But there really was disgust in her expression. "Men like you would take the leavings of others by taking cheap whores to your bed. Are you so anxious to taste another man's scent on a woman you would rub your own flesh against? Or would it be better to taste your scent over and over on a woman you have marked as your own? Bedding many women does not make you a man, Hugh de Winter. It makes you as cheap as they are."

He was out in the landing now, his expression nothing short of furious. "What would you know about men?" he snarled. "Get out of my sight before I kill you."

She smiled, a dangerous gesture. She knew she shouldn't have pushed him; God knows, in hindsight, she knew it. But he was such an arrogant ass that she couldn't help herself. She could already see how to goad him, to drive him to the brink. So she pushed the button without regard for what would come next, only the satisfaction of putting him in his place.

"Your brother might have something to say about that," she murmured. "So ply me not with empty threats. I doubt you are man enough."

He was on her in a flash. Her last coherent recollection was of stars bursting in front of her eyes.

CHAPTER TEN

LADY KATHARINE WAS having a difficult time keeping her composure. She gazed at her youngest son, standing wearily across from her in the lavishly decorated solar of Hollyhock, a four-storied manor on the edge of the River Thames. Hugh had appeared early that morning, just as the sun rose, looking gray and exhausted. She had demanded to know the purpose for his visit, alone and without his brother or their armies. It was just Hugh; he hadn't even been dressed in armor. And then he told her.

It was a shocking revelation. Now, she was struggling as she gazed up at the man who resembled her dead husband to a fault. She was beginning to feel sick and terrified because she knew what was to come.

"Tell me again what you have done, Hugh, so there is no mistake," she tried to sound calm. "I would understand completely."

Hugh was spent. He faced his mother on his feet because she would not let him sit. "I killed Davyss' wife," he said hoarsely. "Mother, you must help me get away. Davyss will come for me and he will kill me."

Lady Katharine sighed faintly. "Why did you kill her?"

Hugh was beginning to shrink in on himself, realizing what he had done the moment he had done it and fleeing Wintercroft immediately so that his brother would not kill him. And he knew the man would. He began to grow agitated.

"Because… because she was a hateful bitch," he insisted, running his fingers through his dark hair. "Everything would have been all right had Davyss not returned for her. But he did return and somehow, she bewitched him. He changed. She did something to his mind, Mother. He was not the same brother I knew."

She watched him through steady eyes. "How did he change?"

Hugh began to pace like a wounded dog. "I... I do not know, really."

"You must know; otherwise, your statement is ignorant and foolish."

He looked at her, his dark eyes flashing. "He had little time for his men or for me. Ever since he returned to Thetford for her, he acted as if nothing else in the world existed but her," he jabbed a finger at his mother. "He killed two of Gloucester's men because of her and ordered all of the serving wenches out of Wintercroft because she wished it. She cast a spell on him, I am telling you; he would not have done such things otherwise. She was a witch!"

Lady Katharine digested his words carefully. In that short burst, she was coming to see something that Hugh was not. It was not something she had expected but pleased to hear it.

"He is focused on her?"

"Aye."

"And he ordered the serving wenches away from Wintercroft? The whores that plague the place?"

"Aye!" Hugh stopped pacing and went to her. "I must go to France, Mother. I need money and safe passage."

Lady Katharine regarded him, mulling the situation over in her mind, pondering, digesting. She was, of course, gravely concerned. She was concerned, as Hugh was, of what Davyss would do. She did not want to see either one of her sons dead but she knew Davyss' temper. More than that, there would be a matter of honor that would render the man a killing machine to the one who wronged him. Her calm demeanor wavered.

"What did you do to Lady Devereux, Hugh?" she demanded quietly. "How did you kill her?"

A pained expression crossed Hugh's face. "We were arguing," he said hesitantly. "I... I struck her and she fell down the stairs. She must have broken her neck."

Lady Katharine struggled not to lash out at him. "You struck her?"

He couldn't look her in the eye. "Aye."

"I raised you better than that, Hugh. You do not strike women."

He was growing agitated again. "I do not know why I did it," he fell to his knees before her. "All I know is that we were arguing and it… it just happened. I do not even remember doing it. One moment, she was standing at the top of the stairs and in the next, she was lying lifeless at the bottom."

"Do you know for a fact she is dead? Did you check her to make sure?"

He shook his head. "Nay… I saw her fall and I ran. I did not stop to see if she was dead or alive."

"Then you assume she is dead."

"She fell down the Tower stairs. If she survived the fall it 'twould be a miracle."

"I happen to believe in miracles," Lady Katharine's regarded her son carefully. "What did she say to you that made you strike her?"

He closed his eyes, collapsing in a miserable heap on his knees. "I do not know."

"You are lying. You just killed a woman, your brother's wife, and you cannot tell me what she said to make you snap?"

His head came up. "She provoked me!"

"Then you do remember. One more lie and I shall not help you at all."

His expression grew painful again. "Oh, God," he breathed, drawing a breath for strength. "We… Davyss and I fought earlier in the evening because I called his wife a bitch. I said it because I was angry; angry she had sent the serving women away from Wintercroft. Angry because Davyss had listened to her. Devereux came to me to try to explain how she had bewitched Davyss into doing it and I would not listen. She… she told me that devotion to one woman is better than bedding many, or something like it. She said I wasn't man enough."

Lady Katharine watched his lowered head, feeling anxiety such as she had never known. But she also felt great sorrow; if what Hugh said was true, then Lady Devereux had been attempting to teach her sons something that she had never been able to. If the lady was indeed dead, then she felt the loss deeply. Slowly, she rose from her chair and moved away from her youngest.

"You will stay here," she told him, her old voice hoarse with emotion. "You will stay here and seek atonement for what you have done. Davyss will come, of that I have no doubt. I will not help you to flee. You have shamed yourself enough. Now you must be a man and face your punishment."

Hugh was on his feet, his eyes wide. "But Davyss will kill me!"

She turned to look at him, her dark eyes piercing. "It is less than you deserve," she snarled. "You are a disgrace to the de Winter name, Hugh. Stay here and face your brother when he comes or leave and never return. I will not see you again if you leave. You have my vow."

Hugh looked like a child who was about to face his greatest fear. "Please, Mother," he begged.

She wouldn't look at him. "Go to your chamber. Bolt the door and stay there. Do not leave until I call for you."

Hugh was torn between extreme fear of his brother and his mother's threat of disownment. He couldn't actually believe his mother would allow Davyss to kill him, so perhaps the best place for him to be was indeed here under his mother's protection. She was the only person alive who could talk Davyss out of killing him.

When Hugh fled her solar, Lady Katharine sat for quite some time, pondering the situation. She wasn't sure she could dissuade Davyss from killing his brother if, in fact, Lady Devereux was dead. She knew that the relationship between the brothers would never be the same from this point forward and rather than see her youngest murdered by his own brother, she began to suspect there was only one answer. She had to keep Hugh alive yet unreachable by Davyss. Perhaps Hugh had been right; he needed safe passage to save his life. As a mother, her loyalty was to both her children. She must keep Hugh alive. And then she must see Davyss.

Hugh went north within the hour, heading to the bosom of an old family friend.

CB

"YOU WILL NOT kill him."

Davyss stood with his hands on his hips, gazing down at his wife with great displeasure. Lucy and Frances were tending her as she lay in their great bed after having taken a nasty fall down a flight of stairs which, Davyss learned, was Hugh's doing. To say he was furious was not strong enough. The only thing keeping him from raging out of control was the anxious expression on his wife's face. That alone was keeping him from ripping Wintercroft apart.

"You will not tell me how to handle my brother," he told her sternly. "He did this to you."

Devereux was actually quite well after having fallen down a flight of stone steps. Fortunately, she hadn't broken any bones although the spill had knocked her unconscious for a short time. She had a bruised cheek, a lump on her forehead, and was generally battered, but she was alive and well for all intent and purposes. And she was having a horrendous time keeping Davyss calm; she could see the rage in his eyes.

"As I told you," she said patiently while Lucy held a cold compress over the lump on her forehead. "Since you would not speak with your brother, I felt strongly that I must speak with him in your place. Your argument was about me, was it not?"

The anger in his eyes flickered. "That is not your business."

"It is if the quarrel was about me. Be truthful and tell me."

He pursed his lips angrily. "Do not lecture me on being truthful. You would not even tell me what you were doing in the Tower. I heard it from a servant who happened to hear you and Hugh arguing."

"If you did as I asked and resolved your quarrel before you retired, then I would not have felt the need to speak with him."

He just rolled his eyes and huffed, posturing angrily, but he did not retort. Truth was, he had never felt more fear in his life as he had when

Andrew had brought his wife's unconscious body back into their bedchamber. He had been sound asleep, both ashamed that he hadn't known she was missing from his bed and gravely concerned that she was injured.

When Devereux had regained consciousness, she wouldn't tell him what had happened but Andrew had pressed a couple of male servants in the Tower who had told him what they had heard and seen; Sir Hugh and Lady de Winter arguing, Lady de Winter's fall and Hugh fleeing in the dead of night. It didn't take a genius to figure out what had happened.

"You will not blame me for your actions," he said, more quietly. "No one forced you to go to the Tower. It was your choice."

Devereux thought on that a moment. "Aye, it was," she winced as Lucy pressed too hard on the compress. "But I had to try and calm the situation between you and Hugh."

Davyss didn't say anything; he just stood there, watching the women fuss over his wife, his initial anger and terror fading into something odd and mixed. He was so angry with Hugh that he couldn't think straight; all he wanted to do was murder the man. But the stronger emotion was worry for his wife and respect for what she had tried to accomplish.

She was a peacemaker, a peace lover, and he knew that. He, on the other hand, was not. War was his vocation, his life, his behavior. This woman was so intriguing and honest on so many levels that he found it difficult to fathom. His mind didn't work the way hers did. The fact that she would try and help him by solving his problem with his brother went beyond comprehension. Did she truly think enough of him, after everything he'd put her through, to do that?

"I appreciate that," he said, his manner softening somewhat. "But I will ask you a question and I want you to be perfectly truthful. Will you do this?"

She hesitated slightly. "Aye."

"Did he strike you?"

She sighed faintly and lowered her gaze. "Aye."

"The bruise on your face?"

"Aye."

Davyss turned on his heel and began to walk from the room. Devereux, realizing that he was more than likely going after his brother, leapt off the bed as much as her aching body would allow. Lucy and Frances tried to grab her but she was swift, racing after her husband. She grabbed him before he could leave the chamber.

"Wait," she dug her heels in and he came to a halt. "Where are you going?"

He almost told her that it was none of her business again but knew better. He was a fast learner. If she thought it was her business, then nothing he could say would deter her. He was quickly coming to learn that she was as stubborn as he was.

"I am going to find my brother," he told her.

She shook her head and pulled hard, trying to pull him back into the room. "Nay, Davyss," she said quietly, firmly. "Come back to bed. It is still a few hours until morning and I am exhausted. Please come and sleep."

He patted her hand, trying to be calm with her through all of the rage he was feeling. "You return to bed and sleep. I am going to find Hugh."

"I cannot sleep if you leave."

He sighed heavily, glancing at Lucy and Frances, standing a few feet away with fear and anxiety in their expressions. He looked at Andrew, Edmund and Philip, standing in the chamber door, waiting for orders. Nik was already in the stables having the chargers saddled. Then he returned his focus on Devereux, holding his arm and gazing up at him with those bottomless gray eyes. It occurred to him that the lure of staying with his wife was stronger than his sense of vengeance at the moment. As he gazed into her lovely face, his sense of thanks that she was well overwhelmed his anger at Hugh.

So he nodded, weakly, and Devereux pulled him back to the bed.

Lucy and Frances scampered from the chamber, taking the cluster of knights with them, as Devereux threw back the coverlet on the bed and climbed in, still holding on to Davyss. He sat on the bed, pulling his boots off with some weariness, before allowing her to pull him back down on the mattress. She pulled the coverlet over him, tucking him in as one would a child, before snuffing out the taper and lying down beside him.

They were lying side by side like two nuns, with the coverlet pulled up properly around their necks. Davyss lay next to his wife, looking over at her and struggling not to grin. She looked uncomfortable lying next to him as if unsure what more she was supposed to do.

With a smirk, he rolled onto his side and captured her in his enormous arms. She yelped as he jostled her, unused to being held tightly against a man. She was still coming to know that part of marriage. But she knew one thing for certain; she would grow to like it. He was warm and wonderful, comfort and security such as she had never known. He was the Davyss she had tried so hard to resist. Now she almost couldn't remember why. She was asleep before she knew it.

He was gone when she awoke in the morning.

CHAPTER ELEVEN

T HE CHURCH WAS dark at this hour, two fat tapers the only light in the dark and shadowed vestibule. The place was cavernous and haunted, smelling of incense, as Davyss slipped from the side entrance and into the shadows of the Temple church. The stone walls were cold, the floor dusty, and he moved through the musty darkness like a wraith. His senses were highly attuned as he wedged himself into an alcove that held a large stone receptacle of holy water. He was well out of sight and blending with his dark surroundings. He simply stood there, still as the stone surrounding him, and waited.

It wasn't long before he noticed movement on the opposite end of the sanctuary. It was a cloaked figure in the darkness near the altar; he could see the folds of the material when the figure moved slightly. They rippled in the weak light, like the ripples of a pond. Davyss made his way, in perfect stealth, in the direction of the movement. In the darkness, he came up behind the figure and put a dagger at its throat.

"Any sounds from your lips and you shall die," he hissed quickly. "State your purpose."

The figure grunted. "*Si j'étais un plus jeune homme j'arracherais vos bras et vous bats à la mort avec eux.*"

Davyss dropped the dagger. "Even when you were a younger man, you could not rip my arms off," he snorted softly. "I think you tried, once."

The cloaked figure turned to Davyss in the darkness. He did not remove his hood but exposed his face; the strong, weathered features of Simon de Montfort gazed steadily at his godson.

"I did try," he insisted. "But your mother stopped me. She threatened to beat me to death and she frightened me."

"She is a frightening woman."

"Still?"

"Good God, must you really ask that?"

Simon's hazel eyes glittered. "I do not," he murmured, drinking in his fill of the man he loved like a son. His humor faded. "'Tis good to see you again. I have missed you."

Davyss was in business-mode; he didn't like these clandestine meetings but he did not want to appear rude. All politics aside, Simon was the only link he had to his long-dead and adored father. He had a soft spot for him, which explained why he was willing to risk his life to meet secretly with him. But their time was extremely limited and he hastened to conduct their business before they were discovered. He reached out and put his hand on the old man's arm, squeezing it.

"What's this about, Uncle Simon?" he whispered. "Why did you need to see me?"

Simon latched on to his hand and held it tightly. "Because I am a weary old man. I need you, Davyss."

Davyss could see the old argument rearing its ugly head. He wasn't surprised that it was immediate. His expression turned stiff.

"Is that why you sent for me?" he growled. "We have been through this too many times to count. I cannot help you."

"But you must. It is crucial." When Simon saw that he was making no headway, he grabbed Davyss by the arm with his old, strong fingers. "Davyss, listen to me. I do not want to see your death, boy. I could not bear it. You have brought three hundred men with you to London and another two thousand wait for you near the Tower. Can you not sense what is happening, lad?"

Davyss' hazel eyes took on an odd flicker. "Of course I know what is happening. I know everything."

Simon sighed sharply, hanging his head a moment and struggling to explain what he must in another way so that Davyss would understand the importance. His head came up and his dark eyes focused on his godson once more.

"Davyss," his grip on the man lessened. "We are amassing. Your beloved Henry is refusing to honor the terms he agreed to six years ago at Oxford and...."

Davyss pulled away from him. "I am a soldier, not a politician. I do not dictate the king's decisions nor do I care. I simply serve him, Simon. You know this."

"He is bringing about another war."

"Then I shall fight it."

"And you shall die," Simon grabbed his arm again and held fast even as Davyss tried to move away. "Listen to me, lad; there are many barons angered by the king's refusal to honor the terms that he signed at Oxford and they are ready to do something about it. We have given the man six years, Davyss; six years to come to his senses and honor his word. But he has not. Do you not understand? An explosion such as you have never dreamed is coming and I do not want you to be a casualty of it."

Davyss stopped yanking and stared at the old man. "Listen to me and listen well," he rumbled. "I serve the king. I am his sword. If Henry goes into battle, then I lead the charge. I will not join you, Uncle Simon. I do not know how much plainer I can be."

Simon remained calm, his wise old eyes regarding the man. His grip moved from the man's arm to his hand, and he held it tightly.

"You are like a son to me," he murmured. "Your father gave you over to me at birth to guide and to bless. I have done so, have I not?"

Davyss nodded slowly, fighting off old and tender memories. "Aye."

"I love you as my own."

"I know."

"I would risk my life for you."

Davyss just stared at him, struggling to fight off the increasing emotion. "And I, you, under normal circumstances. But do not ask me to betray my king. I cannot and I will not. I would be a man without honor if I did."

Simon hung his head. It seemed as if he wanted to say something more, something crucial. He was struggling. Davyss didn't understand why until the old man opened his mouth again.

"Hugh has joined me," he whispered. "Your mother sent word a short time ago. Hugh is now with me. You have lost his sword."

That revelation received a reaction; Davyss' eyes bulged and he yanked his hand away from Simon.

"You lie," he hissed. "Hugh would never...."

He abruptly came to a halt, unable to finish his sentence. All of the trouble with Devereux and Hugh came crashing down on him and suddenly, he felt extremely ill. The room swayed. He put out a massive arm, bracing himself against the stone wall. Simon could see the weakness and, like a good warrior, swooped in for the kill.

"I was told that Hugh murdered your wife," he whispered urgently. "Your mother sent him to me for protection. Davyss, whatever has transpired between you and Hugh, a woman is no reason to hate or disown your brother."

Davyss reached out and grabbed Simon by the neck; Simon was a big man but not as strong nor as big as Davyss. Simon could see, in that instant, that there was much more to this than the missive Lady Katharine had sent him. Simply by his expression, Davyss was as passionate as he had ever seen him.

"Shut your mouth," Davyss snarled. "You know not of what you speak."

"He is your brother, Davyss."

"And she is my wife," Davyss let go of Simon's neck, roughly, his hazel eyes flashing. "In spite of what Hugh tried to do, she is not dead. She is alive and well. But Hugh will suffer my wrath and all of the protection in the world will not prevent that. If you protect Hugh from me, then you are against me. If you are against me, then we have nothing more to discuss."

Simon's eyes took on a pained look. "I will never be against you, lad. Neither is Hugh."

"My entire family has apparently turned against me."

"But what of this wife? Is she so valuable to you that you would put her above your brother?"

It was a difficult question to answer, considering Davyss had been wrestling with that very dilemma for a few days. "That is not your business," he snapped. It was the best answer he could come up with.

But Simon was beginning to see why Davyss and Hugh were divided and it wasn't simply a matter of honor. There was more to it from the look on Davyss' face.

"Nay, Davyss," he said patiently, as if trying to explain things to him. "A woman must not come between you and your brother."

Davyss was feeling ill; he simply waved a hand at the man as if to stop all further words and turned to leave. Simon followed.

"Please," the old man begged softly. "Will you at least not consider my words? We need you, lad. *I* need you."

Davyss was feeling fury along with his disorientation. Simon had him on the run and he didn't like it. He suddenly whirled on Simon and the old man almost plowed into him.

"If my mother is involved in this, then she has betrayed me as well," he hissed. "She would send Hugh to you to keep him from my punishment and you would use him to try and convince me to join you. Understand this, Simon; I am a man of honor. I will not break my oath to the king nor walk away from a post I have worked so hard to achieve. Hugh is jealous of my wife and tried to kill her; he must and will face my punishment no matter if God himself hides him. I will find him. And I will not join you and your rebellious barons because the true king sits upon the throne of England and it is he whom I serve. All of the men in my arsenal could join you and still, I would serve Henry. I must. It is a matter of personal honor."

Simon understood a great deal in that passionate statement. He almost mentioned the fact but he kept his mouth shut; he would not display his thoughts nor his intentions, as Davyss was a smart man and would pick up on it immediately. So he kept silent, watching Davyss as the man blew out of the church like an angry black wind. And that was the end of it.

When Simon returned to his quarters, he sent a missive to Lady Katharine immediately.

Who is Davyss' wife and where may I find her? It may be necessary....

CB

DEVEREUX HAD AWOKEN with the worst belly ache she could imagine. Moving around only seemed to make her more nauseous, but it was her first full day in her new home and she did not want to spend it lying in bed, so she forced herself to rise. Lucy and Frances were waiting like impatient children for her to awaken and when she did, they immediately set about preparing her morning toilette. Devereux felt awful but she allowed them the pleasure. They seemed so eager about it.

So she sat in the bathing room while they fussed over her. Lucy rubbed oil on her skin while Frances brushed her hair. As the women worked, Devereux sat in a fog, her mind on Davyss and the fact that he had more than likely gone to do his brother great bodily harm. The thought made her feel even worse. With her aching head and rolling stomach, she very much wanted to return to bed. Half-way through her toilette, she could no longer stand it.

"I am sorry, ladies," she stood up from the little stool they had her seated on. "I believe my harrowing night has taken its toll. I must lie down for a time."

Lucy and Frances were very concerned. "Are you ill, Lady de Winter?" Lucy asked fretfully.

Devereux nodded as she went back into the bed chamber and climbed back into bed. "Please see that I am not disturbed."

Frances and Lucy helped pull the coverlet up around her, passing anxious glances.

"Shall we send up some wine and bread, my lady?" Frances asked.

The thought of food made Devereux feel ill. She shook her head as she lay down. "Nay," she sighed as she settled in. "No food. Just let me

152

sleep for a time. I am sure I will feel better in a little while."

"Do you require the surgeon?"

"Nay. Just sleep."

There was nothing more that Lucy or Frances could say. They left Devereux asleep in the great bed, although they made sure that one of them was outside of the door at all times in case she needed something. When Davyss returned sometime before noon, Lucy was waiting anxiously for him with a tale of woe.

He raced to the master's chamber to find Devereux sound asleep. The tapestry was lowered, blocking out the light from the windows and the room was dark and musty. He was very quiet as he leaned over his wife, putting a gentle hand on her forehead to make sure she wasn't running a fever. He was deeply concerned, shooing Lucy and Frances out of the room. He followed shortly. Once outside the door, he spoke.

"Did she eat this morning?" he asked.

Lucy shook her head. "Nay, my lord. She did not want anything to eat."

He cocked an eyebrow. "I see," he frowned, thoughtful. "What did she say her symptoms were?"

"She did not," Frances answered. "She only said she must lie down. But she has been asleep all morning."

Davyss digested her statement, the situation in general. He exhaled sharply, blowing out his cheeks. "I can only assume that last night was too much for her," he said. "She is exhausted and injured, and we will let her sleep until she feels better."

"Of course, my lord," Lucy nodded eagerly. "We shall sit with her in case she requires anything."

Davyss shook his head. "Nay," he informed them. "I will sit with her. Send food up to my chamber, please."

The women nodded and fled. Davyss went back into the darkened chamber and tried to stay quiet as he wearily removed his boots. He set the first one down silently but the second one made some noise. He froze, watching Devereux, but she remained still. He resumed removing his tunic, quietly, tossing it over near the wardrobe. By the time he sat down next to the bed, Devereux was awake and looking at him.

"You make enough noise to wake the dead," she mumbled.

He grinned down at her, smoothing a big hand across her forehead. "Enough to wake you, at any rate," he removed his hand, gazing sweetly down at her. "I heard that you were not feeling well. Is there anything I can do?"

She looked up at him with her brilliant gray eyes and the humor in her expression faded. "Aye," she whispered. "You can tell me that you did not kill your brother."

His grin disappeared, the hazel eyes intense. "I did not kill my brother."

"Then where did you go?"

He continued to gaze steadily at her. "On an errand," he replied. "But you need not concern yourself with that. I am more concerned with your health. How do you feel?"

She did not press him on where he had disappeared to; there was no need to if he had not gone to murder Hugh. Devereux realized that she was simply glad to see him.

"Better now that you are here," she smiled wearily. "My head pounds something fierce and my stomach is lurching like waves crashing upon the shore."

His grin returned and he sat on the edge of the bed; she rolled into him, pressed against his thigh.

"Let me send for Lollardly," he said. "He can give you something for your head."

"Lollardly?" she repeated, confused. "Is he not your priest?"

"He is our surgeon also."

She made a reluctant face. "Very well."

He winked at her and kissed her forehead, sending Lucy, hovering just outside the door, for Lollardly, the man of many talents. She almost plowed into Frances in her haste, who was bringing food to Davyss. Since Devereux chased off the serving wenches, Lucy and Frances were doing double-duty. Davyss lifted an eyebrow at the near-collision, watching Lucy scamper off. Frances presented him with a large tray of edibles. Davyss took it back to his wife, who was now sitting up, albeit slowly, in bed.

"Do you feel like eating something?" he asked.

She peered at the tray he offered, noting the cheese, bread, small apples and some kind of meat. She made a face and waved him off as she climbed out of bed.

"No, thank you," she stood up, weaving unsteadily. "I will get dressed and have you show me Wintercroft. I have not seen the entire place. Just the tower stairwell, you know."

He couldn't help but grin at her, the funny way she delivered the last sentence. He was coming to see that she had a delightful sense of humor. "I know," he replied with a mixture of resignation and disapproval. "Are you sure you want a tour? Perhaps you should rest today."

She shook her head, stretching out her stiff muscles as she moved for the bathing alcove. "I am fine," she insisted. "Please eat your meal and I will dress."

"I would like for you to eat something also."

She mumbled something he didn't hear as she moved into the bathing alcove. With a shrug, he delved into the meat on the tray. He hadn't taken two bites when he heard her retching. Pushing the tray aside, he moved swiftly into the bathing alcove to find her bent over the basin, dry heaving. His concern returned full-force.

"Are you all right?" he asked anxiously.

She nodded, holding her hair back as she continued to dry-heave. When the heaves passed, she took a deep breath and wiped at her mouth with the back of her hand.

"I am fine," she muttered.

"You do not look fine."

Her gray eyes widened. "I look terrible?"

He noted the distress on her face and shook his head, putting his hands on her shoulders and steering her back into their chamber. "You are still the most beautiful woman I have ever seen," he assured her. "I simply meant that you are obviously not fine. Lie back down and eat some bread. Perhaps it will make you feel better."

She didn't argue with him until he tried to hand her the bread. She resisted until he put it to her mouth himself and gently ordered her to take a bite. She did, but chewed as if it was made of wood. Davyss was torn between the humor of her expression and concern for her physical state, but she managed to choke down four bites of bread before falling back to the bed and covering her head with the pillow. He did grin, then, and ate the rest of the bread as he sat next to her. He put his free hand on her back, stroking her hair until she dozed.

Lucy and Lollardly arrived some time later. The old priest had a bag with him and entered the bed chamber with Lucy in tow, his old eyes moving back and forth between Davyss and the lump under the covers beside him.

"Lady de Winter is feeling poorly?" Lollardly asked Davyss. "What seems to be amiss?"

Davyss looked over at the bundle of covers beside him. "Her stomach aches and her head hurts," he said. "Give her something to heal her."

Lollardly lifted an eyebrow and went to the other side of the bed for better access to Lady de Winter. He peered at the bump under the covers, trying to get a look at her without lifting any of the material. Finally, he gingerly reached down and lifted up the pillow. Lady de Winter's disapproving face was looking back at him.

"Well?" she lifted an eyebrow. "Do you have something to cure what ails me?"

Lollardly began to rummage through his bag. "What, in particular, ails you, my lady?"

She sat up slowly, covering her mouth when a burp threatened. "Everything," she groaned. "My head throbs and my stomach aches."

Lollardly listened to her before digging into his bag and removing a couple of crude leather pouches. He had Lucy bring him some wine and he dissolved first a white, then a brown, powder into the wine. He handed it to Devereux. She eyed it suspiciously.

"What is this?" she asked.

"Drink it."

"I want to know what is in it."

"Magic. Mysterious stuff. You would not understand."

She pursed her lips at him. "Then explain it so I will."

Lollardly was losing his patience. "Do you want to feel better?"

"Of course."

"Then stop talking and drink it."

She was gearing up for a sharp retort but Davyss, grinning, intervened. "You had better tell her or we will be here all day," he told the old man.

Lollardly frowned, displaying great disapproval as he focused on Devereux. "White willow and coriander," he replied. "Now will you drink it?"

She eyed him as if to emphasize that she was not complying particularly willingly, but she accepted the cup and drained it. Davyss smiled his approval and helped her lie back down.

"Now," he kissed her on the forehead. "Go to sleep. You will feel better when you awake."

She snuggled down into the coverlet and sighed wearily, gazing up at him. "Will you stay with me?"

His smile faded. "For a while," he said. "But I have business in London I must attend to and I am leaving tonight."

She bolted up again into a seated position, fighting the nausea that swelled like the tide. "Business?" she repeated, concerned. "How long will you be gone?"

He was very touched to see the concern in her eyes, as if she did not want him to leave. He never thought to see that expression on her face, ever. It was then that he began to realize that the past few days together might have accomplished exactly as he had hoped; she had warmed to him. Perhaps with time she would actually….

"I do not know," he said quietly, stroking her pale cheek. "Will you miss me?"

She studied him, fighting the urge to lie. She wanted to deny him. But she found that she could not. "Aye," she said after a moment. "I believe I will."

He grinned and kissed her cheek, then her mouth. "I never thought to hear that from your lips.'"

She met his grin reluctantly, closing her eyes in sheer bliss when he kissed her cheek again. "And I never thought to say it," she lifted her hand, putting it against his stubbly cheek "Can I come with you? I have never been to London before."

The denial was on his lips. He tried to speak it but could not make the words come forth. Gazing into her lovely gray eyes, he knew he was going to comply. Although he knew very well that she should stay at Wintercroft, he realized he wanted her with him no matter what.

"You may be spending a good deal of your time alone," he tried very weakly to discourage her. "I have business with the king."

Her eyes widened. "The king?"

His smile returned and he chuckled. "Aye, the king," he lifted his eyebrows. "Surely you did not forget that I am his champion."

She shook her head; then she nodded. "I must confess that for a moment, the fact did escape me," she replied. "Are you really going to see him?"

"Truly."

"Will… will I meet him also?"

"More than likely."

Her eyes bugged and she suddenly propelled herself out of bed. "I must pack," she said anxiously, motioning to Lucy standing just outside the open chamber door. "Come, Lucy, and help me!"

Lucy was as skittish as a bird. She flew into the room, following Devereux as she bolted into the bathing alcove. Mildly startled and slightly confused at the burst of activity, Davyss stood up from the bed and scratched his dark head at the crazed women darting around him.

"Your trunks have not been completely unpacked since our arrival," he called out to his wife helpfully. "You do not need to fly into a frenzy."

She rushed out of the bathing alcove with a small box of toiletries in her hand. "Aye, I do!"

He chuckled as she ran past him, towards the neat row of trunks against the wall. "I thought you were feeling poorly."

She dumped the box into the trunk and whirled on him. "I am," she insisted. "But that will not stop me from going with you."

He watched her as she raced past him, stepping back so she wouldn't run him over. "Are you sure?"

She disappeared into the bathing alcove. It wasn't two seconds later that he heard retching again.

CHAPTER TWELVE

W INTERCROFT WASN'T TOO far from the heart of London city. As they neared the jewel city of England and the early morning sun glittered off the River Thames, Devereux was enraptured. The structures this close to the heart of the city were built close together, crowded upon each other in some areas, but there were some lovely buildings that Devereux found very interesting. One of them was a beautiful abbey, which Davyss apologized for not being able to stop at. He was overdue at the Tower of London and could not make the king wait any longer, but he promised he would take her afterwards to see all of the pretty buildings to her heart's content.

At Devereux's insistence, Lucy and Frances were along on the trip, much to Philip's pleasure and Nikolas' indifference. Davyss had brought a carriage for the women because Devereux still wasn't feeling particularly well and he didn't want her riding a palfrey. So the three ladies idled away the trip in the carriage belonging to Lady Katharine, finding both the trip and the company agreeable.

Devereux was coming to know Lucy and Frances fairly well in just the few days she had known them. There wasn't much more to do to occupy their time than talk, although Lucy brought a spectacular piece of *petite poi* to work on. It was a gorgeous piece of work of a woodland scene and she worked it very carefully as the carriage lurched and bumped over miles of road. She never even pricked her finger, which amazed Devereux. She would have cut herself to shreds by now. Lucy also chattered constantly, making it all the more amazing that she never stabbed herself with her sewing needle. Devereux leaned back against the cab, listening to Lucy speak on all things foolish, smiling faintly at her silly but sweet new friend.

Frances, however, was another matter. She was quiet, humorless and efficient, and would not warm no matter how much Devereux tried. Devereux wondered what could make a woman so joyless; having seen how she interacted with her husband, it was apparent there was little affection between them. Devereux wondered if Frances' demeanor was the cause or the result. No amount of jesting or storytelling could coerce a smile from the woman. She was very serious and, Devereux thought, very sad. It was puzzling.

As she'd been told, Hollyhock was the Lady Katharine de Winter's home in London, close to the heart of the city and downriver from Westminster Cathedral. It was a beautiful home that soared four stories into the sky, built of great blocks of stone rather than the wood and mortar that was so popular in the city. It sat on its own expanse of land along the river, guarded by a big stone wall, dogs, and a small army of sentries.

When Davyss brought the column to a halt in front of his mother's house, he bailed off his charger and ordered the men to hold station. Like a mother hen, Lollardly began to take up his lord's call and squawked Davyss's commands to the entire group. As the old priest barked, Davyss made his way back to the carriage.

Devereux's sweet face was the first thing to greet him; she was staring from the carriage window, drinking in the sight of the four-storied monstrosity before her. But she tore her eyes away long enough to smile at her husband as he approached.

"Well," he glanced at the manor, gesturing with a gloved hand. "This is where you shall stay. Welcome to Hollyhock, my lady."

Devereux was more impressed with this place than she had been with Wintercroft; Hollyhock was a home of astounding architecture and beauty. A lovely garden surrounded the home from what she had been able to see through the great iron gates with forests of colorful hollyhocks and foxgloves reaching to the sky.

"'Tis lovely," she said sincerely. "I do not blame your mother for preferring Hollyhock over Wintercroft."

Davyss gave her a lop-sided grin. "I can see that you do as well."

She met his grin, shaking her head. "It *is* beautiful," she insisted weakly. "Is your mother in residence?"

He nodded. "She comes to Hollyhock for the summer because everyone who lives in town in the summer usually leaves because of the moist heat from the river. She likes the quiet streets. Moreover, Mother swears the moisture soothes her skin so she prefers Hollyhock in the summer."

Devereux, nodding with interest, moved to open the cab door but Davyss stopped her.

"Not yet," he secured the door and kissed her on the cheek. "Wait here. I shall return shortly."

Leaving Philip and Nik in charge of the women, he entered the stately gates of the manor and made his way to the front door. It was a massive door, made with strong English oak and reinforced with great bars of iron. He used the enormous iron knocker which, when pounded, resonated throughout the entire house. Eventually, the massive door creaked open and Davyss entered.

The entry hall was wide, cool, lavishly decorated. Fresh flowers from his mother's garden were everywhere. It was an elegant home, just the way Lady Katharine liked it. Everything reeked of sophistication. He went into the room directly to his left, a massive solar, beautifully appointed, where his mother sat with her two little dogs. Her ladies lingered in the shadows, quiet as ghosts. Lady Katharine barely looked up from her needlework as he entered but the dogs barked furiously.

"Mother," Davyss went to her, bending over to kiss her wrinkled cheek and fighting off the happy dogs in the process. "You look well on this day."

Katharine finished the stitch and gave him her full attention. "You have not come to tell me how well I look," she told him flatly.

He lifted an eyebrow at her, folding his massive arms across his chest. "So much for pleasantries," he muttered, then louder: "'Tis your guilt speaking."

Katharine matched his lifted eyebrow. "I have no guilt to speak of, Davyss de Winter. If you are here to harass me, you can go along your way. I'm sure the king is waiting for you with great impatience, unable to govern the country without his mighty champion by his side."

She said it sarcastically. Davyss couldn't decide if he was angry or humored by her attitude. After a moment, he paced over to the enormous Gothic-style window, complete with precious glass. Very few homes had such opulence. He gazed from the window, seeing a portion of the carriage through the iron gates.

"I would assume Hugh has been here," he said.

Katharine dropped her needlework entirely. "He has," she was honest, moving straight to the point because she knew that was why he had come. "What he did was not right, Davyss. I told him so. But it is my impression that it was an accident more than he was actually trying to hurt her."

Davyss looked at her. "What are you talking about?"

"Your wife. Hugh did not mean to kill her and I forbid you to seek vengeance against your brother."

Davyss' eyebrows lifted. "You *forbid* me?" he repeated, incredulous. "I am a grown man, Mother. The time has long since passed that you could forbid me anything."

Katharine was on her feet, collecting her cane from where it was propped against the luxurious chair she had been seated in.

"I am sorry for your wife, truly," she said with great sincerity. "It is a great tragedy. But what is done is done. Seeking revenge against your brother will not bring her back."

Davyss watched his elderly mother approach. "She is not gone."

Katharine's old eyes widened with surprise. "She is not dead?"

He shook his head. "Nay," he told her. "Not in the least, although she does have a bruise on her face from Hugh's fist."

Katharine suddenly came to a halt, looking exceedingly relieved. "Praise God," she murmured, hand to her heart, before speaking to her son again. "I thought you were here to kill your brother over his actions."

Davyss watched her carefully. "Where *is* Hugh?"

Katharine waved a careless hand. "Gone," she said vaguely, hoping he would not pursue it. "I sent him away. I did not want you to find him here."

"Where did you send him?"

She looked pointedly at him. "Away." She would say no more, changing the subject instead. "Where is your wife, then? Did you bring her with you?"

"I did," he replied, stepping aside so she could look from the window. "Mother, where is Hugh?"

She didn't look at him, pretending to look out of the window instead. "I told you; I sent him away."

"I want to know where he is."

"I will not tell you until your anger against him cools."

"I am not angry," Davyss assured her as calmly as he could. "But I wish to know where my brother is."

He heard his mother sigh faintly. After a moment, she turned to him. "I sent him to Simon."

At least she didn't lie to him about it. He felt marginally better about that. But the confirmation still hit him in the gut.

"You realize, of course, that you are pitting your sons against each other," he told her in a low, calm voice. "I ride with Henry to Sussex, probably tonight. Simon knows this; he is moving his supporters to engage. Hugh and I are riding into battle against each other."

Katharine's steady gaze didn't waver. "There is no difference if you ride to battle together or against each other," she replied. "I stand no greater chance of loss. Either way, I may lose one or both of you. That has always been the case."

Davyss sighed faintly, moving away from the window. He paced to his mother's fat chair and sat heavily, his big body suddenly weary. The little dogs jumped on his lap happily but he did not pet them; he was too focused on his heavy thoughts.

"I do not want to kill my brother," he muttered. "I cannot believe he is siding with Simon."

Katharine moved in his direction, her cane making dull noises against the wood floor.

"He is not siding with Simon," she said quietly.

"Simon told me that he was."

"You already knew I had sent him to Simon?"

He nodded. "I did," he glanced up at her. "I wanted to see how truthful you would be about it."

"And did I meet your expectations?"

"You did," he replied. "And you met my expectations about something else."

"What is that?"

He should have had a difficult time swallowing his pride, but he found he did not. "You were right," he murmured. "About Lady Devereux. You were absolutely right."

Katharine rather liked the sound of that, although her conversation with Hugh had given her some indication about how Davyss and his wife were getting along. She sat on the chair next to him, leaning on her cane.

"What was I right about?" she asked softly.

Davyss smiled faintly. "You said once that I needed someone to show me that the true meaning of manhood comes from dedication to one woman, not many." He suddenly shook his head as if amused by the irony of it all. "I did not believe you; not in the least. But this woman I have been married to for just a few weeks has very quickly come to mean a great deal to me and I am coming to understand what you meant."

Lady Katharine struggled to suppress a grin. "I can hardly believe my ears," she said softly. "Explain."

He shrugged his big shoulders. "I am not sure if I can. All I know is that she is kind, compassionate, humorous and blindingly beautiful. When I look at her, my heart thumps against my ribs and my hands sweat. I kiss the woman and she consumes my being. I want to make her happy; Sweet Jesus, there is nothing more on earth that I could wish for than to make her completely, utterly happy. I cannot explain my feelings to you any more than that."

Katharine's smile broke through and she put a gnarled hand on her son's dark head. "I am pleased, Davyss," she murmured. "Very pleased."

He looked at her, making a wry face. "I knew you would be."

"Are you happy?"

He lifted his eyebrows, nodded his head and shrugged all at the same time. "I am. I truly am. I do not exactly know why I should be, but I am."

Katharine patted his cheek and struggled to stand up. Davyss rose and helped his mother gain her footing.

"Where is your wife?" Katharine wanted to know. "Bring her inside so that I might speak with her. The only conversations I have had with the woman have not been pleasant ones."

He let go of her when he was sure she was not going to teeter. "You will have ample opportunity to make up for unpleasant conversations," he told her. "I will be leaving her in your care while I am away."

Katharine lifted an eyebrow. "Hmmm," she grunted. "Do you suppose she is going to want to spend endless boring hours with a frail old woman?"

"What do you mean?"

Katharine looked at him as if he were an idiot. "What about her charity? Perhaps she would rather spend her time there. It was my understanding that it consumes most of her time, anyway."

He looked as if the thought had not occurred to him. "Perhaps it has in the past. But now her time is spent with me."

"Do you so arrogantly presume that your shining presence will erase any longing she might feel to return to The House of Hope?"

He frowned. "I have provided amply for the place," he told her. "Before we left for Wintercroft, I supplied the place with enough money to see to its needs for quite some time. There are others who can adequately run the place in her stead."

Katharine could see that he did not understand any priorities but his own. She shook her head faintly. "All I am saying is that if you truly wish to make her happy, then you should ask her where she wishes to spend her time while you are away," she eyed her son. "You may be away for quite some time."

Davyss' expression took on a distant look. "Long indeed," he muttered. "Perhaps permanently."

Katharine didn't react other than to pet the dog that suddenly jumped up beside her. "Have you discussed that possibility with her?"

He shook his head. "Nay," he replied. "We are only just coming to know each other. I am not sure that is an entirely appropriate subject at the moment."

"You are a warrior. She knows there is the possibility of you going to war and not returning."

"But I do not want to discuss that with her just yet."

"Why not?"

He looked at her, frustrated. "Can I not simply enjoy this marriage for a few short hours? Why must I immediately speak of war and death to her? She does not want to hear it, anyway. She does not like conflict."

Katharine lifted a gray eyebrow. "She has married you," she replied pointedly. "War and death are part of your life. Whether or not she likes it, it is a reality. What happens if you do not return, Davyss? What shall she do? You must make your wishes clear to her."

He abruptly stood, heading for the door. "I will," he said as he walked. "But not right now."

"If you leave with Henry tonight, you do not have much time."

Davyss didn't reply. He continued through the elaborate foyer and to the great oak door. Throwing it open, he emitted a piercing whistle between his teeth and motioned to Nik and Philip when they turned to look at him. The Catesby brothers, at the back of the column, began to shout and move the men as Nik and Philip went to the carriage. Philip opened the door as Nik extended a hand to Devereux.

"Lady de Winter?" he said politely. "Your husband has requested your presence."

Devereux climbed out of the cab, her eyes still on the elaborate home. Davyss met her at the gate, taking her from Nik and kissing her hand sweetly before tucking it into the crook of his elbow.

"We will only be here a short time," he told her as they approached the mammoth stone entry. "I must attend Henry sooner rather than later and I intend to bring you with me."

Devereux gathered her skirt as they mounted the steps. She was wearing one of the surcoats he had given her for their wedding, a pale blue confection with silver embroidery along the neck and sleeves. With her blonde hair pulled back and secured with a blue-glass comb, she looked enchanting. But Devereux wasn't so sure.

"Am I appropriately dressed to meet the king?" she wanted to know, smoothing down the skirt when they reached the door. "Should I change into something else?"

He shook his head. "You are exquisite," he kissed her cheek before encouraging her into the house. "We will say a few pleasantries to my mother and be on our way."

Devereux still wasn't convinced that she shouldn't change into something more elaborate and put on every jewel she had, but if Davyss said that her appearance was acceptable, then she would trust him. Upon entering the magnificent four-storied foyer, Lady Katharine's two little dogs suddenly rushed Devereux in a barking frenzy. The first thing they did was grab the bottom of the surcoat with their sharp little teeth and begin ripping.

Davyss swooped down and grabbed them both by the scruff of the neck. He would have thrown them through the window had his mother's sharp voice not stopped him.

"Hurt those dogs and I will disinherit you this day," she boomed as much as she was able. "Put them down, Davyss; do it now."

Davyss' jaw was ticking as he looked to the dogs squirming in his grip. "These are vicious little beasts, Mother. If I put them down, they may do more damage."

"Put them down."

"If they bite her, I will kill them."

"Put them *down*."

He did, but not before kicking one of them. He actually shoved the dog with his foot more than he kicked it; the little creature skidded across the floor, barking furiously at Devereux until Katharine's sharp voice silenced it. Then the dogs did nothing more than sniff at Devereux before trotting obediently back to their mistress. Devereux watched them with big eyes, not at all pleased that the savage little rats had just wrecked her skirt.

"It is ruined," she whispered to her husband, trying to get a good look at the damage. "I will most definitely have to change before we see the king."

Davyss, extremely displeased at his mother's wild animals, gently took her into the solar where his mother now sat with her two body-guards. Lady Katharine's gaze was intense upon Devereux.

"My lady," she greeted. "I apologize for the dogs. They do not like strangers. I will replace the dress, of course."

Devereux smiled weakly. "It is of no matter, my lady," she replied, dipping into a gracious curtsy. "I am honored to be in your home."

Katharine watched her very carefully; the last time she had seen the lady, she had been distraught and harried. The woman before her was lovely, graceful and calm, which was something of a pleasant surprise. Even though Davyss had told her that he was coming to appreciate his new wife, still, given their rough beginning it was difficult to comprehend that the situation was easing between them. She indicated the chair next to her.

"Will you sit?"

Devereux planted herself carefully into the chair, sitting straight and properly, hands folded in her lap. Katharine watched her expression, the body language, before speaking.

"You are looking well," she said. "I understand that marriage agrees with my son. Does it agree with you also?"

Devereux' eyes widened briefly at the blunt question. "It seems to, my lady," she replied honestly. "Davyss has done much to make it agreeable."

"Excellent," Katharine nodded with satisfaction. "Then it would not be too much to hope for a grandson very soon?"

Davyss intervened; he had to. He clapped a disbelieving hand on his forehead, reaching to take his wife's arm and pull her from the chair. "Sweet Jesus, Mother," he muttered. "We have only just arrived and already you are speaking of grandchildren?"

He had pulled Devereux to her feet. Katharine watched the pair indignantly. "And why not?" she demanded. "The purpose of this marriage is to perpetuate the House of de Winter and I see no offense in asking a true question."

Davyss gave her an exasperated look, putting his hand on Devereux's back to gently guide her towards the door.

"You could have just as well asked me," he scolded her. "Of course you can hope for a grandson in the spring. Or perhaps the summer. Perhaps it will be a girl and not a boy. Whatever the case, we have done our duty, as you are well aware. The House of de Winter will continue at some point."

Katharine lifted an eyebrow. "At some point, indeed. I am an old woman, Davyss. I do not have time to waste."

Davyss was carefully pushing his wife along but Devereux abruptly stopped, turning to face Lady Katharine. She put her hand on Davyss' arm, stilling him, when he tried to turn her back around.

"I will do my best, Lady Katharine," she assured her. "I understand that my role in this marriage is to breed strong sons. I will try not to disappoint you."

Davyss just looked at her, somehow hurt by her words. Perhaps in his mind, that too had been her only role in this marriage. But that idea ended a few days ago when he returned to Thetford. In just the past few days, she had come to mean much more to him. He almost didn't care about children; he simply wanted to get to know her better because what he knew so far had him captivated. When Devereux turned around to leave the room, he shot his mother a reproving look. Lady Katharine was unremorseful.

"I am sure you will not, my lady," she replied evenly.

Davyss refused to let the conversation continue. He took Devereux from the room and to the wide stone stairs that were built into the house, leading to the upper floors of the manse. He left his wife standing at the base of the stairs while he went to the door and ordered all of her trunks brought inside. Then he escorted Devereux to the third floor, took a left turn, and ended up in a wing of dark wood and musky smells. This was Davyss' domain at Hollyhock, the lair of the eldest de Winter male. It had the feel of power, virility and intimidation.

The four rooms on this level were his; two on the west side of the house and two on the east with a central hall down the middle. There were small rooms in between each pair of rooms for dressing and bathing. Davyss' male servants slept here when he was in residence. He took his wife to the first room on the left.

The first thing that greeted Devereux was an enormous bed made from strong English oak. It had four giant posts and a canopy of heavy fabric curtains that encircled it. He paused by the door as she continued inside, inspecting the big, well-furnished room. She ran her hands over the bed post, feeling the quality of it.

"This is my bedchamber when I stay at Hollyhock," he told her. "If you wish to change anything about it, feel free to do so. It is a room for a man and I am sure you would like to change that."

She smiled faintly as she turned to him. "Why would I?" she asked. "The room reminds me of you and that is not a bad thing in the least."

He grinned. "I am flattered," he replied, stepping into the room. He closed the door softly behind him. "This room shall serve us well as we practice making those grandchildren that my mother is so eager to have."

Devereux's smile faded and she lifted an eyebrow at him, suddenly looking very weary. As Davyss watched with curiosity, she sat heavily on the bed and blew out her cheeks as if her exhaustion had abruptly caught up with her. Davyss thought she looked a bit apprehensive and he began to wonder if his mother's comments this early in their marriage had somehow offended her. He was about to find out.

"I do not believe that shall be necessary," she said after a moment.

His brow furrowed. "Why not?"

She wouldn't look at him as she rubbed her belly. She seemed to find interest in everything else in the room but him, unable to meet his eye. It took her some time to reply and when she did, her tone was laced with hesitance.

"Because…," she tried again. "Because I do believe your mother can already expect a grandchild in the winter."

Davyss stared at her a moment as the words sank in. His smile vanished completely and the hazel eyes widened.

"What?" he couldn't keep his jaw from dropping. "Are you serious?"

She sighed heavily, nodding. Then she tipped over sideways and ended up supine on the bed. Exhaustion and apprehension gave way to teary eyes which she quickly wiped away.

"Aye," she murmured, her hand still on her belly. "I have not been feeling my best the past few weeks and it is only growing worse. I thought it was the shock of our marriage, or the travel, but I cannot deny that I was feeling poorly before you returned to Thetford. Right now, all I want to do is sleep and that is not like me. I am exhausted, my head throbs and my belly aches constantly, which leads me to believe that I may be with child."

He was suddenly on his knees beside the bed, his face a mask of shock. "So that is why you have been retching?"

"I believe so."

"But… but we have only… not more than a few times, and…."

She met his eye, then. "It only takes once, Davyss," she couldn't help but smile at the expression on his face. "It would seem that your virgin bride conceived on that day we do not like to speak of. Perhaps something good came out of that day, after all."

Davyss was stunned. He remained on his knees beside the bed, trying to reconcile her news in his own mind. Eventually, a massive hand came up and began gently stroking her arm. For several long moments, he couldn't seem to manage anything else. He really didn't know what to say.

"Do you truly believe this is the case?" he asked softly.

She couldn't figure out if he was appalled or thrilled by the news. "I do," she acknowledged. "My cycle has not come since that day, either. I am therefore fairly certain."

That bit of information seemed to seal his thoughts. He pulled her towards him, kissing her mouth with gentle passion. His hands were on her face, in her hair, as he gently and tenderly kissed her.

"I honestly do not know what to say to all of this," he whispered against her lips. "I had not imagined that we would be so soon blessed."

Her eyes were open, watching him as he kissed her. "Are you pleased, then?"

He stopped kissing her, fixing her in the eye with his intense gaze. For a long moment, he didn't answer her. He just stared at her.

"Aye," he finally whispered. "I am utterly overjoyed. Stunned, but overjoyed."

"Truly?"

"Truly."

She offered him a timid smile and he resumed his kisses, now more passionate and lusty. In little time, his hands were fondling her breasts and she flinched. He froze in his onslaught.

"Did I hurt you?" he demanded softly, looking at his hand still covering her breast. "I did not mean to."

She put her small hands on his face and kissed his cheek. "I am a bit tender," she admitted.

"You did not say anything two days ago when I disrupted your bath."

"That is because the tenderness is bearable."

He watched her expression a moment just to make sure she was telling the truth. Then a slow smile spread across his face.

"That is good," he pointed out. "You should know that I do not intend to keep my hands off you for the next several months. It would be an impossible task."

She giggled softly, not knowing what to say to his bold declaration. She was still too new to love games to concoct a smooth reply. He saw her uncertainty and laughed softly.

"But I will leave you to your rest if I must," he said softly, his eyes drifting over her lovely face. "I should not want to do anything to jeopardize the health of my son. Even as I say it, I still cannot believe it."

She lifted her eyebrows. "Nor can I," she admitted. "I am sorry I did not tell you sooner. I suppose I have suspected for some time now but I did not want to admit it."

"Why not?"

She shrugged, averting her gaze, watching his enormous hands caress her arms. "Must you truly ask that?" she murmured. "Until a few days ago, I was bound to a marriage I did not want and to a man I did not...."

She trailed off, unwilling to risk upsetting him, but he knew that. He smiled faintly, his grip on her tightening. "I know," he whispered. "I was beastly and selfish. I have tried to right things with us. I hope that I have at least made some progress."

She met his gaze again, smiling gratefully. "You have made a world of progress," she said. "And I am deeply appreciative for all you have done."

He eyed her; it was his turn to avert his gaze, looking pensive as he studied the shape of her neck and shoulders. "I will make you a promise, Devereux," he said softly, sincerely. "I will do my very best to make an excellent husband and father. I want to do this very much."

She squeezed his big fingers. "You are well on your way."

He glanced at her, grinning reluctantly. "Am I?"

She nodded with certainty. "Aye," she replied. "You do not seem like the same man I married in Thetford."

He wriggled his eyebrows sheepishly. "I am the same man," he assured her. "But perhaps... perhaps that man has matured a bit. Perhaps he realized that the lovely woman he married was the path to something in life he never imagined to exist."

She smiled, cocking her head sweetly. "And what is that?"

He lifted his big shoulders. "Heaven and happiness," he said frankly, grinning when their eyes met. "I cannot explain it any more than that."

Devereux smiled sweetly at him, stroking a rough cheek. Davyss lowered his head and kissed her again, with extreme gentleness, as his hand resumed very carefully fondling her breast. As he moved to climb onto the bed next to her, there was a loud knock at the door.

Leaping to his feet, he adjusted his arousal as he made his way to the door and opened it. Several men were in the hall with Devereux's trunks and he directed them to put them in the chamber across the hall. When they were done slamming the trunks to the floor and generally creating a ruckus, he returned to his chamber and once again shut the door. But the moment he turned to the bed, he stopped in his tracks.

Devereux was dead asleep, an arm over her forehead as she lay on her back and snored very, very softly. Davyss stood there a moment, hands on his hips, smiling as he gazed down at her. He was still having a difficult time believing the news. Six weeks ago, he thought his life had taken a turn for the worse. Never had he imagined that he would be seeing an entirely new, joyful side of life that was beyond his imagination.

He had never been the emotional type when it came to women. He'd spent the majority of his adult life with women throwing themselves at him, well-insulated against the female emotions. More than one woman had fallen in love with him and he hadn't cared in the least, not even for the baron's daughter who had borne him twins. Love was a fool's emotion, or so he thought. He had never fallen in love with a woman, not once. But as he gazed down at his sleeping wife, he knew that particular fact was about to change.

It already had.

CHAPTER THIRTEEN

The Tower of London

H ENRY THE THIRD, King of England, was a fairly tall man with reddish-gold hair and a droopy eyelid. He wasn't feeble by any means, having been a warrior most of his life, and even in his advancing years managed to be tough and agile. Devereux was quivering so badly when Davyss introduced her to the king that she nearly fell over when she curtsied. But she managed to hold her balance, holding it further when she was introduced to Prince Edward, the king's eldest son and heir to the throne. Edward was tall and lanky, a big man with a crown of blonde hair and a big booming voice.

Although the pair was polite, it was clear that their attention was on Davyss. Edward joked with him like a brother and Henry seemed almost eager to communicate with him. Although Devereux knew that Davyss was the king's champion and had known that from the onset of their association, it was still difficult to believe. Davyss handled them both with cool respect.

A few minutes into their introductions, it was obvious that Henry and Edward had more important things to speak to Davyss of, and without the company of his wife. But Edward's wife, Eleanor of Castile, unexpectedly joined them, belaying the opportunity to speak to Davyss alone. Eleanor was a very pregnant woman who, by all accounts, had a reputation of being aloof and disinterested in her husband's English subjects. Born in Spain, she was rather frail-looking with dark hair and pale skin. Married to Prince Edward, a tall, blonde and intimidating man, they made an unusual looking pair. She chatted amiably and delayed the war conference even longer, but Edward didn't seem to mind.

KATHRYN LE VEQUE

From the onset, Devereux could see that Edward was very affectionate towards his wife, which caused Devereux to see the man in a completely different light. She had come into the meeting at the dark and foreboding Tower of London thinking on her hatred for what she had once called the tyrannical king, but the politeness of Henry and the devotion of Edward had swiftly caused her to rethink her opinion. Perhaps she had been ignorant as Lady Katharine had once accused her of being; perhaps there was more to Henry, Edward and Davyss than blood-thirsty men. She was starting to see it.

Davyss eventually left his wife in the company of Eleanor and her ladies, all Spanish women with dark Spanish eyes. They spoke in a language that Devereux did not understand, eyeing her suspiciously. She kept hearing the words *puta inglesa* but had no idea what they meant. She suspected, from the way they were looking at her, that it could not be good.

They had moved into the small ladies' solar on the fourth floor of the White Tower that was luxurious and pretty, but Devereux was uncomfortable with the women from the onset. They appeared haughty and arrogant, and made no attempt to speak with her in her own language. They whispered among themselves and pointed. Eleanor spent the first several minutes of their association being made comfortable by her snobbish women; she was a little woman with a very big belly and her discomfort was clear. But she eventually settled down, turning her dark-eyed, pale-faced attention to Devereux.

"*Mi señora encantadora,*" she smiled at Devereux. "Sir Davyss has been a friend of my husband for many years. We are pleased that he has finally married."

Devereux smiled faintly. "Thank you," she replied. "It seems to be an agreeable arrangement for us both."

Eleanor lifted a dark eyebrow. "Is this true?" she asked. "I do not mean to make offense, but I did not think that Sir Davyss would find any marriage agreeable."

Devereux's smile faded. "Perhaps that was true before we were married," she replied steadily. "But I assure you that his opinion has changed. I believe he is quite content."

One of the princess' women, hovering behind the princess, suddenly thrust herself forward and began jabbering at the princess in Spanish. It appeared to be an angry exchange until the princess harshly shushed the woman. When she refocused her attention on Devereux, it was almost apologetic.

"As I was saying," she continued. "I did not know that Sir Davyss was the marriageable kind. I have known him for years and he seemed... well, most devoted to the knighthood."

Devereux sensed cattiness in what the woman was saying and the manner in which she said it. She suspected she would eventually run up against this type of attitude regarding her husband but was surprised to find it coming from the princess. Her husband's past was about to rear its ugly head; she could feel it. She struggled not to show any hostility or disrespect as she replied.

"You are putting it most kindly, my lady, but I know the truth of my husband just as you do," she answered. "He has been completely honest with me so there is nothing regarding his past I do not know. But we do not speak of it; we only speak of our future together and of happy things. There is no use lingering on that which we cannot change."

Eleanor nodded her head, appraising Devereux as if not quite sure she believed her. "You are quite pretty," she said. "I am not surprised that Davyss selected you as his mate. He always preferred the prettiest girls."

It was evident that the princess was going to push the subject of Davyss' wandering eye and Devereux was feeling rather ill about the entire conversation. She didn't want to delve into an undoubtedly uncomfortable topic so she attempted to shift the focus.

"I have not yet heard of a man who prefers ugly ones," she said lightly, changing the course of the conversation. "I understand you are from Castile, my lady. Is your home so different from England? I would be interested to know."

Eleanor's women were jabbering again and the princess flicked a wrist at them to shut them up. "There are many mountains where I come from," she replied politely. "But we were speaking of your husband. I understand that his brother likes to chase women as well; the de Winters are well-known for their conquests. Do you suppose Sir Hugh will settle down someday also?"

Devereux was struggling to maintain her polite attitude but it was slipping drastically. She finally gave up because it was apparent that the princess wished to speak of nothing more than Davyss's shortcomings. Devereux couldn't figure out if she was trying to extract an emotional response from her or simply garner more information for the rumor mill.

"My lady, if there is something more you wish to say about my husband, I would appreciate it if you would come forth with it rather than ply me with innuendoes and impolite remarks," her attitude grew clipped. "I grow weary discussing my husband's past behavior. If you cannot converse on a more suitable subject, then perhaps we should not converse at all."

Eleanor's dark eyes cooled as her women exploded in nervous and outraged chatter. The artificial civility that had existed at the beginning of the exchange was gone completely. Eleanor sat up on her couch as much as her swollen body would allow.

"Do you believe me impolite?" she asked, outrage evident in her voice. "You foolish girl; do you truly believe that in marrying Davyss de Winter, the man will suddenly cut loose his wandering eye and devote all of his time and attention to you?"

Devereux didn't back down. "I do, to both questions."

Eleanor's eyebrows flew up in disbelief. "Is this so?"

"It is," she said flatly. "And if you cannot converse about something other than my husband's past, then I will assume you have nothing more intelligent to discuss and bid you a good day."

She rose to her feet as Eleanor's women began to scream at her.

Spanish insults were flying fast and furious. Devereux went into full defensive mode and jabbed a finger at the pack of snarling women.

"And all of you; shut your mouths," she roared. "You have been rude and imperious from the start and if this is an example of Spanish hospitality, then I want nothing more to do with that barbaric country or with you."

The collection of women was momentarily taken aback, but only briefly. One of them rushed at Devereux with an open hand but Devereux beat her to the punch, literally, and slapped the woman so hard that she toppled over. More women rushed at her and Devereux began swinging at them, knocking off jeweled hair pieces and shoving others back by the face. Spanish bums ended up on the floor as Devereux launched a full offensive, ripping out hair and scratching faces. She was absolutely furious. In the middle of chaos, the princess began screaming and the doors to the solar flew open.

Knights and soldiers rushed in, putting themselves in the very precarious position of separating the women. Someone grabbed Devereux by the arms and she shrieked, preparing to fight back when she saw that it was her husband. Davyss had his big arm around her, pulling her from the room.

In the corridor a safe distance away from the princess' room, Davyss faced his snarling wife. His hands cupped her cheeks as he visually inspected her.

"Sweetling," he sounded frightened. "Are you well? What happened?"

Devereux was still furious. Her fists were clenched and her lovely mouth was in a flat, tight line, but she was without a scratch in spite of the screaming and slapping that had been going on.

"All she wanted to talk about was your... your womanizing," she told him angrily. "I tried to change the subject but she would not speak on anything else. And her women were rude and horrible; they kept calling me *puta inglesa*. I do not know what that means, but I am sure it was not a compliment. When one of them tried to strike me, I struck her first."

Davyss's fright cooled instantly as he realized what had happened. He stared at Devereux for a long moment, his expression morphing into something deep and regretful. He could still hear the angry Spanish voices in the chamber and the princess' high-pitched pleas over the commotion. He sighed heavily and hung his head a moment.

"I am sorry," he murmured, lifting his face to her. "I should have… I did not think she would be so tactless."

Devereux was calming, but not much. She pulled away from Davyss, throwing the dark hair still clutched in her hand onto the floor. He stared at the tangled bundle of long, dark hair as she faced off against him.

"What does *puta inglesa* mean?" she demanded.

He looked at her, his hazel eyes soft with remorse. "You must understand that they are jealous," he whispered sincerely. "You are by far the most beautiful woman in England, something that has not escaped their notice. You have what they want and being petty, jealous women, they are going to punish you for it."

"You did not answer my question."

He gazed at her, not wanting to answer. But he found that he could not lie to her. "It means 'English whore'."

Devereux met his gaze, not surprised by his explanation. But she was still stung by it. The fight and anger drained out of her, replaced by a deep and genuine hurt.

"Did you bed any of those women in there?" she threw a hand in the direction of the now-calming chamber. "Is that why they were so hostile towards me?"

Davyss felt trapped and sick. But if this marriage had any hope of surviving, he could not lie to her. Although he had hoped their conversations over the past few days would have put this subject to rest, or at the very least prepared her for what she might face, he suspected that would not be the case. He could possibly be facing many more of these shameful moments with her and he knew there was nothing more he could do than face them head on. He wanted to be truthful with her and he wanted her to forgive him. He very much wanted to be the virtuous husband that she deserved.

After a moment, he nodded faintly to her question.

"Aye," he whispered. "That is very possible."

She stared at him and he could see the disappointment on her face. She didn't say anything for quite some time and when she did, her voice was tight with emotion.

"I will accept that," she whispered. "You have explained your behavior in the past and I will not comment on it further. There is no reason to. But I will ask you this; when you bedded these women, these low-life trollops whose legs were probably open for every man at court, did you touch them as sweetly and tenderly as you touch me? When you make love to me, is it just as meaningless?"

She suddenly broke down, tears spilling from her eyes and streaming down her cheeks. Davyss watched her, his heart just about breaking. He reached out to embrace her but knew it would probably not be well met. So he clenched and unclenched his gigantic hands, opening his mouth to reply when Eleanor suddenly spilled out of her bower. The princess spied Davyss and Devereux, several feet away.

"¡Usted!" she pointed an imperious finger at Devereux. "¡Dejará mi vista y nunca regreso!"

Davyss put himself between Eleanor and Devereux, his expression like stone. "Your women attacked her first, my lady," he said calmly. "She has done nothing wrong."

Eleanor was furious. She glared at Davyss, marching upon him and slapping him hard across the face. Although Davyss didn't react, Devereux heard the slap and, without thinking who she was about to attack, charged towards the pregnant princess with her claws bared. The princess shrieked when she saw her, recoiling as Davyss grabbed his wife and forcibly turned her around. Without another word, Davyss took Devereux from the battle zone.

It was cool in the late afternoon as they entered the massive bailey of the Tower of London. Davyss had his wife in a firm grip, leading her toward the stables where the carriage and charger await. When they were half-way across the dusty, rocky yard, she abruptly yanked herself from his powerful embrace. They came to an uneven halt, eyeing each other unsteadily.

"You do not need to hold me so tightly," she spat, avoiding his gaze. "I do not plan on turning and running."

Davyss wiped a weary hand over his face; he wasn't sure how the situation had veered so out of control but he knew he had to put a stop to it before damage was done.

"Devereux," he murmured calmly, struggling for calm himself. "Listen to me and listen well; I am sorry you were subjected to the princess' bitter women but there is nothing I can do to erase what I have done in the past. We have already discussed this and I told you that there would be occasion when my past indiscretions would come to light. I can only apologize for your humiliation at such occurrences. I wish I could do more, but I cannot."

She was looking at the ground, her delicate jaw ticking with fatigue and displeasure. "You needn't apologize," she said. "I suppose I am simply going to have to grow accustomed to these occurrences so that I may deal with them more gracefully in the future."

She sounded so hurt. Davyss' heart ached for her, wanting very much for things to be right between them.

"Though I cannot undo the past, I can make a vow for the future," he whispered. "You asked me once to swear that I would be faithful to you. Do you recall? It was when we supped at the Fist and Tankard."

She sighed faintly, thinking back on that day. "I remember."

"Then you also remember that I failed to answer you." He took a few steps, suddenly standing very close to her. He gazed down on her lowered blonde head. "Sweetling, please believe me when I swear that I will always be faithful to you. I will never shame you by straying from this marriage and I have never touched a woman with the same reverenced that I have touched you. What I feel for you is unique unto itself. There is no comparison."

She continued to stare at the ground. When she spoke, her voice was hoarse with anguish. "I feel... I feel so cheapened that so many others have sampled what has become so precious to me. You gave yourself to so many that by giving yourself to me, 'tis as if you have nothing else to give. I am simply one of the many, existing on the dregs left by others."

He shook his head, feeling increasingly despondent. "That is not true," he insisted softly. "There is something I have never given anyone, something more valuable than king or country or even God himself."

He watched her brow furrow though she had yet to look up at him. "What is that?"

"My heart."

Her head snapped up, the silver eyes suspicious yet encouraged. "You... you have never loved any of those women?"

He smiled gently, shaking his head. "Not one," he murmured. "That is the one thing I did indeed save for you."

Confusion creased her expression. "But you cannot simply give it to me as one would a gift. I must earn it from you just as you must earn it from me."

"You have already earned it. I will love you and only you until I die."

The gray eyes widened and he could read her surprise in the brilliant depths. As he watched, her eyes filled with a lake of tears.

"You...," she swallowed hard and the tears streamed down her face. "You *love* me?"

He reached up to wipe the tears away. "You are my angel. I would kill or die for you without hesitation."

She swallowed again, moving back from him and shaking her head as if confused by the entire circumstance.

"That is only because of the child," she told him; she sounded very much as if she was trying to convince herself, too. "You only say you love me because you believe I carry your son. If I had not...."

He cut her off, grabbing her by both arms and pulling her against him. His hazel eyes were intense as his arms snaked around her slender body.

"My feelings for you were strong before you ever mentioned the child," he insisted. "I do not need for you to bear me a son in order for me to love you."

She stared up at him, feeling his warmth envelope her with blissful comfort. It was enough to cause her to forget about the princess and her vicious women. All she could see and hear, at the moment, was Davyss.

"Oh… Davyss," she sighed, her hands moving to his stubbled cheeks. "How is this possible? Do you realize what you are saying?"

He wrapped her up in his enormous arms. "Of course I do," he nuzzled her cheek, her neck. "Although I have never been in love before, the feelings I have for you are so strong that they can be nothing else."

She put her hands on his face and stared at him. It was more than a simple gaze, however; she was inspecting him, the lines of his face, the shape of his nose, and the depths of his eyes to determine if he was telling her the truth. Her thumbs began to stroke his cheeks.

"Then I want to reiterate something from our list," she said.

He grinned, wriggling his eyebrows. "Ah, yes," he muttered. "The list. I have nearly forgotten the hundreds of items that are surely on it by now."

She returned his smile, reluctantly. "You had better not."

He hastened to assure her, like a man who is afraid of his wife. "Only a jest, sweetling," he pulled her closer. "What more do you wish to reiterate from our gigantic, ungainly list?"

She couldn't help but snort at him, pretending to strangle him. He grinned and kissed her.

"You put an item on our list once," she said softly. "You asked for the complete and honest truth when you asked a question. Do you recall?"

He nodded. "I do."

"I would like the same courtesy as well. When I ask a question, I want a completely honest answer without hesitation."

"And you shall have it."

"Did you tell me you love me simply to ease my anger?"

He shook his head. "Nay. I told you because it is the truth."

She wouldn't press him; to do so would be to doubt his word. But she did stare at him for several long moments. "Then I will be truthful with you as well," she whispered. "I cannot guarantee my composure should the next Spanish whore come at me with tales of bedroom exploits with the great Davyss de Winter. It is a matter of honor. I will not have these women so cheaply throw about that which means the world to me; *you* mean the world to me."

He smiled sadly at her, understanding completely. But there wasn't much he could do or say about it. "If I could erase it all, believe me when I tell you that I would. Had I known that someday I would have been married to a woman I adore, I might have thought twice before… well, doing whatever it is I did."

She snorted softly at the way he said it; so guilty, yet so sorrowful. The subject was finished as far as she was concerned. So she kissed him on the cheek gently.

"I wish to go home and lie down now," she said softly. "It has been an exhausting night of battling the Spaniards."

He laughed softly as they resumed their walk to the stables, arm in arm. "I am not entirely sure you can expect an invitation to the princess' chamber any time soon."

She grinned, laying her cheek against his enormous bicep. "What do you think your mother will say?"

Davyss laughed. "She shall build a shrine dedicated to you."

CHAPTER FOURTEEN

W HEN DEVEREUX AWOKE, it was either very late or very early; she couldn't tell. It was dark outside and difficult to judge the time. She looked around the darkened room, orienting herself, not knowing where she was for a moment. But recollections of Hollyhock came to mind and she remembered that she was in Davyss' rooms at Hollyhock, snuggled cozy in his enormous bed. But she was quite alone.

A single small taper burned low on the table next to the bed, giving off enough light to see by. Devereux sat up, curious as to where her husband was. He had been lying next to her when they had returned from the Tower of London after her battle with the Spanish. She had been exhausted and he had lain down next to her, holding her close as she promptly fell asleep. Now he was missing and she wanted to find him. She felt oddly alone without him beside her, as if he had been sleeping beside her for one hundred years. Her comfort level with the man in just the few days they had spent together had grown tremendously. She felt rather lost without him.

Groggy, she rose from the fat mattress, dressed in the soft linen dressing garment that she had changed into when they had returned from the Tower. It was a lightweight shift with long, belled sleeves and deeply V'd neckline that was cool and comfortable in the humidity of the river. The moment she stood up, however, her nausea returned full-force and she covered her mouth, burping unladylike as her stomach lurched. She didn't feel particularly well at the moment. Quietly, she moved to the door and carefully opened it, peering out into the hall.

She could hear Davyss' voice the moment she opened the door. It was coming from further down the hall to her left; she could see an open door and light streaming out of it. Tiptoeing down the wide-planked wooden floor, his voice grew louder as she approached and she paused outside the door, wondering if she should announce herself. It was apparent he wasn't alone in the room and she didn't want to disturb him. But she couldn't help but linger simply to hear the sound of his deep voice. It was beautiful and comforting.

"As I told you earlier, because we already know that de Montfort and his barons are moving south, the king has sent thousands of infantry to camp at St. Pancras," Davyss was saying. "Edward and I will stash the cavalry at Lewes Castle, about a mile north of the priory, and await de Montfort's arrival. But my army must move out of London by dawn if we are to make it to Sussex before de Montfort; we need to be ready and waiting for him when he arrives. Are there any questions so far?"

Lollardly and Andrew were standing closest to the map table, their eyes riveted to the yellowed hide that had a detailed map of the Lewes area on it. Prince Edward had given it to Davyss so he and his men could study it. The plan that Davyss spoke of had been hatched earlier in the day when Davyss had briefly met with the king and the prince, before the women went to battle. At the moment, it was imperative that Davyss brief his knights on what was to come. They had little time to prepare even though they knew this confrontation had been brewing for some time. Now, it was upon them.

"Do we know for certain who rides with de Montfort?" Lollardly asked quietly.

Davyss' hazel eyes never left the map. "Gloucester," he told them. "Guy and Henry de Montfort, and Lord Marshall Segrave."

Andrew tried not to look too surprised. "The Lord Marshall of England rides with de Montfort?" he shook his head. "How is the king taking that bit of news?"

Davyss shrugged. "He is resigned. Truthfully, there is nothing he can do. But he plans to strip the man of his title once he gets his hands on him."

"What about Hugh?" young Edmund spoke from the shadows near

the windows. "Where is he in all of this? Will he not join us at Lewes?"

Andrew shot his younger brother a withering look, to which Edmund visibly shrank, but Davyss did nothing more than look up from the map. There was no emotion on his face when he spoke.

"Hugh will not be joining us," he said quietly.

Andrew turned to look at him. "Do you know this for certain?"

Davyss lifted an eyebrow, refusing to look at him. "Fairly certain."

"Do you know where he is?"

"I do."

"Where."

Davyss looked at him, then. "With the enemy. I will say no more."

Andrew sighed heavily and stepped away from the map table, pondering thoughts he would not voice. Nik and Philip, standing several feet from the map table, came into the light, studying the layout of the town. Nik finally looked up from the map, focused on Davyss.

"I cannot believe he would fight against us," he said quietly.

Davyss grunted with displeasure. "And I cannot believe that he would strike a woman, any woman, but he did. Perhaps there are many things we do not know about my brother. Perhaps... perhaps I have indeed lost him."

"Over your wife?" Andrew couldn't keep silent any longer. "Davyss, you know your brother better than any of us. What he did was out of character for him, I will admit that. Hugh was never the battering kind, at least to women. He was upset because you took your wife's side over his and I cannot say that put in a similar position, I would have been less offended. Perhaps he is not entirely to blame for the situation he finds himself in."

Davyss' hazel eyes flashed. "What does that mean?"

Andrew was Davyss' oldest, dearest friend; only he could talk to Davyss in such a manner and get away with it. But he knew, perhaps better than anyone, how attached he had become to his wife over the past few days. Having known Davyss the majority of his life, he could just see it in the man's face.

"Do not become agitated, my friend," he backed down a bit. "I simply meant that there was no easy transition. One moment, you and Hugh were of the same mind and in the next, you were taking the side of a woman you very much protested to marry. You sent us with Lespada to the marriage ceremony, you consummated the marriage regardless of the lady's feelings, yet suddenly she beckons and you move heaven and earth to obey her wishes. Hugh was caught off-guard; we all were. Only Hugh reacted with jealousy and hurt. Perhaps a word from you would have soothed him. He loves you, Davyss; you know this. You are all to him and suddenly he found himself sharing you with a woman you had once professed to detest."

Davyss watched his auburn-haired friend in the weak light. He sighed heavily, scratching his sweaty scalp and wondering if Andrew wasn't speaking the truth. He shouldn't have cared about explaining himself to his men but he found that he wanted to. Perhaps Andrew was correct; the situation with Devereux had changed and he wanted to be honest. Perhaps it was all part of him growing up and becoming the man his mother had spoken of.

"Then allow me to tell all of you what I should have told Hugh," he muttered. "To be plain, I was wrong. So wrong I cannot comprehend what a complete idiot I was. Lady Devereux is worthy of your respect and more; she is an accomplished woman with grace, humor and beauty. I have learned to adore her and I hope you will as well."

His knights gazed back at him with various expressions of disbelief and approval. Lollardly was actually grinning. But this was a war council, not a gathering of friends, so Davyss cleared his throat loudly and with some embarrassment. He didn't like being so sentimental in front of his men; still, it had been necessary. He was glad he had cleared the air about Devereux for all to hear.

"So with that subject laid to rest, let us focus on the coming con-frontation," he gestured at the map. "The Earl of Cornwall is bringing thousands of men to Sussex as we speak. He will be entrenched at the priory as well. Once we have our front lines defined, it will be up to de

Montfort to engage or retreat. Our sources tell us that he is seriously undermanned compared to the king's forces so I expect this to be an easy victory."

"How many cavalry do we carry?" Andrew wanted to know.

"Five thousand; half of which are knights. Any more questions?"

The men shook their heads, still gazing at the map, very much entrenched in their own thoughts. Satisfied that everyone knew their tasks, Davyss nodded his head.

"Very well," he said. "Then be prepared to depart before dawn. We have a long ride ahead of us so I suggest you make all necessary preparations now."

Out in the hall, Devereux knew that was her cue to leave. Quickly, silently, she raced back down the hall and into their bedchamber. Shutting the door quietly, she ran to the bed and threw herself atop it, pulling the coverlet up and settling in quickly. True enough, she soon heard the pounding of heavy boots and the chamber door opened very quietly. As she lay there and pretended to be asleep, the boots entered the room quietly and shut the door. She heard the bolt thrown.

As Devereux lay there with her eyes closed, she heard Davyss move around the room, presumably removing his clothing. She could hear the soft brush of fabric as it hit the floor, the boots as he took them off one by one. Then, the bed rocked slightly as he slid in beside her. Very, very carefully, he put his arms around her and pulled her against his naked chest. When he looked down to see if he had disturbed her, he saw big gray eyes gazing up at him.

He smiled at her. "I am sorry if I woke you," he whispered. "Go back to sleep."

She smiled in return, snuggling up against his naked body. "I feel like I have been asleep for days," she murmured. "What time is it?"

"Very late. There is perhaps only a few hours until dawn."

She sighed, her cheek against his warm, smooth skin. "I have slept away the afternoon and evening," she yawned. "This baby is exhausting me."

He put an enormous hand against her belly, still tight and flat. "I still have a difficult time believing it."

"Have you told your mother yet?"

"Nay," he answered, his lips against her forehead. "I wanted us to tell her together."

"If you are leaving before dawn that might be difficult."

The hands caressing her suddenly stopped and Devereux felt him tense. Lifting her head, she smiled at him as she propped her head on a bent-up elbow.

"I am sorry," she said softly. "I woke up earlier and heard you down the hall. I heard you say that you were leaving before dawn."

He could see she wasn't being malicious about it. In truth, he didn't mind her eavesdropping; now he would not have to break the news to her. He reached up and gently tweaked her nose.

"Next time, do not linger in the hall," his hazel eyes glimmered. "Simply come in and announce yourself. I do not mind having you listen in. If I do not want you there, I will tell you."

She watched his mouth as he spoke, his lips smooth and full. "I just wanted to hear the sound of your voice," she whispered. "I truly wasn't listening to what was being said as much as I was simply listening to you speak."

He reached up, tucking a stray bit of blonde hair behind her ear. "Sweet words, Lady de Winter. I do not believe you have ever spoken any to me. I believe I like it."

She leaned forward, capturing his luscious lower lip between her own. She kissed him sweetly, suckling gently on his lip before slowly releasing it. Davyss didn't say another word; he pulled her against him in a crushing embrace, slanting his lips hungrily over hers. He kissed her with roaring passion, one hand drifting up her arm and coming to rest on a full breast. He could feel the hard nipple through the fabric and pulled the top of the garment off one shoulder until a nipple was exposed. Then he left her delicious mouth and nursed hungrily.

Devereux gasped with pleasure as he suckled. She couldn't explain why she wanted the man so badly at the moment; never in her life had she known such overwhelming sexual desire. All she knew was that the smell of him, the feel of him, fed her into a frenzy. Soon, she was hiking up her dressing gown, shifting her pelvis so that Davyss' big body wedged itself between her legs. As he nursed furiously against her nipple, she could feel his powerful manroot pushing against her thigh.

Sitting up slightly, she reached down to grasp his throbbing organ, capturing his mouth in her own when he lifted his head. Davyss groaned when her hands closed over his heated manhood, groaning again when she guided it into her slick folds. Pushing her back onto the mattress, Davyss thrust firmly into her welcoming body.

Devereux was so highly aroused that she felt herself climaxing within the first few strokes. Davyss felt her tight walls throbbing against him as he ripped her dressing gown off over her head, throwing it across the room as he fell back down upon her. He didn't want any barrier between his skin and hers. Devereux grunted as his weight came down on her slender body, throwing her arms around his neck and holding him fast as he repeatedly thrust into her. She was hot and wet, and he coiled his powerful buttocks as he pounded her with the proof of his desire.

Devereux climaxed twice more before Davyss finally released himself deep into her womb. As his member twitched and throbbed in its final pleasurable throes, Devereux climaxed yet again as she felt him pulse deep within her. It was wildly arousing to feel him release his seed. Exhausted, emotional, she attached herself to his mouth and kissed him deeply as their last of their passion cooled.

Davyss was overwhelmed with her physical response to him; he'd never experienced anything like it. The woman had an innate sense of what he needed physically, her body responding to his as if she had been doing it all her life. He held her tightly, kissing her gently, dragging his lips over her cheeks and neck. When the kissing faded, he simply lay there and held her tightly, his face in the side of her head.

"Davyss?" Devereux's voice was soft.

He was half-asleep, wildly content. "Hmmm?"

"This battle you are anticipating. Will it be bad?"

He lay there a moment. Then his eyes opened as he pondered the deeper implications of her question.

"Battle is never a pleasant thing," he muttered. "This confrontation has been a long time in coming."

"With de Montfort?"

"Aye."

"But what of Hugh?" she wanted to know. "Is he truly the enemy now?"

He sighed heavily. "How much of that did you hear?"

"I heard you say that he was with the enemy, but that is all. Is that true?"

"I would not lie."

"I did not mean that. I simply meant… would he really do such a thing? Does he hate me so much that he would feel the need to punish you for it?"

He shifted so she was tucked against his shoulder. His hazel eyes stared off into the darkness of the room. "He does not hate you," he murmured. "I believe Andrew was correct when he said that Hugh was jealous; jealous that I would listen to your wishes over his. As I had to grow up, so must Hugh, only he does not yet realize that."

She fell silent a moment, contemplating his words and the deeper meanings. She could do nothing about Hugh but she hoped, for her husband's sake, that he would come around soon. But as she thought on Hugh, she also thought on something else, something that had been lingering in her mind as she had listened to her husband talk to his men. It was something she did not want to face but knew she must.

"What… what if you do not return from this battle?" she finally whispered. "Do you have any instructions for me?"

Davyss pulled back and looked her in the eye, seeing that the great gray orbs were filling with tears. He shushed her softly, cupping her face and kissing her cheek tenderly.

"I want you to do what makes you happy," he stated. "I want you to live where you are comfortable living and raise our son in the manner you feel best. I trust you. But remember he is a de Winter, the heir to a great family name. If I could make one request, it would be that you allow him to fulfill his destiny as a de Winter. That would make me proud."

She couldn't help it; she blinked and fat tears coursed down her cheeks. Throwing her arms around his neck, she pulled him down against her.

"I love you, Davyss," she whispered against his ear. "Please know that I love you very much. I will always do my best to honor both you and the de Winter name."

His arms tightened around her, holding her so tightly that she could barely breathe. "And I love you," he murmured. "I will do my very best to return to you whole and sound."

She sobbed softly in his ear and he pulled back, wiping at her cheeks and kissing her tears away. He didn't want their last few hours together to be spent weeping. In truth, he was overwhelmed by her declaration of love, so much so that he could hardly think of anything else. He could hardly believe the joy that the last few days had brought, the discovery and happiness. If someone had told him on his wedding day those weeks ago that he would grow to love the beautiful spitfire of a woman he had married, he would have laughed at them. But the proof of that love was in front of him, something so unexpected and strong that it overshadowed everything else. When he should have been focused on an impending battle, he found he could only think of the woman in his arms.

"Now," he said, kissing her nose as he wiped the last of her tears. "I must ask you something very serious."

She sniffled, wiping at her nose. "What?"

He looked semi-serious. "I had assumed you would stay here at Hollyhock while I am away, but my mother says that I should ask you where you want to go. She says she doubts you will want to spend endless days with a frail old woman."

Devereux appeared puzzled by the question, a smile playing on her lips. "I do not know. I have not thought on it. Why? Where would you have me wait for you?"

He lifted a big shoulder. "Wherever makes you happy. Do you want to return to The House of Hope?"

A light came to her eyes. "Would you let me?"

He could see, in those few words, how much it meant to her to return to her charity. His mother had been right again. "If that is your wish," he said. "But I will send you back with a contingent of soldiers. My wife must be amply protected."

She nodded eagerly. "Anything you say, Davyss. I would like to go home, only...."

She averted her gaze and he gently tapped her chin, forcing her to look up. "Only what?"

She pursed her lips as if she knew foolish words were about to spill from her mouth. "Only I was wondering... will you and I have our own home together, a place to raise our children, or will we always travel between Wintercroft and Hollyhock like a band of gypsies?"

He laughed. "If you wish for us to have our own home, then we shall. There are several of my holdings to choose from for just that purpose."

"Holdings?"

"Aye," he nodded. "In addition to Wintercroft, there is Castle Acre Castle...."

She shook her head vigorously, making a face. He nodded swiftly. "So you do not like Castle Acre Castle; I understand. There is also a small castle at Threxton and, of course, Norwich Castle."

"Norwich? I have heard my father speak of it. Is it not the king's castle?"

"It is mine. I am the garrison commander for the king."

She appeared to mull over the information. "Then I suppose I shall have to see these two places in order to make a decision. But it must be before the baby arrives. I do not want to be moving around after he is born." She pursed her lips thoughtfully. "Do you think the men will listen if you tell them that you must hurry up and get the battle over with so that you may return to your pregnant wife?"

He cocked a dark eyebrow, a wry expression on his face. "Not at all," he said dryly. "Every man there has a wife and will undoubtedly understand my dilemma. I believe it would be a fair statement to say that we all fear our women more than each other."

Devereux grinned in response. They lay there until just before dawn, with gentle touches, conversation and sweet kisses between them. When Davyss finally rose to dress, Devereux rose with him. In between dry heaves, she dressed, assuring her concerned husband that she was well enough to see him off. He wasn't entirely sure but did not dispute her. When they were both dressed, he escorted his pale and weary wife downstairs.

Lady Katharine was already waiting for them in the foyer. Her little dogs rushed Devereux, who this time tried to outsmart the dogs by kneeling down and speaking sweetly to them. If they didn't like strangers, then perhaps it was up to her not to be one. Her behavior confused the little beasts for a moment but soon the tails began to wag. Before she realized it, the dogs were jumping on her and licking her hands. Lady Katharine watched with approval while Davyss just rolled his eyes.

"Mother," he turned to Katharine as his wife played with the little dogs. "My wife would like to return to The House of Hope while I am away. I will send fifty men later today to escort her back to Thetford. She will stay at her father's house."

Katharine waved a gnarled old hand. "No need," she said. "She may stay at Breckland Castle."

Davyss shook his head. "She does not want to stay at Breckland, Mother. She wants to stay at her family's home."

Lady Katharine opened her mouth to insist that Davyss' wife stay in her luxurious castle but recounted her own word from the day before about letting the woman stay where she was more comfortable. So she veered off that subject and onto the next. "As she wishes," she replied. "But there is no need for you to feather men from your troops, men you will need in your upcoming conflict. I will send her with my own personal guard."

Davyss pursed his lips irritably. "Your personal guard is full of old men and cripples. I do not want those men guarding my wife."

Katharine's thin eyebrows shot up. "Yet they are good enough to guard your mother?" she said, outraged.

Davyss leaned down and kissed her on the cheek to soothe her ruffled feathers. "Although I thank you for your very kind offer, you will keep your soldiers. You need them. I can spare a few from the thousands at my disposal."

Lady Katharine eyed her son, not entirely soothed, but kept her mouth shut. Davyss winked at her, moving to Devereux as she remained crouched with the dogs.

"Can I tear you away from your new friends for a moment?" he asked, taking her elbow and helping her to stand. "I have a long day ahead of me so let us say our farewells now."

Devereux gazed up at him, forcing a smile. Tears stung her eyes but she fought them; she didn't want his last memory of her to be of hysterics. She wrapped both hands around his enormous arm, laying her cheek on his mailed bicep as they walked to the front door. As they passed the elaborate solar, she could see Lucy and Frances inside the chamber, seated on one of the many luxurious chairs before a blazing hearth. She waved at them but only Lucy waved back. Frances seemed her usual dour self. Proceeding to the massive oak-door entry, they were met with pale gray fog as Davyss opened the door.

"Will you send word to me?" Devereux asked him softly.

He nodded. "If I can," he replied, moving to take both of her hands in his massive gloved ones. "It should take us several days to reach Lewes and, after that, I have no way of knowing when or if I will be able to send a missive you. But I promise I will try."

She smiled bravely, her heart breaking but refusing to show it. She had never faced this kind of separation before and was unsure how to deal with it; Davyss was going to war, something she detested yet something she was bound to by marriage. Never had she imagined she would be facing this situation; seeing off someone who had come to mean the world to her. It was possible he would never return. But more tears would not magically stop him from going so she was determined to be brave. She squeezed his hands, standing on tip-toe to kiss him on the cheek.

"I shall miss you," she whispered. "Please take care of yourself. Try to stay away from flying arrows and sharp blades."

He smiled in return. "I will do my best," he replied softly, his gaze moving over her lovely face. "I have much to live for."

He leaned down to kiss her cheek but that wasn't good enough. He wrapped his arms around her, pulling her against him and lifting her off the ground. Devereux wrapped her arms around his neck, her feet dangling a foot off the floor.

"I love you," he whispered in her ear.

"And I love you," she breathed.

Davyss gave her a good squeeze and set her to her feet. By this time, Lady Katharine had walked up beside them. Davyss bent down and kissed his mother again.

"I will send word to you when I can also," he told her. "Take good care of my wife."

Lady Katharine waved him off. "You needn't worry. I have a feeling she can take care of herself."

"That may be, but there is no longer just her to consider. We must consider your grandson as well."

Lady Katharine's eyes widened but that was as far as she went in displaying emotion. "What are you saying, Davyss?"

His eyes glimmered warmly as he took Devereux's hand, kissing it sweetly one last time. "It means that we have granted your request. You will meet your grandson in the winter."

"Do you know this for certain?"

"Fairly certain."

Katharine's gaze turned to Devereux, who only had eyes for her husband. She could see the radiant look on her face in spite of the paleness. She remembered that look, once, years ago when Grayson was still alive. Katharine had that look, too, when she was pregnant with Davyss. A faint smile creased the old, wrinkled lips.

"Excellent," is all she would say.

Davyss knew his mother had much more to say about it but, being a rather austere lady, she would not become emotional in public. He winked at his mother, kissed his wife's hand again, and trudged off into the early morning fog. Devereux stood in the open doorway, listening to her husband's voice as he barked commands. It filled her with comfort and pride. She continued to stand there, listening to him, as the army eventually moved off in the fog.

Even when the last man was gone, she continued to stand there, listening to the army move in the distance but unable to see them through the mist. When the sound vanished completely and all seemed eerily still, she realized that Katharine was standing next to her.

She turned to the old lady with a timid smile. "I would hazard to say that you have spent many a moment such as this, watching your menfolk go off to war."

Katharine nodded faintly. "Many a moment, indeed," she said quietly. "My father, my brother, my husband and my sons. It never becomes any easier."

Devereux's smile faded. "I have never had to do this before."

"It will not be the last time."

Devereux's gaze lingered on the old woman before returning her attention to the open door and the fog. She stood there, gazing out into it as if hoping to see Davyss suddenly returning. Her heart hurt for so many reasons that she could not isolate just one; all she knew was that it ached fiercely. She turned back to Katharine.

"May I speak, my lady?" she asked.

Katharine lifted a thin eyebrow. "Of course. You do need permission to speak to me."

Devereux gave her a lop-sided smile, somewhat humbled, and continued. "When you and I first met, it was not under the best of circumstances," she said. "I… I suppose I simply wanted to apologize for the harshness between us on that day. I was not on my best behavior."

Katharine's old lips flickered with a smile. "I seem to remember a very angry woman telling me that she would not marry into a family so entrenched in oppression and politics."

Devereux half-nodded, half-shrugged. "Forgive me. When you accused me of ignorance, you were correct. I did not know both sides of the situation."

"And you feel that you do now?"

She nodded faintly, moving to close the massive oak panel. "I believe I am learning," she said truthfully. "Your son has helped me understand a great deal."

Lady Katharine took Devereux's elbow as they moved towards the warm solar, smelling of fresh bread and rushes. It was the first time that Katharine made a companionable move towards Devereux, who did not take it lightly. She patted the elderly woman's hand.

"And you have helped my son learn a great deal," Katharine replied. "I believe this marriage has been good for you both."

"It has."

"Excellent," Katharine said as they entered the solar. "I am pleased to hear this."

Devereux's smile broadened as she and Lady Katharine exchanged knowing glances. Silent words of understanding and approval passed between them, establishing the beginning of a relationship between them. By this time, Lucy was on her feet, moving to greet Devereux. Lady Katharine moved to her favorite chair, ringing a little silver bell for her servants and her dogs. Devereux went to the table set with fine dishes of food, trying not to become ill at the sights and smells.

Lucy chattered and Frances remained predictably silent as they broke their fast, but Devereux couldn't follow the conversation. She was still focused on Davyss, her longing for him growing by the minute. She had grown inordinately attached to the man since his arrival at Thetford and now his sudden absence had her feeling hollow and sad.

Eventually, Lucy's prattle pushed her to the point of agitation and she excused herself quickly, retreating to the bedchamber she and Davyss had shared. Stretching out on the mattress, she could smell him on the sheets and she inhaled deeply.

The tears quietly came. She missed him already.

CHAPTER FIFTEEN

Lewes Castle
May 15, 1264

"**H**E WILL SHOW you complete absolution and mercy, Davyss," Hugh's young face was grave. "It is over. All of it is over. Why must you be so stubborn?"

Davyss wasn't shackled or bound as some of Henry's other knights were, something he should have been grateful for. Even now, Philip, Andrew and Edmund were bound and guarded. But they had stripped Davyss of *Lespada* and the rest of his weapons, items that were in Hugh's possession now. Davyss stood amidst a cluster of tents in the early morning hours, facing off against his brother as chaos went on around them.

The Battle of Lewes was over on the morning of the fourth day. The fields surrounding the small town and castle ran red with blood from de Montfort and Henry's troops, and in the end, it had been a bad decision by Prince Edward and a bright one by de Montfort that led to Simon's victory.

Even though Henry's troops were nearly double the size of Simon's, the Earl of Leicester had made the smarter choices with the limited men he had. Edward, ever-confident, had failed to listen to Davyss' advice and it had cost him the battle. Henry and Edward's men were being corralled and processed, prisoners of war now that the battle was concluded. It had been a disaster for Henry's forces and now they were all prisoners, including Davyss.

Davyss answered his brother. "My allegiance is to the king, Hugh," he said quietly. "I cannot change loyalties as easy as you can."

Hugh's face flushed. "I had no choice. I had to pledge to de Montfort or you would have killed me."

"Do you truly wish to delve into that subject right now? I would advise against it."

Hugh's face flushed deeper. "It was not my intention to hurt your wife but she should not have confronted me. Had the woman known her place, none of it would have happened."

Davyss was starting to lose his cool. Exhausted and beaten, his patience was limited as they veered off the subject at hand and into very dangerous territory.

"If you say another word about my wife, I will kill you where you stand," he growled "Do you hear me?"

Hugh couldn't help himself, perilous as it was. "I am glad that she is not dead," he said firmly, extending a hand to his brother to emphasize his point. "Uncle Simon told me that she survived her fall. But I will not apologize for a confrontation that she started."

"I warned you, Hugh."

Hugh's mouth worked furiously but he wisely heeded his brother's final warning. It was as far as he dared push him. He sighed heavily, raking his hands through his dark hair and struggling to get control of himself. He was exhausted, as they all were. It had been a difficult few days. He eyed his older brother.

"How is your shoulder?" he asked.

Davyss' hazel eyes regarded his brother before looking away, gingerly rotating his right shoulder. "It is well enough," he said. "The arrow did not damage anything vital."

Hugh nodded faintly, his mind still whirling with the situation, with de Montfort's proposal to Davyss. He couldn't help but press the subject; out of desperation, perhaps fear, he couldn't help it. The world as he knew it was upended and he was frantic to make sense of it.

"Please, Davyss," he pleaded quietly. "Please consider Simon's offer. Join us and you will be Simon's most honored advisor. He offers you the lordship of Uppington, for Christ's sake. It is a great honor, Davyss. You know this."

Davyss looked at him as if he'd lost his mind. "Uppington?" he repeated. "It is nothing compared to the de Winter holdings and well you know it. He cannot offer anything that interests me."

"Nothing?"

"My loyalties cannot be bought."

Hugh took a few steps back, putting distance between him and his brother, before emitting a piercing whistle. Four big knights standing near Simon's tent came to Hugh's side when the man beckoned. Davyss recognized the knights, men he had known and fought against for years. They were seasoned and strong. He was curious why Hugh had called them over.

"Listen to me well, brother," Hugh said with the safety of four heavily armed men at his side. "Simon has loved you all of your life. Your achievements have been a great source of pride. But he has never been able to stomach the fact that you support Henry and Edward. He is willing to go to great lengths to gain your fealty."

Davyss put his massive fists on his hips. "What does that mean?"

Hugh sighed faintly. "It means that he will use your wife if he has to. He has the means to obtain her."

Davyss' expression tensed and his eyes narrowed dangerously. The enormous fists came off his hips and he began to clench and unclench his hands, working up his building fury.

"If you do not tell me what you mean, I will rip your head from your body," he snarled. "Your bodyguards will do you no good."

Hugh put up his hands. "He does not want to do this, Davyss, truly, but he also does not want to see you waste your life. He will do what is necessary in order to save you."

"Save me?" Davyss repeated, incredulous. "I do not need saving. Now, what in the hell did you mean that he will use Devereux?"

"I will not tell you unless you calm down."

"Hugh, I swear I will snap your neck and worry over the consequences later if you do not answer my question immediately."

Hugh struggled not to appear fearful of his brother. But in that fear was deep curiosity, something he'd not truly felt until this moment. He could see the expression in his brother's face when he spoke Devereux's name. There was something in his tone that Hugh had never heard before. He studied his brother closely for a moment.

"What…," he started again. "What happened to you, Davyss? Does this woman mean so much to you, then?"

"She does," Davyss said flatly.

Hugh stared at him, seeing his brother through new eyes. This wasn't the Davyss he knew. "Are you serious?" he hissed. "You care for her?"

Davyss could see that Hugh was more focused on his feelings for Devereux than in answering questions about Simon. Perhaps he needed to take Andrew's advice; perhaps he needed to be clear with his brother. Perhaps then Hugh would understand and things might be better between them. He was willing to take the chance.

"I love her, Hugh," he said, with less fury and more sincerity. "I love her with all my heart and she carries my child. I cannot express the joy I feel when I am with her because it defies words. She is everything to me. Does that answer your question?"

Hugh nodded but he still looked stunned. "It does," he murmured. "But I wish you hadn't told me."

"Why?"

"Because it makes Simon's plan far more effective against you."

Davyss' expression hardened again. "You will tell me what he plans to do.'

Hugh paused a moment, taking a deep breath before speaking. It was clear he was torn. "He has written Mother to know your wife's whereabouts."

Davyss struggled to keep his fury in check. "She will not tell him anything."

"She will if she feels that it will save your life."

"What do you mean?"

"Now that Simon has captured Henry, your choices are few; either side with Simon and remain free, or remain loyal to the king and become a prisoner as he is. If Simon holds your wife, which side will you choose? And which side do you think Mother will choose for you?" Hugh shrugged his broad shoulders. "Perhaps he will release you if Mother provides your wife as a hostage against your good behavior."

Four knights were not enough to prevent Davyss from seriously injuring his brother. Only a blow to the head from a fifth knight disabled him, enabling the others to restrain him.

⋈

"DEVEREUX? DID YOU hear me?"

In truth, she hadn't. She had been daydreaming again. It seems all she had done was daydream since returning to The House of Hope three weeks before, her mind no longer centered on the charity she supported.

Standing in the entry of the old barn, she had been gazing off across the green expanse of Norfolk and remembering the day when her husband had come riding into the dusty yard with his brother and knights. She remembered fearing the sight of him, being wary of his return. But Davyss had changed her mind in just a few hours. He had tried so hard to make amends for their rough beginning. It was probably that night, as they supped at the Fist and Tankard, that she started to fall in love with him. It was a feeling that had grown deeper by the day.

But she pushed thoughts of her husband out of her mind, wiping her hands off on her apron as she faced Stephan. She was supposed to be collecting eggs from the chicken house but she hadn't made it that far. Stephan knew this; his fair face smiled at her.

"From the look on your face, I do not believe you heard anything I said," his grin broadened.

Devereux smiled sheepishly. "I am sorry," she said. "Just... thinking."

Stephan's smile faded. He knew what she was thinking of and he was still fighting the disappointment he felt. Disappointment that she had returned from London apparently very much in love with Davyss de Winter. Not that Stephan had ever had a chance with her and he knew it; still, her happiness hurt his heart somewhat even if he was glad for her. She seemed truly happy.

"I said that your father is here," he repeated. "I saw his carriage arrive."

Devereux immediately moved back through The House of Hope, dodging people and tables as she headed for the north entrance. Her father would not use the main entrance, as he feared he would be seen. He'd spent so much of his time announcing his dissatisfaction with his wife and daughter's charity that he didn't want to be perceived as a hypocrite to the townspeople. He had a station to uphold, after all. So he always came in through the less-used entrance.

St. Paul Allington had been a handsome man in his youth. He had faded blonde hair and gray eyes, and it was clear to all who his daughter resembled. He was standing outside the north entrance with two of his men, old knights who had served him in his position as Sheriff of the Shire for years.

Devereux emerged from The House of Hope, dutifully greeting her father with a kiss on the cheek. He was a petty, vain and selfish man who struggled to make correct and moral decisions. If it didn't benefit him, he was more than likely not in favor of it. He only cared about his daughter's marriage so long as it brought him prestige and honor. He didn't even care if she was happy and he wasn't even moderately excited about his impending grandchild. Devereux had struggled all of her life not to disapprove of the man.

"Greetings, Father," she said pleasantly. "How may I be of service today?"

Her father gazed steadily at her, an odd expression on his face. "I came to tell you that...," he suddenly turned to the pair of old knights behind him. "Here now, John; you tell her. You are the one who heard the news."

For some reason, Devereux was put on her guard by her father's statement. Something in the pit of her stomach began to rumble unsteadily and she didn't like it one bit. She looked at the old knight.

"What did you hear?" she asked.

John de Ravensworth took a few steps towards her, bowing respectfully. "Lady de Winter," he said. "You are looking fine this day, my lady."

"What did you hear?"

Devereux was in no mood for conversation or pleasantries. John cleared his throat quietly, his gaze moving between Devereux, Stephan and her father. He cleared his throat again.

"I was in town earlier today and several of Norfolk's knights were riding through on their way to Norfolk," he said, somewhat nervously. "I met them on the edge of town to know their business, and they told me that de Montfort is now king."

Devereux's eyes widened. "What?" she breathed, horrified. "When did this happen?"

"Nearly two weeks ago, my lady."

Devereux was quickly growing panicked. "What else did they say?"

The old knight shook his head. "They said de Montfort is now king and he is calling all of the barons to London. They were riding for their liege to summon him."

Devereux could hardly breathe; she put her hand to her breast, feeling her chest heave as it became increasingly difficult to catch her breath.

"What happened to Henry?" she could hardly bring herself to ask. "What of my husband?"

John averted his gaze; he couldn't even look at her. "Captured at Lewes, they said," he replied hoarsely. "Edward with him. They made no mention of your husband. Henry is now a prisoner of de Montfort."

Beyond horrified, Devereux took a step back, tripping on her own feet and ending up in Stephan's arms. But she pushed him away, struggling to maintain her equilibrium and her sanity. The hands on her chest flew to her mouth.

"'Tis not true," she muttered, bordering on panic. "'Tis not true, I say. I would have known before now. Someone would have sent me word. It cannot be true."

St. Paul moved towards his daughter with uncertainty. "Perhaps you should come home and rest, Devereux. We will send word to Lady Katharine and see what she knows."

"Lady Katharine!" Devereux suddenly burst as if the thought had just occurred to her. "She will know something. I must go to London right away."

Stephan tried to take charge of her. He went to her, attempting to steady her. "You will not go," he said firmly. "You cannot risk it. We will send one of Davyss' men to London to find out what he can."

He was speaking of the thirty-eight men that Davyss had assigned to his wife's protection. Even now, they lingered all around The House of Hope, patrolling for any threats against Lady de Winter, while some were in town at the various taverns. All in all, they were a seasoned group and very attentive to Lady de Winter. Stephan began to shout for the sergeant of the contingent, knowing the man was somewhere within earshot. He always was.

His name was Brovus. He was an older man, burly, missing an eye, and loyal to Davyss to the core. He had been lingering just out of sight when John had spilled his tale and was therefore not surprised when Stephan repeated everything for his benefit. The old soldier eyed the knight, Stephan and St. Paul, before focusing on Devereux. He could see that she was clearly distraught.

"I cannot leave, my lady," he told her steadily, "nor can any of my men. My scouts on the road south have returned to tell me that a large group of knights has been sighted in Welnetham and are heading this way. I will not leave you until I know this threat has passed."

"A large group of knights?" St. Paul repeated, looking fearful. "Why did you not tell us before now?"

"Because there is nothing to be done. The lady will stay to her charity and the rest of us will stay out of sight until we know their purpose. To prepare with all manner of arms upon their arrival might invite conflict and I will not do that until I know their intentions."

St. Paul still wasn't convinced. "Perhaps we should return home. It is far more fortified than this pile of wood."

Brovus nodded. "It would be wise, my lord."

Devereux, pale and shaken, shook her head. "I will not leave," she said quietly. "What if it is my husband returning? I must be here."

Brovus spoke before the others. "I do not believe it is your husband, my lady," he replied, somewhat gently. "If it was, my men would have recognized his horse."

Devereux's bright gray eyes were fixed on the man. She went to him, her expression imploring.

"Have you heard that de Montfort is now king?" she asked earnestly.

He gazed steadily at her. After a moment, he sighed faintly. "I have been told that Henry was captured, my lady," he admitted. "It was not my place to tell you. I am a soldier, not a herald. That news should come from those more important than me."

Her eyes widened. "So you knew this and you did not tell me?"

He appeared both contrite and sad. "As I said, it was not my place to tell you. It could be rumor, after all. I did not want to upset you, not until we know for certain."

"But you should have told me."

"To what good, my lady?" he wanted to know. "You would live your days in angst and fear until you received more reliable word. Lady Katharine will tell you the truth, have no doubt. She will tell you what you need to know."

Devereux couldn't think any longer. Her mind was becoming overwhelmed with thoughts of Davyss' fate. She turned away from Brovus, feeling the world sway beneath her. If what these men said was true, de Montfort was now king and Henry was a captive. But the king would only be a captive if Davyss was not there to champion him. And that would only happen if Davyss was dead.

She hadn't taken two steps before she lost consciousness.

CHAPTER SIXTEEN

T HE LAST TIME they had seen the Allington manse, a great battle had gone on inside of it. Lady Devereux had proved more than a suitable adversary for the de Winter knights. This time, the situation was decidedly different.

Davyss knocked on the massive oak door, rattling the entire structure with the big iron knocker. The door was built like a fortress itself with big iron bracing strips riveted across it. He'd never actually seen the manse but his men had. He glanced over his shoulder at Hugh, Andrew, Edmund and Philip. Obviously absent were Nik and Lollardly; Nik had been seriously wounded in the same archer wave that had hit Davyss, struck in the eye. He lost the eye and even now lay on death's door with a raging fever as a result of the injury. Lollardly remained at Nik's side, nursing the knight and hoping to pull him through. Davyss felt their absence deeply.

He also noticed the men he had sent to protect his wife lingered on the perimeter of Allington manse. Brovus, the sergeant, had come out of the trees to greet him. In fact, he'd had his crossbow trained on Davyss as the group had moved towards the manse, not recognizing his liege's charger. Davyss explained that his horse had fallen in battle and he had confiscated another one. Brovus had waved his liege onward and skulked back into the bramble.

Davyss had to knock on the door twice before the small sliding door set within the massive panel slid open. A pair of fearful eyes stared back.

"I am Davyss de Winter," Davyss said. "Where is my wife?"

The fearful eyes widened and the sliding door slapped shut. Davyss heard the bolt thrown and suddenly the massive panel was lurching open. A little old man stood in the doorway, bowing profusely, as another man abruptly came barreling forth from an adjoining room.

"My lord!" the man nearly crashed into Davyss in his haste. "I heard you... you are Davyss de Winter?"

Davyss nodded, sizing the man up. "Who are you?"

The older man extended an eager hand. "I am Devereux's father, St. Paul Allington," he replied, shaking Davyss' hand enthusiastically. "We have never met, my lord, but I have met your mother on many occasions."

Davyss nodded faintly, seeing the family resemblance in the man's gray eyes. Then he glanced into the manse beyond, darkened in the late afternoon. "Is my wife here?"

St. Paul nodded and shoved the old servant back so that Davyss could enter. "She is here, my lord," he replied, suddenly seeming nervous. "But... well, that is to say, the physic says she must stay in bed."

Davyss looked at the man. "Bed? Why?"

St. Paul was wringing his hands. "You will have to ask the physic," he replied. "I believe it has something to do with the baby."

Davyss felt a wave of dread wash over him. "Where is she?"

"Up the stairs; first door to the left."

Davyss bolted up the stairs directly in front of him. The narrow flight doubled back on itself and he ended up in a narrow upstairs corridor. The first door to his left was open and he tried to slow his pace as he entered. But he realized, as he passed into the room, that he was shaking.

The bed was immediately to his left, the head against the wall. It was a big bed with lovely curtains around it, very much a woman's bed. His wife was curled up on her side, facing away from him, and in the corner of the room sat an older, red-haired woman. She had some kind of mending in her hand but when she saw Davyss enter, she immediately bolted to her feet.

"Who are you?" the old woman hissed. "Get out of here. You'll not disturb her."

Davyss lifted an eyebrow at the woman's tone and put up a hand to calm her. "I am the lady's husband," he said softly. "Is she ill?"

The old woman faltered as Devereux suddenly rolled onto her back. Her big gray eyes were wide with astonishment and shock.

"Davyss!" she gasped.

He flew to the bed, half-falling and half-sitting upon it as he pulled her into a crushing embrace. Devereux burst into tears, sobbing dramatically as she threw her arms around his neck and clutched him tightly. The smell, the feel of him, had her overwhelmed to the point of hyperventilation. She couldn't catch her breath.

"All is well, sweet girl," he kissed her cheek and head furiously. "I am here now. All is well."

Devereux pulled back to look at him, running her hands all over his face and hair as if to convince herself that he wasn't a ghost.

"Are you real?" she breathed, kissing his nose, his mouth. "I cannot believe it."

His hands were shaking as he gently cupped her face, kissing her with deep and painful longing. "I am real," he murmured, stopping in his zeal to take a good, long look at her. She looked pale but delicious. "Why are you in bed? What is wrong?"

Her smile faded somewhat. "The physic says that the baby is making itself known," she told him. "It is nothing that a little rest will not cure. You needn't worry."

He touched her head, her cheek, moving his hand down her arm as if to make sure for himself that she was not about to fall apart. She felt warm and soft and wonderful.

"Then a physic has examined you?"

She nodded. "There is a fine surgeon in town, the one who volunteers his time to The House of Hope," she said. "He says our son is due around the New Year."

Davyss smiled faintly, with great joy, as he kissed her cheek gently. "Then your suspicions are confirmed."

She nodded, wrapping her arms around his neck and pulling him against her tightly. "My joy is complete now that you have returned safe and whole to me," her smile faded as she let him go and gazed into his eyes. "Are you all right?"

"I am fine."

"You were not injured?"

He didn't want to lie to her; she would see the scar at some point. "I took an arrow to the shoulder but it was not serious."

She looked worried. "Are you sure? Let me see."

He shook his head, kissing her hands as she tried to get a look at his neck area. "No need," he assured her. "I have healed."

She had to take his word for it, at least for the moment. "And your men? Did everyone come through unscathed?"

He sobered somewhat. "Nik took an arrow to the eye," he told her honestly. "He lingers near death. Lollardly has remained with him at Lewes Castle. We did not want to move him in his condition."

Devereux looked stricken. "Does Frances know?"

Davyss reached up, smoothing the mussed hair from her face in a gentle gesture. "Nay," he admitted. "I have not sent her word. I will not until I know which direction Nik will take."

Devereux shook her head, distressed on Frances' behalf. "That is not fair to her," she insisted softly. "She will want to know. If it were me, I would want to know."

Davyss simply shrugged, not giving her an answer one way or the other. He seemed more intent on inspecting the ends of her hair, her fingers, kissing them one by one. Devereux watched his face, seeing exhaustion and emotion in the strong lines. It was evident that he was distracted, concerned and tense. There was much on his mind.

"We were told that Simon de Montfort is now king," she said softly. "Is this true?"

He looked up at her, the beautiful hazel eyes lined with fatigue. After a moment of studying her sweet face, he averted his gaze.

"Aye," he whispered. "De Montfort is now ruling England."

She could see, through all of his strong military façade, that he was greatly distressed by the thought. For the great Davyss de Winter to have to admit defeat must have been a bitter thing for him indeed and she felt a great deal of sympathy for him.

"What happened to the king?" she asked softly.

"Captured along with Prince Edward."

"My God," she breathed. "Davyss, what happened? How did you escape being captured yourself?"

He looked at her, then, his hazel eyes riveted to her. He wasn't sure he could tell her all of it but, in reflection, perhaps she should know all of it and understand just how serious the situation was. She thought she had married the perfect warrior; perfectly arrogant, perfectly skilled. But the truth was that she hadn't; she had married a man who had grown up over the past few months. He was a better person now, a stronger man that she had helped create. He wanted her to know everything that had happened and hoped it was the right decision to tell her.

"I *was* captured," he told her, taking her hands in his own. "But there is something you must know, sweetling; Simon de Montfort is my godfather. He and my father were the best of friends and Simon is very close to my family."

Devereux's eyes widened. "Is this so?" she was truly astonished. "You… you have never said anything about this."

"I know. It is something I did not want you to know."

"But you are telling me now. Why?'

"Because it is important that you understand the dynamics of what has happened."

She fell silent a moment, thinking, wondering if she was ready to hear everything. "But… but you are Henry's champion. You fought against Simon."

"Aye, I did," he replied. "I fought against Simon because I made a choice long ago to support the king, not a baron's rebellion. Simon has been trying for years to convince me to switch allegiance but I would not do it. Even when faced with the prospect of fighting against my brother."

Devereux watched him with sad, concerned eyes. "Is Hugh all right?"

"He is fine. He is with me, in fact, outside with the horses."

"He is here?" she repeated, digesting what he was trying to tell her. Things weren't making a lot of sense. "If you were captured, why are you here? Did Simon release you because you are his godson?"

He sighed faintly. "As I said, Simon has been attempting to gain my fealty for years," he said softly. "Nothing he could say or do would convince me. But something finally did."

"What?"

"You."

Her eyebrows lifted. "Me? How did I convince you?" She suddenly put her hands on his big arms imploringly. "Surely you did not heed all of those things I said to you when we first met, about not believing in absolute rule or how I distained the knighthood because they used their power for war rather than unity."

A smile played on his lips. "Are you saying that you were wrong?"

She pursed her lips wryly, unable to look him in the eye for the moment. "I was wrong about a great many things," she said, her expression turning earnest as she looked at him. "But the most important thing I was wrong about was you. You are a great man, Davyss. You told me how great you were and I did not believe you. But you were right. And I was wrong about something else."

"What?"

"You said once that most women would see marriage to you as a great honor," she reached up to touch his face. "Your greatness does not come from your deeds or victorious battles. You could be a pauper and I would still consider marriage to you a great honor. It is the man I love, not the warrior."

He kissed her hand sweetly, closing his eyes to the power of her words. He was deeply touched. "Thank you," he murmured. "And I am greatly honored to be your husband. So much so that I would do anything to protect you, including ruin my reputation."

Her gentle smile faded, his words bringing dread. "What does that mean?"

He held her palm against his mouth as he spoke. "It means that Simon threatened to take you hostage unless I joined him. I could not allow this to happen; I could not take the chance of you becoming deeply involved in a deadly game. So I agreed to swear fealty to him on the condition that he leaves you untouched."

Devereux stared at him. As he watched, the gray eyes filled with tears that spilled over onto her cheeks. She suddenly threw her arms around his neck and held him tightly.

"Oh, Davyss," she sobbed. "I am so sorry; so very, very sorry that I caused this."

He held her close, stroking the back of her head with one great hand. "You did not cause anything, sweetling," he assured her softly. "I made the decision; not you. It was my choice completely."

"But you made it because of me."

He sighed faintly. "As I feel you warm and safe in my arms, I would make the same choice a thousand times over." He pulled her back, holding her face between his two big hands as he fixed her in the eye. "Had this happened before I met you, I would have died rather than switch allegiance. It would have been a matter of pride more than honor; Davyss de Winter cannot be coerced into anything no matter what the circumstances. But with you involved... there was no pride or honor involved. I made my decision solely based on the fact that I would do anything to protect you and my family. My agreement to Simon has allowed my knights to be released, my brother and I to serve together again, and has guaranteed your safety. To have thought of only me, and to have been stubborn about it, would have had negative consequences for everyone around me. I cannot only think of myself any longer. Does that make sense?"

She sniffled, tears fading as she digested his words. "Aye," she replied. "But what does it all mean? What will happen now?"

He thought a moment. "I must return to London because Simon is convening all of the barons in England."

Her eyes grew intense. "I am coming with you," she told him firmly. "When do we leave?"

His brow furrowed. "But what about… well, what the physic told you?" he wanted to know. "Do you not need to stay in bed?"

She began tossing the covers off, her lips molding into a pout. "I am going with you," she repeated. "There are just a few things I must pack and then we can leave."

He put his big hands on her, stilling her motion. When she looked up, his handsome face was tense with concern.

"You know that there is nothing more in the world that I would wish for than for you to be with me at all times," he said softly, firmly. "But until I speak with the physic and hear from his mouth what your troubles are, you are not moving from this bed. Your health is of utmost importance to me and I will not risk it."

She looked as if she was about to burst into tears. "But I do not want to stay here without you."

He patted her cheek, rising from the bed as he still held her hand. "Do not fret," he told her. "I shall find the physic right now and speak with him. Do you know where he is?"

She tossed off the covers again and jumped from the other side of the bed so he couldn't grab her. She ignored him completely, snapping off orders to the red-headed woman still in the corner.

"Find Kerby right away," she commanded. "Tell him that my husband is here and he will not take me to London until he speaks with Kerby. He has very important business in London that cannot wait. Go!"

The woman fled, nearly running down Davyss in her haste. When she was gone, Devereux smiled timidly at her husband, who looked the least bit perturbed.

"Dora will find him," she said confidently. "Until then, I will get dressed so you will not have to wait overly for me."

Davyss lifted an eyebrow, resting his enormous hand on his slender hips. "You will tell me why the physic has you in bed."

She averted her gaze, moving with lethargic movements to the massive wardrobe against the wall. Pulling open the door, she pulled forth a white shift as she sighed heavily.

"Because I have not been feeling very well, as you know," she said simply.

He regarded hers suspiciously. "The retching? The headaches?"

"Aye."

"There must be more than that. He would not confine you to bed for an upset belly and headaches."

She shrugged, laying the shift out on the bed. "And... well, I have had fainting spells."

"Fainting spells?" he repeated, his suspicion turning to genuine concern. "Are they frequent?"

"Frequent enough. If I am too tired, or upset, sometimes I become overwhelmed."

He was coming to understand. "And my being away has not helped your situation."

She smiled weakly. "My worry for you has been great."

He went to her, pulling her into his enormous embrace and kissing her forehead. "I am sorry, sweetling," he murmured. "I know the strain has been difficult."

She snorted softly, wrapping her arms around his narrow waist and hugging him tightly. "Compared to what you have endured, I am ashamed to mention my troubles at all," she said. "They seem inconsequential."

"Yet they are not. They are more important to me than anything." He kissed the top of her head and laid his cheek upon it. "Will you please return to bed until the physic arrives? It would give me comfort."

She sighed heavily and he knew he had her. With gentle coaxing, he got her back into the bed and covered her up. But she would not lie down, instead, sitting up and demanding he sit beside her. He did without hesitation, pulling her into his massive embrace and holding her close. And that was how the surgeon found them almost a half hour later.

He was a small man with red hair and a red beard. His movements were sharp and quick, like a little bird. He entered the room, his aged gaze falling on the crowded bed. His eyebrows lifted.

"That is why you find yourself in difficulties in the first place," he was looking at Devereux as he pointed a finger at Davyss. He focused on the enormous warrior. "Lord de Winter, I presume?"

Davyss released his wife, eyeing the blunt old man as he climbed out of the bed. "You are correct," he stood up, hands on his hips. "You have examined my wife?"

"I have, my lord."

"Then tell me why my wife is confined to bed. I cannot get a straight answer out of her."

Kerby cocked an eyebrow. "Because this child is draining her strength, my lord. If she does not rest, she may do herself and the child serious harm. But the difficulty is in having her obey me. She does not want to listen."

Davyss listened to the old man seriously. "If I take her to London with me and promise that she will stay in bed until this child is born, would that be acceptable?"

The old surgeon looked at Devereux, who was gazing at him anxiously. After a moment, he exhaled sharply.

"This pregnancy is tenuous, my lord," he told the man bluntly. "Your wife bleeds daily which tells me that the pregnancy is not secure."

Davyss' eyes widened. "Is that why she is fainting? Because she is losing blood?"

The old man shrugged. "Partly," he replied, looking between Devereux and her husband. "Some women are better suited for child bearing than others, my lord. Perhaps your wife is not. With all of the blood she continues to expend, the child might already be dead for all I know. Only time will tell."

Devereux sat down on the bed, facing away from them, and succumbed to quiet tears. Davyss passed a sympathetic glance at her before turning an angry one to the physic.

"I will take her to London and have the finest physics in England examine her," he was already moving towards the old man as if to physically remove him from the room. "She and the child will be fine."

Kerby could see how agitated the man was; he also knew who Davyss de Winter was. With the king's recent defeat at Lewes, the news of which was swiftly traveling the country, he was frankly surprised to see the man at all. As the king's champion, the man was powerful and legendary, now shamed by a stunning defeat at Lewes. Much was happening in Lady de Winter's life contributing to a pregnancy that was slowly draining the life from her.

The old man slipped from the room just as Davyss slammed the door shut behind him. With his hand still on the latch, Davyss turned to his wife, still seated on the bed with her back to him. He watched her shoulders gently heave, his heart heavy as he went to her.

"I will pack for you," he said softly. "I will take you to Hollyhock and have my mother's surgeon examine you. Do not worry so."

Devereux wiped at her nose, her cheeks. "I... I am sorry I did not tell you all of it," she whispered. "I did not want to disappoint you."

He knelt beside the bed, his big hand on her head. "Sweetling, you could never disappoint me, not ever," he kissed her wet cheek. "I told you that I did not need for you to bear me a son in order for me to love you. I meant it."

She looked at him with her sad gray eyes and he kissed her again, pulling her forehead to his lips gently. Then he took her feet and put them back on the bed, pulling the coverlet over her.

"Now," he tried to sound firm and confident. "You may lay there and direct me to your heart's content. What must be packed?"

Devereux leaned back against the pillows, wiping at her nose. "You truly do not have to pack for me. I can have the servants do it just as well."

He smiled at her. "You may never have another opportunity to order me around like this," he winked at her. "I suggest you not let this chance slip away."

She grinned at him in spite of herself, finally pointing a finger to the wardrobe. "Everything in there must go," she said. "The servants have my trunks stored in the cellar, I think. There are four of them."

Davyss swung into action and soon it was he who was ordering around a fleet of servants from the Allington manse. St. Paul remained stationed in his solar, unwilling to get in Davyss' way and unwilling to be roped into packing for his daughter. He was secretly glad the man was taking her simply so he wouldn't be burdened with an ill woman. He didn't want the responsibility.

Even the knights were forced into service, lugging Devereux's trunks to the wagon that Davyss had confiscated from the Allington stables. Davyss wouldn't let them into her chamber because Devereux did not want to be seen in her sleeping shift, so they stood at the top of the stairs as Davyss lugged out the trunks and handed them over. Only Hugh wasn't given a trunk to haul and that was because Devereux wanted to see him.

When most of the possessions were removed from her chamber, Hugh stood in the hall with a guarded expression. Davyss finally reached out and grabbed his brother by the shoulder, dragging him into the room that looked very much like a woman lived there. Hugh stood by the door and wouldn't go any further.

He and Devereux regarded each other; the last time they had met was under violent circumstances. Hugh wasn't sure if he was in for a verbal lashing so he stayed close to the door in case he needed to get away quickly. After a few moments of uncertain staring, Devereux finally spoke.

"I am thankful that you were not hurt in the battle," she said.

Hugh's gaze flickered nervously. "Thank... thank you, my lady."

He was stiff and wary. Devereux glanced at Davyss before continuing. "Hugh, I wanted to apologize to you," she said. "Back at Wintercroft, I should not have confronted you as I did. You were upset and I fear my attempts to soothe the situation only worsened it. Please understand what I did, I did so that you and your brother would not be at odds. It was not my intention to upset you further. Please believe me."

Hugh stared at her, seeing an incredibly beautiful woman and understanding why she had his brother so smitten. But her apology had him confused and on edge. Women, at least in his experience, were usually very good at manipulating men. He couldn't be certain that Devereux wasn't making the attempt.

"I understand," he said evenly. "Is that all you wished to speak to me about?"

To his right, Davyss grunted irritably but Devereux shot him a quelling look. It was enough to cause Davyss to move away from his brother, finding interest in the view outside the window so he would not jump down his brother's throat. Devereux waited until he was well away before returning her focus to Hugh.

"We cannot go through life hating each other, Hugh," she said quietly. "I wanted you to know that I was sorry for my words or deeds that offended you that night. I should like it if you and I could at least be civil to each other, for your brother's sake."

Hugh's jaw ticked as he gazed at her. "You are my brother's wife," he said. "For no other reason that than, I will be civil to you. But do not expect more."

Devereux watched Davyss clench and unclench his fists out of the corner of her eye; she knew he was working up his temper.

"Please tell me what it is I have done that has offended you so?" she asked Hugh. "Whatever it is, I will apologize for it. I will take the blame."

"Blame?" Hugh repeated, incredulous. "Where shall I start, lady? The very first moment you saw me, you rudely slammed a door in my face. And that was just the beginning."

Devereux thought back to that dark day in this very manse. It was jumbled full of emotion, but she remembered it quite clearly. As she did so, something began to occur to her.

"As I recall," she began thoughtfully, "when I opened the door downstairs to find you standing there, you told me that it was my lucky day and if I behaved in a manner that pleased you, I could have both de Winter brothers for the price of one."

Hugh's face flushed a dull red as Davyss swung on him, his features taut with outrage. "Did you say that to her?" he bellowed.

Hugh began backing out of the room, the very reason he had refused to fully enter the chamber in the first place. He knew his brother's temper. He wanted to be able to make a fast retreat.

"I… I do not recall," he stammered. "I might have said something… but I did not mean it the way it sounded!"

Davyss was charging across the room towards his brother. "You bastard," he snarled. "You hate her because she did not succumb to your foolish proposition? Is that it?"

Devereux bolted up from the bed, jumping on the mattress and taking a flying leap at her husband as he passed by. She slammed into him and he teetered off balance, hitting the wall as he threw his arms around her simply to keep her from falling to the floor.

"Nay, Davyss," she begged, awkwardly clinging to him. "You will not strike him."

Davyss was so furious that his nostrils were flaring. "Did he really say that to you?"

She nodded hesitantly. "But I did not give it a second thought, not until this very moment. It was not the reason I slammed the door in his face. I slammed the door because I did not want to marry you but we both know that has since changed."

She was smiling by the time she was finished speaking and Davyss stared at her expression a moment before sighing heavily, possibly in resignation. He shifted his grip on her and carried her back to bed, gently laying her upon the mattress.

"You should not have done that," he wagged a finger at her.

She looked up at him innocently. "What? Slammed the door in Hugh's face?"

He scowled. "Nay," he snapped without force. "Jump on me like that. You could have hurt yourself."

"I shall do it again unless you promise me you will not charge your brother."

He rolled his eyes but offered his irritated compliance when she pressed him again. His gaze lingered on Hugh, still near the door, before turning back to the window. When Devereux was sure he wasn't going to charge Hugh again, she returned her focus to the younger brother.

"Hugh," she began. "Let us be completely honest with each other. You do not hate me so much as you are angry with me; angry that I did not succumb to your charms the day you came to escort me to my wedding and angry because I asked your brother to remove the whores from Wintercroft. Is this statement any way untrue?"

Hugh's brow was furrowed and he refused to look at her. "It... it was not your right."

She gazed steadily at him. "You are correct; it was not my right," she said softly. "I did it for selfish reasons and for that, I am sorry. I did not want those women around because I was uncertain of my relation-ship with your brother at the time, uncertain if he would prefer me over them. Now that I know he would never do anything to shame me, I understand that what I did was completely self-serving. If I were to allow those women to return to Wintercroft, would it make you happy?"

He looked at her, then. He could see that Davyss had turned away from the window and was looking at him, too. In fact, Davyss moved away from the window and sat on the bed next to his wife, pulling her into his arms and burying his face in the side of her head. Hugh watched the affection, the completely adoration, in his brother's actions and he was surprised by it. He'd never seen his brother behave in such a way before. There was something about it that made him strangely jealous. He felt the fight, the anger, suddenly draining out of him.

"Perhaps," he replied belatedly. He suddenly seemed disinterested and distracted, anxious to leave. "Is there anything else you wished to speak with me about?"

Devereux wouldn't push him. It was the first conversation in a line of many she intended to have with him, so she let him go for the moment.

"Nay," she replied. "Thank you for your time."

Hugh's gaze traveled back and forth between his brother and his brother's wife before silently departing the room. Davyss held her in his arms, thinking many different things at that moment; he felt like the most fortunate man alive. Devereux had shown him so much of life that he had never imagined to exist, her wisdom and kindness without measure. He knew his brother would come around eventually. He squeezed her gently before letting her go.

"You tried to right things with him," he said quietly. "I applaud your attempt."

She wriggled her eyebrows. "I do not know if I did any good, but I hope so," she said. "I should not like to be at odds with your brother for the rest of my life."

"I am sure you will not be," he said. "He will eventually see the error of his ways."

Devereux kept silent on that matter; Hugh seemed to be even more arrogant than Davyss had been so she wondered if he would ever overcome it.

"Perhaps," she said vaguely, changing the subject. "When are we leaving for London?"

He stood up from the bed, scratching his head wearily. "Do you suppose it would be too much to ask that we sleep here tonight and get an early start in the morning?"

"Of course not," she said. "I will tell the servants that we will all be supping here tonight."

"I can do it," he was moving for the door, pointing a finger at her. "I want you to stay there and rest. Is that clear?"

She nodded obediently. "Aye, sweetheart."

"Good."

He winked at her as he quit the chamber, leaving Devereux alone in the room, smiling at the mere thought of him. She could not adequately describe the joy in her heart for the man, the love she felt for him defying explanation. She had so much in her life to be grateful for, and grateful she was. Her happiness was nearly complete and she thanked God repeatedly for it.

Later that night, she miscarried the child.

CHAPTER SEVENTEEN

T HE GREAT HALL of the Tower of London was full of the nobles and fighting men of England. Davyss had spent hours in conference with de Montfort's barons, men he had fought with and against for many years. They were all surprised to see a de Winter at de Montfort's side, but the older barons who had known Grayson de Winter also knew that he and Simon had been the best of friends. To them, it was therefore not so surprising. Still, Davyss de Winter had been a staunch supporter of Henry. It was odd to see him on the other side.

It was evident very early on that de Montfort was determined to give the rule of England to the people through their representatives. He insisted that each borough send two elected representatives, something that seemed to upset the nobles because they were concerned that it would affect their rule over their own lands. Those who had strongly supported de Montfort were now secretly wondering if they should have supported someone who intended to give the country back to the people and not directly back to the nobility. Davyss had listened to their growing dissention for several days now, digesting it, and preparing plans of his own.

He ended up back at Hollyhock, telling his knights to meet him in a half hour up in his solar. The evening was humid and he was sweating rivers as he made his way into the house and up to the third floor. He didn't even bother greeting his mother, who was down in her solar with her ladies and her dogs. Hugh went in to see her but Davyss did not. His one and only thought at the moment was to see his wife.

He found Devereux sitting in the lounge chair of their massive chamber, positioned by the window to catch the last rays of the dying sun. She was wearing a lovely yellow surcoat, her luscious hair pulled to the nape of her neck as she focused on a piece of needlework in her hand.

Davyss entered the chamber, pulling his damp tunic over his head as he approached her. But the moment the tunic came over his head and his gaze focused on her, he came to a halt.

"What is that?" he jabbed a finger at her.

Devereux looked up from her sewing, having no idea what he was talking about until she followed his focus. At the foot of the lounge, lying very contentedly, was a small puppy with fuzzy orange hair. She smiled at her husband's outrage.

"Your mother gave him to me," she said. "Isn't he sweet?"

Davyss made a face as he tossed the soiled tunic to the floor. "Are you serious, woman?" he began to unhappily unlatch his armor. "A dog?"

Devereux giggled. "His name is Louie. You must be very nice to him."

Davyss continued to make faces as he removed his armor, eyeing the dog. In truth, he wasn't all that mad about it; it was the first time she had smiled in days. Devereux had been depressed and sad since her miscarriage two weeks before, a state he had tried desperately to pull her out of. Leaving The House of Hope with Stephan Longham and his brothers in charge, he had taken her to London in the hope that it would improve her health and spirit. But it had worked the opposite effect; she refused to leave Hollyhock at all, staying to their rooms and only coming downstairs to eat when Lady Katharine pleaded. She had been reclusive and quiet, something that disturbed Davyss tremendously.

Davyss had also been worried about his mother's reaction to the loss of an heir, adding to his stress, but his mother had been surprisingly sympathetic. He found out why one night after they had both imbibed too much wine; Lady Katharine had suffered four miscarriages prior to Davyss' healthy birth. He'd never known that. Moreover, she had another two miscarriages between Davyss and Hugh. So his mother understood well what Devereux was experiencing.

Katharine reassured her son that there would be more children someday. Davyss didn't care about any more children at the moment; he simply wanted a happy, healthy wife again. Even with all of the turmoil going on with de Montfort, it was all he could think about.

Therefore, the addition of the little dog didn't distress him as much as he pretended it did. When he bent over to kiss his wife in greeting, the puppy rolled over, struggled to his feet, and barked. Devereux laughed as Davyss scowled.

"You foolish little mutt," he scolded. "You shall not chase me from my own wife."

The dog growled and wriggled its tail, finally taking the hem of his wife's gown and chewing enthusiastically on it. Devereux continued to laugh as Davyss just shook his head at the puppy's antics. He went back to the chamber door and called to the servants for hot water.

"Did you have a pleasant day, sweetheart?" Devereux asked as she turned back to her sewing.

He thought on the irony of that question, knowing she had no idea the depth that the answer would contain. So he kept it simple.

"It was busy," he removed the last of his armor and went to work on the damp linen tunic underneath. "What did you do today?"

She sighed faintly, looking up from her needlework to the western sky with his myriad of colors. "I helped Frances pack," she said. "She is going to be with Nik, you know."

"I know."

"Lollardly sent word that he will be arriving on the morrow to take her to Sussex."

Davyss nodded faintly; he knew that. He had been the one to receive the missive, in fact, that Nik was still alive at Lewes Castle. Frances, usually so dour and humorless, had wept profusely at the news of her husband's injury and was eager to be with him. Davyss missed Nik's presence a great deal in these times of trial and tried not to be selfish about it. He was just glad the man had apparently pulled through.

"Is that all you did today, then?"

She half-shrugged, half-nodded. "Aye," she replied, reaching out to pet the puppy. "Louie and I have been very companionable loafing about."

He pulled off the damp tunic, hearing the servants in the small servant's alcove between the rooms as they began to fill a big copper tub with steaming water.

"I have heard something that I think might interest you," he said casually, unlacing the top of his breeches. "Perhaps you will not want to loaf around when you hear it."

She didn't seem particularly curious. "What is it?"

"Well," he sat on the bed and began to remove his heavy boots. "With all of the nobility in town, someone brought up the bright idea to have a tournament celebrating de Montfort's victory. Everyone seemed to think it was a brilliant idea."

"Why would that interest me?"

"Because I have been goaded into competing."

She stopped what she was doing and looked at him. "What?" she looked horrified. "You... you are going to compete in a tournament?"

He looked at her, amused. "And why not? I am the reigning grand champion at the tournaments in Greenwich, Oxford, Banbury, Thetford and Northampton. I am fairly good at it."

She just stared at him a moment before turning back to her sewing. "Of course you are, sweetheart," she murmured softly.

He was about to remove his breeches but stopped when he heard her tone. He went over to her, bare feet against the wooden floor.

"What is wrong?" he asked quietly.

She shook her head even though she wouldn't look up at him. "Nothing," she insisted weakly. "I... I am simply hungry. It should be time for sup soon. Aren't you hungry?"

He lifted an eyebrow; he didn't believe her for a moment. He gently shoved her over on the lounge, sitting down beside her and taking her into his powerful arms. Devereux surrendered to his warmth and power, collapsing against him and burying her face in his sweaty, musky chest. It was like heaven.

"Do you not like tournaments?" he asked softly, giving her a squeeze. "They are very exciting and great sport, I might add."

She shifted so the left side of her head was against his chest. She could hear his heart beating strong and steady.

"Nay," she whispered. "I do not like them."

"Why not?"

She sighed faintly, thinking. "I saw you compete in a tournament three years ago in Acle," she said softly. "Do you recall that tournament?"

He grunted. "Of course. I won the joust."

"I know," her voice was faint. "It was the first time I ever saw you, though I cannot recall paying terribly close attention. It was my first tournament and my father insisted I attend, so the entire spectacle was rather overwhelming. I do believe my father wanted me to attend because he wanted to attract a husband for me. This was before your mother approached him with a contract. Three years ago, I was still very much an unattached maiden."

He grinned, hugging her tightly. "Thank God that no one approached your father before my mother could get to him," he kissed the top of her head. "I am surprised that I did not notice you. Usually, I...."

He suddenly stopped before he could get himself into trouble. Devereux grinned, lifting her head from his chest to look him in the eye.

"You usually... *what*?" she pressed.

He shook his head and tried to get up, but she sat on him and pushed him down. "Let me see if I can finish your statement," she teased. "Usually you spied all of the beautiful women within the first hour of your arrival and picked off your conquests one by one, as a good hunter would, until none were left standing in the end. Am I right?"

He started to laugh, only he didn't want her to see that he was laughing so he covered his face with his hands and tried to turn away from her. Devereux responded by digging her fingers into his gut, tickling him mercilessly, which prompted him to shoot off the lounge and nearly dump her on her arse. She laughed uproariously as he steadied her by stilling the tickling fingers. They laughed at each other as she tried to tickle him again, but he threw her into a big bear hug and ended her onslaught.

His mouth was by her ear, hot and breathless. "I told you never to do that again."

She was giggling, not trying too hard to squirm away from him. "I told you I would only do it in times of great need. This was one of those times."

He growled, nibbling on her tender neck until she squealed and begged for mercy. Still grinning, he swung her up into his arms and carried her into the small bathing room adjoining the chamber.

It was steamy and moist in the small room because of the bath. Davyss set Devereux to her feet and removed his breeches, plunging into the tub and causing water to slosh over the sides. Devereux turned to the small table where the bathing implements were contained; she picked up a lumpy white bar of soap that smelled of pine, a bristly brush, and began to lather it up.

"Continue your story," he told her as he splashed water all over his head and neck. "You were telling me about the tournament in Acle."

She came to him with the soapy brush and began to lather his hair. He sputtered water from his lips, closing his eyes as she began to scrub.

"I remember seeing several knights injured," she said, thinking back to that day and the distaste it had provoked. "One man who was competing in the joust was knocked from his horse with such force that he broke his arm. I remember seeing the bone stick out."

Davyss grunted. "Such are the hazards of the sport. It is not for the faint of heart."

She lifted an eyebrow at him in disgust as she moved to soap his face and neck. "In the final matches of the tournament, I seem to recall that one knight was speared through the face with a broken lance," she shuddered as she remembered the horror from that moment. "I heard later that he had died. It was so…needless, so wasteful."

She rinsed the soap from his head and Davyss rubbed at his eyes to clear them of water. The hazel orbs opened, remembering the day she spoke of.

"His name was John Swantey," he murmured. "He served the Earl of Warwick."

"You knew him?"

Davyss nodded faintly. "It was my lance that speared him."

She paused in her scrubbing, a look of pain crossing her features. "Oh, Davyss," she breathed. "I am sorry. I did not mean to condemn or criticize. 'Tis simply that it was a death that did not have to occur. I realize that men like to compete and although I do not contest their need for competition, I cannot tell you how devastated I would be if something were to happen to you like it happened to John Swantey. It would absolutely destroy me."

He found a soapy hand and kissed it. "I understand your concern," he told her. "I will not compete if it will upset you."

For the second time, she paused in her scrubbing. She moved around to the front of the tub to look him in the eye, her gray orbs wide with surprise.

"I would never ask that of you," she said sincerely. "I will never ask you to be less than what you are, Davyss."

A warm smile creased his lips. "You are not," he assured her. "I have achieved my share of glory. It is not as if I need another tournament to prove my worth. My worth is well known."

She returned his smile, kneeling by the tub and getting her yellow surcoat wet from the water on the floor. "You are worth everything to me," she whispered. "But… but I think perhaps that you should compete. With everything that has happened over the past few weeks, perhaps it is important for you to."

He lifted an eyebrow. "Why would you say that?"

She shrugged, averting her gaze and beginning to scrub his chest. "Because you said that you had ruined your reputation when you swore allegiance to de Montfort. Perhaps you need to regain some of that honor in the eyes of your peers and perhaps this is a way to do that." She suddenly shook her head. "Forgive me; I do not know what I am saying. I do not mean to tell you how to conduct your business."

He gently pinched her chin between his thumb and forefinger, forcing her to look up at him. The hazel eyes were intense. "Your wisdom is astounding," he declared. "You do indeed understand my business well."

She sighed. "If I had my choice, I still would not want you to compete," she said. "But I understand if you must."

He leaned forward and kissed her, a sweet gesture quickly turning in to something hot and lusty. Whatever attraction flowed between them was quickly sparked and his mouth began doing wicked things to her neck, collarbone, and ears. Wet hands found her breasts through her yellow surcoat but just as quickly as he fondled her, he abruptly stopped.

"I am sorry," he straightened her bodice. "I know we cannot... well, that I cannot touch you for a few more weeks but I must say that it will be the most torturous wait of my life. I want you so badly that I can taste it."

She touched his cheek, thinking of the child so recently lost and of Kerby's instructions that she be given several weeks to heal before they resumed intimate relations. In truth, she wanted him to touch her more strongly than she could explain. Perhaps it was the need to feel his love for her after such a devastating loss, reassuring her that she was still wanted and needed. As she pondered her thoughts, tears filled her eyes.

"I do not care what he says," she wrapped her arms around his damp neck. "I need to feel you, husband. I need to...."

She trailed off and lowered her head, tears rolling down her cheeks. Davyss put his big hands on her face, forcing her to look at him.

"What is wrong, sweetling?" he whispered, kissing her cheeks.

"Why do you weep?"

She burst into soft sobs. "I do not know," she wept. "All I know is that I feel... I feel rather useless as your wife. My only purpose in this marriage is to bear children and...."

He'd heard enough. Abruptly standing from the tub, he swept her into his arms as water sloshed out all over the place. He carried her back into the bedchamber, holding her tightly as she wept against his neck. Wet and all, he lay down on the bed with her, holding her against him as tightly and as closely as she could go. His heart was breaking into a million little pieces as he listened to her tears.

"Devereux," he whispered against her hair. "I have told you before that I do not need for you to bear me a child in order for me to love you. Do you believe that?"

She nodded, her weeping deep and sorrowful. "But that is not fair to you. You must have an heir, Davyss. If I am unable to provide that, I am worthless to you."

He gave her a squeeze. "Do not say that," he rumbled. "I do not ever want to hear you say that again. You are my shining star, the heart that beats within me. Without you, I am nothing. If I must choose between children or you, I would choose you every time. Your ability to bear children has nothing to do with my feelings."

She lifted her head to look at him, her gray eyes watery and red. But the sobbing had eased. "But you need a son. Davyss, it simply isn't fair to you."

He smiled, kissing the tip of her nose. "'Tis not as if we know for certain that you cannot bear children," he said. "There still may be sons in the future. Remember that my mother lost several children before I was born. There is still every chance in the world that we will end up with twelve children, all female, and all driving me to the brink of madness."

She returned his smile, realizing how fortunate she was to have married such a gracious and compassionate man. The day she met him, she would have never believed he was capable of such depth. In one of her darkest hours, he was a beacon of comfort and hope. She put her small hands on his face, stroking his cheeks tenderly.

"Thank you," she murmured, kissing him sweetly. "For everything you have done for me, I thank you. And I love you very much."

His smiled broadened as he dipped low, kissing her passionately. Devereux didn't care that the physic told her she needed to wait a few weeks before having relations with her husband; she threw herself on the man, taking the offensive and returning his kisses lustily. She began to pull off the wet surcoat, not letting him speak when he tried to voice his opposition. Soon enough, the surcoat and shift were off, her naked body against his, and Davyss knew that he was lost.

Still attached to his mouth, Devereux parted her legs and pulled him down into intimate places. Davyss, having been seriously aroused since the bathtub, buried himself deep inside his wife, trying not to be rough with her but unable to rein his passion. Devereux threw her arms around his neck and held him fast against her, moving with him as he thrust into her, climaxing twice before he spilled his seed deep. As he grunted in the throes of release, she whispered hotly in his ear.

"Give me all of it," she hissed. "Give me your son, sweetheart. I can feel your seed even now seeking root. I feel it hot and deep within me."

Her words sent his heart to racing, eroticism as he had never experienced it. His mouth fused to hers, kissing her so ferociously that he drove her teeth into her soft gum, drawing blood. He lapped at the blood, his body buried in hers, feeling himself growing hard again in little time. Something about the woman drove him out of his mind with lust and he began to thrust into her again, releasing himself a second time as she begged for his seed in his ear.

Their passion, their lust and love for each other, went well on into the night.

CB

HUGH, ANDREW, EDMUND and Philip were in Davyss's solar when the man finally arrived just before midnight. He looked exhausted but elated, an odd combination. He grinned sheepishly at his men as he went to a sideboard that held a pitcher of wine and several fine cups. He poured himself a measure of wine, drinking deeply as he approached the map table.

"Well?" Hugh asked, peering closely at his brother. "Where have you been? Or dare I ask?"

Davyss cleared his throat softly, glancing at Andrew as he did so. "I have been with my wife," he focused on the map table. "I apologize on keeping you waiting."

Andrew snorted and slapped him on the shoulder while Edmund looked rather lost. He was still very young, his focus on the knighthood at the moment and not women, so he was fairly oblivious to the innuendos. Hugh studied his brother's expression, his body language.

"I thought you were supposed to leave her alone," he muttered.

Davyss' hazel eyes flicked to him. "I will never leave her alone."

Hugh just shook his head, focusing on the map before them. He thought it might be best to change the subject since they still could not agree on Devereux, in any fashion. It was best not to discuss her.

"Most of the country's barons are in London right now," he pointed out. "Simon has received favorable responses to his summons for elected officials from each berg."

"But the barons are threatened by this," Philip pointed out. "It seems that they were well on board with de Montfort and his ideology until they realized that, by summoning elected officials from their own people, they would be limiting their power."

Davyss nodded, bracing his enormous arms on the table and leaning on them. He stared at the map; it was of the entire country, pockmarked from years of use. It had once belonged to his father. As he stared, he let out a heavy sigh.

"They have made their bed and now they must lie in it," he muttered. "But I intend to change that."

The men around the table looked at him. "How?" Philip asked.

Davyss stared at the map a moment longer before turning away. "I know the majority of you did not agree with my allegiance to Simon but, out of respect for me, you followed," he looked at the men around the table, his friends. "I would have you know that my loyalty to Henry has not ended. Although I have sworn to Simon, the purpose was two-fold."

"What purpose?" Philip was still confused.

Davyss began to pace the floor thoughtfully. "As a captive sworn to Henry, I would be powerless," he lowered his voice. "My knights would be imprisoned, my family's lands possibly confiscated, my wife taken. This I could not allow. But as a free man sworn to de Montfort, I can accomplish much more for Henry's cause."

Hugh stared at him. "You swore, Davyss," he hissed. "You swore to Uncle Simon that you would serve him. Are you saying you intend to go back on that pledge? What kind of man are you if you do not honor your bond?"

Davyss' features tensed. "I am a man who would accomplish what he must for the safety of his family and the strength of his country," his passion was gaining momentum and he threw his arms out. "Do you not see what is happening, Hugh? Simon is giving England to the people, a mindless rabble who have no concept of how to run or maintain a country. This was how the country was back in olden times, before the Bastard, when different kingdoms reigned throughout the country and there was no unity. It was madness. One king and one country bring peace and prosperity to all. De Montfort threatens to ruin that and I will not stand for it. I do not think Father would have, either."

Hugh lowered his gaze, jaw ticking. He was reluctant to admit that what Davyss said made sense. "But you gave your word."

Davyss just looked at him. "Is that all the de Winter name means to you? Our word above sanity? You used to believe as I did, once. Has everything changed between us now, brother?"

Hugh shrugged irritably and looked away. "If he catches wind of subversion, he will kill you."

"I know," Davyss nodded. "That is why what I say now will not leave this room. Is that clear, Hugh?"

Hugh looked at him with exasperation. "I do not want to see your death, brother. Do you truly think I would run back to him with this information? Of course not. Truth be known, I do not disagree with you. But whatever happens must be carefully planned and executed."

Davyss went to his brother, putting his enormous hands on the man's shoulders. He shook him gently.

"As much as I do not relish being subversive to Uncle Simon, I cannot, in good conscience, follow his politics. I do not agree with them." He shook his brother again. "Stay with me, Hughie. All will be well in the end."

Hugh smiled reluctantly; he adored his older brother. Their separation had been hard on him although he was coming to think that perhaps he had been entirely to blame for it. Still, he wasn't ready to voice those thoughts yet.

"I am with you," he assured him softly. "It sounds as if you already have something in mind."

Davyss smiled and pulled him over to the table. "I do," he thumped the map. "Gather 'round, good men. I have a plan."

"What plan?"

"It involves Roger Mortimer, the king's cousin, and us."

"But Mortimer is a supporter of de Montfort."

Davyss shook his head slowly. "Not too strongly, which will work well in our favor."

In the darkness of the night, the de Winter conspirators gathered tight and bred insurrection.

CHAPTER EIGHTEEN

T HERE WAS A massive tournament field about a half mile west of the
Tower of London, a great arena where knights plied their bloody
games. On this busy day, banners of competing houses snapped in the
brisk wind as hundreds of people milled about, preparing for the
spectacle that was soon to take place.

It was a dusty bowl of a field surrounded by great banks of lists,
fairly well built. There was a royal box on the east side of the field,
center line, and other boxes for the dozens of nobles that would view
the games. The guide was not yet planted in the center of the field
because the mêlée would come first and they needed the field clear.
Marshals and pages ran to and fro across the field, preparing it,
memorizing it, getting ready for the first round of the day. A surgeon
and his helpers set up on the south side of the arena.

The tournament field was close to Hollyhock but Davyss brought
his full complement of gear, tents and accessories to the arena. He
wasn't going to go home to rest in between bouts, instead choosing to
have his tents and colors raised high for all to see. He was announcing
the de Winters as loudly as he could, one of the most prominent
families in the country and a name to be proud of. He was there to win.

Lady Katharine, surprisingly, had chosen to attend the games.
When Davyss and his men returned from the tournament field after
setting up, they were met at the door by Katharine, Lucy and Devereux.

Lady Katharine was dressed in her traditional black garments with
traditional black wimple, while Lucy was dressed in a lovely red surcoat.
Devereux looked stunning in the de Winter colors of black, gray and
red. Lady Katharine had a surcoat and shift especially made for
Devereux for this day and the results were spectacular. She looked

delicious.

It was an effect not lost on Davyss. While Hugh escorted his mother to the carriage and Philip helped Lucy, Davyss went straight for his wife. He kissed her hands sweetly before kissing her cheeks.

"You are breathtaking," he told her sincerely. "I shall be the envy of every man at the tournament."

Devereux blushed prettily. "And I shall be the envy of every woman at the tournament," she grinned impishly. "What a pair we make."

He kissed her, leading her towards the carriage. "The happiest pair in all of London, I would wager."

She smiled as he led her up to the elegant de Winter carriage and helped her inside. Her surcoat had quite a train on it and he tucked it into the carriage after her. With a wink to his wife, he shut the door and slapped his hand on the side of the carriage. It was the driver's signal to depart. Davyss mounted his new Belgian charger, a great black beast with hairy fetlocks, and cantered after the carriage as it rumbled down the avenue.

After some morning fog, the day had bloomed surprisingly clear. The sky was brilliant blue with great cotton puff clouds skittering across it in the brisk breeze. Although there was some humidity, it wasn't overbearing. Lucy had only to been to one tournament and her excitement was palpable; she kept pointing and jabbering about the knights, their ladies, and anything else that captured her interest. She wanted to eat custard and drink sweet wine. It was like being accompanied by a five year old with all of the chatter going on and Devereux just sat back and smiled. She was lovely and funny.

Lady Katharine, however, did not think so, and Lucy soon realized that the elder de Winter woman was growing annoyed with the constant conversation. About the time they reached Davyss' encampment, Lucy had shut her mouth completely.

There were three tents raised; a large one and two smaller ones. The tents were made from very fine brocade in an elaborate black and gray pattern. On the door flap of the larger tent was a giant red de Winter dragon. There were soldiers guarding the area and several squires running about, young men that Devereux had seen traveling with her husband's army. When the carriage came to a halt, Davyss suddenly appeared to help the women from the cab.

Lady Katharine exited first and went straight into Hugh's capable hands. While he led his mother away, Lucy was handed over to Philip and Devereux was brought out last. Davyss took her straight into the large tent.

It was well appointed and comfortable inside. Devereux was properly awed by the opulence of the de Winters, as she always was. There was apparently no end to their money. Davyss sat her down on a small stool while he called two of the squires to help him dress.

His armor was on a stand in a corner of the tent and the two squires went about dressing him. Clad in linen breeches, a padded linen tunic and his heavy boots, he put his arms up as the squires placed the mail coat.

"The mêlée is first," he told his wife. "That should go for the rest of morning. After the nooning break, the joust will commence."

She cocked her head. "I have heard that the mêlée is to be outlawed. Is this true?"

He shrugged. "The Church is attempting to outlaw it. In years past, the mêlée could be quite violent. Men would be captured and held for ransom, much like real combat, and people tend to get carried away with the spirit of the thing. I have seen a few men fall to serious injury all in the name of sport."

"But what of the mêlée today?" she wanted to know. "Will it be violent as well?"

He shook his head. "Men are not so voracious these days. It will be mock combat and nothing more." He looked at her and shrugged in disappointment. "They pin flags on our backs, put clubs in our hands, and expect us to call it honorable combat."

She thought on that a moment and, satisfied, moved on. "Do you know who you are competing against in the joust?" she asked as the squires pulled the mail hood over his head.

He shook his head and his shoulders, settling the heavy chain mail on his body. "Aye," he grunted as the mail chaffed. "My first card is against Sir Paris de Norville, who rides for the Earl of Northumberland."

"Do you know him?"

Davyss grinned. "I have known de Norville for many years," he replied. "A more arrogant man you will never meet. I look forward to bragging rights when I plant him on his arse."

"Do you not like him, then?"

Davyss laughed. "I like him a great deal," he looked up and winked at her. "But I am still going to send him to the ground."

Devereux smiled at her husband, who seemed truly devilish about the entire thing. She continued to watch as his squires suited him with other pieces of armor, including massively armored gloves. Davyss also had the advantage of having pieces of plate armor, which most knights did not have. These were newer measures of protection, expensive and heavy pieces of metal that covered his chest and arms. Over that, the squires draped him with his tunic bearing the de Winter coat of arms.

Davyss was a very large man, made larger by the mail and armor he wore. It was a truly intimidating sight. When he was properly and completely dressed, he turned to his wife with a smile.

"Are you ready for an amazing spectacle, my lady?" he asked.

She stood up from the stool, suppressing a smile at his enthusiasm. "I suppose," she sighed dramatically. "But if you end up with bumps or cuts or your brains hanging out, I will not lift a finger to help you. Not one finger."

He scowled good-naturedly. "You cruel woman," he scolded. "'Tis your duty to tend me if I am injured."

She shook her head firmly. "Not when you naughty little boys run about and try to hurt each other. I have no sympathy for men who will not grow up."

He laughed at her, taking her hand and kissing it sweetly. Their eyes met and she melted into him, smiling broadly and kissing his cheek.

"Please be careful today," she whispered as she kissed him again. "I should like my husband whole and healthy tonight."

He nodded. "I will do my very best," he promised. "I shall endeavor to make you proud."

Her smile faded as she gazed up into his spectacular face. "You already make me proud."

Davyss' smile faded as he met her gaze, feeling the heat from the gray orbs. He held her hands tightly and kissed her mouth gently, his eyes closed as he savored the feel and smell of her. It was enough to set his heart to racing.

"I love you, Lady de Winter."

"And I love you."

With a final kiss, he took her out into the sunshine of the new day.

C�

DEVEREUX, LUCY AND Lady Katharine had a box right next to the royal box, which contained none other than Simon de Montfort. When Devereux arrived, Lady Katharine was seated next to Simon in his box, involved in a serious conversation with him from the expression on both of their faces. Devereux took a good, long look at the man who now ruled the country before taking her seat next to Lucy. He looked old and careworn, this man who had taken on the burden of an entire country in an effort to effect change.

There were people everywhere, piling into the lists and cheering wildly for their favorite competitor. Lucy already had her hands full with custard and spun sugar, eating to her heart's content as she pointed out different knights to Devereux. They had no idea who the men represented with their fancy shields and tunics, but it was quite a sight to see with all of the colors. Devereux was caught up in the pageantry of it all, feeling the excitement build, until Lucy suddenly stiffened beside her.

She thought it rather odd that Lucy suddenly stopped talking and looked as if she had seen a ghost. She was looking over to her left where the general population was sitting. Devereux's brow furrowed with curiosity as she tried to follow Lucy's gaze to see what had the woman so rattled. She finally nudged her.

"What is the matter?" she asked. "Why do you look so?"

Lucy, realizing she was being watched, abruptly faced forward. "Nothing is the matter," she said unconvincingly. "I do believe the mêlée is about to start. Do you not want some refreshment before it begins?"

Devereux wasn't stupid; something had Lucy shaken and she peered around the woman's backside to see what she could see. All she saw were people everywhere; men, women and children all trying to get a good seat for the coming spectacle. She saw nothing out of the ordinary. She was about to turn away when a young women suddenly approached the edge of the box and began waving her hands frantically.

"Lucy!" the woman called. "Yoo hoo; *Luuuuuuuucy!*"

Lucy looked frozen with fear. Devereux, at a loss with the woman's behavior, nudged her again.

"That woman is trying to gain your attention," she pointed it out as if an obviously screaming woman wasn't enough. "Do you know her?"

Lucy looked sickened as she turned in the direction of the woman. Weakly, she smiled and waved, but that wasn't enough; suddenly, the woman was ducking under the barrier of the box. But she wasn't alone; as she stepped up onto the benches, she pulled two little girls along with her.

Devereux watched with curiosity until one of the little girls jumped up onto the steps in a very independent gesture and turned in Devereux's direction. Staring back at her were Davyss' features lodged within a tiny, beautiful face. And there was a second child who looked just like her. The longer Devereux stared at the girls, the more she gradually came to realize who they were.

The battering ram hit. The hammer dropped. Devereux suddenly couldn't breathe as she gazed at those two small little faces. *Dear God,* she thought to herself, *it cannot be.* But there was no mistake as the dark-haired, hazel-eyed twins drew near. As Devereux reeled with shock and Lucy tried not to panic, the woman came upon the pale pair with the lovely little girls in tow. She bent down and kissed Lucy on the cheek.

"I have been looking everywhere for you," the woman exclaimed. "I saw the de Winter tents and knew you would be around here somewhere. 'Tis good to see you again."

Lucy wished a hole would open up in the ground and swallow her up. "'Tis... 'tis good to see you too," she gulped. "Are... are you here with your father?"

The woman nodded. "He is competing in the joust," she said. "He says he will leave the mêlée to the younger men like Davyss and Hugh."

Lucy didn't dare look at Devereux as the woman suddenly fixed on her and smiled brightly.

"My lady," she greeted with a small curtsy. "I am the Lady Avarine du Bois. These are my daughters, the Lady Isabella and the Lady Angela."

Devereux stared up at the woman as if she had just spoken to her in tongues. It was difficult to process anything at the moment as she struggled to deal with her surprise. Avarine was a pretty woman with blue eyes and dark hair, and seemed genuinely friendly. As Devereux looked at her, all she could see was her husband making love to the woman and producing twins. It was selfish and foolish, she knew, but that was all she could see at the moment. Her sweet husband all over this woman's body, touching her and kissing her... it was enough to set her head to spinning.

"My lady," Devereux forced herself to respond.

But that was as far as she went. Avarine smiled and planted herself next to Lucy as Davyss' twins sat on the bench in front of Devereux and began pulling each other's hair. Avarine stilled the fighting hands as she turned to Lucy.

"It has been such a long time since we last saw one another," she said to Lucy. "I have seen Hugh and Philip, over by the tents. Is Davyss here?"

Lucy was quickly growing horrified. "Aye," she said in a strangled voice. Then she pointed in Devereux's direction. "This is...."

But she was too late; Avarine didn't hear the muddled start of the introduction to Davyss' wife and she spoke over Lucy's words. She was clearly wrapped up in her own world, her own excitement.

"He has not seen his girls since they were very small," Avarine said. "Do you not think he will be surprised? They have grown so much. They are so lovely and smart now, a perfect tribute to their father. I know he will be proud of them."

Lucy thought she might faint, trying to hush the woman discreetly but Avarine was oblivious. She rattled on.

"My father hopes to speak to Davyss again regarding marriage," she was gazing out over the arena, her blue-eyed gaze searching eagerly for the powerful form of Davyss de Winter. "I know that Davyss does not want to marry, but that was years ago. Perhaps he has changed his mind. It is only right that we marry, after all; we already have two children together. We would make a lovely family, don't you think? And I think a son next year in the image of his father would be wonderful."

Lucy grabbed the woman by the wrist, so hard that she clawed into Avarine's tender flesh. But she didn't still the woman's rattling mouth before Devereux shot to her feet and bolted from the box. Lucy let go of Avarine and began to run after her.

"Devereux!" she cried, tripping over a bench and falling to her knees. "Devereux, wait!"

Devereux heard Lucy's cries but she could not respond. She was verging on complete hysteria, listening to Avarine speak of Davyss and of the children they had together. It hurt so badly that she couldn't breathe. She was Davyss' wife but she had miscarried his child. Avarine had two children by Davyss and wanted more. It was Davyss' right to have more children like the beautiful twins.

Hearing the excitement in Avarine's voice as she spoke of Davyss drove dagger after dagger into Devereux's heart. She felt so worthless, so inadequate. She hated herself terribly at that moment.

Devereux jumped off the lists, hit the ground, and began running.

Seated in the royal box, Lady Katharine heard the shouting and turned in time to see Devereux disappear from the lists. She saw Lucy go after her but was prevented from paying closer attention by a strong hand on her arm.

"Was that Davyss' wife?" Simon asked.

Lady Katharine nodded, looking rather concerned that the woman had just bolted off. "It is," she replied.

"I only caught a swift glimpse of her, but she looks lovely."

"She is," she answered. "Davyss is very much in love with the girl. Perhaps I should go and see what the matter is."

Simon shook his head. "No need," he replied. "You cannot move as fast as she does and you will only hurt yourself, so it is best if you let your son handle his wife."

Lady Katharine shot Simon a menacing glare with her faded hazel eyes. "Watch your tongue, man. I may not be able to run swiftly but I can still use a dagger quite adequately."

Simon laughed softly. "You are still a firebrand after all of these years."

Lady Katharine lifted an eyebrow at him. "You think so?" she slapped the hand on her arm and he removed it, still laughing. "And you are still as I remember; selfish and bold."

Simon's humor faded as he beheld Katharine's angular profile. "Is that all you remember?" he asked softly.

Katharine refused be lured back to the days when she and Simon believed themselves in love with one another, when she was a young maiden and only pledged to Grayson de Winter. It was a futile romance but one that had burned hot at one time.

"I will not reminisce with you," she said flatly. "There is no need."

Simon knew that but it was still something he lived with, something he thought on every time he saw Davyss. "Did you ever tell him, Kate?" he murmured.

"Nay."

"Why not?"

"Because he is a de Winter. What purpose would it serve to tell him otherwise?"

Simon sighed faintly, knowing there was truth to her statement. He wouldn't push the issue, now thirty four years old and beyond any resolution. He averted his gaze, flicking imaginary pieces of dust off his breeches. "No purpose," he agreed quietly. "But someday, I should like him to know."

Katharine was in no mood for Simon's attempt at reflection. In fact, she wanted far away from the subject. "Finish what you were saying about my son and be quick about it," she told him. "He will be competing shortly and I want to watch."

Simon lifted his eyes, regarding the woman's profile again. She was such a strong woman, deeply dedicated to her sons. He knew why she had never told Davyss of his true parentage but it never eased his ache. And it was for that very reason that Simon knew he must press his issue.

"Davyss was most reluctant to swear fealty to me after Lewes," he lowered his voice. "As I said, I believe the only reason he did it was because I threatened to hold his wife hostage to ensure his good behavior. As much as I hate to move against Davyss in such ways, I still feel it is necessary."

Katharine's jaw ticked. "So you do not trust his word?"

Simon was careful how he replied. "I would trust Davyss with my life, as you well know. But the man's loyalties have always been with Henry. Even though he has sworn allegiance to me, I feel there is no harm in reinforcing that oath. Since the only reason he swore to support me was because I threatened his wife, I feel it necessary to force him to honor his pledge."

Lady Katharine sighed heavily. "Simon, if you feel the only control you have over your men is to coerce and threaten them, then you are a poor leader indeed. If you take Devereux, it will only make Davyss hatefully mad. He will kill you."

Simon's gaze moved over the arena, watching as the marshals began to call the combatants forward. "Nay, he will not," he muttered. "But he will want to, make no mistake. Katharine, do you wish to see your son live to be an old man? He'll not live much longer by Henry or Edward's side. They are both ruthless men and willing to battle at every turn. What I offer is peace."

"Peace?" she snapped.

"Aye, peace," he snapped in return. "Peace for the entire country because the common man will have a say in how his country is managed. It is the only way to achieve harmony."

Katharine held up a hand. "Spare me your logic, Simon. I am an old woman and care not for the politics of the crown. But I will say this," she turned to the man. "If you harm Davyss or his wife, in any fashion, my wrath shall be limitless. You need not fear Davyss at all; your biggest fear shall be me. Is this in any way unclear?"

Simon gazed deep into the eyes of the women he had known the majority of his adult life. "What would Grayson say to all of this?"

Her eyes narrowed. "You know what he would say; he would kill you himself before he allowed you to target one of his sons."

Simon drew in a long, thoughtful breath. Then he leaned back in his chair, eventually chuckling.

"Still a spitfire," he muttered.

Lady Katharine continued to eye him, even as he pretended to find interest in the combatants taking the field. She didn't trust the man for she had known him too long; he would eventually have his way if he thought he could get away with it. When Simon started up a conversation about the last tournament he competed in, she paid little attention. There was something in his manner that was unsettling.

She didn't like it.

CB

THE MÊLÉE WAS about to begin. Davyss was poised with his team, comprised of his own knights, Northumberland's men, men from Chester, York and Nottingham. There were also a few bachelor knights, men with less experience but full of heart, and they were thrilled to be included on the mighty de Winter squad. The field marshals were calling the teams onto the arena floor and just as Davyss moved forward with his men to take his position, Philip suddenly came up behind him and grabbed him by the arm.

Davyss turned to the man, speaking before Philip could bring any words forth.

"Where have you been?" he demanded. "You disappeared when the marshals were filling the match cards. What happened?"

Philip looked grim. "Lucy came to me," he said urgently. "Drop what you are doing, man; we have problems."

Davyss first reaction was confusion. But his second reaction was dread; Philip was not one to panic for frivolous reasons. "What are you talking about?" he demanded.

Philip yanked on him even as the men around him were pouring onto the field. Hugh paused, however, standing next to his brother because Philip looked so serious. He raised his visor and peered at the big blonde knight.

"What is wrong with you?" Hugh demanded. "We are due on the field."

Philip shook his head. "Davyss, you must come. It's Devereux."

Those were the magic words. Davyss was already moving, heading for the lists because that was the last place he saw his wife. "What is wrong? What happened?"

As they neared the edge of the arena, they could all see Lucy standing at the edge of the field, her hands to her mouth. As Davyss drew near, he could see that her eyes were red and there were tears on her face. Panic seized him.

"Lucy?" he reached out to grab her. "Where is Devereux? What has happened?"

Lucy was sobbing deeply. "She... she ran away."

Davyss' eyebrows flew up. "Ran away?" he repeated. "Where in the hell is she?"

He was starting to get frantic. Philip pulled his wife from Davyss' iron grip because the woman was already close to swooning. She would not survive Davyss' anger.

"We do not know," he said in a low, swift voice. "Lucy says that Lady Avarine appeared in the list with the twins. She apparently did not know or realize who Devereux was and said many things that upset her. Devereux ran off."

Davyss stared at Philip in complete, utter disbelief. "Avarine is *here*?"

Philip nodded grimly. "With the girls," he replied. "You will recall that she and Lucy were friends long before Avarine met you. Avarine saw Lucy in the lists and naturally went to her."

Davyss' gaze was wide on the man. He wasn't angry; he looked completely devastated. "My dear God," he finally breathed, clapping a hand to his face in incredulity. His mind was whirling with a million different thoughts, easily overwhelming him. He began to walk. "Which direction did Devereux go, Lucy?"

Lucy was walking beside her husband, struggling to keep up with the long-legged men. "I do not know," she wept. "I saw her disappear in the direction of the food vendors but I did not see where she went after that."

Davyss felt sick. "What... what did Avarine say to her?"

Lucy sniffled as Philip pulled her along. "She spoke of the twins," she replied. "She said that her father was competing and he was going to speak to you again about marrying his daughter because you are the father of her children."

Davyss rolled his eyes miserably. "And she said all of this in front of Devereux?"

"Aye," Lucy started to weep again. "She did not know that Devereux was your wife."

Davyss didn't say anymore. He was afraid to. He could hear the marshals yelling for him but he ignored them, instead marching to his tents with his men in tow. He yanked open the entry to the larger tent but it was empty. Andrew and Philip checked the other two; they were empty as well. Fear welled in Davyss' chest until he could hardly think straight.

"Where else could she go?" he asked the general question to those around him. "She is not familiar with London. Where else could she have run off to?"

Andrew was with him. "I shall go to Hollyhock and see if she has returned there."

Davyss stopped him. "Nay," he half-hissed, half-commanded. "I will go. You, Edmund and Philip return to the arena. I will search for my wife."

Andrew's brow furrowed. "But you may need help. If she is not at Hollyhock, there is no telling where she has gone and you will need help looking for her."

Davyss knew that, but he was so shaken at the moment that it was difficult for him to settle his thoughts. "If she is not at Hollyhock, I will send you word," he slapped the man on the shoulder as Hugh bellowed for Davyss' mount. "Go, now. I will return when I can."

Although Andrew wasn't entirely certain, he did as he was told. A groom brought about Davyss' charger and he mounted, charging from the encampments and out into the streets beyond.

CB

SHE WAS STANDING by the river's edge as it banked along the border of Hollyhock, watching the waters of the Thames flow gently along. Birds cried overhead and the clouds intermittently blocked out the sun. She stood there, staring at the water, wondering if she was strong enough to throw herself in simply to rid herself of the pain in her heart.

She had run the mile or so from the tournament field back to Hollyhock. It had been foolish to run away; she knew that. But she had a habit of running from situations that went beyond her control. When her emotions were raging, there was no telling how far she would run. She had tried to run when Davyss' men first came to escort her to her wedding, she had run when Davyss and his men had gotten into the fight at the Fist and Tankard, and she had run again when the woman who bore Davyss children had come around. She was always running. Sometimes she just had to.

She could hear the distant cheers from the crowds at the tournament arena. She knew that the mêlée must be well under way and she was sure that Davyss and his men were winning. With a heavy sigh, she knew that she needed to return to the field before the mêlée ended so that Davyss would not know that she had run off again. But she could hear Avarine's words over and over in her head, like a battering ram, pounding the meaning and pain of the situation deep into her heart. Still, she would have to reconcile herself eventually. Davyss had other children. She had given him none.

With another sigh, she turned away from the river. But there was a body directly behind her and she gasped with fright, startled to see Davyss standing a few feet away. She had never heard him approach.

Devereux gazed into his beautiful hazel eyes, looking so forlornly back at her. She didn't know what to say, feeling flushed and startled by his appearance. She realized that Lucy must have told him what had happened and, like any good husband, he went to search for her. No matter where she went, he always found her. She opened her mouth to say something but the words wouldn't come. The sobs, however, did.

She burst into tears and threw herself against him. Davyss wrapped his arms around her tightly, feeling his own eyes sting with tears. There were layers of mail, armor and tunics between them, but Davyss could not have felt closer to the woman than he did at that moment. His relief, his sorrow, was indescribable.

"I am so sorry," he murmured into the top of her head. "Dear God, if I could take back everything in my life that would even remotely bring you shame, I would do it gladly. I cannot apologize enough for your shame and hurt."

She continued to weep, painfully deep, as he rocked her gently. "I... I am sorry I ran," she sobbed. "I just did not... I could not... what she said. She was so happy, so thrilled to have borne your children and she wants to be a family with you."

He suddenly grasped her by the face, forcing her to look at him. The glow from the hazel eyes was powerful.

"But I do not want to be a family with her," he shook her gently to punctuate his words. "How many times must I explain this to you, Devereux? It is you that I love and adore, children or no. The day I married you, all other women in the world ceased to exist for me. There will be times when women like Avarine speak of me, for whatever reason, and you must tell yourself that whatever they speak of is all in the past. I would never stray from you and I do not hold feelings for anyone but you. How in the world can I prove this to you? Please tell me, for I do not like seeing you in pain like this. Please help me understand what I can do to convince you that you are the only woman I will ever love."

By the time he finished his speech, her sobs had calmed. She gazed back at him, with an occasional hiccup, wiping her cheeks and nose with the pretty red satin handkerchief she had intended to give to her husband as a favor in the joust. After several moments of digesting his words, she finally shook her head.

"I know you love me and I know you will not stray," she whispered. "It had nothing to do with that. After what happened with our child, seeing the beautiful girls you had fathered simply made me long for our baby. I want so much to be a good wife and to provide you with children. Seeing those girls... it simply reminded me of what we had lost."

He pursed his lips sadly, kissed her, and pulled her back into a fierce embrace. "I understand," he answered. "But you are not to blame for the loss. It was simply God's will. There will be more children for us;

I am sure of it. You must have faith."

"I am trying."

"Besides… the fun is in the practice."

It took her a moment to realize what he said and she gasped softly in feeble outrage, swatting his mailed behind. Davyss laughed low in his throat.

"I cannot feel anything with all of this armor on," he told her.

She made a face at him. "You are a vulgar beast."

"A vulgar beast?" he repeated, his eyebrows lifting. "Since when is a man who lusts after his wife a vulgar beast?"

She shook her head, unwilling to answer, and he grinned as he pulled her into his arms once again and kissed her. He was simply glad that her tears were easing. He buried his face in the top of her head for a moment, relishing the feel of her, so glad he had found her safe and unharmed. The woman had become his whole damn world.

"Will you promise me something?" he requested.

She nodded, head against his chest and arms around his waist. "Of course."

"No more running off. It scares the wits from me."

She sighed faintly. "For that, I am sorry. It seems to be my reaction when situations become overwhelming. But I promise I will not do it again."

"If you do run off, at least run to me and not away from me."

"I will."

"Thank you." He kissed the top of her head and pulled back to look at her. "Can we return to the field? I would like to provide you with a deliciously fattening meal before my competition this afternoon."

She smiled unenthusiastically. "As you wish."

With an encouraging smile, he walked her back over to where he had tethered his charger by the gates of Hollyhock. Mounting her on his charger, he vaulted on behind her, holding her close, and took the long way back to the tournament field.

CHAPTER NINETEEN

D AVYSS AND DEVEREUX returned to the tournament arena in time to see the last of the mêlée. They found a spot by the south side of the field and remained on the charger for a better vantage point.

The scene spread out before them could only be called a mess; the combatants were not allowed to fight with real weapons; hence, all they had were wooden clubs and wooden swords, so they were essentially beating one other. There was a good deal of blood and bruising, but no one was seriously injured. The rules stated that once a man was down, he had to stay down. Consequently, the arena floor was littered with men sitting on their bum, watching what was happening and cheering their teammates on.

Devereux had to admit that it was rather like watching little boys run amuck. Out of Davyss' men, the only one down was young Edmund and he was clearly unhappy about it. Andrew, Hugh and Philip were still in the running, clubbing men, tripping them, or shoving them around. Devereux looked at Davyss and they grinned at each other, humored by the spectacle. Somewhere in the fighting, Hugh spied his brother and waved to him, making his way to the edge of the arena and nearly getting pushed over in the process. But Hugh was fast and made it through the masses unscathed.

Davyss dismounted the charger, tethered it, and made his way over to the edge of the field to meet his brother. But as he approached him, someone came up behind Hugh and clubbed him brutally between the shoulder blades. As Hugh staggered, Davyss leapt over the railing and began pounding the knight with his massive fists. Within the first three blows, the man fell to his knees and the club fell from his hand. Davyss picked up the club and brained the man over the helm. The knight fell to the ground, knocked cold.

Hugh was grinning when he finally regained his balance and stood next his brother, surveying the fallen knight. Davyss returned his brother's grin before looking over at his wife, who was still astride the charger and looking rather shocked. He waved at her and she swallowed her shock at what he had just done, finally shaking her head in disapproval. It was all of the encouragement that Davyss needed to jump back into the fracas feet-first. Devereux watched him with a reluctant smile on her face.

Other than pound his brother, Devereux had never seen Davyss fight and it was truly a sight to behold. The man was extremely powerful, dropping men right and left with his heavy blows. He was also very agile, dodging men who would come at him and then turning the tables on them and sending them to the ground. As Devereux watched with a proud smile on her face, a soft voice interrupted her thoughts.

"Lady de Winter?"

She turned to see a knight standing behind her, big and strong. He was very well dressed in expensive mail and protection. She nodded without a second thought. "Aye," she said politely. "May I help you?"

The knight bowed crisply. "Lord de Montfort has requested to meet you. Would you accompany me, my lady?"

Devereux slid off the charger and into the man's upstretched hands. As she straightened her surcoat, the knight extended an elbow but she hesitated.

"My husband is nearly finished with the mêlée," she said. "Should we wait for him?"

The knight shook his head. "Lord Simon has already met your husband," he said, rather lightly. "He would like to meet you."

Devereux passed a glance at her husband as he pummeled some hapless fool who had challenged him. It made her grin. With a shrug, she took the knight's offered elbow and followed him.

Since she had seen Simon in the lists earlier, she was not surprised when the knight took her to the royal box. Simon de Montfort was seated in an elaborate wooden chair, rising to his feet when he saw Devereux approach on the arm of the unknown knight. Devereux mounted the steps to the box, dropping into a neat curtsy.

"Lady de Winter, my lord," the knight announced.

Simon's yellowed eyes inspected every curve, every line, as he stared at her. He'd only caught a fleeting glimpse earlier and had no idea what a beauty Lady de Winter was. As the sounds of the mêlée began to fade as the event drew to a conclusion, Simon indicated for Devereux to sit next to him, which she did. She faced him expectantly as he continued to study her.

"I had heard rumors of your beauty," he said. "I can see that they were not exaggerated."

She smiled modestly. "Thank you, my lord."

"Has your husband told you of me?"

She blinked, not sure of the answer he was looking for. "He told me that he is your godson, my lord."

Simon nodded, deciding his next line of questioning. He was interested in this woman who had captured Davyss' arrogant heart.

"I am told you are from Norfolk," he said. "Lady Katharine de Winter has told me of your charity. 'Tis noble work, my lady, and uncommon for a woman of your breeding to attend."

At that moment, Devereux could see something of her father in Simon de Montfort; arrogant, possibly judgmental. Simply the way he asked the question put her somewhat on her guard.

"My mother started the charity, my lord," she replied evenly. "I am happy to attend to the needs of the poor."

Simon waved a hand at her. "I did not mean to sound critical, my lady," he sensed he had offended her. "I only meant that most noble women do not tend to the needy as you do. Sometimes it is best to leave the needy to those better suited to that lifestyle, like the clergy. You give a great deal of yourself and that is an uncommon trait."

Devereux wasn't quite sure how to respond. "T-Thank you, my

lord."

Simon's intense gaze returned. "What does your husband think about your charity?"

"He has generously supported it, my lord."

"That is surprising."

She stared at him, once again struck by the man's arrogance. In fact, it was beginning to infuriate her. "Nay, it is not," she deliberately left out "my lord". "He is extremely generous and understanding of my charity."

She sounded angry and Simon sat straight in his chair. "I meant no offense, Lady de Winter," he insisted. "It is simply that I have known Davyss for a great many years and he is not the generous or unselfish type."

Devereux was beginning to boil. "Did you summon me simply to speak ill of my husband?" she asked. "I can assure you that you do not know my husband if you believe him selfish or ungenerous. He is the kindest, most compassionate and understanding man I have ever met and I will not permit you to disparage him. And you? Do you not care for those in need? I was under the impression that you cared for all of England, not simply the rich or noble."

Simon could see he had a situation on his hands and he moved quickly to ease it. "My lady," he said steadily, "I assure you that I would never disparage Davyss. I love him as my son. And in answer to your question, I do indeed care for those in need. I believe I have proved that with my actions and deeds."

Devereux eyed him, sensing that de Montfort was not at all the man she thought he was. She could just tell by his manners, the way he spoke. She shook her head and faced the arena where the combatants were starting to trickle out.

"Are you a man of the people, my lord?" she finally asked.

"I would like to think so."

"But if your own daughter was to immerse herself in charity work, you would disapprove?"

He drew in a long, deep breath, knowing this was a tricky question. He was coming to see how Lady de Winter's mind worked and he was quite impressed. "I would encourage my daughters to be generous with charity."

"But you would not encourage them to wipe up after an ill peasant or spoon feed a dying woman, is that it?"

His yellowed eyes twinkled at her. "This is a battle I cannot win with you, my lady. You and I have differing opinions on the matter."

Devereux looked away, seeing her husband at the far end of the arena speaking with the field marshals. She thought back to when they first met and how she had brow-beat him over an arrogant king and a saintly de Montfort. Lady Katharine had accused her of being ignorant and it was obvious she was; she had gone on rumor and what others had told her more than actually experience or personal knowledge. She was coming to feel like a fool.

"I always believed that the Earl of Leicester was a man of the people," she turned to look at him. "I believed that the king was a tyrant and that you had the good of all men in mind. I see now that perhaps I was mistaken."

Simon's lips twitched with a smile. "You were not mistaken, Lady de Winter," he assured her softly. "But this is a conversation I should like to continue with you away from this field. Shall we return to the Tower?"

Devereux shook her head. "Thank you, but I must decline. My husband has promised me a fattening meal and I do not want to miss his joust match."

Even as she said the words, the unnamed knight was taking her gently by the elbow and pulling her to her feet. Simon rose as well, gesturing to the knight that now had a firm grip on her.

"This is Sir Darien de Russe," he introduced the pair. "He will be your escort to the Tower. I shall follow shortly and we may continue this conversation."

Devereux looked at the knight and tried to tug her arm away. "As I said, I do not wish to go," she said, firmer. "I must go to my husband now. The battle is over and he will be hungry. Perhaps we may speak later if it pleases you."

The knight didn't let go. He began to pull, soon putting two hands on her. Frightened, Devereux suddenly turned into a wildcat.

"Release me," she demanded, slapping at his hands. "Let me go!"

Simon continued to smile, waving the knight on as if completely ignoring her demands. Devereux, terrified at being taken against her will, balled a fist and swung with all her might at the knight's face. She caught him in the nose, causing him to release his grip enough for her to pull away. She darted in the opposite direction.

"Davyss!" she screamed. "*Davyss!*"

Devereux dodged to the edge of the royal box and flipped herself over the rail, landing in the dust about eight feet below. She wasn't hurt and bolted to her feet just as Darien hit the dirt beside her. She scrambled away from the man as he made a swipe for her, screaming her husband's name as she ran.

She was creating quite a scene. Those still in the lists after the end of the mêlée strained to get a better view of what was going on. All they could see was a lovely woman running from a big knight. Devereux eventually found an opening in the railing that lined the arena floor and she bolted through it with Darien in pursuit.

The moment she began running across the dusty arena floor, however, she could see Davyss charging in her direction. She was fully prepared to throw herself into his arms but he rushed right by her. When she came to an unsteady halt and turned around, she could see that he had gone after Darien. Davyss tackled the knight so hard that they both went hurling to the ground, sliding several feet through the dust before coming to a stop. Fists began to fly and as Devereux shrieked in fear, Hugh and Andrew suddenly bolted past her. They all went down on Davyss and Darien and the crowd erupted happily as a massive brawl escalated.

Devereux stood with her hands to her mouth, her eyes wide with shock as she watched a huge dust cloud fly up around the clashing men. A gentle hand suddenly took her by the elbow and she shrieked again until she saw that it was Edmund Catesby.

His young face was wide with concern. "Are you well, my lady?" he asked her. "What happened?"

Devereux didn't even know what to say; what *had* happened? She began to stammer. "I… I do not know what happened," she grasped for words. "One moment, I was speaking with Lord Simon and in the next, he was ordering his knight to return me to the Tower. I told him I did not want to go but he would not listen. He tried to force me."

More men were charging on to the field as de Winter and his men lost themselves in combat against a lone knight. A few of de Montfort's men tried to intervene and suddenly, a four man brawl turned into a multi-man scuffle. Men were rushing in from all angles of the field and soon, the swords came out. Field marshals began to rush to the fighting mass, pulling men apart and trying to calm the situation. And at the very heart of it was Davyss.

Devereux could see clearly when the sea of men cleared and he pushed himself off the ground. De Russe was underneath him and not moving. As Davyss turned around and began to walk back to his wife, Hugh decked one of de Montfort's knights and the fight started all over again. But Davyss removed himself from it; he was only concerned with his wife at the moment.

He came upon her, reaching out to grasp her by the arms. He was dirty and dusty and had a cut on his lip, but was unharmed for the most part. The hazel eyes were potent.

"What happened, sweetling?" he half-demanded, half-pleaded. "Why was de Russe chasing you?"

Devereux had been rather brave up until that moment. Suddenly realizing she was safe, she struggled to blink away the tears. "Lord Simon summoned me," she told him. "We were speaking and suddenly he ordered that knight to take me back to the Tower. I told him that I did not want to go but he would not listen. He began to drag me away and I became scared. I ran from him."

Davyss listened to her explanation, an ominous feeling of dread coming over him. "He tried to abduct you?"

She shrugged her slender shoulders. "I do not know, exactly. All I know was that I told him I did not want to go to the Tower and he tried to force me."

Davyss' nostrils flared, never a good sign. He put his arm around her shoulders and began to lead her out of the arena. As Devereux clutched him tightly and struggled not to cry, Davyss issued orders to Edmund who was walking next to her. The young knight acknowledged Davyss' directives and departed. In silence, Davyss led his wife all the way back to his still-tethered charger.

He still didn't say a word as he untied the animal and began to lead it, and Devereux, back to his tents. She continued to cling to him, refusing to let him go until he gently coaxed her to sit. As his wife sat in gloomy silence, sniffling intermittently, he began to remove is armor. She had been looking at her lap until she heard the mail hood hit the ground. Then she looked up at him, startled.

"What are you doing?" she asked.

Davyss was focused on removing his protection. "Undressing," he told her. "We are returning to Hollyhock."

She felt somewhat guilty. "But you have been looking forward to this," she said, watching him pull off his gloves. "I pulled you away from the mêlée and you have not even jousted yet. I will have ruined your entire day."

He suddenly stopped, an odd twinkle in his eye. "Is that what you think?" he asked her. "That you have ruined my day?"

She half-nodded, half-shrugged, looking extremely guilty and he went to her, cupping her chin in his big hand and forcing her to look up at him.

"Sweetling, you have not ruined anything," he assured her softly. "I do not like that Simon tried to take you against your will. The next time, you might not be so fortunate to get away. I intend to have serious words with the man this evening but, for now, I wish to return home."

In truth, Devereux was somewhat disappointed. She wanted to see him joust in spite of her fears, for what she had seen of her husband's fighting abilities during that day had greatly impressed her. He was rather exciting to watch. But she couldn't disagree with his assessment of her encounter with Simon.

"Where is your mother?" she asked as he removed his tunic. "I did not see her or Lucy in the lists when I was speaking with Simon."

Davyss tossed the gray and black tunic to the floor. "Philip took them both back to Hollyhock," he told her. "It seems that neither one of them were feeling particularly well."

"Oh," Devereux said quietly, watching him struggle with the mail coat. "Can I assist you with that?"

Davyss bent over at the waist and extended his arms to her. Devereux stood up from the stool, took hold of the mail on his arms, and pulled with all her might. The coat inched off and she yanked again, this time ended up on her bum as the coat abruptly slipped free. She laughed as Davyss reached down and pulled her back to her feet.

"The object is to brace yourself when you pull," he told her. "Do not throw all of your weight behind it or you will shoot through the wall next time."

She shrugged with a grin. "I do not have much experience with helping knights dress."

His eyes narrowed, though it was without force. "Well and good that you do not, lady."

She smiled at him as he proceeded to remove the rest of his protection himself. Devereux reclaimed her stool and sat, watching him as he stripped down to his padded tunic and breeches. One of the de Winter squires entered the tent and began collecting the armor and mail, taking it away to be cleaned.

Davyss stood there with his hands on his hips, gazing into space thoughtfully as the squire worked around him. Devereux also sat quietly, her hands fidgeting in her lap, uncertain of her husband's mood. In spite of what he said about not ruining his day, she still felt badly about it.

"Do you really believe that Lord Simon was attempting to abduct me?" she asked quietly.

He was still lost in thought, jolted from his trance by the sound of her voice. He shifted on his big legs, joints popping as he moved to her.

"I cannot be completely sure that it was not his intent," he said quietly. "In any case, it concerns me."

Devereux was watching him intently. "But you said that the entire reason behind pledging to Simon was so he would not try to take me hostage to ensure your good behavior."

He nodded, looking rather disgusted with the entire thing. "That is exactly why I did what I did," he rubbed his chin thoughtfully. "But if Simon intends to try and abduct you regardless, then it would make sense to get you as far away from London as possible and locked up safe."

She drew in a long, deep breath and looked at her hands again. "Where will you take me?"

He began rolling up his sleeves. "Hollyhock and Wintercroft are out of the question," he answered. "They are too easily breached with a large army. They are fortified manors and not meant for heavy combat. Castle Acre Castle or Breckland would be acceptable, but you do not like Castle Acre Castle and my mother would disown me if Breckland was compromised. And Threxton is too small."

She looked up from her hands. "Then there is nowhere to go?"

He heard distress in her voice and took a knee beside her, taking her soft hands into his enormous calloused ones. "Of course there is," he stroked her blonde head. "I shall take you to Norwich and heavily fortify it."

She gazed steadily at him. "And you? Where will you go and what will you do?"

He kissed her on the forehead and stood up. "I will do what is necessary."

It was a vague answer but she didn't press him. As she stood up and smoothed her lovely surcoat, the one that she had been so proud of bearing the de Winter colors, Andrew suddenly stuck his head into the tent.

The man's dark blue eyes lingered on Devereux a moment before moving to Davyss. He had an odd look on his face.

"Davyss," he cleared his throat. "May… may I have a word with you?"

Davyss turned to look at him as he stripped off his padded tunic. "What about?"

"Outside, please."

Davyss didn't give a second thought to the man's tone or request. He tossed the padded tunic to the ground and pulled a clean lighter-weight, egg-colored tunic from a small traveling trunk. He pulled it over his head as he walked to the tent flap.

"I shall return shortly," he told Devereux. "Do not leave this tent."

She shook her head and sat back down on the stool. "I will not," she assured him. "May we eat when you are finished with Andrew?"

He grunted. "Of course," he said as if he had completely forgotten he had promised her a fattening meal. "I apologize. I will have food sent to you and then we shall leave for Hollyhock."

She smiled her thanks and he winked at her, quitting the tent. As he followed Andrew and fumbled with his clean tunic, he failed to see a woman and two small girls standing a few feet away. He was busy pulling on the sleeves and adjusting the collar. When he finally lifted his eyes and saw Avarine, he stopped dead in his tracks.

Avarine smiled radiantly at him. In each hand, she held a small girl, both of whom looked back at Davyss with varied degrees of curiosity and boredom. Davyss struggled to recover his shock as he resumed walking, moving more slowly as he approached. When he was a few feet away, he stopped completely.

"Avarine," he didn't know what else to say. "It has been a long time."

Avarine was overjoyed to see him. "Davyss," she breathed the name as if it were the most beautiful thing in the world. "I saw you in the mêlée. You were wonderful."

Davyss nodded faintly as if to thank her, or possibly agree with her, looking to Andrew and silently pleading for the man's help. But Andrew imperceptibly shook his head; *what would you have me do?* Other than create a diversion so he could run away, Davyss wasn't sure. He was trapped. He took a deep breath and squared his shoulders.

"You are looking well," he said, finally looking to the identical girls beside her. He felt his heart soften in spite of his shock. "I cannot believe how much they have grown. Last I saw them, they were barely walking."

Avarine was bursting with pride. "Aren't they beautiful?" she cooed, looking to each girl. "They look so much like you. And they act like you, too; they are very brave and strong."

Davyss nodded his head, watching one of the twins stick her finger up her nose. That brought a chuckle. "They are most definitely a de Winter," he agreed. "I see much of my father in them."

Avarine smiled broadly. "Can you spare a moment to speak with them?" she asked. "I would like for them to know their father."

Davyss looked at the woman, seeing so much more in her expression than mere talk; that had been the trouble with Avarine. She already had them married the moment she first met him and the birth of the children only compounded the problem. She should have been absolutely ashamed that she had borne children out of wedlock, but instead, she waved it around like a banner. He'd spent years avoiding her missives and demands from her father, but at this moment, he could not escape her. He should have known she would be in attendance at the tournament, watching and waiting for her moment to speak with him. Davyss always attended the high-profile tournaments. He felt like the spider cornered by the fly.

"Is that truly all you wish, Avarine?" he asked, a hint of impatience in his tone. "Simply for me to speak with the girls?"

She tried to look innocent but couldn't quite manage it. "It is right that they come to know you," she batted her eyelashes at him. "And… and I thought that you and I could speak as well. There is much to say."

"I have said all I am ever going to say to you," he said, trying not to be unkind. "There is nothing more I wish to speak of."

A disappointed expression crossed her face. "But… time has passed, Davyss, and still I have not wed. The girls need their father. I was hoping we might speak… well, speak on such things. Our future, perhaps?"

Davyss opened his mouth to reply but he caught movement out of the corner of his eye. A soft hand slipped into his palm, holding it tightly. Startled, he turned to see Devereux standing next to him.

She was focused on Avarine, her beautiful face surprisingly calm. Davyss wondered how much of their conversation she had heard. Before he could say a word to her, Devereux spoke.

"I am sorry that we were not property introduced earlier in the lists," she said to Avarine. "There was much happening at the time and I am afraid I was a bit distracted. I am the Lady Devereux de Winter, Davyss' wife."

Avarine's smile vanished as Devereux's word sank in. Her eyes bugged and her face took on a sickly color.

"W-wife?" she repeated, dumbfounded. "But… but I did not know…that is to say, I had not heard that Davyss took a wife."

Devereux smiled up at her rather stricken-looking husband. "He did indeed," she said, returning her attention to Avarine and the girls. "We were married two months ago."

Avarine suddenly looked as if she was about to cry. She turned her attention to Davyss, her eyes wide and accusing.

"But…," she stammered. "You told my father you did not want to marry. You told him that you would never marry!"

He was calm. "At the time, it was true. But time has a tendency to change one's outlook."

Avarine went from sickly pale to brilliant red. "But I bore your children," she spat. "If anyone should have been given marital consideration, it should have been me. Why did you not call for me? *Why not me?*"

Her voice was growing loud and the little girls looked up at their mother, frightened by the tone of her voice. Before Davyss could reply, Devereux suddenly stepped forward and grabbed the woman by the arms.

"Still yourself, lady," she hissed. "Look at your children; look how frightened you have made them with your screaming. If you have been pining over Davyss for the past five years, then that is your misfortune; he was never yours to begin with. So still your crying voice and get ahold of yourself, because what you wish for can never be and the sooner you understand that, the better for you and your children."

It all came out as a rapid-fire, lowly spoken tirade. Avarine stared at Devereux with shock, her mouth working as the girls on either side of her tugged and whined. But Avarine ignored the girls; she seemed to having great difficulty breathing as her chest heaved.

"But...," she gasped. "But we have children together and...."

Devereux cut her off. "Any whore can give a man children," she snapped. "It does not endear you to him any more than any other woman he has bedded. Did you think you were special? Are you truly so stupid? Your children are beautiful and he will, of course, see to their needs, but my advice to you is to grow up and move on with your life. There are other men out there who would be honored to marry a woman of your beauty. But think no more on Davyss de Winter, for he is married and out of your reach."

Avarine took a step back; she had to. Devereux's words slammed into her like blows from a mighty fist. She began blinking back tears as she thought on the brutally frank words that Lady de Winter had so honestly delivered. It was harsh but true.

"My God," Avarine suddenly hung her head, closing her eyes tightly. "I am so ashamed."

Devereux wasn't without sympathy; she had, after all, what the woman wanted. She put her hand on her shoulder briefly. "No need," she whispered. "We have all had our moments of foolishness and weakness."

Avarine simply hung her head. With a lingering glance at the woman, Devereux turned around and headed back for Davyss' tent.

"I shall await you inside, sweetheart," she said, head held high. "Take whatever time you need."

Davyss watched her go, fighting off a grin of such astonishment and pride that it was difficult for him to conceal. He was constantly amazed by the caliber of the woman he had married, so much love for her in his heart that he couldn't begin to describe it. As she disappeared into the distant tent, he turned back to Avarine, who was still rooted to the spot with a somewhat dazed expression.

Davyss took some pity on her; after all, she had just received a fairly impressive tongue lashing, truthful though it might have been. With a faint sigh, he moved to within a few feet of her and knelt down, focused on the little girls.

Two pairs of hazel eyes gazed back at him, curiously, and he smiled. "Who is Isabella and who is Angela?" he asked gently.

The little girls looked confused a moment before timidly pointing at each other. Davyss laughed softly lowered himself to the cool green grass, getting comfortable.

"That did not help me in the least," he told them. "Let me try again. Who is Isabella?"

One twin pointed to the other. Davyss' smile grew and he held out a hand to the little girl. "Isabella, would you like to sit with me?"

Isabella took a timid step forward but Angela was faster.

"I want to sit!" she announced, plopping onto her bum.

Davyss nodded with approval. "Thank you, my lady," he said sincerely. "I do not like to sit alone."

Isabella fell to her knees, grinning at him when he looked at her. Then she inched forward. Angela, seeing that her sister was moving closer to the enormous man, inched forward also. Isabella suddenly launched herself into Davyss' lap and he grunted as the child hit him in the chest and groin.

The girls giggled as he groaned. Davyss ruffled the hair of the child in his lap, thinking they were indeed lovely little girls. It made him think of the child Devereux had lost and he felt a brief stab for the loss, but nothing more. He hadn't really thought about a family with many children until this very moment, but with two little girls sitting on his lap, he realized he could come to like it very much.

Devereux peered from a crack in the closed tent flap, watching the interaction between Davyss and his girls. It made her heart swell to see him speaking to the children, his manner gentle and warm. She smiled as she watched the child in his lap pop up and accidentally ram him in the chin. When he fell over, mortally wounded, the girls pounced on him with squeals and Devereux laughed softly at the sight. He was going to make a wonderful father to their own children and suddenly, she wasn't so terribly hurt over their loss. Watching Davyss with his girls oddly eased her. She was confident there would be others, just as he was, and very much looking forward to it.

Thoughts of hazel-eyed children were her last coherent idea before the world turned painfully, abruptly black.

CHAPTER TWENTY

DAVYSS DIDN'T WAIT to be admitted entrance. He charged into the king's solar in the White Tower, ramming aside a knight who had been foolish enough to try and stop him. *Lespada* was flashing wickedly in his hand and he gored the next man who came at him right in the chest. The ancient blade of the de Winter male line dripped with blood.

People were screaming and running as Davyss, followed by Hugh, Andrew and Philip, charged into the room and slashed anyone who got in their way. At the other end of the chamber sat Simon, calmly watching his godson wreak havoc. He had been expecting this moment and was prepared. As Davyss approached him, sword aloft, Simon merely lifted an eyebrow at him.

"If you kill me, you shall never know where she has gone," he told him.

Davyss was indeed mad enough to kill; he had killed at least three men who had tried to bar him from the Tower and injured countless others. Dressed to the hilt in complete battle armor, he was formidable and terrifying. It was de Winter at his worst. He came to an unsteady halt several feet from de Montfort, flipping up his visor to display blazing hazel eyes.

"Where in the hell is she?" he boomed.

Simon glanced behind his godson, seeing the carnage and destruction left in his wake. Servants were dragging away the dead knight and others were helping the wounded. He could hear people weeping and groaning. He sighed heavily and refocused on Davyss.

"She is perfectly safe and unharmed," he told him evenly. "She will be my honored guest for a time. I insist."

Davyss' jaw ticked violently. "Give her back to me or I will tear this place apart."

"Tear it apart and you will never see her again."

Davyss' jaw stopped ticking and his hazel eyes widened. "Why?" he demanded, sounding more like a plea. "What in God's name have I done that you would do this to me? I gave you what you wanted; I swore my fealty. Why would you take my wife?"

There were several armed knights in the room, men that had rushed in to protect de Montfort from Davyss' rage. But Simon sent those men away with the flick of his wrist, unafraid of Davyss' wrath. He knew his godson was hot headed and rash, but he wasn't foolish. He knew that *Lespada* would not end his life.

"Send your men away, Davyss," Simon said quietly. "I will speak only with you."

Davyss turned to the heavily armed men behind them, sending them off with a nod of his head. They followed the path they had taken when they had entered, leaving the room in disarray and chaos. When the last of the injured had been removed and Hugh quietly shut the door, Davyss turned to Simon.

"You had no reason to take her," he told him, sounding more hurt than angry. "I want her back. I need her back."

Simon lifted his hand. "Davyss, Davyss," he murmured, sing-song. "Sit down before you fall down."

"I will not. I want my wife back immediately."

Simon sighed heavily, looking up at him. After a moment, he rose wearily and Davyss took a step back; Simon was wily and cunning. He didn't trust that the old man wouldn't have a dagger wedged in his palm somehow. Simon saw Davyss back away and he smiled thinly.

"Davyss," he paused, gazing into the younger man's face. "I did not get where I am in life by being a fool. You know this."

Davyss' jaw was ticking again. "Tell me why you took her," he asked hoarsely. "Just tell me why."

Simon lifted an eyebrow. "You know why."

"If I did, I would not be asking. Tell me."

"Because people live longer when they do not completely trust their friends and family," Simon tapped his right temple. "I know you, Davyss; lest you forget how well I know you. I know that you have always disagreed with my politics. The only reason you swore fealty to me was to ensure your wife and family's safety. But I know, in your heart, that you do not truly support me. Yet, if I hold your wife, it is insurance against you doing anything, shall we say, foolish."

Davyss' cheeks took on a ruddy glow. "You doubt my word of honor?" he hissed. "I am a man of my word; I always have been. If you do not trust me, then you should not have forced me to swear fealty."

Simon shrugged as if to concede the point. "Yet I did, you did, and now you wonder why I have my doubts. I love you, Davyss, but it is better if I do not trust you completely. Surely you understand that."

Davyss began to wonder if Simon knew of his meetings with his men, discussing plans to free Prince Edward from captivity. But there is no way the man could know because Davyss knew his men; he knew they would never betray him, not even Hugh. So he could only presume that Simon was going forward on caution and suspicion only. He hated to lie to the man's face but, feeling betrayed himself, he didn't feel an over amount of guilt.

Davyss sighed heavily, studying Simon's strong, wrinkled face. "I swore fealty to you and I shall honor that commitment," he said. "There is no reason to hold my wife hostage to ensure my good behavior. She is... not well. I must have her back."

Simon's eyebrows lifted. "Not well? What do you mean?"

Davyss' jaw resumed its nervous tick. "She recently miscarried our child. She has not recovered from that. I want her back, Uncle Simon. Please do this for me."

It was the first time Davyss had lowered his guard. He was no longer the angry warrior but the begging husband. Simon could see the young man, the young boy, the child he had once known in just those few words. He began to feel some remorse but he fought it.

"I am sorry for you, my son," he said softly, sincerely. "I promise you that she is in no danger. She is well cared for and looked after."

"I want her back."

"Perhaps... in time."

Davyss' jaw began to tick again, so hard that he almost broke his teeth. Wearily, he removed his helm and planted himself in Simon's chair all in the same gesture. Simon watched as Davyss held his head in his hands, a gesture of desolation and defeat. What the old man wasn't prepared for, however, was what came next.

Davyss began to sob. Softly at first, but by the time Simon realized what was happening, Davyss was sobbing deeply and painfully. Stricken, he went to the knight, wondering if attempts at comfort would be well met. He'd never seen Davyss show any measure of disappointment or sadness much less cry. He was beyond shocked; he was shattered.

"Davyss," he whispered earnestly. "Nay, boy... don't...."

"I want my wife," Davyss sputtered, suddenly wiping at his face as if ashamed he had broken down. "You have no reason to hold her. I have given you everything you wanted, Uncle Simon. Why can you not give me back the only person that has ever meant anything to me? She has done nothing wrong. Why must you punish her?"

At the end of the chamber, the solar door creaked open and a small figure stood there, surveying the room with calculated eyes. There was blood on the floor and Davyss was collapsed in a chair, weeping. Lady Katharine knew the situation; although Davyss had not returned to Hollyhock before making his way to the Tower in search of his wife, she had heard through Davyss' soldiers what had happened. Lady Devereux had been taken from Davyss' encampment and her son was bent on murder.

So she stepped into the chamber, her fine slippers making their way through the blood smeared on the floor, her cane making a rhythmic thumping as she moved across the wood. She could see Simon standing over Davyss, who seemed truly distraught. She was nearly upon them by the time Simon heard her.

He turned sharply, only to be faced with a furious woman. Although her expression hadn't changed much from its normal countenance, he knew just by looking in her eyes that she was livid. Davyss looked up, saw his mother, and lowered his head into his hands again.

Katharine's hazel gaze lingered on her shattered son. Then the wise old eyes moved to Simon, who visibly stepped back from the woman. If looks could kill, then he would be a dead man.

"I told you to leave his wife alone," she muttered. "You did not listen to me."

Simon stood his ground. "I told you why."

Davyss' head shot up, his wet eyes accusing at his mother. "You knew what he was planning?" he demanded. "You knew and you did not tell me?"

Katharine lifted a thin eyebrow at her son. "Be still," she hissed, returning her attention to Simon. "You and I will come to terms before I leave this room or you will leave more than your share of blood on the floor. If you want a valuable hostage to ensure de Winter support, then you could have done much better than Lady Devereux."

Simon's expression flickered with uncertainty. "What are you saying?"

"Me, you fool," she snapped. "You will take me and release Davyss' wife."

Davyss closed his eyes and hung his head again as Simon staggered. "I will not," he gasped. "You... you are...."

"More valuable than that young woman by leaps and bounds," she jabbed a finger at him. "I carry the wealth of the de Winter empire, you idiot. She carries nothing but my son's affections. You will release her immediately and take me instead."

Simon stared at her. Then he walked away; he had to. Katharine was a tiny woman but her presence was overwhelming him until he could hardly breathe. He paced several feet away and came to a halt, turning to face the pair. Davyss was still hanging his head, sniffling now and again as he stared at the floor. Lady Katharine stood next to her son, more powerful at that moment than the mighty Davyss de Winter could ever hope to be.

"And if I do not accept your offer?" Simon had to ask.

"Then Davyss withdraws his support, as do all of the de Winter allies. You will lose at least five thousand men. If this does not concern you, then by all means, do not agree to my terms."

Simon's jaw tightened. "Do you actually think to threaten me?"

"Absolutely."

Simon was furious but he stopped short of reacting violently. It was clear that he knew he was cornered. He finally shook his head, almost comically, lifting his hands in resignation.

"And just what am I supposed to do with you?" he wanted to know. "You will not go where I want you to go. You will stay locked up in Hollyhock and absolutely nothing will change."

Lady Katharine shrugged her bony shoulders. "Replace my personal guard with men of your own choosing. Confine me to my own home with your men as my jailers. There is no shame in that arrangement, for either of us."

Simon rolled his eyes. "Ridiculous," he spat. "You will go to Eleanor."

"I do not like your wife."

"She does not like you."

"I will not go to her. I will stay at Hollyhock."

Simon couldn't believe the ridiculous terms. "You are my hostage yet you dictate the terms of your captivity?"

"I do. And you will agree."

Simon just shook his head, frustrated and defeated. "I do not believe I am getting the better end of this deal."

Lady Katharine didn't say a word. She hobbled over to him, her cane clicking against the floor, before suddenly lashing out with the cane and knocking Simon on the side of the head. The man went tumbling as Davyss bolted to his feet and put himself protectively between his mother and Simon, who was now struggling to get off the floor. But the world was rocking so he stayed on his arse, gazing up at Katharine with a baffled expression. She glared daggers at him.

"You are getting the services of Sir Davyss de Winter," she snarled. "You are by far getting the better end of this deal and you will not forget it."

Simon wouldn't.

CHAPTER TWENTY-ONE

May 1265 A.D.
Norwich Castle, Norfolk

"WHAT HAVE I told you?" Davyss was wagging a finger in her face. "You are not to run about and tire yourself. I thought I was clear."

Devereux gazed up at her husband, properly contrite, but it was only for show. She shifted the basket of blooms to her other hand, grasped the finger that was wagging at her, and kissed it.

"I am not exhausting myself," she insisted calmly, turning away from him and continuing along her way. "I feel fine."

Davyss followed her, watching her shapely backside as she walked. To look at the woman from the back, one would never know she was pregnant. But when she turned around, she had a belly as big as a pumpkin.

He sighed, making faces as he followed her through the enormous garden at Norwich. When she stopped to cut more flowers, this time big fat pink blooms, he firmly pulled the basket from her arm.

"At least let me carry this," he fumed, watching her smile. "You are the most stubborn woman I have ever met; do you hear?"

She grinned up at him, truly radiant in her pregnancy. Her cheeks were round and rosy, her eyes bright. Davyss had never seen her more beautiful and he fell in love with her more deeply with every day that passed. He sighed with exasperation and kissed her, continuing to follow her as she did exactly as she pleased.

The day was sunny, the weather remarkably mild for this time of year. The spring flowers had been blooming like mad for the past week and Devereux had cut bushels of them. There were flowers in every room of the castle. Although Norwich was a functional military garrison, it was starting to look more like women had taken over every inch of the place. Between Lucy, Frances and Devereux, female traits of flowers, fresh rushes and fine furnishings were everywhere.

But Davyss didn't particularly mind. He was simply glad to have his wife with him. The past year had been particularly difficult with de Montfort's rule and Henry's captivity, but Davyss had stayed bottled up at Norwich with his wife, leaving only when he was summoned by de Montfort. Even then, he left Devereux closely guarded, terrified that Simon would betray him again and take her. But Simon had Lady Katharine, the solitary reason why he had not made another try for Devereux. Lady Katharine ruled Simon more than God did.

Even so, Davyss had not been out of the political picture entirely. He and Roger Mortimer had been in constant contact over the past nine months, speaking of politics, of kings and of barons. Roger was a supporter of de Montfort but recent months saw his support wane. Davyss had sensed this right after the Battle of Lewes and was smart enough to capitalize on it. Now, it was Davyss and Mortimer who were allies. De Montfort had nothing to do with it.

Mortimer knew where Henry and Edward were being held captive and it was out of Mortimer's mouth that a plot for release eventually sprang. Davyss had spent the past several months planting the seed of escape through conversations and innuendos, so when Mortimer finally discussed a plot, Davyss' job was done. He would facilitate whatever Mortimer had planned. Even now, he was waiting for Mortimer to arrive at Norwich so they could begin their deed. Time was growing short.

Hugh, Andrew, Edmund, Philip, Lollardly and Nik were well briefed and awaiting Mortimer's arrival as well. Nik had recovered from his near-mortal injury at Lewes with hardly a reminder except for the patch he now wore over his missing left eye. If one good thing had come out of his injury, it had been that he and Frances had drawn closer together and she was now three months pregnant with their first child. Nik was thrilled, as was Frances, but she had been so ill through the pregnancy that it was difficult for her to show much joy. Mostly, she stayed to bed and Nik spent a great deal of time with her.

But Frances' pregnancy was completely unlike Devereux's; in the month of November, Devereux had discovered she was with child again and Davyss' joy had known no limits. However, he had insisted that she stay in bed almost immediately and it had been a six month battle to keep her in bed when she did not want to stay there. Lollardly, Davyss' resident surgeon, had examined Lady de Winter and insisted she was perfectly healthy, but it wasn't good enough for Davyss. He didn't want anything to go wrong and insisted that bed was where she needed to be.

His wife cooperated for the first three months but after that, she insisted that she felt fine and there was no reason to keep her supine day and night. Davyss divided his time between his duties and watching out for his wife as she went about her own, exhausting him to the point of frustration. Even on this fine and sunny day, he continued to follow her about as if afraid something horrible would happen the moment she was out of his sight.

"Davyss," Devereux's voice brought him out of his morose thoughts. "I have been thinking about something."

He lifted an eyebrow at her, holding out the basket so she could lay the fat pink flowers down. "No doubt," he muttered. "I am afraid to ask what it is."

She smiled as she cut another stalk. "Why are you so irritable all of the time?"

"Is that what you have been thinking?"

She laughed. "Nay," she turned to him. "But I have been wondering where you intend we should raise our son after he is born. Remember? We discussed this once. I told you I did not want to be traveling around like gypsies."

He shrugged. "What is wrong with Norwich?"

She lifted her shoulders and turned around, picking at the next flower. "Norwich does not belong to you. I want to raise our children in a castle that belongs to you, some place that we will never be forced to leave or surrender. I was raised at Allington; it is my home. It will always be my home. I want our child to feel the same sense of security."

He took the flower that she handed him. "I was raised between Wintercroft, Hollyhock and Breckland before fostering at Kenilworth. I did not suffer overly because I did not have a single place of residence."

She put her hand on her belly, turning to him with a pout. "Little William must know the security and safety of one home."

He fought off a smirk. "So it is William today, is it? What happened to Henry Thomas?"

She made a face at him. "I like William," she insisted, turning back to the last flower. "I like the way it flows over the tongue; William. *William.* Still, I have always liked the name Titus."

"*What?*" he rolled his eyes in disbelief. "My son shall not be named Titus."

"Tiberius?"

"Nay."

"Roland?"

"Silly wench," he rolled his eyes again and took the last flower from her hand. "If you cannot think of a suitable name, I shall be forced to do it."

She put her hands on her hips. "Is that so?" she sneered. "And just what brutally masculine name would you choose?"

He pretended to think as he took her hand with the intention of returning her to the keep. "My father's name was Grayson."

"I like that name but I do not want to name our son after your father. He will be forever confused with his grandfather." She cocked his head. "What was Grayson's father's name?"

"Davyss."

"Oh," she thought on that a moment. "What about your mother's father?"

"Hugh."

She threw up her hands. "Do you de Winters go along naming the entire family after each other? Where is the originality?" she demanded to his chuckles. "My father's name is St. Paul and our son will *not* be named St. Paul. It sounds as if he should go around performing miracles."

Davyss' laughter grew. "We still have time yet. Do not worry your-self over it."

She grinned in spite of herself, allowing him to reclaim her hand, kiss it, and take her into the massive keep of Norwich.

Norwich was truly a massive compound. The keep sat on the top of a natural rise that was augmented by a giant motte, surrounded by a deep moat and separated from the rest of the castle by an enormous drawbridge. Devereux had never in her life ever seen anything so large; not even the Tower of London, which was enormous in of itself. Norwich sat like a huge sentinel surveying the countryside and could be literally seen for miles in any direction as if daring someone to try and breach it.

The keep was cavernous inside. Davyss and Devereux had the mas-ter's chamber on the fourth floor of the keep, a room that was probably as big as the entire House of Hope. It was monstrous. The soldier's hall, or great hall, was situated on the second floor and covered more than half of the floor space while several smaller rooms, including a kitchen, knight's room and garderobes, covered the rest of the floor.

As Davyss and Devereux entered the keep, Davyss handed the flow-ers off to Lucy, who happened to see them entering from the garden. As she happily skipped off with the flowers, he continued to carefully lead his wife up two flights of spiral stone steps to the fourth floor. Their chamber lay on the north side and he took her inside, hoping to convince her to rest now that her gardening was finished.

But Devereux had other ideas; once inside the chamber, she went straight for her massive wardrobe as Louie, the little orange dog, jumped frantically at her feet. She finally picked the little beast up as she opened up the wardrobe door.

"I would like to change my coat and go into town," she informed him.

He eyed her. "Why?"

Her brow furrowed. "Because the last time we were in town, there was a new merchant from Brussels. Do you remember?"

He nodded and she continued. "He had fabric from Athens and all sorts of wonderful things. I want to see what else he has. Maybe he has new things that I have not yet seen."

Davyss sighed heavily; it would do no good to deny her or argue with her, so he resorted to a tactic he had used much more as of late. He bargained.

"I will take you," he said, "on the condition that you rest for a couple of hours first. Please, sweetling; it would make me happy."

She gazed up at him, drinking in his handsome face. She didn't feel like being particularly belligerent; not when he was trying so hard to be kind and gentle with her. The man had barely left her side for months and they were very much attached to one another, shadows that followed one another around in love and harmony. She couldn't remember what her life was like before she met Davyss de Winter. She set the dog down and went over to him.

"Very well," she kissed him sweetly. "If that is your wish."

Davyss returned her kiss, putting his hand on her belly as he suckled her lips. There was something profoundly intimate and erotic about the gesture, feeling the life they had created together. He had been terrified to make love to her for the first three months but when Lollardly assured them that the pregnancy was secure, he had taken great delight in inspecting his wife's changing body. Her gently swollen middle aroused him tremendously and he would turn her onto her side, facing away from him, and make love to her. All the while, he would hold her belly in his hands, feeling the fruition of their love. Never in his life had the act of sex meant more to him emotionally than physically. But it did with Devereux.

Even now as she changed out of her surcoat, his hands were all over her. She pulled the coat over her head, followed by the shift, leaving her in her pantalets and hose. Davyss gently pulled her pantalets off, followed by the hose, holding her from behind as his hands moved over her belly and breasts and his mouth feasted on her neck. He pulled his tunic off so their bare skin could touch, the warmth of attraction between them stark and strong. Bending his wife carefully over the foot of the bed, he lowered his breeches and entered her from behind.

Devereux groaned at his entry, sighing with contentment as he thrust carefully yet powerfully into her. His hands were on her rounded belly, holding the child gently as he made love to the mother, and in little time Devereux was climaxing in multiplicity as he continued to thrust. Davyss released himself into her body, his hands moving to her breasts, her shoulders, pulling her up and kissing her soft mouth as she arched her neck over her shoulder, surrendering to his seeking mouth.

When the kisses gently faded away, he went to one of the two massive wardrobes in the room and pulled forth another shift for her, this one heavier and made of pale lamb's wool. It was as soft as a feather. He handed it to her and she pulled it over her head, straightening it out around her growing body. He helped her straighten the bottom when her growing belly made it difficult to bend over. Louie, not to be left out, tried to jump and play under the hem of the long shift until Davyss chased him out. Offended, Louie went under the bed.

"Now," he took her to the head of the enormous bed and pulled back the coverlet. "Lie down and sleep. I shall return to you in a couple of hours and we will go into town."

She didn't argue with him; in fact, given their heated encounter, she was looking forward to resting for a while. Snuggling down into the bed, she began to mutter as he covered her up.

"We must think of names that begin with the same letter as our names," she sighed, her eyes drooping. "Can you think of any?"

He put an enormous hand on her forehead as if to still her thoughts. "Shhhh," he whispered. "Go to sleep."

She closed her eyes, already beginning to doze. "I cannot," she mumbled. "Not until I... think of a name for...our... son...."

She was very nearly asleep. Davyss removed his hand from her forehead gently, so as not to disturb her, and very quietly collected the tunic he had thrown off in the heat of passion. Pulling it back over his head and making every effort not to wake her, he slipped from their chamber.

He could hear men and noise coming from the floors below. It was suddenly very loud as he descended the steps into the soldier's hall, and for good reason; it was full of men. Some he recognized and some he did not, but those who were unfamiliar bore the colors of Mortimer.

Davyss moved through the crowd of soldiers looking for Mortimer himself. He had known the man to be on the approach and was rather perturbed that no one had bothered to tell him that the man had arrived. In fact, when he came across Hugh, he told his brother precisely that.

"Why was I not informed of Mortimer's arrival?" he grabbed his brother by the arm.

Hugh had a tankard of ale in his hand. "Because you were with your wife," he said frankly. "I knew you would come down here sooner or later. Mortimer is in no hurry."

Davyss frowned at his brother but he could not dispute the logic; it had become well known with Davyss' men not to interrupt him when he was with Devereux.

"Give me that," he snatched the ale from his brother and took a heavy swallow. "Where is Roger?"

Hugh snatched the tankard back. "Over there," he pointed near the kitchens.

Davyss continued his path through the crowd of men, settling in with their food and ale. There were so many people that it looked like a celebration. He finally caught sight of Mortimer's dark head near the dais. As he approached, Roger's head came up from the table and their eyes met. Davyss smiled.

"My lord," he greeted. "I apologize that I did not greet you upon your arrival."

Roger waved him off. "No need," he studied him a moment. "How are things at Norwich?"

"Quiet," Davyss sat down opposite the man. "You look well enough. Thank God your injuries healed."

Roger had been badly wounded at Lewes. "Nothing that good food and wine has not healed with time," he gingerly rubbed the spot on his chest where an arrow had nearly claimed him. "And de Nogaret? Is he fully recovered now?"

Davyss nodded. "He is indeed," he replied. "His wife is expecting a child in the fall."

Roger lifted his cup to toast Nik's excellent fortune. "That is good news."

"My wife is expecting, also."

Roger looked at him. Then he broke down into laughter, snorting as he recovered. "Davyss, from what I have heard, you have not left that woman's side for even a moment," he sobered further. "But after what happened with de Montfort, I do not blame you. The man is vain, underhanded and ruthless but when he betrayed even you by holding your wife hostage, I believe his supporters began to realize just how untrustworthy the man was. There were a good many people who pitied you."

Davyss watched him drain his cup. "Shall we go someplace private to speak?"

Roger nodded, grabbing the nearest serving wench with a pitcher of ale. He took it right out of her hand and stood up from the table.

"Lead the way, de Winter."

Davyss stood up and pointed to the knight's hall on the other side of the room. "This way, my lord."

Roger was already on his heels. "It is not necessary to address me so formally, Davyss. You and I share the same rank, Baron Blackheath."

Davyss lifted an eyebrow at him. "The title came through my mother," he said. "I do not even think of it, to be truthful. I do not want the politics that are associated with baronial responsibilities. I would rather serve as a knight than lead as a noble."

Roger slapped him on his massive shoulder. "God's Beard, man," he was evidently well into his ale, indicative of his happy mood. "Your mother's family *is* Surrey. The de Warennes hold the entire shire, plus part of Norfolk. Your father, God rest him, came from a prestigious line of knights that ruled Radnorshire in Wales for centuries. Not only do you hold your father's properties and titles in Wales, including four castles, but also his property in Norfolk as granted to him by Henry. Since when did you become so humble?"

Davyss smiled faintly as Roger followed him into the knight's hall just beyond the soldier's hall. "I am not," he assured him. "I am well aware that my family is older and richer than yours. More handsome as well."

Roger snorted. "Ah; much more like the Davyss I know."

Davyss' smile faded. "I miss my father," he muttered. "But I do not believe he would have been very happy with what Simon is attempting to accomplish."

Roger shrugged. "God should not have taken your father so soon."

"It was not God that took him but disease. The man's heart seized up when he was not much older than I am."

The knight's hall was nearly devoid of people; everyone was crowded into the main hall beyond. Davyss and Roger sat at the heavy table in the center of the room, listening to the loud clamor in the hall beyond. It was the perfect atmosphere to drown out any eavesdropping that might take place with what Roger was about to say; a low voice could not be heard over all of the noise out in the hall.

"So," Davyss faced Roger expectantly. "I do not guess that you have come here simply to speak on my father and my property. I assume our plan is moving forward."

Roger nodded. "I have been permitted to visit Edward in captivity," he said. "As his cousin, of course, it is my right. Moreover, de Montfort is not too restrictive about visitors to Edward as he is to Henry. We have formulated a plan that I believe will work."

Davyss lifted his eyebrows. "You will include me, of course."

"You will lead it."

Davyss nodded, moving closer to Roger so he could hear the man's softly uttered plans over the happy chaos in the room beyond.

CB

THE FEAST WITH Mortimer's men went well into the night. Devereux had awoken from her nap close to sunset and she could hear the noise clear up in her chamber. Rising slowly, she was careful not to step on Louie as she went to one of the long lancet windows that lined the chamber, peering outside to see if she could see what was going on in the upper bailey. There were hundreds of men and their horses, cluttering the upper bailey with their noise and smell. She could see part of the drawbridge that led to the lower bailey and she could see that the bridge was down and men were traversing it.

Although Davyss didn't discuss military matters with her, she had heard him mention that Roger Mortimer was due to visit. Devereux tried to stay clear of in-depth political knowledge because she and her husband could never agree on the need for war versus peaceful solutions to conflict. It was something they had never agreed on, not since they day they had met, so it was best if they didn't discuss the subject too deeply. But she knew enough that Roger Mortimer had arrived, purpose unknown, so she made haste to dress.

She'd had to have several surcoats made recently to accommodate her growing belly. One of them was a lovely pale blue garment made of brocade, and she slipped on a light shift before pulling the surcoat over her head. She still dressed alone and bathed alone, just as she always had, even in this fine massive fortress with dozens of servants running about. She was simply more comfortable alone. But she did call a maid to help her secure the ties on the garment so it draped beautifully over her shoulders and breasts, the one thing she couldn't do for herself. The maid also pulled her hair back into a single braid, which draped elegantly over one shoulder.

Fully dressed and looking like an angel, she quit the chamber and slowly made her way down the spiral stairs. The noise grew louder as she drew near the soldier's hall and by the time she entered, the roar of men and laughter was almost deafening. There were strange soldiers everywhere, drinking and eating.

She asked the first servant she came across where her husband was. The man offered to escort her through the masses and she gratefully accepted, following the rather large servant through the crowd and into the knight's hall beyond. As soon as she entered, she saw her husband seated at the table with a dark-haired, slender man.

Davyss spied his wife the moment she entered the room. He bolted to his feet and went to her.

"Sweetling," he put his arm around her shoulders. "Why did you not send for me? You should not be down here with all of these men."

She waved him off. "I am fine, Davyss; I am not going to break." She smiled at Roger, who rose from the bench and returned her smile. "I am Lady de Winter. Welcome to Norwich, my lord."

Roger bowed gallantly. "My lady," he greeted. "I am Roger Mortimer. 'Tis a pleasure to finally meet you. I have heard many great things about you."

She lifted an eyebrow at him as Davyss helped her to sit. "No doubt you have heard many great things about our child, to be sure," she winked at her husband as he sat down. "His son is all he can speak of."

Davyss kissed her on the temple. "Not all," he said. "I speak of you also on occasion."

Roger laughed softly as Devereux made a face at Davyss. "Do not let him fool you," Roger said. "Davyss is so proud of you that he is close to bursting. From a man who embodies the male trait of pride, I would say that is quite a statement."

Devereux's twisted expression transitioned into a glowing smile at her husband. "He has much to be proud of," she murmured, gently tweaking his chin. "He is a great man. He told me so himself."

Roger laughed uproariously and moved to pour Devereux some ale, but someone was shouting his name from the soldier's hall and his attention was diverted. His men were calling to him and he set the ale down.

"Excuse me, Lady de Winter," he said as he climbed off the bench. "It seems that my men require my attention. I shall return and look forward to having a detailed conversation with you."

Devereux merely smiled at him as he quit the hall, hearing the cheers from his men in the room beyond as he entered the hall. She turned her attention to her husband and her smile faded.

"You know that I do not ask you your business," she said quietly. "But I would like to know why he is here."

Davyss held her hand, rubbing it gently between his two big palms. The gentle expression on his features faded.

"He is here because we are to attend to some business together," he said softly. "When Roger leaves on the morrow, I go with him."

"I see," she wasn't particularly surprised but she was hurt that he had not told her sooner. "And just when did you plan to tell me you were leaving?"

He reached up to tuck a bit of stray hair behind her ear. "Tonight," he muttered. "When all was quiet and still between us, I was going to tell you."

"But you have known for some time that you were leaving."

It wasn't a question; it was a statement. Davyss nodded faintly. "I knew that as soon as Roger arrived, I would be leaving with him. Devereux, I simply didn't want our last days or hours spoiled with my impending departure. You know how emotional you become."

There wasn't much more she could say to that, considering he was right. She averted her gaze for a moment. "How long will you be gone?"

"I have no way of knowing, sweetling."

"You must be here for the birth of your son. That only gives you three months."

He sighed faintly. "I will try, you know I will," he murmured. "There is nothing on this earth more important to me than that. But I cannot promise that I will return in time."

"Where are you going?"

"I do not want you to know for your own safety." He shook his head firmly when she opened her mouth to dispute him. "Please, sweetling. Do not ask me any more questions. I will not answer them."

Devereux just stared at him. She knew she shouldn't be selfish, but she wasn't in a very generous mood. She didn't want her husband to leave her and she certainly didn't want him to be absent for the birth of their child. With a sigh of exasperation, she pulled her hand from his grip and stood up, moving away from him.

Davyss watched her pace away, moving to the extremely long and thin lancet windows that allowed air and ventilation into the room. He watched her until she reached the window and hung her head.

"I do not want you to leave," she burst into soft tears. "You are going away and doing God knows what, but I am sure it involves danger and swords and battle and there is every chance that you will never return to me. I want you to remain with me, where you belong, so you may be here for the birth of your son. This is where you belong, Davyss; not fooling around in silly wars."

He rose from the bench, going to her. He put his enormous hands on her face, forcing her to look at him.

"I want you to listen very carefully to what I am to say because it is important," he whispered. "Can you do this?"

She nodded hesitantly, gazing up at him with big watery eyes, and he smiled gently at her.

"You and I do not discuss political matters because we disagree on them," he said quietly. "But you must listen to me now. I go with Mortimer because the stability of the country and the safety of my family is my priority. I would kill a thousand men if it will keep you and my son safe. But it is not merely you and my son; it is my mother as well. She is being held captive in order to ensure that I do not rise against de Montfort. I must do all I can to ensure that she is safe as well. I cannot sit idly by and hope for the best, Devereux; I must do something. I am Davyss de Winter and my reputation is second to none; I am the most powerful knight in England. What good is that power and reputation if I cannot use it to make this country a safer place for my family?"

By the time he was finished, she was no longer weeping but gazing at him with a serious expression.

"You are indeed the most powerful knight in England," she whispered. "I knew that the moment I met you. But you are also my husband and father to my child, someone I love more than anything on this earth. Even though I understand your reasons, I still do not want you to go. I am afraid you will never come back."

He cupped her face, kissing her cheeks tenderly. "We had this same conversation the last time I departed," he said softly. "Do you remember? I told you that I would do everything in my power to return to you and I did."

She nodded faintly, reaching up to touch his face. She ran her fingers through his dark hair, watching as he closed his eyes to the sweetness of her touch.

"Aye, you did," she agreed. "But not without compromise."

He pulled her into a smothering embrace, opening his eyes to look at her. "And I would do it again if given the same choice. Sometimes compromise means survival, and I mean that my family should survive."

She wasn't going to argue with him; Davyss was doing what he felt was best and Devereux trusted him. But she missed him horribly already. She threw her arms around his neck and held him tightly.

"I do not know what I shall do without you," she hummed against his ear. "The days and nights will be horribly lonely."

He pulled back and looked at her. "You still have Louie."

He said it with some jealousy and she laughed. "Now, you mustn't be bitter because he likes to lie on your side of the bed," she told him. "He is simply a little dog. He does not know any better."

Davyss made a face. "He would know if you disciplined him once in a while," he pointed out. "As it is, I am nearly kicked from my own bed by a dog no bigger than my fist. I am ashamed to tell anyone."

Devereux laughed. "You have never been removed from your own bed," she countered. "I move Louie aside when it is time for sleep."

Davyss pursed his lips, letting her know what he thought about both her sense of discipline and the dog. Louie had become king of the entire keep and his wife allowed it. Although he was a cute little mutt, Davyss wasn't particularly fond of it. He just didn't like small dogs. Not wanting to argue the point of the dog further, mostly because he knew he would lose, he began to nuzzle her cheek.

"I will leave Lollardly here with you," he whispered. "As much as I will miss him, I feel strongly that it is more important he remain here to assist in the birth of my son."

Devereux nodded, closing her eyes as his mouth moved along her jaw. "As you say, husband."

"He will keep you safe."

"I know."

He kissed her neck. "And I will see you every night in my dreams," he whispered. "You will take care of yourself while I am gone and you will not stray from Norwich for any reason. Not even to go back to The House of Hope because you are bored or because you feel the need to go. Is that clear?"

She nodded obediently. "It is."

"Good."

Devereux gazed up into his beloved hazel eyes, loving the man more than words could express. The longer she stared, the more her heart began to ache for what was to come. She didn't want to face it but knew she had little choice.

"Wherever you go and whatever you do, please know how much I love you," she murmured. "I will watch the road every day for your return."

He held her close a moment longer before kissing her, so deeply that it brought tears to his eyes. Davyss didn't want to leave her but, as with Lewes, he knew it was a matter of life and death. For the survival of England and of his family, he knew what he had to do.

Morning came far too quickly.

CHAPTER TWENTY-TWO

August 5, 1265 A.D.

I T HAD BEEN a long and bloody night, following an extremely long and bloody day. The Battle of Evesham was over, the second violent battle he had attended in a little over a year, something that had to be experienced to be believed. Davyss had seen more than his share of battles in his life and had experienced some fairly brutal warfare, but none of that could compare to Evesham. Nothing could have prepared him.

The brutality had been of his own doing. Simon, not realizing that Mortimer and de Winter, among others, had stolen banners from his own son, Simon the Younger, and then rode to battle flying those banners to make the elder de Montfort think that reinforcements were coming, had been shocked to see Davyss and his armies riding with Mortimer and other Royalists. But it had been Simon's last thought before the bloody battle ensued and Davyss, along with Mortimer, began to easily cut through de Montfort's barons. Rather than capture the nobles and ransom them, the Battle at Evesham reeked of vengeance. Davyss and Mortimer killed rather than take captives. It was meant to be a message to all of those who still harbored thoughts of resisting the absolute rule of Henry the Third.

Overwhelmed and undermanned, Simon tried to surrender but the blood lust was too great. He had been killed and dismembered, and even now as dawn broke on the day after the battle, Mortimer, Henry and Edward were deciding what was to be done with Simon's body parts. Davyss, having known and loved the man his entire life, buried himself in organizing the remaining royalist army for the return to London. He didn't want to know what they did with Simon because he wasn't sure how he felt about any of it yet. He struggled to ignore the pain, the guilt.

The sun was just beginning to rise but the day was swamped in a horrible thunderstorm. The storm had rolled in the day before at dawn and the entire battle had been conducted in a downpour. Even now, Davyss stood outside his tent, watching the remaining royalist army attempt to cook a well-deserved meal and trying to remember what it felt like to be dry again. It had been a very long three months since his departure from Norwich, having entrenched himself in Prince Edward's release from captivity and the battle preparation for Evesham. It had been Davyss who had provided the horse for the prince's escape and Davyss who had rode interference when the prince's jailers tried to follow. Once they had Edward free, it was only a matter of time before they would also have Henry.

And now they did. Henry was king once more and the winds of fortune had once again shifted. Davyss glanced up at the storm clouds, raining buckets on the already-saturated ground, his mind whirling with a million different thoughts and emotions as he tried to reconcile himself to the change in political tides. Hugh suddenly appeared through the sheets of rain, water dripping off his face as he pushed past his brother on his way into the moderately dry tent. Philip, Nik, Andrew and Edmund followed, all looking sloppy, muddy and soaked. They had been up all night and were showing their exhaustion.

Davyss moved aside as his grumpy, weary men piled past him. He turned to watch them throw their gear on the ground, trying to stay out of the damp grass and pulling out bedrugs in preparation for sleep. Their mail was already rusting and each man struggled to pull his free, knowing it was going to be a massive job for the squires to remove all of the rust that had accumulated over the past few days. The mail coats went into piles in the corner.

"God's Blood," Hugh sighed, pulling off his wet tunic and throwing it into the same pile as the mail. "I could sleep for a week."

"You only have the morning," Davyss told him. "We meet with

Henry and Edward at noon."

Hugh groaned, flopping down onto his bedroll. "Are you not going to sleep, brother?"

Davyss' hazel gaze returned to the storm outside. "In time," he muttered.

Hugh twisted his head so he could look at him. "What is troubling you?

Davyss shook his head. "Nothing."

By this time, Andrew was watching Davyss from the other side of the tent. Being closer to Davyss than the others, Hugh included, he could fairly read the man's thoughts.

"There was nothing you could have done, Davyss," he told him quietly. "Simon was in pieces before you realized what they had done. You cannot blame yourself."

Davyss' head snapped to him, the hazel eyes blazing a moment before quickly cooling. "I do not blame myself," he replied. "Such are the perils of war. But...."

Andrew lifted an eyebrow. "But... what?"

Davyss shook his head. Then he answered. "I was simply wondering what my father would have said to all of this."

Andrew walked up beside him, also gazing out at the downpour. "He would have said the same thing you did," he replied. "Such are the perils of war. Simon knew that the moment he took up arms, it might end this way. Do not pity the man."

"I do not," Davyss assured him. "But I would be lying if I said that his death has not saddened me. He was the last link, other than my mother, that I had to my father. I miss him already."

"Would you have stopped his slaughter if you could have?"

Davyss drew in a long, heavy breath. "I do not know for certain," he said honestly. "More than likely, I would have tried."

Andrew clapped a hand on his shoulder, not knowing what else to say to that. He decided it was best to shift the subject. "Have we heard anything from Norwich?"

Davyss shook his head, turning to watch Andrew regain his bed roll. "Not since the last missive, almost four weeks ago," he said. "Lollardly says that the child is massive and that all my wife does is cry and sleep. He curses me for having left in the first place." His smile suddenly faded and he turned to the rain outside once more. "God, I would give my right arm to be with her. Surely the child has been born by now."

Hugh lay on his back, staring up at the ceiling of the tent as he listened to his brother's lament. "Have you sent word to Mother yet?" he wanted to know, completely off the subject. "She is no longer a prisoner of Uncle Simon."

Davyss glanced over at his brother. "She has not been for several weeks."

Hugh looked up at him, a confused expression on his face. "What do you mean?"

Davyss lifted an eyebrow. "Because I had Lollardly send a missive to Hollyhock addressed to Darien de Russe. He was mother's primary jailer. You remember Darien, do you not?"

As Hugh nodded, Davyss continued. "Since Lollardly is our priest as well as our surgeon, I had him send a missive on behalf of the Bishop of Norwich requesting that Lady Katharine de Winter be released to the custody of the church so that she could travel to Norwich and attend her son's wife in childbirth. If all has gone as planned, Mother has been at Norwich for several weeks now. I have not yet heard from Lollardly to that regard but I am sure that de Russe would not go against a request from the Bishop of Norwich."

"Brilliant," Hugh approved. "So Mother is now safe at Norwich."

"Presumably."

Davyss stepped away from the tent flap again, seriously considering getting some sleep before his meeting with Henry in a few hours. Reaching his bedroll, he sat heavily. He could already hear Philip snoring. With a weary sigh, he lay down and stretched out, the first time he had done so in two days. Exhaustion was finally catching up to him. Just as he was drifting off, there was a call from the tent flap.

Andrew was up, moving for the entry. As he peeled back the cloth, he found himself looking at a soldier he recognized. The man was one of Davyss' men, left behind at Norwich for Lady de Winter's protection. Andrew's face lit up with a smile.

"Ah!" he said happily, turning to Davyss. "Look what we have, Davyss; news from Norwich."

Davyss was on his feet faster than lightning. He didn't even remember getting up, but suddenly, he was up and at the tent entry. He, too, recognized the man, and all he could feel at the moment was terror and elation. He didn't even give the man the chance to greet him before he was pounding into him with questions.

"Well?" he demanded. "Where is my missive? Has my son arrived yet?"

The soldier was exhausted. His face was pale and stubbled as he focused on his liege. Only Andrew seemed to sense that the man was hesitant to speak, which immediately put him on his guard.

"I carry no missive, my lord," the soldier said. "Your mother has sent me with a personal message for you."

Davyss' brow furrowed slightly. "So my mother is at Norwich?"

"Aye, my lord."

"Excellent," Davyss, either too exhausted to notice or too focused on the news the man carried, didn't sense the soldier's reluctance. He pushed him. "Well? How are my wife and son?"

The soldier took a deep breath, water from the driving rain dripping off his helm and on to his face. "Your mother says to tell you that two male children were born to you as of three weeks ago," he said. "She congratulates you on your healthy children. She also says to tell you that your lady wife did not fare well in the birth and that you should come home immediately."

All of the joy abruptly drained from Davyss' face as the man's words sank deep. The ground suddenly became unsteady and he began to grab for something to steady himself with, which happened to be

Hugh and Andrew. As his joy turned to horror, he literally could not stand as his legs turned to water.

"My wife?" he breathed. "My sweet God… is she dead?"

"Nay, my lord."

"What happened?"

The soldier shook his head. "I was not privy to such knowledge, my lord. There was not time for your mother to draft a missive so she bade me to ride hard for Evesham and deliver the news to you personally."

Davyss thought he might become physically ill; in fact, it was some time before he realized that Hugh and Andrew had lowered him onto the ground. He sat there, his face a mirror of horror and shock, as Andrew and Edmund bolted from the tent and began calling for the chargers. Davyss heard them but he couldn't think straight; all he could do was stare at the soldier who had delivered a message he had always known might be a possibility yet had not truly anticipated.

"You do not know what happened to my wife?" he pleaded.

By this time, Hugh had pulled the soldier into the tent and closed the flap so prying eyes from outside would not see Davyss in his weakened state. The soldier shook his head to Davyss' question.

"All I know is that your wife delivered twins in mid-July," he replied. "All we knew was that she had two boys and did not fare well in the birth. Lollardly has called in physics from Norwich, Great Yarmouth and Acle to tend your wife. Your mother told me to ride swiftly to find you and tell you to come home right away."

Davyss struggled to think, to plan what he must do next. All he could feel was stark, unadulterated panic and he struggled to shake it off. He could not let it overwhelm him. He had to get to Devereux.

Somehow, he found his feet but he was still unsteady. All he could think, feel or see was his wife and the thought that something horrible had happened to her threatened to undo him time and time again, but he pushed the negative thoughts away, listening to his brother's instructions because he couldn't seem to do for himself. Hugh seemed to be doing everything for him, helping him to dress, telling him that

Andrew and Edmund were securing the horses.

It was Hugh who strapped the scabbard around his waist, the elaborate leather sheath that contained *Lespada*. Davyss absently touched the hilt of the ancient sword, thinking that all of the battles in the entire world seemed rather insignificant now; family, life and love were so much more important. All he wanted to do was get to his wife. That was the only thing that mattered. As he moved past the soldier who had delivered the devastating news, he grabbed the man by the arm.

"My sons," his voice was faint, hoarse. "They are well?"

The soldier could see how shaken his liege was and, truth be told, he felt a good deal of pity for the man. They all did. All of Davyss' soldiers knew how deeply in love he was with his wife and her failure to come through the birth of his children unscathed had sent all of Norwich into a depression.

"Well, my lord," he assured him softly. "Lollardly and your mother have had quite a time with them. They scream at all hours and eat constantly."

Davyss looked more stricken, if such a thing was possible. "My mother is not caring for them, is she?" he demanded. "The woman can barely walk. I do not want her carrying around a newborn infant."

The soldier shook his head. "Lady Lucy and Lady Frances have care of the infants. They have also hired a wet-nurse from town. Your boys are well taken care of, my lord, I assure you."

That seemed to ease Davyss somewhat but he was still horribly pale. He continued to clutch the man's arm as if the soldier was some odd link to everything back at Norwich. He didn't want to let him go.

"Do...," he began again in a whisper. "Do the boys have names?"

A faint smile crossed the soldier's weary lips. "Your wife has named them Drake Davyss and Devon Grayson," he replied. "Your mother says they are the image of your father but I have heard tale that they are fair like your wife."

That was all Davyss could take; he closed his eyes and tears rolled down his cheeks, mingling with the pouring rain. Hugh, concerned, tugged on his brother and got him moving. The soldier followed because Davyss couldn't seem to let go of him. Together, the three of them traveled to the livery area of the encampment where Andrew, Nik, Philip and Edmund already had the chargers saddled and about five hundred men preparing to move out for Norwich. It was Hugh who ran to Henry and Edward to tell them what had happened.

Henry let Davyss go without question.

CHAPTER TWENTY-THREE

O N THE MORNING of the sixth day since leaving Evesham, the massive white block of Norwich Castle's keep came into view.

Davyss had pushed his men hard for the long trek back to Norwich. The column had made around thirty-five miles a day before stopping only to rest the horses and then proceeding on. Davyss seemed to have no sense of exhaustion although his men certainly did. After weeks of traveling and fighting, they were all deeply exhausted but pushed on for Davyss' sake. They knew what was at stake and not one man disagreed with him. So they rode on, fighting the intermittent thunderstorms and sometimes stifling moist heat, until the great keep of Norwich was finally sighted on the horizon.

Once Davyss caught sight of it, he spurred his charger into a thundering gallop. Nothing on this earth was going to keep him from Devereux any longer and he rode the already-exhausted horse into Norwich's double-baileys, leaping off the horse when he reached the keep and taking the steps two at a time. He burst into the soldier's hall only to be met by Lollardly.

The old priest threw his arms around him. "Davyss, boy," he squeezed him and let him go. "We saw your army on the horizon. Praise God that you are safe."

Davyss grabbed the old man by the arms, his fingers biting into the flesh. "Devereux," he demanded. "What happened? Where is she?"

Lollardly could see how edgy Davyss was. He struggled to calm him. "Listen to me," he gripped him. "You must calm yourself or you will do her no good. Do you hear me?"

Davyss shook him so hard that he nearly snapped the man's neck. "Enough," he roared, moving for the stairs that led to the upper chambers of the keep. "Tell me how she is. What happened to her?"

Lollardly was trying to keep the man from bolting up the stairs. "Davyss, I cannot tell you all that I must if you are running up those stairs," he yanked on his arm. "Stop a moment and listen to me. It is important."

Davyss heard the plea through his desperate haze and he came to an unsteady halt, facing the man. "What is it, then?"

Lollardly knew he would only have his attention for a short amount of time before he was demanding to see his wife again, so he spoke quickly. "Your wife went into labor two weeks early," he lowered his voice. "She labored for two days to bring forth your enormous children, Davyss, so much so that I believed I was going to have to cut into her to remove them. The physic from Great Yarmouth agreed with me. But finally, she gave birth to your first son and we were shocked to realize that there were two. Never did I feel two children when I examined her; only one. Your wife was so weak already by the time the first boy was born that it was nearly impossible for her to gather the strength to birth the second child. But that wasn't the worst of it."

Davyss' expression was wrought with horror. "Dear God," he breathed. "What happened?"

Lollardly sighed heavily, his manner turning gentle. "Your second son was born feet-first," he murmured. "Your wife did not have any strength left to push so we were forced to… well, we had to pull the child out by his feet, Davyss. It was the only way. Then we could not detach the nourishment sack from her body and she bled profusely until we were able to pull it free. She lost a great deal of blood and the difficult birth seriously injured her."

By this time, Davyss' hand was at his mouth as if to hold in the gasps of horror. The hazel eyes filled with tears. "How is she now?"

Lollardly lifted his shoulders. "She lives," he said honestly. "But she has not recovered. All she does is sleep. She barely eats. If she does not start showing more improvement soon, I am afraid we… well, we may lose her."

Davyss blinked and the tears rolled down his cheeks, just as quickly wiped away. He took a deep breath, digesting Lollardly's words, struggling to acclimate himself to the situation.

"May I see her?" he whispered.

Lollardly simply nodded. He followed Davyss up the stairs to the fourth floor. As Davyss approached, he could hear babies crying and his tears returned en force. As he stood at the top of the stairs, gazing into the chamber where both of his lusty sons were being tended, he sobbed deeply.

Lollardly stood behind him, his hand on Davyss' shoulder as the man observed the activity of the room. It was a smaller chamber with a large bed in it, and Frances sat on the bed changing the swaddling of one twin while Lucy paced the floor with the second twin. Both boys were screaming at the top of their lungs and Lucy was attempting desperately to calm the baby in her arms until she saw Davyss.

The surprise on her face turned to joy before immediately turning to distress. The enormous man was filthy and exhausted as he stood at the top of the stairs, tears running down his face and dripping onto his dirty tunic. Lucy went to him.

"Davyss," she was torn between being very glad to see him and deeply concerned as to why he was crying. She could see that he was looking at the baby in her arms and her focus turned to the child. "This is your son, Drake. Your mother swears that he looks just like your father."

Davyss gazed down at the baby, struggling to stop his sobs. As Lucy unwrapped the boy so he could get a better look, his sobs turned into weepy laughter at the vigorously screaming baby. He was absolutely furious. Davyss reached out a tentative finger, pushing it into a waving hand and being rewarded when the infant gripped him tightly.

"He is very strong," he commented, feeling the warmth of joy wash over him as he gazed into the little face. "But why is he so angry?"

Lucy grinned. "He is hungry; he is *always* hungry."

Davyss was overcome with emotion as Drake continued to scream.

Lucy watched the man's face, seeing the complete adoration, the pain. It was enough to bring tears to her eyes. She knew how much all of this meant to him and to Devereux.

"Would you like to hold him?" she asked softly.

Davyss shook his head. He bent over, kissing Drake on the forehead. "Not at the moment," he whispered. "I want to see my wife first."

Lucy understood. With a lingering look at Devon, screaming on the bed, Davyss quit the room and went to the master's chamber. The door was closed and he very quietly opened it.

The room was dark inside, big oilcloth curtains covering the long lancet windows. It smelled of cloves and rushes and as he entered the room, his gaze was immediately drawn to the enormous bed. His mother was seated to the left of the bed, the needlework in her hands falling to her lap when her old eyes beheld her son. The little dogs at her feet stood up, tails wagging furiously.

Davyss' gaze moved between his mother and the still figure on the bed. He finally focused on his mother when the woman stiffly stood up.

"Davyss," she breathed, inspecting his dirty mail, his stubbled face. "Thank God you have returned. Are you well?"

Davyss nodded shortly, his attention moving to the bed. "How is she?"

Lady Katharine knew it would do no good to ply her son with foolish questions that could just as easily be answered later. He had come for one reason and one alone; Katharine's gaze trailed down to the blonde head buried amongst the coverlets.

"She sleeps," she whispered, turning to her son. She noticed that Lollardly had come in behind him. "I assume Lollardly told you of her condition?"

Davyss' tears were returning as he gazed down at his wife's extremely pale, sleeping face. "He did," he breathed, collapsing beside the bed and clutching one of Devereux's outstretched hands. "Dear God... she looks so pale."

Lady Katharine put her hand on her son's dirty hair, something completely out of character for the woman who normally showed no affection. But this was an exception; she grieved deeply for her son at the moment. She knew well what it felt like to love someone and face the prospect of losing them.

"She is a very sick woman," Katharine said softly, running her thin fingers through her son's hair a moment before removing her hand and gathering her cane. "I will leave you alone with her and go and see my grandsons. They sound a good deal like you did as an infant, Davyss."

Davyss couldn't even respond as his mother left the chamber, taking Lollardly and the dogs with her. When the door shut softly and the room was suddenly very still, he pulled Devereux's hand to his lips and kissed the soft flesh reverently.

"Sweetling, can you hear me?" he whispered, his tears pelting her flesh. "Devereux? I am here, sweetling; I am here. All will be well again, I swear it."

She continued to lie still, breathing heavily. Davyss watched her, feeling more anguish than he ever imagined possible. They had spent so much time focused on his battles and her worry over him not returning that it had never occurred to him that she would be the one facing life or death. It just wasn't fair. He felt cheated.

Davyss had everything he had ever wanted out of life; power, honor, prestige. He had the arrogance and the following to prove it. Now he had a beautiful wife and two strong sons. But that joy was threatened and he knew that he would give it all up, without question, if it meant Devereux would live. He could deal with the loss of wealth and even power. He could live without a pristine reputation. But he could not live without his wife. He let go of her hand and began to remove his armor.

"I have thought of nothing but you for the past three months," he mumbled as he pulled his tunic over his head and began stripping off his mail. "Every moment of every day, you were always in my heart. So much has happened since we have been separated I do not even know where to start. But I swear to you that I will not leave you ever again.

Not ever."

The mail coat hit the floor and he stood up, pulling off his boots and continuing with his one-sided conversation. "I have seen the boys," he told her as the boots hit the floor with a heavy knock. "They are magnificent, Devereux. I am so humbled by your sacrifice that I cannot put it into words. It… it seems like all you wanted was to provide me with sons. You got your wish, sweetling; we have two beautiful boys."

The room remained quiet as he fell silent, removing his breeches. Naked, sweaty, dirty and all, he climbed into bed with Devereux and with extreme care, pulled her into his arms. The moment he felt her soft warmth against him, alive and breathing, he burst into tears. The anguish was more than he could stomach and his emotions flooded from every pore of his body.

"God," he sobbed, his face in the back of her head. "Please do not take her from me. I have done things in my life that I am not proud of and things I should show repentance for. I am sorry if I have failed You. But my wife… she is the one gift you have given me in life that outshines everything else I have ever known to exist. I am completely unworthy of her and I know it, but please, God, do not take her away from me. I love her with all of my heart. I cannot go on without her."

His last sentence was barely recognizable through the sobs. He held Devereux tightly against him, his tears wetting her hair. His hands stroked her but he made no attempt to elicit a response from her. He was simply grateful to be with her, holding her, feeling her heartbeat mingle with his. But the tears wouldn't stop; he didn't even try. He let them come.

As he lay there and held his wife, he realized that something was happening. Devereux wasn't limp any longer; in fact, she was moving. Startled, Davyss lifted his head, propping himself up on an elbow so he could see for himself what was going on. As he lifted himself, Devereux rolled sluggishly onto her back.

Davyss was stunned to see the big gray eyes gazing up at him. He didn't know what to say; in fact, words, at the moment, seemed oddly out of place. He just stared at her, an enormous hand coming up to gently touch her face. He stroked her velvety cheeks with his thick fingers, gazing down at her as she smiled faintly. He returned the gesture and, without provocation, the tears came again.

Devereux shushed him softly when she saw his reaction. She put a weak hand to his face, watching as he kissed it fervently and held it fast against his cheek.

"You have come home," she whispered.

He nodded, trying to hold off the sobs. "I have missed you so much," he wept softly. "I love you, Devereux. More than anything on this earth, I love you."

She put up her other hand, fingers against his lips as the tears rained down. "And I love you," she whispered. "Have you returned to me unscathed?"

He burst out in to ironic snorts, mingled with the sobs. "How can you ask me that when I return to find you on death's door?" he suddenly lay down against her, his face buried in her neck and his warm tears on her flesh. "I cannot lose you, Devereux. I would not survive such a thing."

He was sobbing heavily and Devereux wrapped her weak arms around him, shushing him gently. Though she was horribly drained and barely able to move, her husband's tears had her playing the role of the comforter. His tears had her deeply touched and deeply distressed.

"I will not leave you," she assured him softly. "I simply need time to recover, 'tis all. Surely you saw those two enormous children I birthed."

She was making an attempt at humor and he lifted his head, kissing her so sweetly that his head swam. "I did," he kissed her cheek, her chin, silently conveying the love and adoration he felt for her. "I am humbled, Lady de Winter. Truly humbled. Words cannot describe how pleased and grateful I am."

She smiled faintly and he heard what he thought was a laugh. "Since when are you a humble man?"

He stopped kissing her, lifting his head up to look into her dark-circled eyes, still so beautiful to him. "Since I married you," he answered. "I remember an angry woman telling me once that I should be humble and gracious and endearing because those qualities will cause people to bow at my feet and my wife to respect me. I once thought all I wanted was your respect but, somehow, I got much more than I ever dreamed of. I am still not sure how that happened."

Her smile grew, the gray eyes glimmering. "I am not sure, either," she admitted. "One moment I was loathing you and, in the next, I could not live without you."

He returned her smile, feeling the warmth between them, the love, and his eyes started to water again. He simply couldn't help it; he couldn't imagine life without her.

"Please," he begged softly, his smile fading. "Please get well. I cannot stomach the alternative."

She sighed faintly, reaching up a weak hand to stroke his handsome face. "Nor can I," she murmured. "I do not want to watch you leave to war ever again. Please, Davyss; tell me that these wars between Simon and Henry are ended."

He thought of Evesham, of Simon's body in pieces over the green English grass. "They are over," he declared. "I swear it."

"Then you will not leave again?"

He kissed her cheek. "Not unless I have your permission," he said. "And even then, I will not stay away long, I swear it."

She sighed faintly, feeling weak yet joyful. The past three months had been particular hellish, not knowing if Davyss was dead or alive, only hearing about him periodically by way of quickly written missives. It had not been enough to sustain her. The birth, though difficult, had not drained her as much as the thought of her husband's fate did. Perhaps it was her distress over Davyss' whereabouts and activities that had contributed the most to her loss of the will to live. The twins, as strenuous as their birth had been, had only compounded the problem.

Gazing into Davyss' eyes, she knew for a fact that they were going to live long and healthy lives together. She felt stronger simply by having him in the room. She wrapped her arms around his neck weakly and he enfolded her with his strength, his massive arms blocking out all of the evils and deeds of the world. It was a safe and protective cocoon.

"Thank you, Davyss," she murmured.

His face was buried in the side of her head. "For what?"

She smiled even though he couldn't see it. "For marrying me on that day so long ago, even when I said such horrible things to you."

He grinned, shifting on the bed so that he was lying beside her. "Our wedding was quite a show," he agreed. "The only one who wasn't complaining or fighting that day was *Lespada*."

"He is so cold and sharp. He makes a terrible husband." Davyss laughed; it was so good to be with her again, to enjoy her humor. He pulled her close, kissing the tip of her nose. "I have an idea on how to rectify that, if you will allow me."

"Of course I will."

On their wedding anniversary in March of the following year, Davyss arranged a massive wedding in Winchester Cathedral that turned out to be the social event of the year. Everyone was in attendance, including the king and queen, and between Hollyhock and the Tower of London, the celebration went on for three long and glorious days.

This time, the groom attended the wedding instead of his sword.

EPILOGUE

1271 A.D.

The House of Hope, Norfolk

D EVEREUX HEARD THE thunder and the boys began to run.

"It's Da, it's Da!" they screamed.

Devereux caught up to her children in the yard of The House of Hope, making a futile attempt to quiet them as they jumped up and down like lunatics. Devon and Drake were nearly six years old, enormous children for their age with blonde hair and hazel eyes. Feature for feature, they looked mostly like their father and they acted like him, too; whenever Davyss was away, it brought Devereux great comfort simply to look into their handsome little faces. And Davyss had been gone, this time, for nearly a month. She had looked into those little faces often.

Their three-year-old brother Denys, for some strange reason, was the image of his Uncle Hugh. He was a handsome dark haired, dark-eyed lad who tended to be quite aggressive, and Hugh adored the boy that looked just like him.

Even now, Denys was slugging it out with his older brothers and Devereux had no idea why. She simply put her hand in between the boys to still the boxing fists. When Denys bit Drake out of pure spite, she swatted him on the behind and he plopped onto his bum in the dirt and began crying.

The thunder of horses was drawing nearer. Devereux sighed at the sight of Denys weeping in the dust, thinking of picking him up but stopping short of it. He would never learn his lesson if she was constantly coddling him. Besides, she already had her arms full with their two year old sister; gorgeous dark-haired, gray-eyed Lady

Katharine was clearly the beauty of the family.

Named after her grandmother, her father was particularly enamored with her. She was a sweet girl who seemed to bring out her brothers' gentler side. They would slug each other and then turn around and play very sweetly with her. Perhaps it was because their father had threatened them if they so much as touched her. Or perhaps it was because Katie was a truly sweet, calming creature.

The chargers finally plowed into the dusty stable yard, the de Winter war machine at its finest. Noticeably missing knights were Nik and Philip, perhaps having gone ahead to Norwich to meet up with their wives and children. Andrew and Edmund were riding with the pack, shouting orders to the men. Devereux pulled the boys back from the flying hooves, terrified that they were going to get clipped as the chargers circled.

Davyss was in the lead, as usual, bailing off his horse before it even came to a halt. He charged a path straight for his wife, a gloved finger pointing at her.

"I told you to stay at Norwich," he scolded. "Why did you leave?"

The boys ran at him, throwing themselves into his massive arms. Davyss was momentarily distracted as he found himself picking up Devon, Drake and Denys. But he only had two arms so Denys ended up sitting on his shoulders, holding onto his father's neck tightly for support.

Trying to talk with three young boys hanging on to him was difficult, but Davyss was making the attempt. The boys were screaming his name, trying to hug him and roughhouse with him at the same time. Suppressing a grin at their antics, Devereux went to her husband and kissed him sweetly, glad to see him. He returned her kisses but he still had not forgotten his anger.

"'Tis good to see you, too," she quipped softly, her hands on his face as she kissed him. "I have missed you."

"I have missed you also."

"I love you."

"And I love you," he murmured as she suckled his lower lip. "Now, answer my question. Why did you not stay at Norwich?"

He was unwilling to be distracted with sweet talk. Devereux sighed heavily. "I told you that we were coming to The House of Hope while you were away," she reminded him patiently. "You left me a contingent of one hundred men. Did you forget?"

He growled even as Denys tried to yank his helm off. "I left the contingent to guard you at Norwich, not act as escort as you cavort around the countryside. You were supposed to stay at Norwich."

She lifted an eyebrow at him. "Yet I did not," she dared him to fight with her about it. "Whenever you leave on business, you know that I like to come here. I always do. It is important that our children understand how crucial it is to tend to those less fortunate."

Davyss wasn't really angry more than he was frustrated. He told her to stay at the castle and she was very happy to disobey him, dragging their children along with her. The House of Hope continued on, mostly administered by Stephan Longham with the de Winter wealth behind it, and Devereux was very pleased to have one of the most prominent charities in the country. Just as she had when she had been young, her children helped tend the sick, swept the floors, and fed the chickens. Devereux was positive it would help mold more compassionate and grateful adults.

But Davyss wasn't so sure. As he stewed about it, Denys was becoming frustrated because he couldn't get his father's helm off so Davyss unlatched it and pulled it off for the boy. Setting down all of the children in his arms, he handed his helm to Denys, which instantly became a target for the other two. They all wanted the helm. Screams and fists ensued until Devereux handed Katie to her father and went to break up the fight.

Davyss watched her calm, soothing manner with the three ruffians. Mother had far more control over them than he did and he wasn't ashamed to admit it. It only made him love her more. As he watched Devereux deal with the boys, little hands were suddenly patting his cheeks and he turned to see his sweet little angel smiling at him. He grinned, kissing her loudly on the cheek. Katie put her fat little baby arms around her father's neck and hugged him tightly. He was a man in love and his disobedient wife was quickly forgotten.

Devereux had nearly managed to calm the boys when a larger, more disruptive influence entered the mix. Hugh was suddenly among them, laying down on the dirt and rolling into the boys as if to mow them down like a giant rolling pin. Delighted, the boys began to jump on Uncle Hugh gleefully. Devereux stood back before she got caught up in the mêlée, shaking her head in resignation. She looked at her husband as she pointed at his brother.

"No wonder the boys play so roughly," she said accusingly. "Look who sets the example for them."

Davyss merely shrugged but Hugh lifted his head, trying not to get kicked in the face. He was grinning from ear to ear.

"They are boys," he announced happily. "This is what boys do."

Devereux's eyes narrowed. "When you have your own children, Hugh de Winter, I shall make sure to remember that. And when we join your bride at Wigmore Castle next month for your wedding, I shall be sure to remind her of my retribution for your behavior."

Hugh tried to get up but the boys wouldn't let him; he ended up down in the dirt again, fending off an attack. "I will not be blamed if you drive her away," he sounded very much like a reluctant man. "In fact, I still may drive myself away. I have not decided yet."

Devereux fought off a grin; Hugh and Roger Mortimer's youngest daughter, Isolde, were to be wed the following month at Wigmore Castle, Roger's seat. Hugh and the very lovely Isolde had met at Davyss and Devereux's second wedding ceremony and it had taken Roger years to convince Hugh to marry his daughter. He even promised him the baronetcy of Audley to entice him, but still, the de Winter stubborn streak was strong. Only when Lady Katharine threatened to disinherit him did he start taking the marriage proposal seriously.

"You cannot fool me, Hugh," Devereux lifted an eyebrow. "You are more excited about this wedding than your bride is and I am looking forward to a lovely event."

Hugh took a direct hit in the chin from Devon, finally deciding he'd had enough and was struggling to crawl away.

"Mother was more excited than any of us," he finally made it to his feet, fending off a charge from Drake by pushing the boy away by the forehead. "I regret that she did not live to see it."

Devereux's smile faded, thinking on Lady Katharine and the illness that had swiftly claimed her life six months before. The woman had been the rock of the de Winter family and her boys were still struggling to adjust to life without their mother. Devereux moved to her husband, still standing with Katie in his arms, and wrapped her hands around his enormous bicep.

"She lived to see four grandchildren born, including her namesake," she tried to comfort the sons. "She lived to see a great deal. I know she was happy; she told me so on many occasions. Which reminds me; did you ever read the missive she left for you, Davyss? The one she had scribed by Lollardly when she lay dying?"

Davyss shook his head. "I have not had the nerve."

"Where is it?"

"In my saddle bags."

Devereux's eyebrows lifted. "Do you mean to tell me that you have been carrying it around with you since her death?"

He nodded, glancing at Hugh as Devon and Drake latched on to his leg and tried to pull him down. He lowered his voice and turned to his wife.

"I have told you this before," he said. "I do not know what she could possibly write to me on her deathbed but I do not like it. I do not want to know."

"Perhaps she only wanted to tell you how much she loved you."

"Perhaps; but I do not think so."

Devereux fell silent a moment, contemplating. "Perhaps you should let me read it. If I think you need to know, I will tell you."

Hugh went down again in a pile of boys as Davyss stepped over him, making his way to his charger. With Katie in one massive arm, he unstrapped the left saddlebag and dug around in it until finally pulling forth a small tube of yellowed vellum. It was tied with gut, sealed with Lady Katharine's stamp. Katie was more interested in what else he had in the bag so he held it open for her as she rummaged around. She pulled forth a strip of leather, nothing of any true value or worth, and began to play with it. Davyss let her have it as he made his way back over to his wife.

Devereux was in the process of telling Denys to stop biting his uncle as Davyss approached, extending the missive to her. She looked somewhat surprised as she accepted it.

"This is it?" she asked.

"Aye."

"Are you sure you want me to read this?"

He shrugged, stepping aside when Hugh rolled into him. "You may as well. I never will."

Devereux paused a moment, indecisive, before finally untying the gut and breaking the seal. Carefully, she unrolled the vellum and began to read.

No one was paying much attention to her as she moved a few feet away so that she could read without getting hit by one of her wrestling sons. In fact, her back was to both Davyss and Hugh. Davyss watched her a moment before setting Katie down, immediately having to protect her from her flailing brothers. When Katie reached down and began to pull Hugh's hair, the man howled in pain and the children laughed loudly. The more Katie would pull, the more Hugh would yell. Davyss just stood there, hands on his hips, and grinned.

But Devereux wasn't grinning. She finished the missive and read it through again, just to make sure she understood what she had read. With a lingering glance at her husband, she turned and headed into The House of Hope. Davyss, Hugh and the children continued to play. When Devereux finally emerged several minutes later, it was without the missive. Davyss glanced up at her, noticing her empty hands. He moved away from the writhing group on the ground.

"What did you do with it?" he pointed to her empty fingers.

Devereux gazed up at him steadily. "Burned it."

Davyss' eyebrows lifted. "What?" he demanded. "Why did you do that?"

Devereux thought on her reply. When she spoke, it was careful. "I did not want it to fall into the wrong hands," she said quietly, wrapping her fingers around her husband's big arm. "If you truly wish to know what it said, I will tell you. Otherwise, my lips are sealed. I will take the contents of that missive to my grave."

Davyss stared at her, feeling some trepidation. His fingers began to toy with hers. "Is it so terrible?"

"I suppose that would depend on your point of view."

"If you were in my place, would you want to know?"

She thought on that. "More than likely."

"Then tell me."

She did. Davyss wasn't particularly surprised to find out that Simon de Montfort had fathered him.

He took the secret with him to his grave as well.

C03 THE END 80

AUTHOR NOTES

Lespada was originally called *Song of the April Rain*, but when the opening chapters were written and the sword played such a major role, the title was changed to *Lespada*, which is Portuguese meaning "sword". Davyss de Winter, almost more than any other Le Veque character, goes through a huge transformation during the book – he starts out as an arrogant, self-centered knight and ends up a devoted and loving family man. His priorities shift with the addition of Devereux, who is clearly as stubborn as he is. She, too, goes through a great transformation as she falls in love with the husband she never wanted. What a sweet love story.

Simon de Montfort, of course, existed. Reading on the Battle of Lewes and the Battle of Evesham make for fascinating military tales. All people related to the battles did, in fact, exist, including Roger Mortimer. He planned an escape for Prince Edward from jail that is worthy of a Hollywood movie. And Roger did indeed have a young daughter named Isolde, who married a man named Hugh, who took on the name Baron Audley. Who is to say that it really wasn't Hugh de Winter…?

This House of de Winter novel includes a tie-in with The Questing.
Drake de Winter, a secondary character in The Questing, is the son of
Davyss and Deveraux.

The Questing

Davyss de Winter also appears in The Thunder Lord.

The Thunder Lord

For more information on other series and family groups, as well as a list of all of Kathryn's novels, please visit her website at www.kathrynleveque. com.

ABOUT KATHRYN LE VEQUE

Medieval Just Got Real.

KATHRYN LE VEQUE is a USA TODAY Bestselling author, an Amazon All-Star author, and a #1 bestselling, award-winning, multi-published author in Medieval Historical Romance and Historical Fiction. She has been featured in the NEW YORK TIMES and on USA TODAY's HEA blog. In March 2015, Kathryn was the featured cover story for the March issue of InD'Tale Magazine, the premier Indie author magazine. She was also a quadruple nominee (a record!) for the prestigious RONE awards for 2015.

Kathryn's Medieval Romance novels have been called 'detailed', 'highly romantic', and 'character-rich'. She crafts great adventures of love, battles, passion, and romance in the High Middle Ages. More than that, she writes for both women AND men – an unusual crossover for a romance author – and Kathryn has many male readers who enjoy her stories because of the male perspective, the action, and the adventure.

On October 29, 2015, Amazon launched Kathryn's Kindle Worlds Fan Fiction site WORLD OF DE WOLFE PACK. Please visit Kindle Worlds for Kathryn Le Veque's World of de Wolfe Pack and find many action-packed adventures written by some of the top authors in their genre using Kathryn's characters from the de Wolfe Pack series. As Kindle World's FIRST Historical Romance fan fiction world, Kathryn Le Veque's World of de Wolfe Pack will contain all of the great storytelling you have come to expect.

Kathryn loves to hear from her readers. Please find Kathryn on Facebook at Kathryn Le Veque, Author, or join her on Twitter @kathrynleveque, and don't forget to visit her website at www.kathrynleveque.com.

Made in the USA
Coppell, TX
04 September 2020